STORM OF DESIRE

As Amy crossed the dining room, Captain Bond stepped inside. He looked tired and drawn, the creases around his eyes pronounced. Amy had a sudden urge to hold him close and smooth the worry lines from his brow. "You look terrible," she said.

"Do forgive my unkempt appearance, Mistress Hawthorne, but I was too busy to groom myself for your approval. I trust your sleep was not disturbed unduly by the storm," he snapped.

The tender feelings she'd just entertained for him vanished. "I intended to complain to you about that, Captain. Kindly steer us away from these storms in the future—they do give me a headache."

Amy saw his lip twitch. "I suppose I deserved that," he said, his eyes softening as he gazed at her. She was so damned desirable that he tried to hide behind an abrupt manner to keep from wanting her.

Amy relented and reached up to touch his cheek. "You haven't had any sleep, have you?"

His hand came up to clasp hers, and, turning his face, he kissed her palm.

Amy's heart began to race. He smelled of wind and rain. The room felt cool and she felt hot. Unconsciously, she leaned closer and his head came down to claim her lips. A jolt of excitement shot through her. Her world spun . . .

SANDRA DONOVAN

RESTLESS PASSIONS

ZEBRA BOOKS
KENSINGTON PUBLISHING CORP.

ZEBRA BOOKS

are published by

Kensington Publishing Corp.
475 Park Avenue South
New York, NY 10016

First printing: October, 1992

Printed in the United States of America

This book is dedicated to three of my best friends:

my mother, Dessie
my sister, Bev
my office partner, Boni

Thanks for supporting every venture I undertake,

And to Molly and Hope.

Chapter One

Amy Hawthorne urged her mount along King Street and directly onto Long Wharf. When she came abreast of the *Rebecca,* her heartbeat quickened. This mighty merchant ship, riding at anchor, was to be her escape. In two days it would carry her away from Boston town to the Bermuda Islands . . . and away from Edward Simpson.

She paid scant attention to the bustling activity around her as she gazed at the clean lines of the vessel and daydreamed. With stolen glances or bold, open stares, busy seamen and dockworkers admired her striking beauty, but all recognized that she was no tavern doxy to be trifled with or approached.

One young sailor, who was waiting patiently for his captain next to a nearby warehouse, thought her the most beautiful creature he'd ever seen. Her bright copper hair was piled high in the latest fashion and had a jaunty little green hat sitting atop. The fitted jacket and full skirt of her riding habit were of the same green wool. And even from a distance he could see the proud tilt of her small chin. He wondered what she was doing

7

there, for well-bred young ladies of quality were seldom seen on the docks without an escort.

At just that moment, two sailors, coming from opposite directions, collided, and one dropped the barrel of nails that had recently sat on his shoulder. The resounding crash caused Amy's horse to dance back and rear. Caught off guard, Amy let out a small cry and fought to keep her seat. The young sailor who had admired her rushed forward and grabbed for the reins, but the black stallion, whose fright was increased by the man's swift approach, rolled his eyes and landed a glancing blow with one hoof in the boy's stomach.

Amy was marginally aware of what was happening as she tried to quiet the beast and keep from falling off, but she was unable to do more than shout "Stay back! He'll trample you!"

The following moment, she was whisked from the sidesaddle and set upon the ground, none too gently. Catching her breath, she stared as a tall stranger grabbed the reins and set about subduing the frightened animal. Amy admired the way each movement and word quieted the horse. The man certainly had a way about him, she thought, and she eyed appreciatively his broad shoulders straining against the black coat he wore.

He handed the reins to one of the men standing by, then turned to her. "If you can't control that beast, mistress, then leave him in the stable." The anger in his slate-gray eyes pierced her. "You nearly got that man killed," he finished, jerking his head toward the young man who'd been kicked.

Startled by his harsh attack, she glanced at the sailor to satisfy herself that he was not unduly hurt. The young man blushed to the roots of his blond hair and started to shake his head in protest. "I'm quite all right, sir—"

8

Amy's admiration of a moment before turned to fury. She interrupted the young sailor with a stinging speech aimed at her rescuer. "You overbearing lout! I didn't ask for your interference or your advice. And what's more, I didn't need it. I can control Caesar without any help."

While the girl delivered her reprimand, Marcus Bond took note of her appearance. When he had pulled her from the horse, the only thing he'd noticed about her was that she was as light as a feather. Now his gaze took in her turned-up nose and large green eyes, which, framed by dark spiky lashes, flashed provocatively when she was angry. And while he appreciated her lively spirit, he was not accustomed to being called names. "We could all see that, mistress. I, for one, was impressed," he replied dryly, crossing muscular arms across his broad chest. The crowd of men that had gathered around guffawed at his rejoinder.

His sarcastic reply further maddened Amy. She could feel an angry flush creeping up her cheeks, and she itched to slap the smirk from his arrogant face. Instead, she whirled about and snatched the reins from the man who held them. Putting her foot in the stirrup, she attempted to climb into the sidesaddle unassisted. It was impossible, but before she could admit defeat, a strong, brown hand lifted her up and guided her knee around the horn. The gesture seemed almost intimate, and she felt a strange stirring in her midsection. Jade-green eyes lifted to meet slate-gray ones, and for a moment something flashed between them. It sent Amy's pulse racing, and she breathed in a barely audible voice, "Stand aside, sir." And with that, she pulled Caesar around and kicked the horse into a canter, leaving the wharf behind. A roguish smile on a handsome face haunted her all the way home.

9

The red, brick mansion on Beacon Street had been home to Amy ever since she was ten years old. Her parents had died in a fire that burned their house to the ground one winter's night. Only she, rescued by a servant, had survived the inferno. Her father's older brother, Thaddeus, had taken her to live with him, and although he was a stuffy bachelor, he had done his best to be a parent to her.

She entered the elegant foyer that afternoon like an angry whirlwind, tearing her gloves off and tossing them onto the lowboy table next to the tall clock. Hannah, her personal maid, appeared from the direction of the kitchen, a frown wrinkling her brow. She was a short woman with graying hair, standing no taller than Amy's five feet, but her waistline was considerably larger, a testament to the fact that she favored Mistress Pierce's pastries.

Hannah bore down with a purpose on the young woman. "It's about time you got back, Amy! Where did you run off to anyway? And why didn't you take Mistress Morgan along? Your uncle would have all our heads if he knew you'd ridden off alone on that devil horse!" She stopped to catch her breath.

Amy rolled her eyes heavenward, in no mood to be further scolded this afternoon. "Since Uncle Thad is apparently not at home, I suppose we shall keep our heads one more day, Hannah," she snapped, and then strode purposefully toward the oak staircase, ignoring the woman's questions. "Although mine is hurting abominably. Please send up some headache powders and don't preach."

Hannah threw up her hands in exasperation and retreated to the kitchen.

Amy swept up the stairs and down the hallway to her room. She sank down on a chaise lounge near the wide windows. It was upholstered in pale pink satin and complemented the small roses in the wool carpet. The high bed was covered with a pink-and-white satin spread, while the posts were draped with delicate cotton lace.

Closing her eyes, she leaned back to rest her head on the pillow, hoping to ease the throbbing. A mental picture of that odious man on the wharf immediately rose up to laugh at her, though, and she sat straight up and hissed aloud, "Be gone, you arrogant devil!" However, her command did little good, for her cheeks burned once again as she remembered his sarcasm.

She had never been treated so ill in her entire life, and the incident stung her pride. If she would have had the wit to demand his name, she could have set her uncle on the rogue for his disrespect.

Amy chewed thoughtfully on her thumbnail for a moment. Well, perhaps she couldn't mention it to Uncle Thad after all, since he would be thoroughly incensed at her for riding Caesar down on the wharf alone. How many times had he lectured her about the proprieties? Anyway, it was comforting to think about that ill-mannered ruffian begging for her forgiveness. She could see him now, hat in hand, a contrite look on his bronze face. Idly, her mind remembered every strong feature of that face . . . and the way his thick hair, black as sin, was pulled back in a simple queue at his neck, an unruly lock falling forward on his wide brow. It was his eyes that were fascinating, though — they were like the silver flash of lightning in summer.

A dreamy expression crossed her face before she caught at her wayward thoughts. Reclining once more, she closed her eyes and reminded herself how fortunate she was that she would probably never see the man again.

But what about Edward Simpson? asked a sly little

voice in her head. He would not be disposed of so easily. Amy groaned at the thought. Of all the bachelors invited by her uncle to their dinner table, Edward Simpson irritated her the most. He was a pompous dandy who strutted about like a peacock thinking to impress her with his authoritative manner. And what was worse was that Uncle Thad favored the dolt as a prospective husband for her! Her uncle had already informed her of his decision: if she hadn't chosen a suitable mate by the time they returned from this pleasure-business trip to Bermuda, he would encourage Simpson to court her with an eye to marriage.

The door opened and Hannah bustled in with a tray. She placed it on a small claw-footed table next to Amy. "Here, dearie, drink this," the maid urged, holding out a glass. "You'll need it. Mr. Simpson is coming for dinner tonight." It was pronounced as a sentence, and Amy felt that indeed she was being punished. Dutifully, she drank the headache concoction and gave the maid a rueful smile. "Thank you, Hannah. Whatever would I do without you?"

The older woman sniffed and busied herself laying out Amy's clothing for the evening. Her back was stiff with disapproval. "I expect you'll be finding out the answer to that soon enough," she said.

Amy could have bitten her tongue for bringing up the sore subject. "I'll have to make do with Fiona on this trip, Hannah dear, but she could never take your place," Amy cajoled, rising from the couch to give the woman a quick hug.

"Don't be trying to get around me with your pretty speeches, girl," Hannah warned as she suffered the embrace. "How can Mistress Morgan see to your needs when she's used to having servants of her own?"

Amy began to undress, working at the tiny buttons on the front of her riding jacket while Hannah re-

12

umed her duties. "She's learning. Why, in the two weeks she's been here, I think she's done remarkably well. You're a fine teacher, Hannah."

The maid took out a pink silk dress from the wardrobe and Amy protested, "Not that one — I want the gray."

"That old thing?" Hannah asked, aghast.

Amy insisted and the older woman did as she was bid, grumbling to herself. She laid out matching shoes and fresh undergarments. Returning to their previous subject, she complained, "I should be going. The girl doesn't know the first thing about taking care of your clothes."

Amy sighed in exasperation and pointed out, "You got so seasick on our last trip I thought you would die. Heavens above, Hannah, be reasonable! Uncle Thad only hired Fiona to save you that fate."

"I know," Hannah grumbled, finally defeated.

"We'll only be gone a few months," Amy promised, then added mischievously, "And perhaps that odious Edward Simpson will have married someone else by then."

Hannah's lips twitched in spite of her effort to keep up a dour appearance. She opened the door to let herself out. "We can hope, dearie, but tonight he's all yours. I'll send up your bath."

Amy had just slipped into her underthings when she heard a soft knock and Fiona Morgan stuck her head around the door. "Could I be of some help, Amy?" the girl asked solemnly, her large brown eyes blinking owlishly behind the spectacles she wore.

"Yes, please," Amy said, picking up the delicately embroidered stomacher from the bed and slipping her arms through it. "This one has hooks in the back."

13

Fiona entered and closed the door behind her. As she began fastening the small hooks, she asked primly, "Will I be needed at dinner tonight? If not, I have some packing left to finish."

Amy stepped into her petticoat, and Fiona grasped the ribbons to tie it in back. "I'm sorry, Fiona. I do need you tonight. Edward Simpson is coming and I can't bear the thought of spending any time alone with him. Promise you'll stay by my side all evening?" Amy pleaded as she slipped her arms into the sleeves of the gray silk gown.

Fiona helped her adjust the dress over the full, matching petticoat. "Of course, Amy. That is why you hired me. I'll finish my packing tomorrow."

"I'll be eternally grateful," Amy said, sitting down at her dressing table. She glanced at her companion's reflection in the mirror as the girl began to brush her employer's hair. Something in Fiona's tone had caught Amy's attention. Was it irritation? Amy didn't know, but she began to wonder if this arrangement would work out. It was unusual, to say the least.

Fiona had been an older classmate of hers at Dalton Academy for Young Ladies in Philadelphia. Amy had returned home from there a few months ago, but before that, Fiona had been mysteriously expelled before completion of the term. The rumors had flown that she was pregnant, had committed a crime, had been caught cheating. No one knew what the truth was, but some of the more malicious had their theories. Amy paid them no attention, for even though she and Fiona were merely acquaintances, she had no patience with gossips.

When Fiona answered Thaddeus's advertisement for a companion for Amy, the girl explained her situation quite honestly. "My father suffered some business reversals," she had said, "and my uncle in Ireland opened his home to our family, but I felt I should start earning my own way."

Amy and her uncle had both been impressed by this attitude and her candor, so Thaddeus had immediately given her the job. Nevertheless, Fiona sometimes seemed a bit peevish about her duties. Since Amy had barely known her at school, she didn't know if Fiona's personality was naturally taciturn or if circumstances had made her thus. Amy sighed and decided it didn't matter. It was too late to change things now.

The dinner guests had all arrived by the time Amy descended to the drawing room. She stood in the doorway for a moment, unnoticed, making sure everything was as it should be. A generous fire made the room invitingly warm, and the crystal chandelier was glowing with dozens of candles. Clara, one of the young maids, was circulating with a tray of Madeira. The room was quite large, designed for entertaining, with several settees and numerous stuffed chairs all upholstered in various shades of rose-and-green silk or satin damask. Above the large fireplace on the wall hung a needlepoint picture that Lucy, Amy's mother, had worked for Thaddeus the Christmas before she died. It depicted his cottage in Dedham on the Charles River, where the family spent time in the summer. Rose-and-green damask silk covered two walls, and mahogany panels adorned the remaining two. For a large room, it was comfortable and inviting.

Tonight was a sort of farewell party, and her uncle had invited close friends . . . and then there was Edward Simpson, she thought.

Spying her, Thaddeus excused himself from Captain Simpson, Edward's father, and made his way to her side. He was still a handsome man at fifty years old.

15

Tall and lean, he was wearing a brocade banyan coat of rich colors, a white linen shirt and black velvet breeches. His powdered wig hid a head of thick, gray hair.

Amy knew that he was not pleased with her late appearance, so she smiled brightly at him. "Good evening, Uncle Thad."

His sharp brown eyes sent her a warning before he gave her a dutiful peck on her smooth brow. "My dear Amy, how, ah, nice you look tonight," he said, taking her arm and leading her into the room. Before they reached the first cluster of guests, he bent and whispered, "Whose dress did you borrow, pray tell . . . Hannah's?"

A delighted chuckle bubbled up in her throat as she glanced at his dry expression and whispered back, "I chose this just to match Edward's dull personality."

Thaddeus frowned and harrumphed as they reached the rose silk-damask settee. The Jarvis sisters, two elderly spinsters who lived next door, were seated there talking to the Millinses. Amy greeted each one with a smile and a few words.

Mistress Nancy, the younger of the two sisters, being eighty-one, squinted at Amy above her eyeglasses. "Gray is your color, my dear. You look simply divine in that dress."

Mistress Macy nodded her bewigged head vigorously, sending a shower of white powder over the area, and agreed, "Simply divine."

Amy smiled sweetly at the two. "It's my uncle's favorite, and I do love to please him."

Thaddeus gave her elbow a warning squeeze as he excused them. As they walked away, they overheard Mistress Millins comment to her husband that Amy was such a considerate young woman.

Thaddeus chuckled in spite of himself. "I do hope

16

Edward has a strong constitution, or he'll never survive being married to you."

Amy glanced up with the light of combat in her green eyes and admonished, "Now, now, Uncle—you promised we wouldn't settle anything until we return from Bermuda."

"And I always keep my word," he said with a significant lifting of his brows.

Amy swallowed the retort that rose to her lips. She was twenty years old—on the road to spinsterhood, by some standards—and had turned down a host of marriage proposals in the last two years. Thaddeus was growing concerned for her future, since she was his only heir and would inherit a sizable fortune. He wished a proper marriage for her, and a strong-minded husband to tend her and her business interests. Their arguments had been many and heated on the subject, but Thaddeus was her legal guardian and his word was law. Edward Simpson was his choice . . . unless she could produce another suitor whom her uncle approved.

The man in question appeared at her side at that moment, and Amy collected her scattered thoughts. Giving him a bland smile, she said politely, "Good evening, Edward. So nice of you to join us." She deliberately took her uncle's arm lightly with both hands. Edward had an annoying habit of placing on her hand disgusting wet kisses that sent cold chills down her spine.

The gesture was lost on Edward as he bowed briefly. "It's my pleasure, Mistress Amy . . . and may I say you look very charming tonight?"

Amy inclined her head at the compliment, and Thaddeus spoke up. "Your father tells me that your man-of-war is leaving on patrol at the end of the week."

Edward pushed his ruffled chest out a fraction and stated in his nasal voice, "Yes, sir. We've got to keep the sea-lanes safe for decent shipowners like yourself. Those damned—pardon me, Mistress Amy—Spanish privateers are taking too many vessels of late."

Thaddeus nodded in agreement. "I've been very lucky that none of my merchant ships have come under their guns, but a business associate of mine, Harlan Stafford, has lost two that I know of."

As Edward embarked on a lengthy and boring inventory of the firepower of his ship, the *Beaver,* Amy studied him and tried to envision herself married to the pompous dandy. His attire was almost laughable, what with his having more ruffles and furbelows on his shirt than any of the women in the room sported. His red velvet coat and breeches were foppish, and the powdered wig he wore was elaborately coiffured. But his manner was more repulsive than anything else. She gave an involuntary shudder and searched the room for Fiona. Drat it—where was the girl when she needed her? After a moment, she spotted her companion talking to a friend of her uncle's, John Hancock, and his mother. She finally caught the girl's eye and sent a silent message.

Fiona excused herself. Amy watched her cross the room and was again amazed at how the Morgan girl had changed since last year. The cream-colored silk dress she wore was very modest, her hairstyle rather severe, and then there were those wire-rimmed spectacles that gave Fiona a sober look. At school the girl had been the epitome of fashion and elegance. Now it was as if she were a different person.

Both men nodded politely at Fiona, and she dropped a small curtsey and exchanged greetings with Edward. Then, turning to Amy, she said, "I almost

18

forgot — Mistress Pierce wishes to speak with you concerning dinner."

There was a spark of mischief in Amy's green eyes. "Of course. If you gentlemen will excuse me, I'd better see to that immediately."

Edward watched the red-haired beauty glide away from him, a look of disappointment stamped plainly on his face. Just when he thought to hold her attention with talk of his impressive position, she was called away for a silly domestic conference. Deeming it her fault, he cast a jaundiced eye upon Mistress Morgan before resuming his conversation with Thaddeus. Although he felt sure the elder Hawthorne thought of him as a worthy suitor, the man had not given him permission as yet to court the girl. However, he could wait. Her wealth and position equaled his own . . . and then there was that delectable body that he wished to possess . . .

Marcus Bond, captain of the *Rebecca,* rose from the desk and stretched his cramped muscles. He walked to the brass porthole and gazed out at the morning activity on the wharf, not really seeing what was there. Instead, his mind was on the paperwork on his desk — his own personal business. The ship's ledgers had already been put in order and stored away in the wall cabinet. No, what concerned him greatly were the debts from his father's estate. Marcus had carried an ache in his heart day by day this past year. First his father, Jonathan, had been lost in a shipwreck aboard the one remaining vessel in their fleet, the other three ships having been pirated the previous year. And then his mother had died a few months later of a broken heart. The doctor had pronounced the cause of death to be pneumonia, but Marcus knew better. Moreover, the deathbed confession Sarah Bond had made to her son had shaken his very existence.

Jonathan Bond had borrowed heavily to invest in a cargo that would have brought the family business out of a slump. Unfortunately, the *Polly* went down in a storm off the coast of Cuba, and neither the cargo nor the ship had been insured.

A knock on the door ended his disturbing thoughts, and he turned and called permission to enter.

Toby Oakes, his first mate, came in carrying a tray and placed it on a table opposite the desk. Oakes was fifty years old and had a balding pate. He was barrel-chested and muscled from the hard work of a sailor. "Thought ye might be needin' some refreshment, lad," the older man said as he began pouring the raspberry-leaf tea from the silver pot into a thick mug. "I do wish this cursed protest was over with so we could have some decent tea," he grumbled, passing the cup to his captain and pouring one for himself.

Marcus smiled at his old friend and agreed, "This does take some getting used to."

"Mr. Hadley made these spice cakes fresh this mornin' to keep us from fadin' away before the noon meal. They're as fair as I've tasted," Toby commented as he bit into one.

"Where did you find this culinary genius, Oakes? Did you, perchance, steal him away from the governor's palace?" Marcus asked, duly impressed with the cook's talents so far.

Toby sipped at his tea and smiled benignly. "Oh, I have me ways, lad."

Marcus chuckled and slapped the man on the shoulder. "Did I tell you how glad I am that you came out of retirement to be my first mate?"

Toby reached for another cake and cleared his throat, a deep emotion starting to lump there. Offhandedly, he replied, "I think ye mentioned it. But, in truth, ye did me a favor. I wasn't cut out to stay landlocked in no warehouse."

"Aye, Toby, I understand. Although shipbuilding is a fine profession, I too was missing the sea. And besides, this position will enable me to pay off my father's creditors sooner."

" 'Tis a good son ye are, lad. I know Jonathan was ever proud of ye," the older man said as he picked up the tray and departed.

And that was the other reason, Marcus thought grimly, that he'd signed on as captain of a Hawthorne ship. He knew that Hawthorne and Harlan Stafford were partners in several business ventures, and in this position he could get to that blackguard, Harlan Stafford.

The time sped by quickly to their day of departure. Mistress Pierce and Hannah wished the three travelers a tearful goodbye at dawn. Thomas drove them to the wharf in the carriage, unloaded their small bags and then solemnly shook hands with each of them before he returned to the Hawthorne mansion. The trunks had been delivered the day before and stored aboard the ship.

The morning was misty gray and the wharf seemed an eerie place at that hour, but dockworkers and seamen were busy at their chores, darting in and out of the swirling fog, carrying crates to and from the bobbing ships.

As they stood waiting for a gangway to be let down from the side of the *Rebecca,* Amy heard bits of conversation and caught the smell of breakfast coming from a nearby tavern. She shivered from excitement rather than from the damp, cold wind that

21

whipped around her cloak — at last, they were leaving.

The memory of what had happened on this very spot two days ago flashed through her mind as she watched the gangway being lowered by a young sailor. In the fog, it was hard to see anything clearly, but he reminded her of the boy who'd been kicked by Caesar. When the wooden plank touched the wharf, he moved down to help them board and she caught her breath sharply. It was the same young man. She dipped her head, trying to hide beneath the wide brim of her hat.

"Here, lad, get the ladies' bags and I'll carry my own," Thaddeus instructed.

"Aye, sir," he said, moving to do as he was told.

The two women held onto each other as well as the ropes for support in their climb.

"You're awfully quiet this morning, Amy," Fiona observed as they reached the top, where another sailor stood to assist them.

Amy mumbled her thanks and turned to her companion. "I'm still half-asleep. We arose at an ungodly hour, after all," she fibbed.

Fiona smiled and pointed out, "We must sail with the wind and tide."

Amy sniffed. "That's a poor excuse." While she was wondering where the young sailor had gotten to, he suddenly appeared in front of her, holding the light satchels.

She looked directly at him and he smiled, recognition lighting his eyes. Then he blushed and dropped his gaze. "Should I take these to your cabins, mistress?"

Relief washed over her and she replied, "Yes, please."

When he moved away, she called after him, "What's your name?"

He turned, his color still rosy. "Cooper . . . Jeremy Cooper." And then he fled before she could thank him.

Just when she was congratulating herself on the fact that young Jeremy would keep her secret, a familiar voice assaulted her ears. It was deep-timbred and held a note of authority, just as it had two days ago when he had reprimanded her. She swallowed hard and turned to see her handsome rescuer shaking hands with her uncle. She groaned inwardly. In just a moment her escapade would be revealed, and her uncle would be furious with her behavior. It would be one more reason to marry her off to Edward Simpson.

"Captain Bond," Thaddeus said, drawing her forward.

"Let me present my niece, Amy. Amy, Captain Marcus Bond."

Chapter Two

Amy took a deep breath and then looked the captain in the eye with a hint of challenge. She held out her hand and he took it, slowly raising it to his lips while his appreciative eye traveled from her royal-blue hat to the matching shoes that peeked from beneath her blue-and-white silk traveling dress.

Those slate-gray eyes held an amused twinkle, as well as something else she couldn't quite define. "A special pleasure," he murmured.

The warmth of his lips caused a strange fluttering in her stomach. It was such a pleasant feeling that she was sorry when he released her hand. She gave a somewhat breathless reply and introduced her companion.

With the amenities out of the way, Captain Bond became brisk. "Jeremy will show you to your cabins, and should you need anything, ask him. He's on light duty for a few days due to a thrashing he took from a horse recently." His sharp gaze pinned Amy for a brief moment before he spoke again. "We'll be sailing within the hour, Mr. Hawthorne."

They followed Jeremy, who had reappeared to guide them. Once everyone was shown to their cabins, Amy asked for Jeremy's assistance with her small trunk. It had been tucked under the bunk, and she needed more strength than her own to pull it out. When he finished the task, she thanked him and added softly, "I hope you've not suffered a great deal from the incident with Caesar." Her captivating green eyes told him she was grateful for his discretion also.

He backed toward the door shyly. "No, mistress, I'm fine. Will you need anything else?"

Amy assured him that was all for the moment, and he hastened out and closed the door behind him. She shook her head in puzzlement over his apparent fear of her and then promptly forgot about him as she began taking note of the small domain that would be hers for the next few weeks.

There was a candle lit inside a brass lantern hanging on the wall. The bunk was small and covered with a thick quilt. Amy tested the mattress with a push of her hand and decided it was soft enough. Across the small room and built into the wall was a mahogany-doored cupboard. A chair and a small table stood against the remaining wall. Everything was tidy and clean; she was satisfied with it. Crossing the small space, she peered through a tiny brass porthole, but because of the fog she could see nothing.

After removing her hat and cloak, she hung them on a peg on the door. Fiona knocked and entered a moment later. She had also removed her outerwear, revealing a plain brown silk traveling dress. "I'll help you unpack," Fiona offered.

Together they filled the cupboard with Amy's things and had to leave a few items in the trunk for lack of space.

"Why is there always more clothing than space to store it?" Amy grumbled, looking at her beautiful gowns being crushed together. A mischievous gleam lit her eyes for a moment. "I wonder if Uncle Thad has a larger cupboard?"

"No," Fiona said. "His cabin is the same size as this one, and so is mine. Your uncle asked me to tell you that he will be resting and doing some paperwork until the evening meal and doesn't wish to be disturbed."

"Business and more business!" Amy said in an exasperated tone. "Uncle Thad is far too serious for his own good."

Fiona smiled, pushing her glasses a little higher on her nose. "He does work too hard. I've noticed that."

"We should make it a point to see that he relaxes and enjoys this trip. Will you help me, Fiona?" Amy asked.

"I'll do what I can," the girl promised without hesitation.

A smile lit Amy's face. "Perhaps that would take his mind off my future."

"Don't count on it," Fiona warned.

There was a change in the activity above, and hearing shouts of command, Amy suggested, "Let's go up on deck. We must be readying to sail."

Fiona handed Amy her cloak. "Do go ahead. I would rather unpack my things first, if you don't mind."

Once on deck, Amy chose a spot at the rail, well out of everyone's way. She watched as the men bustled about, hauling up the sails and lifting the anchor. The one spot her eyes avoided was the quarterdeck where Captain Bond stood shouting orders. A brief glance at his masculine form in tight black breeches and a white shirt, open at the throat, had sent her pulse racing and her gaze skittering away. It made her feel as if she were twelve years old again.

He was merely a man, like any other, she told herself sternly, but when she glanced at him again to prove her point, his wintry gray eyes caught and held hers captive. She sucked in her breath, and the noise around her seemed to fade away for a few heartbeats.

He gave a brief mocking salute that broke the spell,

26

and she stifled an urge to stick out her tongue at him. Instead, she turned and presented him her back while gazing at the gray silhouette of the city's outline across the bay as it slowly retreated.

The *Rebecca* boasted a small but elegant dining room, which seated ten people. The first night out, Thaddeus, Amy and Fiona sat down to dinner with Captain Bond, Toby Oakes, who was the first mate, and Andrew Williams, a young officer. Jeremy served at the table.

Amy gave the towheaded young man a warm smile as he placed the main course of venison in front of her, and he blushed furiously, something he seemed to do quite often.

"More wine, Jeremy," Captain Bond requested quietly from the head of the table.

"Aye, sir," the sailor said, moving from place to place, filling glasses.

Amy noticed that the captain's deep voice held a gentler note when he spoke to the lad. Perhaps he wasn't all bad, she thought grudgingly.

Amy liked Toby Oakes immediately. He had twinkling blue eyes and a kind smile. He glanced up just then and said to the women, "I hope ye ladies have had a good first day out."

Amy returned his warm smile. "It felt wonderful to be on the sea again, even if the north wind had a bite to it."

"I had plenty to do today and barely noticed its passing," Fiona commented primly.

Amy hid a smile at her companion's peevishness. Andrew Williams spoke directly to Amy, ignoring everyone else. "In a week, Mistress Hawthorne, we'll feel the warmth of the Gulf Stream and enjoy very pleasant weather," he promised, his admiring gaze on her.

27

"I'll be looking forward to that," Amy assured him.

Thaddeus joined the conversation with an announcement. "We'll be stopping at New York town to load more cargo. My merchant ship, the *Emily Jane,* arrived there a few days ago and sent a special messenger to let me know before we left Boston."

"Will there be time for a visit to the shops?" Amy asked hopefully. It had been a few years since she'd visited there.

Thaddeus shook his head. "Not this time, my dear. As soon as we load, we'll be sailing. Our cargo is expected soon and so are we."

Captain Bond spoke up. "There will be time for a short foray ashore while we load. You did want me to speak with your agent at the warehouse."

"Quite right. Perhaps we can work something out," Thaddeus conceded.

Amy glanced up, surprised that the captain was the least bit concerned with what she wanted. She found him carefully concentrating on the food in front of him. "It's not important," she said hastily, her heartbeat quickening. She returned to her meal and changed the subject. "The venison is delectable. I must congratulate Mr. Hadley."

"Indeed it is, Captain Bond," Thaddeus agreed, his eyes twinkling. "We shall be quite spoiled if all our meals are this fine."

The captain nodded. "I wish I could take credit for finding the man, but Mr. Oakes is the one we should thank. He is a veritable genius at ferreting out the right man for any task."

"If King George had a good man like Mr. Oakes to advise him, he would be on better terms with the colonists," Thaddeus jested. A discussion on politics and the latest news from England ensued.

28

"Lor'," Toby Oakes said gruffly, "it's like a bloody slap in the face, these Townshend taxes."

Captain Bond agreed in his deep voice. "I'll wager it will cause more trouble in the future if they're not repealed. If His Majesty would but listen to our grievances and use some common sense, he would be rewarded with our loyalty."

Thaddeus spoke. "King George—I heard from Captain Scott—has decided on advice of his party that the colonies are to be punished for our refusal to buy goods, but I fear that His Majesty will be sorry if he makes an issue of it. I attended a merchants' meeting last evening, and the whole assembly was up in arms."

"Aye, sir," Andrew Williams put in, "everyone is talking. I was at Mrs. Cordis's last evening and heard all about it."

"I should think," Amy said passionately, "that the recent murder of some of our townspeople is more than enough of an issue! Why, young Christopher Seider was only twelve years old—his young life snuffed out like a candle flame by a customs informer. And the other five who died in the King Street affair were killed by soldiers of the Crown. Our fair city has turned into a battleground and it's a nightmare to be sure." There were bright spots of color in Amy's cheeks and a fierce look in her green eyes.

Thaddeus sighed. "It was a terrible waste of lives, I'll agree, my dear. However, I arrived on the scene at the King Street incident just as it exploded. There was an angry crowd flinging clubs and chunks of ice at the soldiers in front of the customshouse and taunting them. What followed, I believe, was an unfortunate mistake. The fire bells had been rung, which is why I was there, for I'm a fire warden, and there were several shouts of 'Fire.' Captain Preston's men, I think, heard the command and mistook it as an order from him. I know Captain Preston personally and he is not the type of officer to lose his head. As it stands, the captain and seven of his men have been taken to jail and committed for the misdeed. I am sorry for that and also for the loss of life."

Captain Bond had been quietly studying Thaddeus and his niece during this exchange. He wanted to dislike both of them simply because they were connected to Harlan Stafford, but he found himself giving them a grudging respect instead. He sipped his wine and commented lazily, "I think, sir, from your speech that you are a diplomat. It would be quite difficult to decide which side of the issue you favor . . . unlike your rebel niece."

Amy bristled, but said sweetly, "Do you prefer, Captain Bond, the company of women who have no opinions except those of a domestic nature? Does a woman with political views offend you, perhaps?" She gave him a challenging look as she lifted her own glass of wine and took a dainty sip.

His interest in her heightened with each word spoken. There was a vibrating warmth coming from her and he felt it to the very marrow of his bones. His mouth curved into an unconscious smile. "Quite the opposite, Mistress Hawthorne. I admire a woman who can think and knows her own mind. You needn't ever be silent on my account."

Thaddeus chuckled and turned to his niece. "I think you've met your match, Amy."

Silently, she agreed with her uncle; however, she ignored his comment and gave the captain a thin smile. "Why, thank you, Captain Bond, for the permission to speak freely. I shall remember in the future that I may do so."

Captain Bond's eyes crinkled with amusement for a

moment as he gave her a brief nod. "Touché, Mistress Hawthorne."

Andrew Williams frowned and abruptly went back to the subject at hand. "If King George would rescind the Townshend duties, all of this trouble would cease."

Thaddeus agreed. "He and Lord North are making a grave error in thinking of Americans as children who must be kept in line."

Captain Bond smiled then at Thaddeus, and his words were slightly cynical. "Are you doing business with the British, Mr. Hawthorne?" He had raised his crystal glass of Madeira pointedly and gazed at the ruby color before sipping.

Amy bristled once again, but Thaddeus did not take offense. "A reasonable question, Captain Bond, considering we are enjoying this fine wine. And my answer is that my cellar was well stocked. I have not purchased one pipe of imported wine in two years. I had this sent aboard from my private stock, sir. As for tea, well, we have learned to improvise, eh, Amy?" He smiled and turned to his niece.

"Since Captain Bond needs an explanation, we drink raspberry-leaf tea," she replied, giving Bond a challenging look. Her tone implied it was none of his business. She and her uncle might disagree on many things, but she would not stand by while anyone cast aspersions on his character. "In fact, sir, just last month, I signed a pledge with hundreds of other women of Boston not to buy any East India tea until the impost is repealed." She was thoroughly irritated by this outspoken man, and it did not help any when she caught a brief flash of amusement cross his face.

"I must beg your pardon, Mistress Hawthorne. I meant no offense by my question," he said smoothly and turned to her uncle, dismissing her altogether. "Or to you, sir. Especially since you are my employer. I was merely curious."

Thaddeus chuckled at Captain Bond's forthright manner, but Amy couldn't resist one last retort. "I trust you've heard what happened to the cat who was also affected by curiosity?" She rose then, and the men, caught off guard, rose hastily. "I feel the need for some fresh air," she said, giving them a brilliant smile. "Please excuse me."

She swept from the room, and Fiona, excusing herself, followed in her wake. When out of earshot, Fiona said, "Do let us get our cloaks before we go topside, Amy. I don't think your anger will keep you warm."

"That man is odious! I cannot imagine why Uncle Thad employed him," Amy said, not bothering to deny her frustration.

"Perhaps he's a good ship captain," Fiona pointed out reasonably as they retrieved their wraps.

Once on deck, Amy replied heatedly, "What does that matter if the man is a lout? He was deliberately toying with us. Do you think he could be a spy for the Crown? He seemed intent on learning where our loyalties lay."

There was a brisk breeze, and the sky was star-filled and cloudless. The two women pulled their cloaks tighter to keep the cold out. Fiona waited to speak until they had passed a sailor on watch. "There are many such spies of late, what with the political climate what it is, but I believe that the good captain merely enjoys an argument. Would you like to know what else I've observed about him?"

Fiona's opinion relieved Amy for some strange reason. Although she disliked him intensely, she couldn't bear the thought that the captain could be so low as to inform on his fellow citizens. She glanced at her companion curiously. "Do go on," she prompted.

"He is attracted to you. He could hardly take his eyes off you at dinner," Fiona said.

Amy stopped and stared at her companion for a moment before speaking. "That's nonsense! I certainly didn't think you were one of those empty-headed romantics, Fiona," she chided, glad that the moonlight would not betray her blush.

Fiona's voice held a smile. "My dear Amy, it's the truth whether you want to believe it or not."

They resumed their walk and Amy said flatly, "Well, it doesn't matter, because he's much too arrogant for my liking. When I choose a man, he will be my equal, not my lord and master." Even as she spoke the words, she felt an unwelcome surge of excitement at the thought of him.

"Men rule the world, Amy. Haven't you realized that yet?" Fiona said, a touch of bitterness edging her voice. "We women must learn to use what we have to survive."

The poor girl, Amy thought. She must have felt betrayed by her father when he lost the family fortune.

Amy's chin pushed out a fraction, and the light of battle flared in her eyes. "You're absolutely right, Fiona. However, I intend to do far more than merely survive."

The *Rebecca* arrived at New York harbor the next afternoon, and after the customs officials were dealt with, the crew set to work transferring cargo from the *Emily Jane* to the *Rebecca*. Standing at the rail, Amy was fascinated by the activity all around her. On the wharf, there were vendors hawking their wares, and the seamen chanted as they worked. She saw fashionable gentlemen and ladies strolling along, as well as scruffy children darting in and out of the crowds. The coffee-houses and taverns emitted delectable smells that mingled with the odor of fish.

Thaddeus came up beside her. "If you and Fiona would like, I'll take you ashore for a bit. We can't get too far afield, however. The loading should be completed in an hour or so."

The scene before her was too tempting to refuse. "I'll go fetch Fiona."

In just minutes, they were back. Thaddeus glanced toward the quarterdeck. "Captain Bond is joining us. He has business at the warehouse."

Amy had hoped he would be gone already, but since that was not to be, she decided to make the best of it. He appeared at her elbow a moment later, and she jumped at his touch. "Ready?" he asked, smiling benignly on all of them. He offered his arm to Amy and she reluctantly took it. She found his nearness disturbing and tried to force her confused emotions into order.

Fiona took Thaddeus's arm, and they led on to the gangway. But they had barely taken a few steps when Fiona let out a frightened cry and pitched sideways. Thaddeus grabbed her around the waist and pulled her firmly back against his chest.

For a moment the two of them swayed, and Amy thought they might fall into the murky water, but Thaddeus steadied them. "Are you all right?" Amy called out, anxious over the near-miss.

Fiona was still holding tightly to Thaddeus and shaking from reaction. "I think so," she replied unsteadily. "I turned my ankle."

Thaddeus was patting her shoulder in an awkward way. "No need to feel frightened now," he assured her.

Fiona straightened herself and looked sheepish. "So silly of me," she said, striving to regain her composure. "Please, let's continue." They started forward, but

Fiona leaned heavily on Thaddeus and gasped, "My ankle—I can't walk."

"Let's get her back on board," Thaddeus turned, supporting her weight. "Can you make it, my dear?"

"I think so," she said, leaning on him as they made their way back on deck to a nearby barrel, where she sat down.

Amy kneeled down beside her. "Let me take a look, Fiona."

She lifted her skirts demurely and revealed a shapely ankle and calf encased in a white silk stocking. Amy didn't see anything misshapen about the ankle, but knew it could begin swelling any time. "The ship's doctor should look at it to make sure there are no broken bones, but I think it's just a sprain."

Thaddeus cleared his throat. "In any case, you'll need to stay off it for a while."

Fiona groaned. "How clumsy of me. Now I've ruined the outing ashore for Amy."

"Nonsense," Thaddeus said briskly. "I'll remain here and see you settled, and Amy can continue with Captain Bond."

"I think I should stay—" Amy began to protest, but her uncle waved it aside.

"I insist, my dear." He turned to the captain. "You don't mind, do you?"

"Of course not, sir. I'd be honored to escort Mistress Hawthorne," the captain replied smoothly, and with a smile he offered his arm to her again. "Shall we?"

"I'd really rather stay," Amy tried again, but Fiona pleaded with her. "I'll feel simply dreadful if I ruin your day. Please go on."

Amy was left with no choice, so she descended the gangway with the captain and stepped onto the wharf. Looking back, she saw Thaddeus, with the aid of a sailor, helping Fiona away.

Captain Bond was gazing down at her in a most peculiar manner when she looked up into his steel-gray eyes. "Where would you like to go?" he asked, his voice revealing a certain gruffness.

Amy looked away and said flatly, "Back to my cabin, but since I was coerced into this, I have no preference."

He laughed outright at her candid reply, and Amy, in spite of her opinion of him, liked the sound. It was deep-timbred and warm and gave her gooseflesh. She found herself smiling in response. "You do speak your mind, don't you?" he said, his eyes crinkling at the corners.

"You did give me permission, remember?" she replied in a dry tone.

The look on his face was warm and appealing as he gazed down at her. "That I did. Well, why don't we take care of my business first, and perhaps then you will have decided where you would like to stop," he suggested.

She nodded and they started off. He matched his long-legged stride to her shorter steps and tucked her hand in the crook of his arm. Amy had a queer feeling in the pit of her stomach as she held his muscled arm. She could feel his strong heartbeat through the heavy black coat he wore and it unsettled her. His change of attitude a moment ago also unsettled her. He could be quite attractive and appealing when he chose to be, and it did strange things to her senses.

She tried to concentrate on her surroundings. After a few moments, she asked, "How long have you been in my uncle's employ? I don't recall his ever mentioning your name."

"I signed on a month ago," he replied, and she could hear a touch of amusement in his voice.

Exasperated, she glanced up at him and confirmed her suspicions. Irritably, she asked, "Do you find me entertaining, Captain? Or are you merely laughing at me?"

He didn't look in the least repentant. "Forgive me, Mistress Hawthorne, for my bad manners. It's just that I find your volatile personality so fascinating. I never know whether to expect a tongue-lashing or an angelic smile."

Somewhat mollified by his explanation, Amy smiled slightly and said, "Speaking of temper, I wish to thank you for not mentioning that you had seen me on the wharf that day."

He grinned. "Was that you? I thought it was some spitting wildcat loose on the docks."

Amy's smile widened at his nonsense, and she pointed out, "You were quite rude to me and deserved what you got. My only regret is that poor Jeremy was injured."

He chuckled. "I'm learning to be wary, mistress. Never let it be said that Marcus Bond has a thick head."

"*Marcus* . . . is it a family name?" she asked, liking the strong sound of it.

His smile slowly faded, and his eyes became wintry for a moment. Abruptly, he said, "No . . . I don't believe it is." He pointed out a building up ahead to the right. "That's your uncle's warehouse."

Amy was taken aback for a moment by his mood change, but since they were at the door of the building, she said nothing. She glanced up and noted the sign that simply stated, "Hawthorne of Boston."

She took a seat near the door to wait. There was a man seated at a desk to the far right, and he rose as Captain Bond approached him. They sat down and a discussion ensued, none of which Amy could hear, so she gazed around. It was dark in the corners of the building, but a few lanterns staved off the gloom at the two desks in the room. Another man worked diligently

37

on some paperwork and didn't bother to glance up.

Amy didn't have long to wait before the captain finished his business and returned to her. They walked back out into a darkening day, the weak sunlight having fled.

"Looks like a storm brewing," Marcus observed in a neutral tone as they began retracing their steps. The wind whipped up in small gusts, and a clap of thunder rolled in from the sea. "We'd best take shelter or risk getting drenched," he said, guiding her into a tavern just as the first raindrops began to fall.

Amy pulled her hood back and loosened her cloak as they crossed the common room to a table beside the fireplace. The warmth was more than welcome after experiencing the damp cold air outside.

Captain Bond slipped the cape from her shoulders, his fingers brushing her neck and sending a warm tingling through her body. Amy tried to ignore the sensation.

After they were seated and their order given, he said, "Your uncle will be pleased that the silks he ordered from the Orient arrived at the warehouse and will be loaded before we sail."

"I had quite forgotten about that. He means to gift the Stafford ladies with several pieces, and I myself intend to wheedle some. I have never seen more beautiful colors than the Chinese produce," Amy told him.

The serving girl arrived with a tray of pastries and a pot of coffee. Captain Bond watched Amy choose one of the delicate morsels before he gave a reply. "If you would like an opinion, I think you should wear only that shade of green," he said softly, his eyes warm and appreciative as they skimmed over her attire. "It matches your eyes." The moment the words were out of his mouth, he could have bitten his tongue. Where was his resolve? Not only did he not want to get involved with any woman at this point, but he especially did not want to be attracted to this woman. Her uncle and Harlan Stafford were business partners, and that meant she was linked to Stafford, if only indirectly. And he intended to avenge his mother — nothing could stand in his way.

His unexpected words were like a caress, and Amy strove to retain her composure. Of all the men who had paid her lavish compliments — and there had been several — not one had broken through her cool reserve. This loss of self-control irritated her. She thought that perhaps Fiona had been right about the captain's being attracted to her. However, she could not possibly be interested in anyone as arrogant and bossy as he. That was exactly what she was trying to avoid. She took a sip of her coffee and gave him a bland smile. "I'll take that into careful consideration, Captain Bond," she said flatly, effectively snuffing the amorous light from his eyes.

They paid exaggerated attention to the food for several minutes before Captain Bond broke the silence with a question. "Are you well acquainted with the Staffords?"

"No, not really. My uncle and Harlan Stafford have been business partners for years, but I met him and his son, Justin, only once when they came to Uncle Thad's for a brief visit. The rest of them I have yet to meet." She raised a fine, arched eyebrow. "Do you know them?"

For a moment she saw a watchful fixity in his face before a smooth mask descended. "No, but I will have my chance before long," he said in a cool tone, then added, "I heard that Mr. Stafford is a widower. Is that true?"

"Yes. I believe it's been five years since his wife died, and he's not remarried. Besides Justin, he has a daughter — my age — Pamela, and a spinster sister, Julia, who lives in the household," Amy related, then added with a smile, "I'm quite looking forward to staying there a month. Uncle Thad is the only family I have, and I've

39

often longed to be a part of a large family — brothers and sisters, you know."

"Blood ties don't necessarily mean anything, Mistress Hawthorne, and it's a fool who trusts without reservation," he said stiffly.

His countenance had begun to rival the storm clouds outside, and Amy was confused by his moodiness, not to mention his dark observation. The man was definitely a puzzle.

The rain had slowed to a light mist when they emerged from the tavern, and Captain Bond suggested they return to the ship, saying the loading should be almost finished. Amy readily agreed. On the way back, they spoke only in generalities, each careful not to touch on any personal subject.

Once on the ship, Amy thanked him for escorting her ashore. He gave her a mock salute and strode off in the direction of the quarterdeck without a backward glance. His indifferent attitude stung her pride, and she watched him for a moment, a gleam of challenge in her green eyes. This would not be a boring voyage, she thought.

Going below, she knocked lightly at Fiona's door. A soft voice from within bade her enter, and she found her companion sitting up on her bunk with her foot propped on a pillow. Fiona smiled wanly. "Did you have a pleasant time?"

Amy frowned. "Not really. But how are you? Is your ankle very painful?" She sat down on the chair beside the bunk and looked at the slight swelling above Fiona's foot.

"No. It's much better now. The ship's doctor looked at it and said it wasn't too bad. I'll have to stay off it for a few days, though." She looked contrite. "I'm dreadfully sorry I won't be of much help to you for a while."

"I can manage on my own, Fiona. I'm just glad

it wasn't more severe," Amy assured her.

She looked at Amy speculatively. "Why wasn't the excursion pleasant? Did you have an argument with Captain Bond?"

"Not exactly. However, the man's attitude is less than cheerful, and he makes a very moody companion." Amy gave her a wry smile then and added, "If my afternoon was ruined, it's your fault for sending me off with the wretch alone."

Fiona chuckled. "I was merely doing a bit of innocent matchmaking. I think you'll agree with me that he's a far more interesting candidate than Edward Simpson."

"Ha! More interesting is not necessarily better," Amy chided, and then she rose. "I'd better go freshen up for dinner or I'll be late." She walked to the door and turned. "I'll have a tray sent to you."

As Amy washed and changed her gown, she mentally compared Captain Bond with Edward Simpson. Both men were arrogant, but where Edward seemed so pompous, Captain Bond wore his authority like a well-made suit of clothes. Which was not to say that he couldn't be irritating. Still, there was something definitely virile and stimulating about him. She paused as she heard the sound of activity on deck. The creaking of rigging meant that they were putting to sea, and she went to peer out the small porthole.

It was dark except for some torches lit at intervals along the wharf. After a moment, Amy realized she'd been listening for Captain Bond's voice commanding his crew. She shook herself and sat down to gaze into the mirror. Her hair was in place and needed no alteration, but she blinked in surprise at the telltale flush on her cheeks and the sparkle in her eyes. "It's merely my excitement over the trip . . . and meeting Justin Stafford again," she said aloud, as if to convince herself.

Her thoughts turned to Justin, and she wondered if

41

he was still as handsome as she remembered him. After all, she hadn't seen him since she was twelve years old, and perhaps her childish eyes had made him seem like a fairy-tale knight just because he'd been charming to her. Amy knew he hadn't married as yet, for her uncle had mentioned that fact — several times. She wondered if he was hoping for a match between her and his partner's son. It would be ideal . . . from his point of view, that is. However, she would reserve judgment on Justin Stafford until she got to know him.

Finally finished, she smoothed a wrinkle from her skirt as she stood up. After brief consideration, she had chosen a pink satin gown with a white embroidered petticoat. Her fingers had lingered on a green silk dress before she realized that Captain Bond would most likely assume she was wearing it for him. That would never do, she thought. The man's ego would grow to beastly proportions.

A knock sounded at the door, and when she opened it, Thaddeus stood there. She gave him her best smile as she stood aside for him to enter. "I missed you this afternoon," she said.

He kissed her cheek. "I'm sorry I couldn't accompany you, but I trust Captain Bond served you well."

"He doesn't have your lively wit, Uncle, but we managed," she told him. Amy sat down on her bunk, leaving the chair for him.

A faint look of concern crossed his face. "I've noticed some tension between you two. Has he done anything to distress you?"

"No, Uncle Thad. It's just that his manner is irritating, and you know how I love to put arrogance in its place. Moreover, he seems quite moody," she told him. And it was the truth. However, she failed to mention how the captain made her heart race or how he shook her normal control. She had barely admitted those

42

things to herself.

Thaddeus nodded solemnly. "If the man is moody, it is certainly understandable due to the severe losses he has suffered in the last year."

Amy's interest sharpened. "What sort of losses, Uncle?"

"His parents died within months of each other. And not only that, but the family shipping business lost three ships to pirates, while their last remaining ship went down in a storm with Jonathan, Marcus's father, aboard. Jonathan had failed to insure the cargo, and every cent they had was invested, not to mention some loans besides. The fates have not been kind to Marcus Bond lately," Thaddeus said. Then he added, "However, he's a resourceful young man and will make his own way in the world. I know also that he would not appreciate pity, so perhaps you had better not mention any of this to him, my dear."

"The poor man," Amy said softly, feeling a twinge of guilt for all the unkind things she'd said about him.

"That's exactly what I mean, Amy. He's very astute and will sense your pity," Thaddeus warned.

Amy nodded in agreement. "I suppose so, Uncle. He would probably make me walk the plank should I show him any sympathy."

Thaddeus smiled. "He's a prideful, stubborn man, but I like him. I knew his parents and they were fine people. Marcus, I believe, will mellow with time." He stood then to leave. "I promised Fiona I'd stop in to see her before dinner. Would you like to accompany me?"

"Do go on — I saw her earlier." For a time after he left, Amy sat ruminating over the tragic happenings in Captain Bond's life. Perhaps, due to his circumstances, he could be excused some rude behavior. She made up her mind to be a little more understanding in her dealings with him.

Chapter Three

Dinner proved to be another culinary delight. Mr. Hadley had prepared roasted quail, herbed potatoes and sweet corn. For dessert, he had made a blackberry pie. The fine fare put the men in an excellent mood, and they discussed their usual subjects, including politics, with enthusiasm.

Amy tended quietly to her meal, however, adding nothing to the discussion. The only time she spoke was to answer a question put to her by Andrew Williams regarding the welfare of her absent companion. Her mood was pensive, due to the distressing story her uncle had related to her about the captain. She watched him surreptitiously from beneath her sooty lashes throughout the meal and noted that he too was quiet for the most part, only adding a comment or opinion occasionally.

Moreover, it seemed to her that he avoided looking in her direction. Wasn't that what she wanted? she asked herself. But a feeling of disappointment pricked her.

During a lull in the conversation when Jeremy brought their brandy, Thaddeus, finally noticing her unusual silence, asked, "Are you unwell, Amy? You look a trifle pale."

As she had been wool-gathering, she gave a small

start and then blushed a rosy color. "No . . . no, not at all, Uncle. I am merely tired, I think."

He smiled solicitously. "Perhaps you should retire."

She nodded and rose. "I think I shall — please, gentlemen, stay seated and enjoy your brandy," she urged and left the room.

When she reached her cabin, she unwound her upswept coiffure and brushed her thick copper tresses a hundred strokes. It helped to relieve the tension inside her. Hanging her dress in the cupboard, she slipped into a white lawn nightrail and got into bed. But as the hours slipped by, she tried in vain to fall asleep. Her traitorous mind kept replaying the afternoon spent with Marcus Bond. She could see vividly his smoldering gray eyes flashing in anger and then again warm and compelling as his gaze swept over her in an intimate way. "Stop it!" she hissed as a warm flush stole over her body.

Punching her pillow, she turned several times in an effort to find a comfortable spot and fall asleep. By sheer will and determination, she pushed the captain from her mind and began to doze, floating lightly to that place where dreams took the place of reality.

Marcus Bond followed her there, however, and a soft moan escaped her lips as his mouth took hers in a warm, passionate kiss that flooded her being with liquid excitement. As he pulled her against his strong, lean body, the ship rolled with a particularly large swell, and Amy tumbled to the edge of her bunk. Instinctively, she grasped the sideboard and her eyes flew open. The dream flashed through her mind, and she found that she was trembling.

Her hands came up to cool her flaming cheeks. Rolling agilely off the bunk, she stood in the center of the small cabin fighting her confusion. Never had she had feelings like this about any man. The dream had fired her blood, and with a woman's curiosity she wondered suddenly what would it be like to . . . She halted her wayward thoughts and pulled a soft, green wool wrapper and slippers from the cupboard. She needed some fresh air to clear her brain, she decided hastily.

All was quiet as she walked silently along the passageway. She peered cautiously around at the top of the steps, but saw no one on deck. She chose a shadowed spot at the rail to stand and gaze out on the ocean. The air was cold, but Amy welcomed the feel of it against her fevered skin.

She chewed thoughtfully at her lower lip as she contemplated this intrusion in her life. Marcus Bond was the most handsome, virile man she'd ever met. And he was also arrogant, opinionated and dictatorial. Oh, he had said that he admired a woman who could think for herself, but she knew he would expect obedience from his woman! *His woman* . . . The thought lingered a moment and made her cheeks flush once again.

"You shouldn't be out here half-dressed, you know. This wind will give you a chill," Captain Bond said, coming up behind her.

Amy gave a violent start and whirled about. That familiar, deep-timbred voice sent a wild shiver through her that had nothing to do with the night air. "I . . . I couldn't sleep," she said. She pulled at the front of her wrapper when she realized it was gaping open. Although the moon was on the wane, she could see a faint scowl on his face.

"A cup of tea from the galley would have been more appropriate, Mistress Hawthorne. I have a good crew, but they are men, after all, and if one of them happened upon a vision like you, alone, in the middle of the night out here—well, I'm sure it would test any man's self-control," he said sharply, as if reprimanding a child.

Amy's eyes narrowed. "Are you scolding me, Captain Bond?" she asked incredulously. "You're nothing but a brutish clod, and I will not be lectured by you on the proprieties." Her anger gained force as she spoke, and she stepped closer to him and poked a finger in his chest. "You, sir, are my employee and will treat me with the respect I deserve or my uncle will hear of it!"

She was truly magnificent in a high rage, thought Marcus, catching his breath. Her loose, wild copper hair tumbled about her slim shoulders, and the sweet fragrance of her filled his nostrils. He gripped her upper arms and yanked her against his chest, valiantly trying to sustain his anger, but it was turning into something quite different. "Don't shout, woman," he growled. "Will you bring everyone up on deck to witness your childish fit?"

Amy gasped in outrage. "Childish fit!" she echoed, her voice barely below a screech.

Marcus realized he'd pushed her too far as she began to beat ineffectively at his chest with her small fists. "Unhand me this instant," she gasped.

The heat of her body struggling against him heightened the ache in his loins, and his control snapped. He dipped his head and captured her warm mouth in an angry kiss. At first, his lips punished hers, but as his tongue forced its way into the sweetness of her mouth, his lips gentled on hers in a quickening of desire.

Amy's struggles ceased for a moment in surprise and confusion, but they began anew when she realized what was happening. Her heart fluttered like a trapped bird as she squirmed and pushed against his superior strength. His hot, probing kiss, unlike any she had previously experienced, sent her world spinning crazily. Without conscious thought, her arms slid up to caress the back of his neck.

Marcus groaned and caught her tiny waist in his strong fingers, pulling her tightly to him. He could feel her soft, rounded breasts crushed against his chest as

47

both their hearts beat in an erratic rhythm. His mind clouded in the heat of their embrace.

Amy strained closer to him, becoming pliant, almost liquid in his arms as she surrendered to a passion she'd never known before.

Marcus finally raised his head and gazed into her flushed face. Amy tried to collect herself, but found she was trembling and her breathing ragged.

Her hands rested still upon his broad shoulders, and he retained his hold on her waist. His composure was no more steady than hers. "I shouldn't have done that," he whispered hoarsely, "but you made me so angry."

Amy felt a prick of annoyance at his words. The kiss had been wildly exciting, and now he was spoiling it with his arrogant attitude. She stepped back and let her arms fall to her sides. Lifting her small chin, she said in an unsteady voice, "You were quite right when you said I could be accosted out here alone. However, sir, you did not need to prove your point in such a . . . physical way. Please consider your warning heeded—goodnight!"

She didn't give him a chance to respond, but stepped around him and went belowdecks. Marcus stepped over to lean on the rail and gaze out at the sea. The moon, very low now, silvered the surface of the water in the ship's wake, but all he could see was the beauty of Amy's perfect features, the wild disarray of her curling copper hair, the slim yet rounded figure with curves that fit his hands. His jaw flexed in frustration. In a few short days, the fiery vixen had managed to wedge herself under his skin like a thorny burr. For that was what she was—an irritation. He scowled for a moment at the remembered sharpness of her tongue . . . and then came the memory of her softness crushed against his hard frame. He groaned inwardly—Mistress Amy Hawthorne had sorely strained the seams of his endurance.

* * *

Fiona was still confined to her bed the next day, and Amy spent several hours with her but finally made her way up on deck in the late afternoon. It was cloudy and the wind was brisk, filling the sails and pushing them along at a good speed. Amy clutched her heavy pelisse tightly and was glad of the warm fur lining. The sailors, busy with their chores, nodded or spoke respectfully as she made a turn around the main deck. She hadn't seen her uncle since breakfast and guessed that he and Captain Bond were talking business. It seemed that was all the two of them were interested in, except politics, of course, and Amy was feeling peevish about being ignored.

Not that she wanted any attention from Captain Bond—quite the contrary! After that scorching kiss last night, she was determined to keep her distance from him. He was an overbearing lout, and she was counting the days until this voyage was over and she would no longer be subject to his boorish behavior.

But as she walked briskly around the deck, her cheeks grew rosy at the memory of how warmly she had responded to his lovemaking. It was merely curiosity, she told herself soothingly. Of all the suitors she'd had, none had given her more than a chaste, tight-lipped kiss—and only after asking permission. She had discarded each man who'd sought her favor as unsatisfactory, all the while yearning for something she couldn't put a name to. She was a woman, after all—not a child any longer—and Captain Bond had made her feel womanly for the first time in her life. However, he meant nothing to her, for she knew that someday the *right* man would come along and he would make her feel loved and cherished above all else.

A voice behind her brought her attention back to the present, and she turned to see Andrew Williams bearing

49

down on her. She smiled at the young officer. "Good afternoon, Mr. Williams."

He gave her a small salute, his expression earnest. "Good day to you, Mistress Hawthorne. I hope you haven't been ill this morning. I usually see you taking your exercise at an early hour."

"No," she assured him with a small smile. "I spent the morning with my companion so that she wouldn't get too lonely while confined to her cabin."

"That's very commendable of you," he said, his manner serious. "How is Mistress Morgan?"

"She'll be up and about tomorrow, I'm sure." Amy smiled again then and added, "If I call you Andrew, will you call me Amy? I don't see the need to be so formal, do you?"

His brown eyes lit up, and he smiled as if he was feeling more at ease. "I'd be pleased, Mistress Amy. And if I might be so bold, you look like a ray of sunshine in that gown."

Amy smiled at the exaggerated compliment on her yellow wool dress and matching pelisse. "Would you like to accompany me on my walk, Andrew? I would enjoy the company."

Before he could answer, something caught his attention just over her shoulder. He snapped to attention, and Amy turned to see Captain Bond approaching.

His dark face was set in stern lines, and his slate-gray eyes bored into the young officer. "I believe you're needed on the quarterdeck, Mr. Williams," he said curtly.

"Aye, sir," the young officer said smartly and then nodded to Amy. "Perhaps another time, Mistress Amy."

She felt sorry for Andrew as he hurried away, for Captain Bond's tone seemed unduly harsh. "I suppose it was a matter of life and death that he get there immediately,"

50

Amy snapped, glancing sharply up at the captain.

His brows drew together in a frown. "My men have their duties, Mistress Hawthorne, and should not allow distractions to interfere with them."

His superior tone set her teeth on edge. "So it's my fault, is it?" she challenged, glaring at him. At this moment, she couldn't understand why she'd ever found him attractive.

He stared a moment at her angry expression, and then a slow smile began to form at the corners of his mouth. "No . . . but I must admit that a man could forget his purpose while staring into those emerald eyes."

His voice was deep and warm, sending involuntary shivers down her spine. The swift change in his mood left her confused once again, and she couldn't think of a scathing retort to his compliment, so she turned away abruptly. "Please excuse me, Captain Bond, I'll just continue my walk. I'm sure you also have things to do."

Ignoring the hint, he took Amy's arm firmly and matched his stride to hers. "Nothing important at the moment. I'll just keep you company."

Goaded by his presumptuous behavior, she said firmly, "Captain Bond, I don't want to appear ill-mannered, but I prefer taking my exercise alone." She jerked to a halt, thereby forcing him to stop also.

A mischievous look came into his eyes, and one brow lifted. "That's not quite true, Mistress Hawthorne. I heard you ask young Williams to accompany you just a few minutes ago."

Amy didn't know which she detested more, his sarcasm or his amusement at her expense. A flush of annoyance warmed her cheeks. "If you were a gentleman, Captain Bond, you wouldn't put me in the position of having to tell you that I heartily dislike you," she said, glowering at him.

"You're still angry about last night," he chided

51

lightly, ignoring the insult, which further exasperated her. "I'm willing to put that unfortunate incident behind us if you are," he suggested blandly.

Amy had to clench her hands at her sides to keep from slapping his smug face. How dare he treat her like a pouting child? And he acted as if they had had a mild disagreement instead of a blazing argument and a passionate kiss. However, she certainly didn't want him to think the interlude had meant anything to her. She lifted her gaze and gave him a derisive smile. "I'm surprised you mention it, Captain. It was but a tiff and I had quite forgotten it."

"Good," he said, grinning, his eyes telling her he knew she was lying. "I'm glad to see you do not hold grudges."

She read his knowing look correctly and ground her teeth in frustration. He always knew exactly what to say to stir her temper. She smiled thinly. "I feel a headache coming on, Captain. Excuse me."

Marcus watched her walk away, admiring the provocative sway of her hips. He felt a tightening in his loins as he thought about the night before and how she'd felt in his arms. It made his mouth go dry when he recalled the stirring kiss they'd shared. "Damned vixen!" he muttered hoarsely, irritated with himself for letting thoughts of her cloud his mind.

On the third day of her confinement, Fiona Morgan sat before her mirror humming a tuneless song as she applied a touch of rouge to each cheek. She assessed her features objectively as if each had a saleable value. The large brown eyes framed by dark lashes were her best asset, she thought. Nevertheless, her small, straight nose and generous mouth seemed to be equally attractive to men . . . and there had been many, many men. However, her last affair had cost Fiona dearly. John Haverley was a wealthy lawyer who owned the estate next to the Morgans' in Philadelphia. He was rich, charming, married . . . and a womanizer. The Morgans and the Haverleys attended the same social functions, and Fiona and John had immediately recognized in each other a base desire for illicit excitement.

She had been sent home in disgrace from Dalton Academy just a month before for an affair with her riding master which her parents had tried to keep quiet. Fiona grimaced when she remembered the terrible scene they'd made over it. Her father had ranted and raved for over an hour while her mother sat by and wept. "You have ever had the morals of a tavern wench and have been an embarrassment to us. The Morgan name," he'd shouted, "has always stood for integrity both here and in Ireland, and I also beg you to remember that I am a deacon in the church! Do you seek to disgrace me before my peers?"

Fiona had sat quietly, eyes downcast through this tirade as if she were repentant, but she seethed inside at the injustice of it all. How dare he speak of integrity and disgrace when she knew he was bedding the upstairs maid and had been for two years. While home for a short holiday the year before, Fiona had happened upon the two of them in the library late one night. She'd been on her way to the kitchen for a late snack when she heard noises behind the door. Carefully, she had opened the door a crack and recognized her father's voice crooning hoarsely to Milly and calling her by name. She couldn't see more than dark tangled shapes on the settee, but ragged breathing and deep moans told the story clearly.

Quietly, she had closed the door and slipped back up to bed. She, herself, had been caught in several compromising situations since the age of fifteen, and her father had always punished her in righteous indignation. This midnight tryst was all the more shocking for that reason.

The following day, Fiona had cornered Milly and frightened the truth from her. Leland Morgan — upstanding citizen, respected banker, deacon of the church — was an adulterer who had forced his attentions on a helpless servant girl. Poor Milly had lived in fear of losing her job, which kept her from starvation. In that time, the girl had sobbed, Morgan, to keep his secret, had forced her to abort the baby she'd conceived.

Fiona was coldly furious at his hypocritical behavior. When she remembered all the pious sermons she'd endured from him, she wanted to scream her ire and lay this knowledge at his feet. However, she thought it over and knew it would do no good. Men retained all the rights, while women were mere possessions to be owned by them. And even if she found anyone who would take her accusations seriously, his punishment would most likely be a mild admonition to do better, and her punishment would have been losing her home and family. So, she'd kept quiet and returned to school.

Her affair with the riding master had been discovered in the stables by the old biddy who taught French and had a habit of bringing apples to feed the horses. The riding teacher had declared undying love for her — until questioned by the headmaster of the school, at which time he promptly assured his superior that Fiona had repeatedly thrown herself at him and had finally seduced him. She was expelled, and her lover was given a stern lecture.

Fiona's lips thinned with displeasure as the memories once again left a sour taste in her mouth. The final drama had been played out when her father found out about her affair with John Haverley. Her large brown

54

eyes stared into the mirror and through her own reflection to the past.

Leland Morgan had called her into his library and coldly announced that she was no longer part of his family. She was to leave that very day and never return. Fiona had been stunned, but managed to collect her wits and ask sarcastically what blame Haverley would receive. After all, he had a wife and children — wasn't he as guilty as she, or more so?

"John Haverley is an upstanding family man who was tempted beyond his endurance by you. A bad seed is what you are, wench — a seducer of righteous men," he shouted, pointing an accusing finger in her face.

With that, her control had snapped. "I suppose that's what Milly is also? A seducer of righteous men, eh, Papa?" she asked heatedly, her eyes narrowing.

Leland Morgan paled to a pasty color and stuttered an unconvincing denial, but Fiona knew she had the advantage. While he might not receive any stiff punishment, he was a hypocrite and didn't want the truth of the affair bandied about the parlors of Philadelphia.

Fiona was sick of her father and wanted to leave even more than he wanted to be rid of her. Hence, she proposed a solution: for a tidy sum of money, she would not only keep quiet, but would move to Boston, never to return. He agreed and she packed and left.

Fiona stood up, slipped a beige satin wrapper loosely over the matching nightrail she wore and sat on her bed, arranging herself to good advantage. Her sable-brown hair, brushed to a shine, floated about her shoulders in casual disarray. The seductive scent of her French perfume filled the small cabin as she had intended. A self-satisfied smile played about her generous mouth as she remembered how easy it had been to obtain the position of companion to Amy. Her main thought when leaving Philadelphia to go to Boston was to find a rich husband in a city where her shady past was unknown.

Upon arriving in Boston, she'd seen the advertisement and remembered that Amy lived with a wealthy bachelor uncle. The rest had been easy. And her sprained ankle was the opportunity she'd been looking for. Thaddeus Hawthorne might have avoided the state of matrimony up until now, but that was going to change.

Fiona knew she'd already caught his attention. But this time she'd been very subtle in her advances. Her first ploy had been the story she'd concocted about her lost family fortunes and her own desire to work and be self-sufficient. That had left Thaddeus with a good impression of her character. From there she'd proceeded cautiously, dressing demurely, acting in a quiet, mature manner. Then came the day she'd conveniently turned her ankle and had held him tightly for support. She'd pressed her firm, ripe breasts against his chest and felt a trembling response from him. Since then, he'd been extremely attentive to her welfare, stopping in to check on her frequently. Fiona's smile broadened. He didn't realize yet that he was attracted to her, but soon . . .

A knock sounded on the door, and Fiona checked her gown to make sure a bit of cleavage was showing. She picked up a book, holding it in her lap, and called softly, "Come in."

Thaddeus stepped inside and smiled warmly. His gaze swept over her seductive appearance and hastily rose to meet her innocent brown eyes. He cleared his throat and moved to sit down. "You're looking very fit this morning, Fiona. I trust you slept well."

She smiled demurely. "Thank you, yes." Sighing, she said, "I am growing rather tired of this inactivity, however. If only I had a cane, I could perhaps get up today and take a walk on deck."

Thaddeus leaned forward eagerly and offered, "I'll

be happy to be your support, my dear. After lunch would be a good time, don't you agree?"

Her face brightened at the suggestion. "How kind you are, Mr. Hawthorne! I shall be ready and waiting."

Her voice was breathless, and the heightened color in her cheeks momentarily arrested him as he rose and excused himself.

As the door closed behind him, Fiona smiled to herself once more and began to hum softly.

Andrew Williams hurried to the dining room early and was waiting when Amy arrived with her uncle for the noon meal. He rose hastily and held the chair next to his for her while Thaddeus shook his head in bemusement. Anytime Amy was about, the young men fell over themselves to give her attention, and the irritating twit took it as her due. As a result, she left many broken hearts in her wake.

Amy smiled her thanks, and Andrew hastened to engage her in conversation. "Have you been on deck this morning, Mistress Amy? The breeze is warming as we head into the Gulf Stream."

"I was attending to some small chores in my cabin and failed to take my exercise, but I certainly shall do so this afternoon, Andrew. Is it warm enough that a light wrap would be sufficient?" she asked, anticipating the more favorable weather.

Thaddeus spoke up. "You had better stay with the warmer cloak just now, my dear. We are not yet in the tropics." He smiled and added, "I've promised Fiona a turn around the deck this afternoon. Perhaps you'd care to accompany us?"

"Is her ankle so much better?" Amy asked hopefully.

Thaddeus was placing his napkin on his lap and nodded. "The doctor said she could begin using it."

"I would enjoy the company, Uncle. Besides, you've been so busy of late, I've scarce laid eyes on you," Amy chided gently.

Captain Bond entered the room, nodding to the assembled company and apologizing for his tardiness. As he seated himself at the head of the table, he rang a small silver bell beside his plate, and Jeremy entered with a bottle of Madeira.

With a glint of mischief in her eyes, Amy said casually, "If your duties are not pressing, Andrew, please join us on our walk."

She glanced at the captain, expecting him to object, but he seemed preoccupied with sampling his glass of wine.

"I'm not on duty until tonight. Thank you for including me," Andrew said, his face brightening.

Jeremy began serving the first course—an onion soup—and Thaddeus turned to Captain Bond. "Since our paperwork is completed, Marcus, I shall endeavor to entertain my niece. She has been berating me for my lack of attention."

Marcus gave his employer a slight smile. "With no house to care for or shops to visit, the ladies always become dispirited on a sea voyage. We men tend to neglect them as our duties press upon us."

Amy blanched at the condescending tone in his voice, but she said coolly, "If I but had some duties to occupy me, I would be far happier than I am now, when forced into idleness. However, my uncle feels that any sort of occupation for a woman of my station in life is the next thing to black sin."

Thaddeus turned a stern eye on her. "She exaggerates her cause greatly, I fear. I merely want for her what her parents would have prescribed, had they lived—a suitable marriage, a home, children."

Marcus noted the high color in Amy's cheeks and the

58

frown on her brow. He couldn't resist prodding her temper. "That sounds reasonable, sir. Most young ladies find those womanly occupations worthwhile and satisfying."

Amy looked archly from her uncle to Captain Bond as she dabbed at her lips with the linen napkin. In her opinion, the views of men tended to be pompous and irritating beyond belief. "It's a matter of choice, gentlemen," she said in a level tone, holding her temper in check. "My argument is that a woman should be able to choose the course of her life, whether it be marriage or business . . . or both."

Captain Bond's eyebrows rose inquiringly. "Merely for argument's sake, Mistress Hawthorne, what course would you choose if you were not so hampered by your wealth and social position?"

His question, phrased thus, made her protests seem petty. She was all the more determined to best him, especially since she detected a flicker of amusement in his eyes. "On the matter of business, I would open an academy for young ladies in Boston. The curriculum would include the sciences, fencing, law and courses in navigation — none of which were taught where I attended. I believe a woman's brains and talents are shamefully wasted in our society," she said firmly, a hint of challenge in her tone.

Marcus couldn't hide a look of surprise that crossed his face. He recovered himself and asked, his voice a shade warmer, "And what would become of the fine arts of sewing, music and household management? Would your students neglect these studies?"

"Of course not, Captain Bond," she said with a dry smile. "They would add the new studies to the present ones, giving them the opportunity to widen their world."

Andrew, who had fallen silent during this exchange,

spoke up. "What a novel idea, Mistress Hawthorne. That sort of thinking is indeed modern — I applaud you!"

Amy gave him a genuine smile. "You, sir, are truly a man of the world."

Marcus, when she glanced at him, had a gleam of interest in his gray eyes. "I find myself agreeing with Andrew, Mistress Hawthorne . . . which I'm sure surprises you."

Amy studied his expression, looking for a spark of insincerity, and when she found none, she felt a delicious warmth steal over her. She didn't understand why, but his opinion mattered to her.

Thaddeus harrumphed loudly. "She's headstrong enough already. Pray, don't add fuel to that fire."

Marcus chuckled and rang the small bell, bringing Jeremy with the next course. The conversation turned to business — their cargo in particular — and Amy settled down to her meal and let their talk flow over her. Barrels of salt cod from Boston barely interested her. However, she became aware that a strange fluttering in her stomach erupted each time Captain Bond spoke. His deep-timbered voice did strange things to her senses.

Chapter Four

Fiona leaned heavily on Thaddeus's arm, pressing herself against him as they walked slowly along the deck. She was wearing a pale blue silk dress with a matching pelisse. There was a becoming rose tint to her cheeks as she smiled warmly up at the older man and said, "What a wonderful change. It feels like springtime."

Thaddeus's gaze traveled over her attractive features, and he found himself extremely conscious of her womanly appeal. "That it does, my dear. And in another day or so, it will feel like summer. There is an amazing change in climate between the colonies and the Bermuda Islands for such a short distance," he said, his voice not quite steady. How long had it been, he thought, since he had taken note of the passing seasons . . . or anything besides business? He realized also that it had been a long time since he'd been with a woman or even thought of one. For years, he'd visited the Widow Harvey when an amorous urge came upon him. It had been a physically satisfying relationship with no commitment expected on either side. And when she had decided to marry another suitor, he'd graciously wished her well. To his surprise, he realized that had been several years ago. Fiona's soft voice brought him back to the present as he picked up the thread of what she was saying.

". . . am so happy I took this post, Mr. Hawthorne. I feel as if I've begun a new and exciting life." She gave his arm a gentle squeeze.

Thaddeus smiled at her enthusiasm and thought how beautiful her large brown eyes were when she didn't have on her spectacles. "You are amazing, Fiona," he said, shaking his head. "You lost your home, family and social position, and yet you are happy and optimistic."

She gave a merry laugh. "Oh, I was a bit frightened at first, but when I found you and Amy, I knew everything would be all right."

Thaddeus gave her a tender look. "I'm glad you did, my dear."

Fiona glanced up ahead at Amy and Andrew, who were strolling and talking. "I certainly haven't been of much help to Amy this past week," she said with a sigh.

"Nonsense. Accidents happen and it's not your fault," he said. Following her gaze, he lowered his voice and added, "I would appreciate your help, Fiona, on a matter concerning my niece. You are levelheaded and seem far more mature than your years, whereas Amy is headstrong and, I fear, somewhat spoiled. Could you possibly help guide her away from the wrong ideas she sometimes gets?"

Fiona looked into his earnest expression and felt a surge of triumph. He was placing her on his level and even confiding in her. She had gained his trust as well as a budding interest. Her plan was working perfectly. "Of course, Mr. Hawthorne. I've grown quite fond of Amy and will do whatever I can to help."

Amy and Andrew were well ahead of the other couple due to Fiona's slow progress. The young officer had been answering Amy's questions about the life of a sailor. As he began a serious discourse on the *Rebecca's* strong and weak points, Amy's thoughts drifted. Andrew was nice looking, well groomed, pleasant and thoroughly boring. Captain Bond's handsome visage floated through her mind and, once again, she felt a surge of excitement. She wondered why he awoke intense feelings in her when the other men in her life had failed.

Her uncle thought she was merely being stubborn about choosing a mate, but that was not true. It was simply that her suitors up to now had either bored or repulsed her. Although she had no experience with intimate relationships, she knew what occurred in the marriage bed — Hannah had explained it to her. Hannah also explained that with the right man she would welcome the act of love. Armed with this knowledge, Amy had tested her feelings with each suitor, but she'd found herself shying away from their kisses . . . until Marcus Bond. She remembered vividly the warm excitement that had raced through her body at his touch, his kiss.

At the edge of her attention, Amy noted that Andrew's speech was coming to an end. "So you can see, Bermuda-built vessels like this one have been proven far superior to any others," he said with confidence.

"I've heard Uncle Thad mention that fact, Andrew. I believe most of our ships were Bermuda-built from the Stafford shipyards," she replied, steering their course to the rail. Looking back, she watched her uncle and Fiona coming in their direction.

A young sailor approached and nodded respectfully to Amy before addressing Andrew. "Sir, Mr. Oakes wants a word with you on the forecastle deck. The weather is changing."

Amy lifted an inquiring brow. "I trust it's not serious," she said.

Andrew smiled and assured her, "Nothing to worry about, Mistress Amy. Please excuse me."

Amy explained Andrew's departure when the others arrived at her side. "It would be rare indeed," Thaddeus said, smiling, "if we completed the voyage without at least one squall." He gazed out over the gently rolling waves. "We're in the Sargasso now, ladies — a sea surrounded by an ocean — and her currents are much warmer. I've made this crossing many times, and the strangeness of these waters is always amazing to me."

"A sea surrounded by an ocean? That hardly sounds possible," Amy said, her interest piqued.

"It is an enigma," he agreed. "There are many stories about this area — ships lost, never to be heard from again, and ghost ships found floating with no captain or crew."

"Good heavens, that gives me gooseflesh," Fiona said, giving a small shudder.

Thaddeus chuckled. "Forgive me, ladies. I didn't intend to frighten you. They are merely tales told by over-imaginative sailors too long at sea and in need of entertainment."

Amy smiled. "It takes more than that to frighten me, Uncle, as you well know. I've always had a fondness for ghost stories. Hannah used to tell them to me at bedtime."

He laughed again. "You are incorrigible, Amy."

Fiona made an involuntary sound, and Thaddeus and Amy glanced at her with concern. "Is it your ankle?" Amy asked.

"It's just throbbing a bit," the girl said apologetically.

"We must get you to your cabin. How thoughtless of me to keep you standing so long," Thaddeus said, frowning. He placed an arm around her waist and she leaned against him.

64

"I'll come along and see you settled," Amy offered.

"Please don't bother," Fiona pleaded. "I'll manage just fine. Stay and enjoy the fresh air."

Amy watched them until they were out of sight, and then turned to gaze at the ocean. Smiling, she thought that Fiona had been more of a companion to her uncle of late. The deep blue of the water fascinated her. Even the foamy caps of the waves were blue. As she watched, a yellow-green fish about four feet long rose up out of the blue water and made a graceful arc before it nosed back beneath the surface. She laughed aloud in sheer delight. It had been years since she'd seen a dolphin, and it brought back memories of other voyages and the wonders of the ocean.

"They are amusing creatures," said a deep voice behind her.

There was no need to turn around, for she knew that voice. Her heartbeat quickened, and she swallowed to relieve the sudden dryness in her mouth. He stepped up to the rail beside her and rested his arms on its width.

She spoke softly. "I'd forgotten how much I loved the sea."

"It can get into your blood," he agreed quietly, then added more slowly, "My . . . father couldn't bear being landlocked for more than a month at a time, and my mother couldn't board a ship without becoming seasick."

Amy could hear an underlying thread of regret in his tone, but she sensed that he would not want her pity. Lightly, she said, "That must have made for an unusual marriage."

"I suppose it was, but they loved each other very much," he said, a smile in his voice.

"My parents were happy too. I can remember how mother's eyes would light up when Papa came

65

into the room. They died in a house fire when I was ten," she said, wistful, her own memories returning.

They were silent for a few minutes, and then Amy asked, "What is that floating mass there? And there's another." She pointed out to the left, squinting to see better.

"It's sargasso weed. You'll see a lot of it before we reach Bermuda. The Sargasso Sea is thick with it. It floats in wide rafts like that," he told her.

"But we're not even near a shore—too far away for seaweed," she protested.

"Some think it grows on the ocean floor here-abouts and becomes so thick it breaks away and drifts to the top. There are stories of the weed tangling and trapping ships as large as this one."

She looked at him for the first time and was struck anew by his handsome profile. The wind and sun had bronzed his skin, and the heavy dark blue coat nearly matched the blue-black of his hair. The effect he had on her senses gave her a moment's pause, but she forced her voice to a normal tone. "Uncle Thad said as much. However, he seemed to think it was merely imaginative tales."

He turned to face her, and his eyes, so changeable in different moods, were as warm as pewter now. "That's possible, but in my travels, I've seen some very strange things."

The eye contact was almost like a physical caress, but she rigidly held onto her composure. "I have always had a yearning to travel the world. Men have such freedom, while we women are compelled to stay at home and tend to domestic chores."

His eyes lit with admiration. "I have never met a woman quite like you, Mistress Hawthorne. If you could, would you captain your own ship in your travels?"

"Aye, Captain Bond, and why not?" she questioned, raising an arched brow.

He gave a bark of laughter and offered her his arm. "Why not, indeed. Come along and have your first lesson."

Amy hesitated only a second before she took his arm and followed him across the main deck to climb to the quarterdeck. Marcus dismissed the sailor at the wheel and moved to take his place.

"Do you know anything of a ship's workings?" he asked.

"I'm afraid not. As I said before, my education is somewhat lacking in certain areas."

"Take the wheel," he instructed.

She placed her hands on two of the extended spokes of the large wooden wheel as he stepped aside. "It controls the rudder that's attached to the hull. This," he said, placing a hand on a wood-and-glass box, "is the binnacle. It houses the compass and gives us our direction."

As she held the wheel steady, she glanced over at Marcus, her green eyes sparkling. "It must be a wonderful feeling to command a vessel and bend it to your will."

He chuckled and leaned a shoulder comfortably against the rail. "I should have known better, Mistress Hawthorne. This taste of power will most likely lead you to mutiny."

Amy grinned mischievously and quipped, "Aye, Captain Bond. You had best beware of me."

His eyes locked with hers as the playful words struck in him a serious note. Indeed, he would need to guard his feelings, for he was surely attracted to the lovely redhead.

An unexpected gust of southerly wind caught the mainsail broadside, causing it to clap like thunder. The wheel lurched, nearly jerking itself free of Amy's hands, and she gave a gasp of surprise. In an instant, Marcus stepped behind her and steadied the wheel in his strong grasp, bringing the prow back on course.

Amy's sweet perfume filled his nostrils, and the press of her soft body against his warmed his blood more than a bit. In a husky voice, he said, "Perhaps we'd best continue the lesson at another time."

Amy took a deep, unsteady breath and hastily agreed. "Aye, Captain . . . another time." Her heart had suddenly begun to flutter like a trapped bird. He dropped one arm, and she moved away from the heady prison to gather her composure.

Marcus scanned the horizon and noted the dark clouds that had gathered there. "We're headed into a storm," he said without looking at her. "I must see to my ship now."

His terse words served to break the spell. "Of course, Captain Bond," she replied. Lifting the skirts of her pink silk gown, she descended the flight of steps to the main deck and made her way to her cabin without once looking back.

The bright sky turned prematurely dark as the afternoon wore on. Amy paced the small cabin for a time, fuming over Captain Bond's high-handed treatment. Dismissing her as if she were a lackey! She vowed that for the remainder of the trip she would give him no more than a civil greeting, and that only when absolutely necessary. She credited her racing pulse to anger, refusing to examine her feelings too closely.

Unable to bear her own company any longer, she went to knock lightly at Fiona's door. There was no answer, and Amy decided her companion must be sleeping. Making her way to the next cabin, she again knocked, hoping to find her uncle free. As she waited,

Jeremy Cooper came along the passageway, his arms loaded with linens. He stopped when he saw her and nodded politely. "Your uncle is on the quarterdeck with Captain Bond, Mistress Hawthorne."

"Thank you, Jeremy," she murmured, and turned back to her own cabin. She stepped inside and retrieved her pelisse from a hook on the door.

Once on the main deck, she moved to stand at the rail, carefully averting her gaze from the quarterdeck. The breeze, although not as chilly as it had been the day before, was growing more brisk. Amy noted that the lazy blue waves had changed to hurrying, shallow ripples that had darkened in color. She felt restless, irritable, and wished the voyage was over. There was hardly ever a time when she wasn't in control of her emotions, but lately one disturbance after another seemed to upset the balance of her life. If only her uncle weren't so adamant about finding her a husband, she mused. Moreover, his choice of Edward Simpson made her shudder. Since she was a practical and intelligent young woman, not many guessed that she possessed a romantic heart. In her private daydreams, she yearned for love — for a man who was not only strong, but gentle, a man who would champion her causes, but not feel it necessary to break her will. She wanted a loving, equal partner.

Amy pulled a wry face. If she was going to find this paragon, it would have to be on the island of Bermuda, for if she returned to Boston unmarried, Edward Simpson awaited her.

Her thoughts turned to Justin Stafford as a possible alternative, but it had been eight years since she'd seen him. She knew not what sort of man he had grown into. She turned at the sound of approaching footsteps and was relieved that it was her uncle.

"We're heading into a storm, according to Captain Bond," he said.

"I trust it won't be a bad one," she replied, glancing at the sky. The dark clouds that had crowded the horizon earlier were moving closer.

"Winter squalls are generally not as violent as summer storms," he said reassuringly.

They turned to lean on the rail and gaze out at the choppy water. A large shape rose briefly out of the water, and a stream of water spewed forth from its back. "A sperm whale," Thaddeus breathed softly, as if afraid to raise his voice and frighten the creature away.

It was an awesome sight for Amy, who had never seen one before. The huge fish dipped below the surface and rose again before disappearing. "It was nearly as big as our ship," she gasped.

"Aye," Thaddeus agreed. "It takes brave lads to go on whaling expeditions. The men of St. David's Island in Bermuda are very skillful whalers, I'm told."

"My adventurous nature doesn't extend that far, I'm afraid," Amy murmured, still awestruck by the sight.

"I can be thankful for that," he said. "Your escapades have aged me beyond my years, and I'll be relieved to see you married and settled."

"You have such a talent for exaggeration, Uncle!" she chided. "You look younger and more handsome than any man I know."

Thaddeus regarded her with amusement. "Don't try to change the subject with your overstated flattery."

Amy laughed. "Very well, but I do mean what I said." She slid her hand comfortably in the crook of his arm and asked, "Speaking of marriage, why did you never enter into that blissful state?"

His brow furrowed. "As I recall, the woman I was interested in when I was a young man married someone else."

"Were you so in love with her that you couldn't care for another?" Amy asked seriously.

He smiled and patted her hand. "Well, at first, I think that was the case, but then I became so involved in business I ceased to think about such things."

There was a wistful quality in his voice, and Amy wondered if he regretted this fact. She also felt a twinge of guilt. "Perhaps the added responsibility of raising me kept you from the normal course of your life."

He was quick to disagree. "Not at all, Amy. You've given my life meaning. After your parents died, I believe I would have turned into a bitter man if not for you."

Amy was touched by his declaration and had to swallow a lump in her throat. Even if she didn't agree with him on some matters, she knew he had her best interest at heart. In a small voice, she said, "I love you, Uncle Thad, and I'll try to cause you no more worry. Mayhap I will soon meet a man suitable to be a husband."

Thaddeus squeezed her hand. "Pray, don't change too much, child," he said, a smile in his voice. "Life would be quite dull."

Amy lifted misty eyes to smile at him, a hint of mischief there. "If you insist, Uncle."

Thaddeus laughed. "That's the Amy I know," he said and then sobered a bit. "However, your future husband is a true concern, my dear."

"Aye," she agreed in a more serious vein.

He was quiet for a time, as if deep in thought. Finally he spoke. "I had a letter from Harlan a few weeks ago. He wants his son to settle down and marry also. He suggested that you would make a proper wife for his heir."

Amy nodded and gazed out at the gray choppy water. "It's strange, but I was just thinking about Justin. When he came with his father to visit us, he was kind to me."

"I remember very well. You were just beginning to get over your parents' death, and he spent most of that afternoon talking with you. I was impressed with his sensitivity."

Amy smiled at the memory. "And I was quite taken with his good looks and charm."

"Perhaps you will feel the same when you meet him again," Thaddeus said hopefully.

"Perhaps . . ." was Amy's noncommittal reply.

Memories of Justin Stafford stayed with Amy through the evening as the full force of the storm buffeted the ship. The entire crew was needed to keep the vessel on course, so Thaddeus, Amy and Fiona found themselves alone at dinner. Mr. Hadley, who did not allow even the elements to interfere with his culinary art, had prepared baked rockfish, which they found very tender and sweet.

Fiona smiled at the two of them across the table. "I am so happy I could join you tonight. It's terribly trying on the nerves to be confined to bed, especially if one is not ill."

"I agree," Amy said, glancing at her uncle. "Remember the time I was thrown from my horse and had to stay abed for a week? That week was at least a month long."

Thaddeus smiled. "It seemed much longer than that to me, for you complained constantly."

Amy chuckled and hastily grabbed for her wine glass as the ship rolled to the right suddenly. Some of the ruby liquid splashed on the bodice of her cream-colored silk gown. "Oh dear," she cried, dabbing at the stain with her napkin. Rising, she said, "I'll be back in a moment."

When Amy returned to the dining room, after removing most of the stain, her uncle was talking about the Staffords. "And besides his business interests in Boston, Harlan owns a shipyard in Bermuda and deals heavily in the salt trade."

Fiona smiled. "He must be an astute businessman

ike yourself to handle such diverse concerns."

Amy noticed that her uncle flushed with pleasure at he compliment, and Fiona's color was high. There was something different about the older girl lately, and Amy realized that Fiona was not wearing her spectacles. Her hair was also arranged in a softer style. She was beginning to look like the girl Amy remembered from school—fashionable and sophisticated. Before Amy could dwell on these changes, Fiona asked a question hat Amy herself had intended to ask.

"I am curious about the other members of Mr. Stafford's household, if you don't mind my asking," Fiona said.

"Of course not. Since we will be staying there for a while, I had intended to tell both of you what to expect. 'm afraid the Stafford family is a bit complex."

Amy spoke up. "That sounds intriguing, Uncle. You certainly have our attention."

"Harlan has a sister—Julia—who never married and has run his household since his wife died. Julia is, well, a bit strange. Moreover, she and Harlan are not close. As a matter of fact, I sometimes think they dislike each other." He paused to take a sip of wine and then continued. "And then there is Pamela, his daughter. She is Amy's age and unmarried as yet. A nice little thing, but painfully shy. Justin, however, is outgoing and quite a charming young man. However, from comments that Harlan has made over the years, I believe both his children are somewhat of a disappointment to him."

Amy's eyebrows rose at his last statement. "Why is hat, Uncle Thad?"

"Harlan is the head of a vast empire and is a strong-willed man. Knowing him as I do, I believe he expects obedience from those he rules, but despises weakness. Neither of his children are strong enough to stand up to him."

Fiona dabbed her lips with her napkin and refused the dessert that Jeremy was offering to each of them. She frowned. "So you're saying that he doesn't respect his children because they obey him?"

Thaddeus nodded. "I know it sounds unreasonable, but that seems to be the situation."

Amy asked, "Is Justin involved in the family business?"

"Yes. However, Harlan refuses to relinquish any control to his son," he said.

Amy remembered the nineteen-year-old Justin who had walked with her in Uncle Thad's garden so many years ago. "You remind me of a hibiscus flower, Mistress Amy," he'd said with a smile. "Your hair is like the scarlet petals, and those green eyes are the color of the vivid leaves." She had been infatuated with his memory for a long time after he went home. And she realized now with adult insight that Justin most likely had a sensitive nature that would seem quite foreign to his strong-willed father.

Suddenly, there was a great splintering noise, as sharp as a gunshot, followed by a violent lurch of the ship. They clung to the table's edge until the room leveled out once more. Thaddeus tried to stand, but found it impossible for several moments. "I'll try to make it topside and see —" he began, when Jeremy came running in, his wet hair plastered to his head, his clothes dripping. "Captain Bond," he gasped, "asks that all of you go to your cabins and stay there. The storm's getting worse."

"What happened up there?" Thaddeus asked in alarm.

Jeremy shook his head even as he was weaving back out the door. "Don't know, sir. I heard it as I was coming through the passageway. Sorry, sir, but I need to get back."

Thaddeus helped the two women to their feet, and the three made their way along the passageway with difficulty, once being thrown against the wall by the force of the rolling ship. Both women refused Thaddeus's offer that they stay with him in his cabin until the storm abated. "I'm not afraid," Amy assured him, and Fiona nodded firmly, saying, "I'll be fine, sir, but thank you."

Amy didn't feel as brave as she had boasted, however, as she finally managed to don a nightrail and climb into bed. For a time she listened to the wind howling and the torrents of rain hitting the porthole. How safe was the crew on deck, she wondered, with the elements tearing at them? There had been many cases of sailors washed overboard during a storm. The violent tossing of the ship frayed her nerves, but beneath the fear, she felt a certain security knowing Captain Bond was at the helm. If anyone could see them through, he could. Why she felt this way, she couldn't say, since he was almost a stranger, but she drew comfort from the fact that he was in charge.

Gray light seeped into Amy's cabin as night gave birth to a weak dawn. The ship was no longer tossing like a leaf on the wind. Instead it rode the swells gently. Amy arose and stretched her sore muscles. Even in sleep she must have subconsciously held on to keep from landing on the floor, and now she felt it in every muscle of her body. There was a dull ache behind her eyes, and she longed fervently for a cup of strong black coffee. This was not a raspberry-leaf tea morning, she thought.

Sitting down in front of the small mirror, she brushed the tangles from her copper hair and slipped on a soft woolen robe over her green satin nightrail. It was so early yet, she had no fear of running into anyone in the passageway, but Mr. Hadley would surely be up and about with a pot of coffee brewing.

Her luck held as she stepped through the doorway into the galley. Just as she thought, the cook was stirring some sort of batter in a large wooden bowl, and the warmth of the stove enveloped her.

He glanced up and scowled at her—a tall, burly hulk of a man with dark hair and a black bushy beard. He had a curving scar on his wide brow that made his look all the more fierce.

Amy smiled tentatively as he growled, "No one's allowed in me kitchen, missy."

Not being accustomed to this sort of reception, Amy was a bit taken aback. "I'm sorry . . . I—"

"Spit it out and be off with ye," he commanded.

"Coffee . . . I just wanted—" she stammered.

"Help yerself—I'm busy," he interrupted, jerking his head toward the stove.

Not wasting any time, Amy grabbed a mug from a rack close by and then let out a gasp as she touched the handle of the hot pot without thinking.

"God's blood!" Mr. Hadley cursed, moving to her side. "Let's see 'ere, missy, what ye did."

Her eyes were wide as she held out her injured hand and he glanced at the angry red line across her palm. "Pesky intruders in my galley," he muttered, and then rummaged in a cupboard until he found a small tin.

"It's starting to . . . hurt." She sniffed angrily to keep from crying. He could have told her the handle was hot! How was she supposed to know these things when Hannah had always brought her hot drinks in delicate china cups?

"Do tell, missy. Ain't you never seen a hot pad?" he said gruffly, taking her hand in his and gently applying some of the clear salve to the burn.

For a moment it stung, and she muttered the only expletive she knew. "Damnation!" Then the burning sensation subsided and the pain was gone. She looked into his eyes and smiled. "That feels wonderful — what is it?"

A brief glint of amusement lit his gaze as he handed the tin to her and went back to his batter. "Don't know what it's called. It comes from a plant in Mexico and I got it when I sailed on the *Amity*. The Indians down there use it for a lot of things."

Amy's uneasiness at being in the company of this mean-tempered bear of a man was fading, and she decided he was not as fierce as he wanted her to believe. She took a pad and poured herself a cup of the coffee. "Well, thank you for the salve . . . and the coffee. I'll not bother you again." Putting the tin of medicine on the table, she turned to leave.

"Take it with ye — might need it later," he ordered as he poured the batter into a long pan.

She smiled and dropped the tin into her pocket.

"Mind ye bring it back in the morning when ye come for yer coffee."

She turned at the door and grinned, but his back was to her as he leaned over the oven. As she crossed the dining room, the door to the passageway opened and Captain Bond stepped inside. He looked tired and drawn, the creases around his eyes a bit more pronounced. He hadn't shaved, and a dark growth of beard shadowed his face, making him look more rugged than usual. Amy had a sudden urge to hold him close and smooth the worry lines from his brow. "You look terrible," she said.

"Do forgive my unkempt appearance, Mistress Hawthorne, but I was too busy to groom myself for your approval. I trust your sleep was not disturbed unduly by the storm," he snapped.

The tender feelings she'd just entertained for him vanished. Annoyed at his jibe, she said sharply, "I intended to complain to you about that, Captain. Kindly

77

steer us away from these storms in the future—they do give me a headache."

They were standing not two feet apart, scowling at each other, and then Amy saw his lips twitch. "I suppose I deserved that," he said, his eyes softening as he gazed at her. "There's no excuse for bad manners." But, in truth, there was an excuse, he thought with a sinking feeling. She was so damned desirable that he tried to hide behind an abrupt manner to keep from wanting her.

Amy relented and impulsively reached up to touch his cheek. "You haven't had any sleep, have you?"

His gray eyes caught and held hers as a warm current passed between them. His hand came up to clasp hers, and, turning his face, he kissed her palm. He saw the burn and frowned. "What's this?" he asked in concern.

Amy was breathless, and her heart had begun to race. For all her resolve, she couldn't seem to control her emotions when he was near. She looked away from his disturbing gaze and placed the mug in her other hand on the table beside them. "It's nothing," she managed, forcing her gaze back up. It seemed, in that moment, all her senses were sharpened. He smelled faintly of wind and rain, while the texture of his white linen shirt felt rough where her arm brushed it. The room felt cool and she felt hot. Unconsciously, she leaned closer, and his head came down to claim her lips. A jolt of excitement shot through her as his warm mouth covered hers. His arms came around her and pulled her to his hard body. She felt his tongue tracing her lips and pressing for entry.

Her world spun as she opened her mouth and tasted the sweetness of an intimate kiss. He boldly explored her mouth as his hands roamed her curves. Amy gave a moan of pleasure as he found her breast, his thumb grazing the nipple through her satin nightrail. She had

78

no thoughts of resisting, wanting only to experience more of these heady sensations.

Marcus felt a surge of desire that was nearly painful as he plundered her sweet mouth and his hands touched the places he'd been dreaming about. His mind warned against her charms while his body partook of them eagerly. The more passionate their kiss became, the more his reason slipped away. He wanted to lay her back on the dining room table and take her then and there. His left arm held her securely while his right hand slipped down to touch the soft core of her between her legs. A white-hot fire seared him as she moved against his questing fingers.

Amy gasped as he touched her, and she felt she would burst with longing. Her body was hot and fluid, and she wanted him never to stop. A strange and wonderful feeling was building inside her, and she was frantically anxious to follow it to its end.

Through the thick haze of passion, Marcus heard a deep voice singing a lusty tavern song in the next room. For a moment he tried to ignore it, but reason reasserted itself in his clouded brain and he remembered where they were. Mr. Hadley was on the other side of the door, he told himself, as he lifted his head and swore hoarsely, "Damnation!"

Amy lifted heavy-lidded emerald eyes, her breath coming in short gasps between swollen lips. "Marcus?" she whispered, not realizing she had used his given name for the first time. She offered her lips again, but he set her abruptly away and scowled at her. Turning slightly, he gripped the back of a chair and asked, "Are you a witch, Mistress Hawthorne? You tempt me beyond my control, it seems."

Amy stared at his rigid profile, her cheeks flushing as she realized how wanton she'd been in his arms. But why was he angry with her? Had this been her fault? She knew about innocent flirting, but had no experience with intimate relationships. Moreover, the intensity of the feelings this man evoked in her was frightening. She would die of shame if he discovered how attracted she was to him. Taking a deep breath, she salvaged her pride. "No, Captain, I'm not a witch. Just a woman forced to endure a boring voyage. I merely sought some small diversion."

Marcus jerked his head about and pinned her with a hard stare. He had been angry with himself and had not expected an answer from her, but her words were like a cold douse of water. "Diversion, Mistress?" he asked. "Do you play these games with any man who takes your fancy?"

His derisive tone hurt, but she forced a stiff smile. "At the risk of flattering you, I would say I'm quite selective." Before another blush could reach her cheeks, she picked up her cup and left the room.

Chapter Five

"We'll just have to manage without the mainsail," Captain Bond said, "but that shouldn't present a hardship. The winds are favorable, and we will reach the Bermudas tomorrow about midday." He glanced at Toby Oakes for confirmation.

"Aye, Marcus," the first mate agreed and then grinned. "That is if we can keep 'er afloat. Sprung a few leaks, we did, in that squall."

They were gathered in the dining room for dinner, and Amy could barely tolerate having to be in the same company with Captain Bond. She would have taken her meal in her cabin except it seemed a cowardly thing to do, so instead she tried to appear as indifferent as possible. So far it hadn't been difficult, since he had all but ignored her.

"Shame on you, Mr. Oakes. You'll frighten the ladies with such talk," Thaddeus said, smiling at Fiona who sat across from him.

Fiona smiled back. "Well, sir. I'm not afraid now, but had I known that loud noise last night was the mainmast splitting asunder, I might have turned a hair."

Jeremy came in with the main course of chicken in a creamed sauce and potatoes. He refilled the wine glasses, and Amy drank liberally from hers. She fervently hoped they reached their destination the next day. It couldn't be soon enough for her. She turned to her left and spoke to

Andrew Williams. "You must have been quite busy, Andrew, for I didn't see you all day."

He sat up a bit straighter and gave her a pleased smile. "Quite, Mistress Amy. What with the storm, every hand was needed to clean up and make repairs."

"The weather was so beautiful today, I could hardly believe we'd had a storm," she said, picking at her food with her fork disinterestedly. Mr. Hadley's culinary skill was wasted on her tonight.

Andrew glanced around the table and noted that the others were engaged in conversation before he said in a low voice, "If I might be so bold, you're the beautiful one. Your eyes are like fine emeralds and your hair—"

"How poetic you are, Andrew," Amy said, interrupting him before he got too eloquent. She wasn't in the mood for flattery.

Undaunted, Andrew's eyes roamed from the slim column of her throat down to the creamy expanse of her bosom, which swelled above her bodice. "Not so poetic as truthful," he corrected, his gaze alight with desire.

His too obvious attention was making her uncomfortable, and the feeling intensified when she glanced up and caught Captain Bond's censorious look. Her cheeks grew warm as she realized what he was thinking—that she was seeking a new diversion with Andrew. While trying to pretend an indifference to his caresses, she'd impetuously given him the impression that she was no better than a tart.

Andrew didn't seem to notice her discomfort as he changed the subject and talked on about his cousin who lived in St. George, the capital of the Bermudas.

Amy lifted her chin a fraction, and her mouth thinned with displeasure. Casually, she returned her attention to the food before her, when something Andrew said penetrated her thoughts. "What did you say, Andrew?"

"About staying with my cousin, Alice?" he asked, cheered once again by her interest.

Impatient, she said, "Something about the crew being stranded several weeks ashore."

"At least, Mistress Amy. The repairs will take that long, I'm quite sure. We can't embark on our next voyage until the *Rebecca* is made seaworthy again," he explained.

Amy felt as if a cold stone sat in the pit of her stomach. She had been counting on Captain Bond's leaving the Bermudas once they disembarked. Now it seemed he would inhabit the islands for weeks. Quickly she told herself that, even so, she probably wouldn't see him. She glanced up at the object of her thoughts and caught in his expression a note of mockery. It was as if, again, he knew what she was thinking.

Amy stood on the forecastle deck with Thaddeus and watched as a speck on the horizon grew in size. It was her first glimpse of the Bermudas—St. David's Island, to be exact. The *Rebecca* was moving closer to the land while still running parallel to it. For the moment, Amy forgot about her unsettling experiences with Captain Bond as excitement overtook her. The noonday sun was as warm as midsummer, and the water an intense sapphire blue.

"We're skirting the outer edge of the coral reef that surrounds the Bermudas. Once we pass these small outlying islands, there's a narrow channel where we'll enter Castle Harbor," Thaddeus explained.

"You make it sound somewhat difficult," she observed with raised eyebrows.

"Not for an experienced captain like ours," he said with a smile.

The mention of Captain Bond reminded her. "I understand from Andrew the *Rebecca* will be dry-docked for some time to make repairs."

"That's true, my dear. It will be done at Harlan's shipyard. The dried cod we have aboard will have to be taken by another vessel to the Caribbean. It will cut into our profit somewhat, but it can't be helped." He turned then and glanced back to the passageway that led to the cabins. "Is Fiona going to join us?" he asked.

"When she's finished packing," Amy told him, distracted by an agile young sailor as he climbed up the rigging. The activity of the crew was increasing, and Amy suspected they were nearing the narrow channel her uncle had mentioned. When the sailor reached the top, he shouted out their position to Captain Bond, who held the wheel on the quarterdeck. For a few minutes Amy felt the tension in the air as the large ship angled into the channel.

On their right some tiny islands appeared, and on the left a larger one, Charles Island. Amy was entranced as the deep blue of the water was changing to a clear aquamarine. Once past Charles Island came Castle Island, and she saw a large fort built on the southern side with gun embrasures and a citadel, rising high above the stone walls.

"The King's Castle," Thaddeus said. "It protects this channel entrance from pirates and Spanish raiders. They've been trying to lay claim to these islands since the first settlement."

"I can see why," Amy said, her gaze sweeping across the panorama of beauty. Inside Castle Harbor proper, the sea had turned to pale green, but the innermost fringe of the tide was lavender-tinged. The pinkish-white sand of the beach blended into verdant foliage dotted with bright flowers.

Fiona joined them, and Thaddeus made room for her at the rail between Amy and himself. Fiona exclaimed over the scenery, and Thaddeus smiled and complimented the two of them. "All the men of Bermuda will envy me the company of two such lovely ladies," he said.

Fiona dropped her gaze and Amy laughed, saying, "After getting a glimpse of this place, I would wager the work of nature commands more attention than a fashionable woman."

Thaddeus snorted. "You, young lady, have a lot to learn about men."

A slight frown creased Amy's brow as she wondered if she really wanted to know more about those hateful creatures.

In a short time, the *Rebecca* dropped anchor just inside a sheltered cove. Amy could see a wharf jutting out from the shore across the small expanse of water, and there was considerable activity was taking place. There were men, small shapes from this distance, scurrying in and out of warehouses on the beach, and wagons moving to and fro along a road that snaked away from the beach and up and over a hill. It was like a slash of white ribbon lying on a bed of green velvet. A small boat struck out from the dock to ascertain the identity and purpose of the ship.

Amy and Fiona followed Thaddeus to their cabins to retrieve the few articles they would be carrying ashore with them. Amy adjusted the small pink-feathered silk hat atop her upswept hair. It matched the pink-and-white striped gown she wore. The dress was one of her favorites—she wanted to look her best to meet the Staffords. Pulling on fingerless lace gloves, she picked up her fan and drawstring purse and left the cabin. Fiona, just coming out her own door, smiled. "I suppose we're ready now. Jeremy has promised to see our trunks safely ashore himself."

"That's good news. I watched the crew loading and unloading at New York town, and I'll admit I was worried about our trunks ending up in the bay," Amy said with a laugh. She hooked her arm through Fiona's as they started down the passageway. She was pleased that her companion had become more friendly of late. It made her separation from Hannah a bit easier.

"I noticed Captain Bond watching you earlier as we

stood on deck. You haven't given the poor man a moment's notice, have you?" Fiona asked as they came out onto the main deck.

"If you like him so much, you may have him. I can't abide his arrogant attitude," Amy said quickly, irritation creeping into her tone.

Fiona laughed. "Dear Amy, he's not attracted to me. You should feel flattered instead of insulted that such a handsome rogue finds you so interesting."

"Rogue is exactly what he is," Amy muttered as they drew near to Thaddeus. The three of them watched as the man from the island came aboard. Captain Bond appeared and spoke briefly with him and then motioned toward his passengers. He moved over to them and spoke to Thaddeus. "John here will take you ashore, sir. Unless you wish to wait for our launch."

"No, we'll go with this good man, Captain. I'm anxious to plant my feet on solid ground again," Thaddeus said, then added, "I'll see you ashore later."

Captain Bond nodded, and Fiona held out a gloved hand to him. "Thank you, Captain, for a pleasant voyage. The food was excellent and the company very interesting."

Marcus gave her a brief smile. "My pleasure, Mistress Morgan." His glance fell on Amy, but she merely nodded and turned away. He felt a stab of disappointment. She boded ill for his plans, yet he couldn't seem to get her out of his mind.

As the three passengers from the *Rebecca* were helped onto the dock by several willing hands, an open carriage pulled by two perfectly matched bays topped the hill and came to a halt at the edge of the beach. Amy took her uncle's arm, leaving Fiona to follow, as they made their way toward the man and woman alighting the carriage.

The man was tall, broad-shouldered, and had dark hair

threaded with silver. He was handsome in a mature way. His dark blue silk banyan coat looked loose and comfortable, and yet appeared elegant at the same time. Harlan Stafford was not a man one would forget. His companion was thin and short of stature. She wore a drab-brown silk dress and a wide straw hat — very effective, Amy supposed, in this hot climate.

"Thaddeus . . . welcome," Harlan boomed in a deep voice as the two groups converged. The men shook hands enthusiastically.

Amy smiled at the young woman and felt a twinge of pity as the girl dropped her gaze self-consciously.

"Harlan, let me present my niece, Amy," Thaddeus said, pulling Fiona forward. "And her companion, Mistress Fiona Morgan."

Harlan nodded politely to Fiona before his gray eyes lit with undisguised admiration as he took Amy's proffered hand. Instead of a brief squeeze, as was customary, he lifted it to his mouth and placed a kiss on it. "Thaddeus wrote me that you had grown into a lovely young woman; however, I fear that description falls woefully short of the mark," he said gallantly with a smile.

"More than likely, he said I had grown into an irritating, troublesome twit, but you are too kind to repeat such a slanderous statement, Mr. Stafford," Amy said.

His laugh was deep and hearty. "What a delightful treasure! It's not every day one finds a young woman with spirit and a sense of humor. Pamela could take a few lessons from you." He turned to his companion as if he had just remembered her presence. "My daughter, Pamela."

Amy was quick to notice the slight cringe Pamela gave at her father's thoughtless remark, and decided on the spot to befriend the shy girl. Reaching out, Amy clasped her hand and said warmly, "I'm so happy finally to meet you."

Pamela barely returned the handshake, but managed to

raise her eyes and smile weakly. "Welcome, all of you, to our home." Her brief speech sounded stilted, but sincere. Thaddeus renewed his acquaintance with Harlan's daughter, and Fiona added her greeting.

Harlan took Amy's arm and said briskly, "Come, we mustn't burn your delicate skin in this noonday sun." He escorted Amy, and the others followed to the carriage.

Harlan and Thaddeus, sitting across from each other, entered into a discussion about the going price of cod, salt, molasses and sundry other products they bought, sold or traded, leaving the ladies to enjoy the scenery. Fiona asked Pamela about a particular flowering bush at the side of the road, while Amy took one last look at the *Rebecca* as the carriage crested the hill. She doubted she would see Marcus Bond again, even though he would be staying ashore for a while, and she told herself that would suit her fine. Why, then, did she feel an odd twinge of disappointment?

Justin Stafford was twenty-five years old and born to wealth. He was of medium height and had a slim build. His light brown hair was streaked with gold from the sun, since he rarely wore his hat, and large gray eyes dominated his handsome square face. When he smiled, which was often, his even white teeth contrasted pleasingly with his sun-bronzed skin. Most women, young and old, found him ingenuously appealing and fell over themselves to please him. He would take a dare or bet on anything, no matter how frivolous, and swilled cheap rum as often as he sipped the finest Madeira. Life for him was an ongoing party, and the only blight on the festivities was his father, Harlan.

Justin's best friend, Patrick Cormac, was the same age, but had been born on the poor side of the blanket; yet their personalities were so similar they should have been brothers. Patrick was blond, blue-eyed and equally as handsome as his friend, but in a bigger, burlier way. Patrick had three mistresses: drinking, wenching and gambling. The major blight on his existence was that he had to work part of the year to support these expensive ladies.

On the very day the *Rebecca* arrived, Justin and Patrick sat in the Boar's Head tavern, in Tucker's Town, at their favorite table against the back wall, drinking rum and playing a desultory game of cards. The wide wooden shutters were propped open, letting in light and a gentle westerly breeze. Three soldiers from the nearby fort on Castle Island, dressed in red coats and white breeches, came through the door and sat at a table near the bar. Justin glanced up and, recognizing one of the men, nodded a greeting.

Patrick squinted at the soldier, frowning in concentration for a moment, and commented, "I think he's the one that cracked me skull last month at that brawl over on St. George's."

Justin was studying his cards. "That's him. He's a good man."

Patrick's eyebrow rose. "And it's a foin friend you are. He could have killed me."

Justin glanced up and said mildly, "You were here the very next night raising all manner of hell, so I hardly think that little tap he gave you was serious. Moreover, you deserved it — breaking up the furniture the way you did."

A smile lit Patrick's face. "We was havin' a foin evening at the Thorn and Thistle, we was."

"Aye," Justin agreed with a wide grin, turning his winning hand up on the table. "Sally Miller sang songs that night that would break your heart."

Patrick winked broadly. "She wasn't trying to break your heart, mate, but warm it a mite, I'm thinkin'."

Justin glanced over at the pretty silver-haired girl who was serving drinks to the soldiers, and said, "Pray, don't say that too loud. You'll bring Megan's wrath down on me, and I don't need that today."

Patrick chuckled. "Me little sister does have Da's Irish temper, to be sure." He held up his cup to attract her attention.

As she walked toward them, balancing a tray on one hand and walking with a natural grace, Justin gave her a tender smile, genuine affection lighting his eyes.

She gave him a saucy look and set a fresh jug of rum down in front of her brother with a loud thunk. "I'm thinking you've had enough, Pat. And besides, I know your pockets are gettin' thin," she stated flatly, turning her gaze to frown at her brother.

Patrick's expression grew pained as he sighed. " 'Tis worse than having a wife, it is. Don't you have better things to do than act as me conscience, Megan?"

"Someone has to do it," she said.

Justin pushed his chair back and raised both hands in mock exasperation. "If you two are going to start brawling, I'm leaving."

Megan chuckled. She took advantage of Justin's position and sat boldly on his lap, wrapping her slender arms around his neck. "You'll not get away that easy, me handsome bucko. I've packed a lunch for us, and we're going to our favorite place."

Patrick snorted. "He doesn't have time for that, silly chit! His da's got him working in the shipyard office now."

Raising fine, arched eyebrows, Megan protested, "But you promised we'd spend some time together, Justin. work every night and you know that."

He gave her a quick kiss on the cheek and stood up, pushing her to her feet. "I know, Meggie, and I'm sorry, but my father ordered me to report to the shipyard this afternoon." He grimaced and added cynically, "He seems to think I need more responsibility to make a proper man of me."

Megan's swift temper flared. "And who does he think he is now? You're the finest man in all the Bermudas, and I challenge anyone to say different!" Two bright spots of color stained her pale cheeks, and her sea-blue eyes shot sparks.

Justin lifted her off the floor in a bear hug and laughed suddenly. "As long as I have you to champion me, Meggie girl, his poor opinion matters little."

She clung tightly to him for a moment and whispered in his ear, "Come back tonight at closin' time."

He set her on her feet once again and winked at her. "If I can" was his vague promise.

Amy was fascinated by the beauty of the countryside as the carriage rolled along the white coral road. To her left was a salt marsh, thick with mangroves that threw their branches down into the dark ooze. To the right, an especially lovely meadow sloped off into a valley carpeted with wild violets and white-gold lilies. Pamela had been drawn out of her shell by the two women, who were asking enthusiastic questions about the local flora they passed. The shy girl warmed to her subject by giving them the names of each tree and flower, and Amy got a glimpse of the attractive woman Pamela could be with a small amount of encouragement.

Although Amy was truly interested in her surroundings, she could feel Harlan Stafford's eyes rest briefly on her several times. Was it merely curiosity, or was he measuring her as a possible daughter-in-law? This type of arrangement was fairly common, especially in the upper classes; however, it made her decidedly uncomfortable. Perversely, she decided any man of their choosing could not possibly suit her.

Presently, they stopped before a set of double-iron gates flanked by tall stone pillars. A low stone wall reached on either side like long arms as far as the eye could see. The liveried footman jumped down and opened the gates so the driver could pass through, and then closed them, climbing agilely back up on the high seat.

The lush vegetation had been tamed in a more formal fashion inside the estate walls. Green lawns to either side of the road led up to a wide circular driveway. A colonnade of royal palms edged the drive, and Pamela explained that her father had had them planted when he took over Stafford House some thirty years before. An oval flowerbed graced the center of the large circle in front of the huge mansion, and Amy voiced her admiration of the white stone and cedar-trimmed edifice.

Hearing her comments, Harlan smiled and said, "I hope, Mistress Amy, that we can make your visit so pleasant you'll not wish to return to Boston." He gave Thaddeus a meaningful glance and climbed out of the carriage, not waiting for her reply.

After the women were helped to alight, Harlan led the way up a short flight of steps to a covered terrace. A black maid opened the door as if on cue, and Harlan stood aside to let them pass. He followed them in and bowed low with a flourish. "Welcome to Stafford House." Glancing around the foyer, he asked the maid, "Where is Mistress Julia?"

The black girl averted her eyes and said hesitantly, "She be resting, Massa."

He frowned. "I see . . . Well, Ivy, show our guests to their rooms." Turning to them, he suggested, "Once you've freshened up, we'll have tea in the drawing room." Pamela gave them a shy smile in parting.

The young maid, clad in a flowered cotton dress and turban, led them across the spacious foyer and up a wide staircase. After the bright sunlight, Amy's eyes were still adjusting to the dim interior, but she noticed the decor was ornate, from the furniture to the silk wall hangings.

The wide hallway on the second floor stretched the length of the house, with heavily carved doors on both sides. Ivy turned to the left, saying, "Dis way, if you please." Her voice was musical, and Amy detected a French accent.

She stopped at the end of the hall. "Massa Hawthorne, dis corner room be yours, and de other two is fo' de ladies."

Amy smiled her thanks and stepped into her room, glancing around. A large bed with graceful cream-colored drapings stood against the far wall, next to French doors that led onto the covered upper terrace. They stood open, and a slight breeze cooled the room. A large mahogany wardrobe with doors and drawers, a dressing table with a filigree mirror, a small writing table and a dainty pink upholstered side chair completed the furnishings. Delicate rose-flocked wallpaper adorned the walls, and a rose wool Persian rug covered the center of the polished floor.

Amy looked longingly at the bed and sighed. The change in climate as well as her tumultuous voyage had left its mark on her, and she suddenly felt spent. However, she would be expected to take tea with the family, and decided it would be rude of her to decline. Besides, she was curious to meet Julia and also hoped Justin would be in attendance.

Fiona appeared at her door and asked, "Do you need my help?"

"No, I don't intend to change until dinner, so you may see to your own toilet."

Fiona nodded and closed the door behind her. Amy removed her hat and gloves and dropped them on the bed as she walked to the French doors and stepped out on the terrace. The view at the back of the house was nearly as picturesque as the front. A wide green lawn spread to the woods. To the left was a quaint cemetery surrounded by a low stone wall. Even from this distance, Amy could see how well tended it was, with flowers and plants growing on the mounded graves and neat white stones marking the heads. To her right, a very tall, slim building stood next to a shorter, wide building, and she could see black women in turbans busily moving between the two. A thin spiral of smoke issued from a chimney atop the shorter structure, and considering the delicious smells filling the air, she guessed it to be the kitchen. Her stomach growled in a very unladylike fashion as she realized she hadn't eaten anything that day. Since she'd met that odious Captain Bond, her normal appetite had gone awry. Thoughts of their last encounter caused a warm flush to creep up her cheeks. The way she had responded to his advances had been positively shameful, yet a delicious shiver raced up her spine as she remembered the way his strong hands had felt on her body. Hastily, she pushed those thoughts from her mind, certain she would never have to deal with him again, and retreated to the dressing table to check her appearance.

Ivy met Amy, Fiona and Thaddeus at the foot of the staircase to guide them to the large drawing room. It was located in the front of the house and had French doors that opened onto the terrace. A green velvet sofa and several brocade side chairs were arranged in front of a deep stone fireplace. A low mahogany table sat in the center of the grouping.

Harlan was lounging against the wide mantel when they entered, and he immediately came forward to greet them. Taking Amy's arm, he led her to the sofa to sit, while Thaddeus and Fiona took side chairs. Another black maid entered with a silver tea service on a matching tray, and following her came Pamela with an older lady.

"Ah, Julia . . . there you are. A trifle late, but then you always are," Harlan said, his tone a bit sharp. Amy glanced up at him and he smiled benignly, as if it were a good-natured jest.

"Better late than never, dear brother," Julia said softly, her eyes narrowing.

Thaddeus stood up politely and smiled. "Mistress Julia, how good to see you again."

Amy had a chance to study the older lady while she exchanged pleasantries with her uncle. She was a handsome, well-shaped woman with dark hair pulled up in the latest style. Her dress was of the current mode, but of black satin which suggested mourning attire. Her face would have been attractive except for the pinched look about her thin mouth.

"This is my niece, Amy," Thaddeus said, performing the introductions, "and her companion, Fiona Morgan. Mistress Julia Stafford."

Julia's gaze fell on her, and Amy nearly shivered at the coldness in the woman's dark eyes.

"It's a great pleasure to meet you," Julia said in a cool tone. "Your uncle has mentioned you quite often over the years."

Amy murmured the proper response and noted that Julia barely nodded to Fiona. Taking the place beside Amy on the sofa, Julia began serving the tea. Harlan sat down in a chair on the other side of Amy and asked her about their voyage. Relieved that she didn't have to converse directly with Julia, Amy launched into her impressions of the trip, recounting the storm. Thaddeus and Fiona joined in, leaving Pamela and her aunt to listen quietly.

"I instructed Captain Bond to take the *Rebecca* to your shipyard, Harlan. Moreover, I hope you have an available vessel to transport the remainder of my cargo on to the Caribbean." Thaddeus helped himself to an iced teacake. "Ahh . . . these apple cakes are as delightful as I remember, Mistress Julia. I take it Tante Belle still rules your kitchen?"

Julia gave him a thin smile and remarked in a cool tone, "Of course, Mr. Hawthorne. My brother is a very possessive man, and he would never sell off a jewel like Tante Belle."

Harlan frowned at his sister and proceeded to answer Thaddeus's first question. "I have a ship leaving day after tomorrow for Barbados, among other places. We will make room for your cargo, my friend."

"That's good of you, Harlan. Perhaps we could visit the shipyard before dinner and I can go over some of the details with Captain Bond."

"Directly after tea, Thaddeus," Harlan said agreeably. He then changed the subject and asked his guests for the latest news of Boston. For the remainder of tea, they discussed politics and the growing unrest in the colonies. Amy gave her opinion freely and enjoyed the lively exchange. She tried to draw the Stafford women into the discussion, but they seemed to have no opinions and remained quiet for the most part. Harlan explained his son's absence, and although Amy was disappointed, she hoped his presence at dinner would liven up the company. Little did she realize just how lively the evening would be.

Chapter Six

As a young man, Harlan Stafford, the son of an impoverished earl, had signed on as a young officer of an English merchant ship that traded with the colonies. For several years, he worked diligently, putting money aside for the purchase of his own ship someday. A man who always recognized and seized every opportunity, he wooed the favor of the captain and, when that was accomplished, began courting the man's daughter. The lovely Sarah Payne was sweet and naive, an easy conquest for one of his practiced charm. She was in love with him and thought he reciprocated her feelings. Moreover, he would have married her had he not been approached by an old friend of his father's who was looking for a suitable match for his daughter. It seemed there was a taint of insanity in the family, and the girl had spent part of her life in an asylum. Her older brother (and heir to the family fortune) had been killed in a hunting accident, which left Martha to carry on the family name and fortune. There were no other male relatives to inherit, and not one of the possible suitors her father brought around could be enticed to marry her once they were apprised of her condition.

Harlan immediately saw the advantages of the situation and cared little about the girl's mental state. He would worry about that later. Martha's father bestowed a sizable amount of money and property in the Bermudas upon them as a wedding gift. Harlan resigned his position with Captain Payne, omitting his reason for doing so, married Martha and wrote Sarah a brief note, telling her regretfully of his marriage. He never knew she carried his child.

Now, thirty years later, Harlan was a wealthy man, he had two perfectly healthy children, and Martha, dead for five years now, had never exhibited any signs of insanity.

The Stafford shipyard was located about two miles from the estate and was a beehive of activity. An extra-long pier, equipped with sturdy winches, jutted out into the deep water of the cove so that a ship could be hauled up for repairs. Not only were there new ships in different stages of construction, but there were constant repairs to be made on the Stafford ships as well as vessels brought in by other parties. Bermuda cedar was plentiful and had been found to be an excellent wood for shipbuilding.

Marcus Bond stood beside Justin Stafford and watched as the cargo of the *Rebecca* was unloaded onto the dock. The two men had just met, and although Justin had tried to be friendly with the captain, Marcus kept his distance.

It was one thing to know you had a half brother, Marcus mused, and another matter actually to come face to face with that person. His anger and resentment must not show, he reminded himself, or he would never get close enough to Harlan Stafford to exact his revenge.

Turning to Justin, he asked casually, "Is there lodging nearby for my men while we're here?"

Justin raised a hand to shield his eyes from the sun as he watched the progress of a large crate being lowered to the dock. "The Boar's Head Inn in Tucker's Town," he suggested. "There's plenty of work here at the yard as well if they're interested in earning some extra money. Most of our men are on Grand Turk for the winter season of salt raking and won't be back for a good while."

"I'll pass the word along to my men," Marcus said, his tone thawing somewhat.

Justin nodded and excused himself and went back to the office while Marcus sought out the master shipwright and consulted with him on the necessary repairs. As their discussion was completed, Marcus glanced up to see a carriage approaching and felt a tightening in his stomach. He recognized Hawthorne and knew instinctively that the man climbing out behind him was Harlan Stafford. They entered the low stone building that housed the office.

Marcus removed his coat and sat down on a wooden piling to wait. Hawthorne and Stafford would seek him out in time, and he wanted to collect his thoughts—and his temper—so that neither showed during the interview.

Unbidden, Sarah Bond's face swam before his vision, and he recalled her soft-spoken confession. Anger rose in his throat like bile, but he forced it back. Her plea had been that he not be angry with her or Harlan, for the man had never known of Marcus's existence, and she had been very happy with Jonathan Bond. Her only reason for telling him had been the fact that he would be alone in the world after her death, without one blood relative.

Marcus wished fervently, though, that he didn't know. He felt compelled now to avenge the wrong done to his beloved mother, and honor forbade him to ignore this knowledge. Somehow, he had to find Stafford's vulnerable point and strike him there.

The sound of voices coming toward Marcus warned

of their approach. He stood up and slung his coat over his shoulder, hooking the collar casually with one finger. Thaddeus greeted him and introduced Harlan. Marcus eyed critically this man who was his natural father, then realized with a start that there was indeed a resemblance. The thought rankled.

Stafford seemed not to notice anything untoward and greeted him in a cordial fashion. "Thaddeus has told me of your capable handling of the ship during the storm," Harlan said.

Marcus shrugged. "I merely carried out my duties."

"Modest as well as able, Captain . . . a worthy combination," Harlan replied easily, a smile lifting the corner of his mouth. "Is this your first visit to the Bermudas?"

"No, I've delivered cargo several times at St. George's over the years," he said.

"I thought as much, since you maneuvered the channel without any problems. That coral reef can be treacherous around these islands."

"You could say I have a healthy respect for it," Marcus responded, and even permitted himself a small smile.

"Only a fool would take these waters lightly," Harlan agreed, and he turned to Thaddeus. "I'll leave you two to discuss your business while I have a word with my son." He started for the office and then turned around. "Come to dinner tonight, Captain Bond. We dine at eight."

More a command than an invitation, Marcus thought harshly. However, he also felt a brief surge of excitement to have made contact with the man so soon after arriving. His plan was evolving more smoothly than expected.

* * *

Amy sat at her dressing table and stared into the filigree mirror, watching as her upswept hair was curled by Fiona. The heat of the afternoon was gone, and a gentle breeze wafted through the open French doors, cooling the room.

The long sausagelike curls grew into a cluster that hung to the back of her head and pleased her far more than the overblown, towering hairstyles most women affected of late. Paris fashions were all well and good, but cow-tail hairpieces stuffed inside one's own hair to imitate the royal ladies of the French court did not suit Amy. "Where did you learn to do this, Fiona? I know Hannah didn't teach you." Amy took a hand mirror to admire the back.

Fiona stood back to inspect her handiwork. "Oh, my maid at home was gifted with hair arranging. I seem to have that common knack as well," she replied with a vein of sarcasm.

"Nonsense," Amy said with a smile. "There is nothing common about you. We women of the upper classes have many talents that we never get to pursue, simply because nice society won't permit it."

Fiona chuckled. "Pray, don't bring that up at dinner, or your uncle will turn purple again."

"Oh, don't worry. I don't relish another lecture," Amy said as she stepped into her hoops and petticoats. After tying them at the waist, Fiona helped her don the matching jade-green silk-taffeta gown. The fan-shaped cuffs at the elbows were trimmed with delicate white lace. She slipped on the French-heeled shoes that had been covered to match the gown.

Once again, she sat down in front of the mirror to apply some rouge to each cheek. "Thank you, Fiona. You may go and finish dressing," Amy told her.

"Perhaps I shouldn't have dinner with the family," Fiona said hesitantly.

Amy glanced at her in the mirror and raised a brow. "Why ever not?"

"Well, Mistress Julia acted quite odd this afternoon at tea. I suspect it was because she had to entertain a mere servant with her other guests."

Amy grimaced. "You call that entertainment?"

Fiona laughed. "You are incorrigible, Amy Hawthorne!"

Amy grinned, not the least bit repentant. "Let me worry about Mistress Julia. And do hurry, or we shall be late."

A small group of musicians played softly in one corner of the large drawing room as Amy and Fiona entered. Quite a number of people besides the Staffords were present, clustered in small groups talking and sipping Madeira. The guests were dressed in the latest finery, the women in bright silks and satins, the men, for the most part, in elegant banyan coats of soft Chinese silk, satin knee-breeches and fine linen shirts.

Harlan was the first to see them and came forward. "Ah, my lovely guests come at last to grace this humble gathering."

Amy smiled and offered her hand. "Your gathering looks anything but humble, sir. I do hope we're not late."

He kissed her hand lightly. "Of course not," he replied suavely. "We were but impatient for your presence. Come, let me introduce you." Offering each of them an arm, he proceeded to introduce them at each small group. Amy could not keep all the names straight, so she simply smiled graciously and returned their greetings. There was a judge and his wife, a sea captain in Harlan's employ, the collector of customs at St. George's, the minister of nearby Trinity Church, and the sheriff of Hamilton Parish with his mother. And those were just a few that she could remember. As they made their way through the throng, she spotted Pamela and Julia talking to a well-dressed gentleman with his back to her. His jet-black hair was pulled back in a neat queue, and broad shoulders filled out the fine coat he wore perfectly. Amy's distracted gaze took in his narrow hips and muscular legs, which were encased in tight-fitting breeches. She thought that this man's tailor must work rapturously on his wardrobe, for he was a superb example of manhood. Her gaze wandered on, trying to locate Justin, but the room was fairly crowded.

Her eye did alight, however, on Andrew Williams, and he, catching her attention, waved. Toby Oakes stood beside the young officer, sipping a glass of Madeira and looking quite pained in his formal attire. A sudden chill ran up Amy's spine as a premonition washed over her, and her gaze swung back to the muscular stranger she'd been admiring.

He had changed position and was now facing her. Marcus Bond! Amy's surprise was replaced by an apprehensive excitement. Their eyes met, and a brief flash of heat passed between them. His gaze dropped to her low-cut bodice, and her breasts tingled as if they had been caressed. It shook her composure, and she hastily turned away from his intense stare. "I . . . I would like some champagne, please, Mr. Stafford. It's rather warm in here," she breathed, interrupting his conversation with a boring government official.

"How inconsiderate of me!" he exclaimed, motioning to a servant.

Amy opened her ivory fan and created a cooling breeze as she sipped the wine, trying to control her nervousness. She could still feel Captain Bond's steady regard even though her eyes were averted.

Fiona lifted her fan and spoke behind it. "Our

Captain Bond is in fine feathers tonight."

"I thought we were rid of him," Amy returned in a low tone. She carefully kept her attention away from him until they went in to dinner, and she breathed a sigh of relief when she found him seated across the table and down a safe distance.

To her delight, Justin Stafford was placed to her right, and he introduced himself as he held her chair. Giving him a bright smile, she exclaimed, "Of course I remember our last meeting. You look the very same."

Justin grinned rakishly as he took his seat. "I most certainly can't say the same thing about you. That shy little girl in braids has turned into a beautiful woman."

Amy's laugh was softly seductive. "I see you have not lost the ability to flatter."

He gave her a mock frown. "You cut me to the quick, dear Amy. It's not flattery, but the truth." As he spread his napkin on his lap, Justin continued, "Please accept my apologies for not being here sooner to greet you. I was detained at the shipyard and just returned a short while ago."

"Oh, I quite understand. My uncle is frequently late for dinner while tending to business. If he would let me assist him, perhaps his stomach wouldn't suffer so much," she said, her green eyes twinkling.

The servants began moving around the table, serving the roasted pork and duckling. Amy finished her wine and indicated a refill. Usually, she drank sparingly of spirits, but she felt the need to imbibe this evening to soothe her nerves.

"Your uncle and my father, I fear, are men of like mind. They think their business interests will not run properly without their complete control," Justin said. Even though he smiled, there was a touch of bitterness in his tone.

Amy was reminded of what her uncle had told her,

and felt an empathy for Justin's plight. Impulsively she lay her hand over his on the table. "At least you are allowed some occupation within the business, while I must languish at home in the parlor," she said.

His left eyebrow rose a fraction. "You're quite serious about this, aren't you?"

"Little good it does me," she replied with a wry smile.

Justin's gaze was admiring as he turned his hand and gave hers a reassuring squeeze. "Life is deuced unfair sometimes. However, I believe you will overcome any obstacles in your path, Amy. You have a determined light in those emerald eyes, and I, for one, would not want to oppose you."

Amy chuckled and drew her hand away. She glanced up at that moment, and her gaze met Captain Bond's frowning countenance. For some strange reason she felt guilty, and that unwarranted feeling irritated her. A warm flush rose to her cheeks before she looked away. For the remainder of the meal, she carefully avoided looking in his direction.

When they returned to the drawing room, Amy was relieved that Justin barely left her side. It pricked her ego, however, when several surreptitious glances at Marcus assured her he was not interested in her presence. Moreover, he was surrounded by females who seemed to hang on his every word. Well, she thought, all the more proof that he was not the sort of man for her. Belatedly, she remembered Fiona's reticence about joining the company, but with relief located her companion in the company of Thaddeus and Harlan. Since her companion seemed quite satisfied, Amy concentrated her attention on Justin, who proved to be as charming as she remembered him to be.

Amy's earlier fatigue had vanished, due to, she

thought, the emotional ups and downs she'd suffered. It was well past midnight, and she lay wide-awake in her large comfortable bed, listening to the foreign sounds of the island. The French doors were open, but the earlier breeze had disappeared, leaving the air sultry. Even her light silk gown felt hot and cloying. Her body was not yet adjusted to the tropical climate. The rolling of the ship had rocked her to sleep each night, and now everything was strangely still. The night birds of the island called out to each other, and she could hear faint sounds like drumbeats in the distance. Her spirit was restless, and she could not put a name to what caused it.

Finally tired of tossing and turning, she arose and slipped on the pale blue robe that matched her nightrail. Quietly she left the room and made her way downstairs and through the sleeping house. Having consumed very little of the delicious dinner, due to her nervousness, she now felt ravenous. Without a candle to guide her, she made her way cautiously, for she had imbibed liberally of the champagne and still felt light-headed.

The pale moonlight streaming through the windows dimly lit her path, but she still managed to brush against a pedestal bearing a bronze bust. She gasped softly as it made a scraping sound, and she had to grab it to keep it from falling. Her heart hammered loudly in her chest for a few moments before she could continue. There had to be a door leading out of the dining room, for she remembered the kitchens were in a separate building. Just as she thought, a winter kitchen lay beyond the dining room, and a door there led outside. It had no bolt, for which she was thankful, so she eased it open. A stone pathway led across the kitchen yard, and she hurried along, hoping no night creatures lay in her way, since she'd forgotten her slippers.

The air was heavy with perfume from the nearby oleander shrubs, and she breathed deeply of the scent. Just before she reached the squat stone b... caught her attention. She stopped and l... but seeing nothing, moved on and opened...

The interior was dim, but she saw the ... shelf inside the doorway. It would be logical to ... and candles there. Just as her hand closed over a ...mp, a large hand closed over her mouth, and a strong arm yanked her close.

Panic seized her, and a scream rose in her throat but could not escape. She struggled and tried to bite her captor while a dozen frightening thoughts raced through her mind at lightning speed. Her heel connected with a hard shinbone, and she and her assailant both grunted in pain.

He held her fast, though, and hissed in her ear, "It's Marcus Bond, Amy! Cease your fighting!" It took a moment for his sharp words to sink in, and when they did, she sagged with relief. His strong arm around her midriff was all that kept her from sinking to the floor. He took his hand from her mouth, and she gasped for air.

Turning her around to face him, his hands slipped to her waist as if he was afraid she'd yet collapse. The darkness in the room prevented her from seeing anything but his outline, but she knew his voice and remembered well the masculine smell of him.

"You nearly frightened me into an early grave," she gasped, her tone just above a whisper.

"I'm sorry, but I didn't want you to scream and wake the household," he said, his tone not the least bit contrite.

"What are you doing here?" she demanded, suddenly realizing his presence was suspicious.

"The same as you, I should imagine—I'm hungry," he lied. That was partially true, he told himself, breathing in her heady perfume. His large hands nearly spanned waist, and the feel of her silk gown spun erotic thoughts through his mind, making him hungry for her. He'd been in Harlan's bookroom, searching for any information he could use, when Amy had slipped past the open doorway. He hadn't been able to resist following her.

"That's not what I meant, you dolt! The dinner guests left hours ago," she snapped.

Grinning in the dark, he said, "Ah . . . I see your confusion. I'm a houseguest, Mistress Hawthorne, like yourself. Mr. Stafford invited me to stay here until the *Rebecca* is repaired."

His words were like a cold dash of water in the face. "You?" she blurted out, wide-eyed. "Here?"

"Aye. Very hospitable of him, was it not?" he said, his voice sounding strangely husky. Her nearness was beginning to stir his senses — the womanly smell of her, the heat of her body beneath his hands — and he should have known better than to follow her.

The initial shock of this whole encounter was wearing off, and Amy realized he still held her. The situation seemed far too intimate for her comfort as the sultry darkness enclosed them. "Take your hands off me. I'm going back to my room," she breathed as she pushed at his chest.

Instead of complying, he pulled her closer. "I thought you were hungry," he murmured thickly. By then their bodies were touching, and he felt as if a fire had been ignited in his loins. Without conscious thought, his hands roamed over the sweet curve of her rounded hips.

Amy drew in a ragged breath as he caressed her. An intense longing rose in her as the heat and hard planes of his body pressed against her. This could not happen, she told herself sternly, yet her body responded to his touch as wantonly as before. "No," she gasped, making another attempt to return to reality, but as the word passed her lips, he claimed her mouth with his own. His tongue boldly pressed for entry, and Amy found herself giving it to him. Her arms slid up around his neck, and her fingers entwined themselves in his thick hair.

Marcus lifted her off the floor and held her hips tightly against his as he deepened the kiss.

Amy's senses whirled as she gave over to the passionate nature she hadn't known she possessed. Marcus Bond attracted and intrigued her as no other man before—he made her feel like a woman. Even as their kiss deepened, her rebellious heart chafed at the restrictions placed on her. She yearned to know what it would be like to have this handsome, virile man make love to her. Edward Simpson's face flashed into her mind. Soon enough, a tiny voice warned, her uncle would choose a husband for her, and then her fate would be sealed.

Marcus drew back and rained small kisses on her eyes, nose and lips. "Come to my room," he rasped deep in his throat. His desire for her was nearly painful, but he forced himself to wait for her response. She was not a tavern doxy who made her living from men, but a young lady of quality, gently bred. And even though he had doubts about her virginity, he wanted to make sure she wanted this as much as he.

Amy hesitated but a moment before she murmured, "Aye."

He kissed her passionately once more to seal the bargain, savoring the feel of her in his arms, then set her down gently. Taking her hand, he led her back to the house and quietly up to his bedroom at the opposite end of the hall from hers. Once inside, he closed the door and pulled her close. "You can change your mind," he offered.

There was a wall lamp lit across the room, casting the two of them in its pale light. Amy gazed up at his handsome features and brushed a stray lock of dark hair from his brow. "Are you saying you don't want me now, Marcus?" she asked, not understanding his reluctance.

He groaned and cupped her small face in his hands. "Never! I just want you to be sure . . . and I know I have no right . . ."

Amy flicked her tongue over her dry lips and said with as much courage as she could muster, "I give you that right."

His eyes smoldered with fire as he wordlessly picked her up and carried her to his bed. He slipped the robe from her shoulders and then removed his own white shirt. Taking a moment to remove his boots, he then joined her, dipping his head to taste her lips.

Uncertain what was expected of her, Amy ran her hand across his dark-furred chest. He pulled back from her mouth and captured her roving hand, pressing a kiss into the palm. She was intrigued by his muscled physique and eyed the bulge in his tight-fitting breeches with a mixture of fear and fascination. "The light . . . perhaps you should — "

"It would be a shame to hide beauty like yours with darkness," he said, his voice growing deeper with desire. "Ah, Amy love, you've tormented my dreams for weeks now. Since that day on the wharf when I first saw you, I've wanted you in my bed."

Leaning forward, he buried his face in her sweet-smelling hair and then nuzzled her neck. His free hand cupped a full breast, and Amy felt it swell beneath his touch. She gasped at the pleasurable sensation and moaned softly when he teased the nipple, already swollen with desire.

A foreign sensation spiraled downward from her stomach to the region between her thighs, and ended in a curious throbbing ache.

His lips followed his hand down to suck gently at the crested peak through the material of her gown. Amy buried her hands in his hair and instinctively arched her hips in response to the passionate longing that gripped her.

Marcus slid her gown up to her flat belly and boldly caressed the softness between her thighs. She sucked in her breath as waves of desire, stronger than before, flooded her. "That feels so . . . oh, please," she moaned.

He paused to kiss her and then whispered his love for each part of her body, while his fingers probed gently through the silky hair between her thighs. His erotic caresses caused her to arch her body in exquisite pleasure. In her mindless passion, her hands moved down his muscled back to the waistband of his breeches and tugged gently. She hardly realized what she was doing. All she knew was that she desperately wanted this mating. The pent up longings that had been building inside her since they'd met were about to explode, and she knew he was the trigger.

"My sweet Amy," he groaned as her brazen fingers slipped inside his breeches. He jerked away as if burned, and stood up, divesting himself of his remaining garments.

Her breath was coming in short gasps as her heavy-lidded gaze raked over his magnificent body. Broad of shoulder and narrow of hip, he looked like a bronze statue. She felt little embarrassment at the perusal, or at the size of his obvious arousal. She was beyond doubt and wanted only the release he could give.

As Amy branded him with her bold curiosity, Marcus felt the blood pump wildly through his veins in answer. Bending forward, he slipped the gown over her head so that he could look upon her fully. Full satiny breasts with rosy peaks rose up, and from a tiny waist flared rounded hips. He lowered himself over her and tantalized her lips with his tongue while drawing her hips against the naked heat of his. Amy's eyes fluttered closed and her world spun crazily as his tongue plundered the softness of her mouth. His hands began to move over her body, stroking her breasts and moving down to the satiny skin of her inner thighs. His mouth left hers to tease a budding nipple, sucking and kissing until her passion burst into a shower of flames. "Marcus . . . oh, Marcus," she whispered, her breathing ragged as she twisted beneath his tantalizing assault. Her movements drove him wild with wanting, and his mouth sought hers once more. She returned his kiss with a passion of her own, even while one last twinge of fear knotted in her stomach for a moment. That quickly melted away with the heat of his tender caresses. She welcomed him as he guided his burgeoning erection to the opening he sought.

Through his haze of passion, he felt her readiness as he pushed boldly into her velvet softness. It took him a moment to grasp the fact that she was a virgin, as a sharp gasp escaped her lips and he felt his first thrust break the small barrier inside her. His movement stilled suddenly. "Amy?" he breathed hoarsely.

Her eyes had flown open at the sharpness of the pain, and she tried for a moment to push him away. Sudden tears sprang to her eyes.

He lifted his head, a stunned expression in his eyes. "My God, Amy! Why didn't you tell me?" he said hoarsely.

An errant tear escaped and slipped down her cheek. "I didn't know it would . . . hurt so much," she whispered.

He groaned and traced the trail of wetness with his thumb. "The pain is over," he said gruffly. Anger and desire warred within his breast. Desire won as she slid her hands behind his neck and pulled his head back down to hers.

"Kiss me again, Marcus." she pleaded softly against his mouth. "Don't be angry . . ."

It was far too late for him to stop anyway, he thought feverishly, as he grasped her hips and began to move slowly within her. His breath quickened at the exquisite pleasure of loving her. His hands resumed their tormenting caresses.

She rose to meet each thrust and clutched at his powerful shoulders. Amy cried his name softly as new and wonderful sensations flooded her body and the rhythm became urgent, until finally the throbbing between her legs exploded in a stormy release.

Marcus felt the sensuous tightening of tiny spasms around his manhood and found his own release. As pleasure washed over both of them in waves, he held her fiercely.

When the world righted itself once more, Amy stretched expansively beneath him, running her hands lovingly over his broad back. She sighed happily as he nuzzled her hair and traced her ear with his tongue. He rolled to his side and pulled her against him, covering them with the sheet. Amy, her head resting on his shoulder, could feel the strong beat of his heart under her hand. She was drowsy and strangely content, despite or because of what had just occurred between the two of them. "It was all I had dreamed and more," she confessed. Of all the men who had courted her favor, not one had excited her passion. Nor had she given a thought to allowing them any intimate mastery over her body. But Marcus . . . he had boldly taken what she offered, and had given her ecstasy in return. She shivered as she thought about what his touch did to her. And for the moment, she didn't want to think about the consequences.

113

"Aye," Marcus agreed, thinking of his own intense pleasure. But he was thinking of more than that as he placed a gentle kiss on the top of her head and idly caressed her hip. There was the guilt he felt over taking her virginity. He hadn't known, but would he have done the same even if he had, he wondered? In an agony of wanting her, had he ignored the signs of her innocence? And now when he was so close to accomplishing his task of making Harlan Stafford pay for his sins, he was getting himself involved with someone closely related to that blackguard. A seed of regret took root in his mind. "Why didn't you tell me?" he asked, more sharply than he had intended.

Amy blanched at his tone and raised up to gaze into his face. "Tell you what?" she asked.

He closed his eyes for a moment, knowing he was being unfair, but unable to help himself. "You've never been with a man," he said flatly. "You purposely deceived me."

Amy drew in a swift breath. "I know I may have given you the wrong impression once, but I was angry at the time. Moreover, I don't understand what difference it makes, Marcus Bond! What passed between us was of my choosing, and you owe me nothing." She jerked away from him to a sitting position, heedless of the fact that she was naked and her breasts heaved with each indrawn breath. Marcus pushed himself up and swallowed tightly at the sight. As she tossed her head, her thick mane of tangled copper hair fell back over her slim shoulders, and her eyes glittered dangerously in the dim lamplight.

Marcus wanted, all of a sudden, to return to the sweetness they'd shared a few moments ago, though he knew that it was impossible. He'd stung her pride, and a woman of her spirit would not let that pass. Moreover, he would be doing her a favor by letting her go. With an iron will, he struck down his desire for her and let a faint sneer color his voice. "I've heard that vow before and count myself lucky to have avoided the matrimonial trap, Mistress Amy."

Infuriated, Amy slapped his face with a resounding smack. "You conceited pig . . . you arrogant, blackguard bastard!" she hissed.

Deftly, Marcus caught her arm, subduing her with ease. He felt he deserved the first blow, but decided this confrontation should end before he weakened and told her the truth. In her glorious anger, she was more beautiful than when soft and yielding, and he wanted her more now than the first time. Steeling himself against the arousal he felt, he gave her a twisted grin. "Aye, Amy — bastard I may be, but a free man. I don't intend to be shackled . . . even by bonds as beautiful and silken as yours."

Amy jerked her arm free and scrambled out of bed. She found her nightrail and slipped into it and grabbed her robe. Turning, she became more incensed when she found him watching her as he lounged casually against the massive headboard. Between clenched teeth, she said, "If you come near me again, I'll see the hide flayed from your worthless back."

Marcus watched helplessly as she left the room, a sickening pain cutting through him like a knife.

Chapter Seven

Fiona stepped abruptly back into her room and closed the door gently. Her heartbeat slowed to a normal rhythm as she listened at the wooden portal. If she'd been a scant minute later, she'd have run into Amy. No sounds came, and she breathed a sigh of relief. Amy must have gone to her own room. Where had she been at this hour? Fiona wondered. Her brief glimpse had told her Amy was in a hurry.

Fiona chewed distractedly at a fingernail while she calculated her young employer's reason for roaming the hallway at one-thirty in the morning. Perhaps she'd been with Justin Stafford, Fiona thought, a gleam of malicious interest lighting her brown eyes. The two of them had been practically inseparable all evening, and young Stafford could hardly keep his eyes from Amy's low cut bodice. He was quite handsome and possessed considerable charm. Mayhap Amy had fallen under his spell.

Fiona left off her musing and quietly opened her door a crack to peer out. She had a mission of her own to attend to. The hall was empty, so she hurried to Amy's door and listened for sounds within, but heard nothing. She moved on to Thaddeus's bedroom, and her eyes sparkled in anticipation. Experience told her he was ready to be seduced. At an opportune moment during the evening, she had taken his arm and pressed her body against him; another time, their fingers had brushed as he'd handed her a glass of champagne, and she'd seen a flicker of desire in his eyes. Aye, he was more than ready.

Easing open his door, she crept in, relying on touches of moonlight to show her the way to the shadowy bed. She could hear light snores and smiled to herself, hoping his heart could stand the shock she was about to give him.

Slipping out of her satin nightrail and robe, she eased under the sheet beside him. She touched his cheek lightly and whispered his name, so as not to startle him unduly.

Groggily, he mumbled and opened his eyes, blinking to focus. Fiona's lips curved in a sensuous smile as she stroked his face gently. "Wake up, my love," she whispered.

For a moment Thaddeus thought he was still dreaming, but Fiona's warm, naked body pressed against his side, while her sweet breath filled his nostrils. He realized this was the real woman, not the ethereal figure that had haunted his sleep for many nights. He turned and pulled her closer. "How did you know?" he asked in a voice husky with sleep and desire.

She pressed her warm breasts against his chest. "I didn't . . . but I'm in love with you and could not help myself," she said in a breathy voice.

Thaddeus's hand caressed her satiny hip and moved up to cup the naked weight of her breast as his heart thudded in an erratic rhythm. "I had hoped, my dear, that you would come to care, but this is beyond my imaginings," he said, his voice low and intense.

"Oh, Thaddeus," she gasped as his hand slipped down between her legs and began to stroke her gently. "I would have died if you'd sent me away."

He rose up and pulled his nightshirt off, tossing it aside. "I'd have been a fool to do so," he growled.

With the sheet pushed aside, his gaze took in her

young, taut body, glistening like satin in the soft moonlight. His member was swollen and throbbing, and for the first time in a long, long time, he felt young and vitally alive. "God's blood, girl, but you're beautiful!" he breathed. He took her lips then in a fierce kiss and covered her body with his own.

Fiona moaned with pleasure as his hands touched her everywhere—her breast, thighs, and the soft down between her legs. In return, her caresses were more innocent and tentative, which further inflamed his passion. Unable to wait any longer, he possessed her with an urgency that belied his years, and they rose to breathless, spiraling heights.

Climbing up from the depths of sleep, Amy squinted bleary-eyed at the maid, Ivy, who quietly placed a tray on the small writing table. The black girl moved noiselessly across the room to push the French doors wider. Raising up on her elbow, Amy asked sleepily, "What time is it, Ivy?"

The girl started at the sound of Amy's voice. "It be almost noon, Missy Amy. I brought tea. You need Ivy to dress?"

Closing her eyes, Amy rubbed her temples for a moment to relieve the pain in her head. "Thank you, no. I can manage." She waited until she heard the door close before she got up. Stripping off her gown, she sponged off with cool water from the bowl provided and then stepped to the wardrobe.

She caught her reflection in the mirror on the inside of the door and blushed, feeling self-conscious for the first time at the sight of her own body. It was almost as if Marcus had left his mark on her. She shivered with remembered pleasure and then felt shamed that her mind betrayed her so. He was a blackguard, and she'd been a fool to succumb to his potent caresses. Her curiosity had once again led her into disaster, and this time she had paid dearly.

Touching her flat stomach, a frightening thought occurred to her — what if their time together had left her pregnant? That sobering question sent her pulse skittering, and she hastily pulled her clothes out and slammed the door. Surely it wasn't possible, she told herself while dressing. There had only been the one time, yet a sly voice inside taunted that he was a bold and virile man.

After donning the white taffeta morning gown, she sat down to brush her hair. A brief knock on the door brought an end to her disturbing thoughts, as Fiona entered. She was dressed demurely in beige satin, and her spectacles were in place. "Let me do that," Fiona said, taking the brush.

"I cannot imagine why I'm such a slugabed today," Amy commented, knowing full well she'd hardly slept a wink the night before. She closed her eyes, enjoying the soothing service her companion performed.

"Perhaps you did not sleep well last night," Fiona suggested casually, working Amy's thick tresses into an upsweep.

"I was restless," Amy agreed finally, trying to ignore the reason for that state.

"Once, I thought I heard you moving about. You weren't ill?" Fiona pressed, hoping Amy had not come to her room and found her gone. She wanted Thaddeus well and truly hooked before Amy was told.

"No, and besides, there would have been nothing you could do. One of us unable to sleep was enough," Amy said. "I believe it was merely strange surroundings that caused the problem."

"You will soon settle in," Fiona comforted. "All finished," she said, and added, "Ivy said Mistress Pamela expects us in the drawing room."

Amy rose and picked up her fan. "I'm ready, then."

Pamela gave them a shy smile as they entered the room. She was seated in a straight-backed chair beside the French doors, a wooden embroidery stand in front of her. Rising, she gestured toward the settee close by. "Please, join me, and I will have tea brought in."

She rang for a servant and gave her instructions before turning to her guests. "I trust you had everything you needed and slept well," she said.

Both girls assured her they had, each lying politely. Amy smiled and said, "You have such a lovely home, and the grounds that I could see from my room are beautiful. I would quite like a tour sometime, if you're not too busy."

A deep voice spoke up from the doorway. "Please allow me to be your guide, Amy." The three women looked up, and Justin continued into the room. Clad casually in a full white shirt and tan breeches, he looked even more handsome than he had the night before. He stopped beside Amy's chair and smiled warmly down at her.

She inclined her head in compliance and returned his smile. "How kind of you to volunteer."

"It will be my pleasure. How about tomorrow morning? You ride, do you not?" he asked.

"Yes, I do—and tomorrow morning would be lovely," she answered.

Justin helped himself to a cup of tea and took a chair. He didn't seem to be the least bit uncomfortable in a group of women. He began talking about some of the important personages who had attended the dinner party the night before, relating some funny and scandalous stories about each. His wit was more mischievous than malicious, and Amy enjoyed his company enormously. Pamela scolded and laughed at him in turns, and Amy could see that she adored her older brother.

As he was recounting a particularly amusing tale

about the Widow Drake and Sheriff Campbell, Amy heard voices in the hall. She glanced up, a feeling of dread washing over her, as Thaddeus, Harlan and Marcus entered the room.

Her eyes met Marcus's for a brief moment before she looked away, pretending to pick up the threads of Justin's story. She pointedly ignored him as the conversation became more general. At least once, she felt his gaze on her, and it took all her willpower not to return his interest.

Julia arrived, excusing her absence with household duties, just before a maid announced the noon meal. Justin stood and offered Amy his arm, and she took it gratefully. He held her chair at the table and bent his head to give her an outrageous compliment on her appearance while viewing boldly the swell of her bosom rising above the bodice of her dress. Not realizing where his gaze roamed, she laughed brightly, chiding him for his exaggeration. He took the chair beside hers, and Amy noticed in dismay as Marcus sat directly across from her and scowled in her direction. Amy gave him a quelling look and turned her attention back to Justin. It would not do to let him know how much he hurt her by the things he'd said the night before. She'd made a colossal mistake, but did not intend to repeat it.

Marcus continued to watch Amy and brooded on the state of affairs. How he wished he hadn't let desire overrule his better judgment. She was beautiful and fine, and he had taken something from her that couldn't be replaced. And what had he to offer her anyway, not to mention his plans for Harlan Stafford? He was penniless and she an heiress. For the greater part of the meal, he surreptitiously watched Amy and Justin as they talked and laughed. A knot formed in his stomach as he noted Justin's outrageous flirting. He had to suppress the desire to throttle the man.

Toward the end of the meal, Harlan spoke up from the

head of the table. "My dear Amy, would you and Fiona care to accompany Thaddeus and me into Tucker's Town this afternoon? I need to conduct some business, and our little town might prove interesting for you."

Amy glanced at Fiona, who nodded her assent, before she said, "I'm sure it would. Thank you, we'd be delighted."

As the plum tart was served, Amy attended to Justin' plans for the shipyard with half an ear while she also listened to Marcus and Pamela's conversation. The girl seemed to blossom beneath his attention, and it surprised Amy that he took special care to draw her out. His consideration was to be commended, yet Amy was annoyed that he had never spoken quite so kindly to her.

"My dear, if you don't mind my saying so, that small confection with a bit of lace and feathers on your head will not keep you from sunstroke," Harlan said to Amy, amusement lighting his silver-gray eyes.

As the carriage rolled along the coral road, Amy turned from the scenery to smile at him. "It wasn't meant to, Mr. Stafford," she said pertly.

He gave a hearty laugh at her quick wit and nudged Thaddeus. "I marvel at the fact that some young buck hasn't taken this delightful creature to wife as yet."

Thaddeus rolled his eyes in exaggeration and snorted. "There've been none able to withstand the slash of her sharp tongue, my friend. It seems her standards are high indeed."

Harlan grinned at her, approval lighting his eyes. "Aye, as well they should be. A woman of spirit as well as beauty is a fine treasure and not to be squandered on a milksop."

"You're making me blush," Amy chided, doing no such thing. She rather enjoyed compliments, even when

122

they were exaggerated. She touched the small blue hat on her head and asked seriously, "Is the sun really so hot here?"

"It is, quite," he replied. "If you've brought nothing suitable with you, might I suggest that you and Mistress Fiona visit the milliner's shop in town. I believe Julia and Pamela find all they require there."

Amy nodded. "The advice is appreciated, and it will occupy us while you gentlemen attend your business," she said, and then added mischievously, "Besides, it's a wonderful excuse to do some shopping."

Thaddeus smiled impartially on both girls and extracted some money from his coat pocket. "Purchase the hats and anything else you both need for the moment. I can't have Harlan thinking I'm a miser where my girls are concerned. He's sure enough that I'm tightfisted when it comes to business."

Amy took the money and slipped it inside her drawstring purse as the men's conversation turned to business. Smoothing the folds of her dark blue afternoon frock, she returned her gaze to the scenery. The well-appointed open carriage rolled smoothly over the road, and they passed an occasional cottage and small farm. The countryside of the interior was not as spectacular as that of the coast; however, it was charming just the same. The road was like a curving white ribbon flanked by low stone walls here and bright-colored hedges there. Amy noticed that the occasional pedestrians they passed wore large straw hats, with the exception of the black women who wore turban-style kerchiefs on their heads. She had packed several parasols, and she realized their purpose would be twofold now, fashionable and useful.

More stone cottages came into view as the party neared the town, and as the carriage turned onto the narrow main street of Tucker's Town, Amy took in the sights. There were quite a few shops lining both sides, with quaint, painted signs proclaiming the type of establishment within. She saw a dressmaker, a bakeshop, a wig maker and a barber before their conveyance stopped at a storefront with the name "Stafford and Son" above the door.

As they stepped down, Harlan pointed up the street a short distance. "The milliner is there, ladies. We shall be here at my offices until you tire of looking or run low on funds, whichever the case may be."

The two women made their way to the small shop and stopped for a moment to look at the artful display of hats in the window. Fiona spoke as they entered. "It was very generous of your uncle to offer to purchase what I need, especially when my salary is more than adequate."

"Uncle Thaddeus is not known for parsimony, contrary to what he says," Amy replied with a smile.

After the bright sunlight, the interior of the shop was dim. A small, birdlike woman came from the back to greet them. "Good day, ladies. I am Madam Burgess. Might I be of service to you?"

Amy glanced around at the array of hats gracing the small tables and spotted a white, full-brimmed silk creation. "Ah, there. We are interested in something like that. And perhaps some in straw."

" 'Tis a fine choice, and aye, I have some in straw as well," she enthused, ushering them to chairs set before tall mirrors, placed so that the customer might enjoy a view of not only the hat, but its total effect on the wearer.

There were soon dozens of hats strewn about while the young women happily tried on one after another, asking each other's opinions and comparing colors and materials.

Amy was admiring a fine straw, closely woven, with dark blue ribbons tied under her chin, when the door opened and another customer entered. She caught sight of the girl in the mirror and was struck by the beautiful, unusual silver shade of her hair.

Madam Burgess glanced up from helping Fiona and said sharply, "I am busy, Megan. Are you in need of something in particular?"

The girl's expressive face darkened, and her eyes narrowed at the slight. "I'll be wantin' to look around, but I *do* have coin in my pocket."

Amy hid a smile at the girl's brisk rejoinder. She had noticed that Madam Burgess's fawning tone of voice had changed abruptly with the new customer and rightly deduced the girl most likely had less money to spend. Most shopkeepers were shamelessly pretentious, Amy knew.

Fiona turned to Amy. "I can't decide between the straw and the blue silk . . . what do you think?"

"Take them both," Amy suggested, trying on yet another.

"If you think 'twill be all right," Fiona answered, a suitable amount of doubt in her voice. At Amy's absent-minded nod, Fiona quickly handed her favorites to Madam Burgess to wrap. "Oh, my dear! You must take that one," the older girl exclaimed. "That shade of green matches your eyes and also the gown you wore last night. I could not help but notice the way young Stafford attended you all evening. I believe he was quite smitten."

Amy's eyebrow rose, and she remarked, "With Justin, it's hard to tell. He's just as charming to every other woman." She heard a sharp gasp from across the room and turned in that direction.

The silver-haired girl's face was flushed as she muttered, "I don't have all day to wait, like some folks." She whirled and slammed the door as she left.

Madam Burgess sniffed indignantly. "That chit has gall! Pay her no mind, ladies, for she's but a tavern maid. And you know what they are."

The little woman's brows rose to emphasize her meaning. Amy, however, did not like her tone. "Perhaps that is the only occupation the woman can find," she suggested.

Madam Burgess gave both girls a knowing look. "To be sure. Serving drinks is not all she does."

Amy did not hold with malicious gossip. She rose and said briskly, "I'll take these three."

As Fiona and Amy walked toward the Stafford offices, Amy caught a glimpse of a silver head and a flurry of skirts rounding a building across the street. She knew it was the girl named Megan and wondered if she had been spying on them and did not wish to be seen. Shrugging, she put the incident from her mind.

When they entered the building, a young man with a pasty complexion rose from a desk near the door and led them up a flight of stairs. The whole second floor was furnished elegantly with deep upholstered chairs, bookcases and a massive cedar desk. Harlan and Thaddeus rose as the women entered.

Amy thanked the young man — whom Harlan called Wallis — and dropped her packages on a chair.

Harlan smiled. "Thaddeus and I were going to visit the wharf and thought you would like to join us. One of my ships is in port to unload cargo."

"That sounds exciting, Mr. Stafford," Fiona said, and then turned quickly to Amy. "That is, if Amy would like to."

"I should enjoy it also. Only first let me put on one of my new hats, ere I get too much sun." She grinned mischievously as she undid her package and replaced her small hat with one of the straws. In front of a wall mirror, she tied the blue ribbons beneath her chin and pronounced herself ready to depart.

Both men dutifully admired the creation before they left the room. They had only gotten midway down the stairs, though, when Fiona cried out softly and clutched at the rail for support. "Oh, dear! I've turned my weak ankle again."

Thaddeus slipped an arm around her waist and gave her support to the bottom of the staircase. He helped her to a chair and frowned in concern. "You cannot walk that distance now, Fiona."

"I will go ahead and tend to my business at the wharf if you want to return to the house with the women, Thaddeus," Harlan suggested.

Fiona looked contrite. "Please, no. I will sit here until you return. Truly, I will be fine."

"I have a solution," Thaddeus interjected smoothly. "I will have tea brought in and keep Fiona company while you give Amy the outing. I'm sure she will enjoy seeing the bay."

With the matter thus settled, Amy took Harlan's arm, letting him lead her out into the sunshine. She was rather glad not to miss this outing, for she was curious to see everything, the islands being so different from Boston. The narrow streets were paved with the local white coral, and most of the buildings were of glaringly white limestone, quarried on the island. Bright red, pink and purple blossoms grew in flower beds, along walkways and in hedges.

Amy tipped her head to the side and smiled up at Harlan. " 'Tis so colorful here in your lovely islands compared to the drabness of Boston, Mr. Stafford."

He gave a mock frown. "It makes me feel such an old man, my dear, when you call me Mr. Stafford . Do you think you could manage Harlan?"

Amy chuckled. "Aye, sir. If that's all it takes to make you feel young, I daresay I can do it."

Harlan grinned rakishly, and Amy caught a flicker of resemblance to Justin in the look. "Sporting a beautiful woman on my arm through town for all to envy will also do much for my reputation," he teased.

"I know now where Justin gets his charming manner," she said, returning his teasing, her green eyes twinkling.

Harlan's eyebrow rose. "So you think my son, charming, eh? I would have you know he's of like mind and more."

Amy looked away demurely, taking note of the pale green bay that was in sight now. Harlan Stafford was not given to mincing words, and it was obvious he desired a match between his son and her. However, Amy balked at being pressured. Carefully, she said, "I hope Justin and I can become good friends." She placed quiet emphasis on the last word in an effort to discourage him.

To her surprise, he changed the subject quite tactfully. Pointing out different ships riding at anchor in the bay, he told her who they belonged to and where they'd been. Some of their cargos were as exotic as the places where they stopped to trade — the West Indies, the Sandwich Islands and as far away as China.

Amy loved the sights and sounds of the wharf, as sailors in all sorts of garbs worked and lounged, calling out to each other with their strange accents. She was receiving much attention, but none felt brave enough to do more than look, for Harlan Stafford was a well-known figure and one to be reckoned with should he become displeased. Pointing just ahead of them, he said proudly, "That's the *Sea Nymph* — my best ship. She's just come back from an extensive voyage."

Amy's gaze skimmed over the two-masted schooner admiringly. Her lines were clean and beautiful, but one thing puzzled her. "Is she a merchant vessel?"

Harlan nodded absently as he signaled to a sailor standing watch on deck. "Aye, Amy."

A gangway was being lowered to let them board as Amy remarked, "By the look of the guns, I would mistake her for a warship."

She missed the surprised look he gave her as he

grasped her elbow to ascend to the deck. Casually, he explained, "Pirates and privateers, my dear. 'Tis a sad state of affairs, but one must be prepared to fend off attacks from these marauders." His tone grew chilly then as he added, "I've lost all I intend to."

Before Amy could question his cryptic remark, a burly seaman hurried across the deck to speak to Harlan. He was dirty, his clothes torn, and a full black beard gave him a fierce look. Amy had to force herself not to flinch when he raked her form boldly with his eyes.

"What's the meaning of this, Stowe?" Harlan demanded, eyeing not only the sailor distastefully, but the unkempt look of the ship. Although his standards were not unduly rigid, he still expected a certain amount of cleanliness and order on his vessels. In short, he was embarrassed that his lovely guest should see his prized ship in such a state.

The sailor had snatched his hat off, and he stood twisting it nervously in his hands, his expression both fearful and agitated. " 'Ere's been . . . a problem, Mr. Stafford, sir. The captain, uh, he's mighty anxious to speak to ye. Told me I should bring ye to his cabin the very minute ye set foot—"

Harlan grew impatient and ordered, "Spit it out, man! What's going on?"

Amy watched curiously as the man talked and shot furtive glances at her. She realized her presence was keeping him from blurting out some serious news.

Stowe cleared his throat nervously and shook his head. "You'll not want the lady hearin' this, sir," he said, frightened of Stafford's wrath, but knowing the news was not for an outsider's ears.

Not being dull-witted, Harlan grasped the situation and nodded. "I'll see Captain Aiken, and I charge you personally with the care of Mistress Hawthorne. Find a comfortable spot for her and fetch some fresh coffee—

and see that no one" — Harlan emphasized the latter command with a piercing look before continuing — "accosts her in any way."

He gave Amy's arm a reassuring squeeze. "I'm dreadfully sorry, my dear, to have brought you into this rather uncomfortable situation. I had a message this morning from the captain to meet him here, but apparently it was more urgent than I knew. Will you be all right for a few minutes? I shall dispense with this business as fast as possible."

Amy glanced at the crude sailor and swallowed tightly, but nodded. "Do not worry about me, Harlan. Tend your business, and I shall be fine with, er, Mr. Stowe."

Harlan smiled his approval and gave Stowe a final warning glance before he went off.

Stowe suggested a shady spot where she might wait, but Amy declined, assuring him she preferred to watch the lively scenes on the wharf from the rail. He called another sailor over and bade him fetch fresh coffee from a tavern on the dock, while he retreated a few yards and took up his watchful position of guard.

Chapter Eight

"You killed every last man on the ship . . . and the women as well?" Harlan repeated, staring incredulously at Captain Aiken. "A British ship! Good God, man—that's murder and treason!"

The color had drained from the captain's face as he recounted the misadventure to his superior, but he flushed at Harlan's tone. "A bloody mistake, sir—that's the way of it! We thought it was one of those Frenchie merchant sloops headin' home from Martinique, so we fired on 'er. By the time we knowed our mistake, it was too late and they was firin' back—I swear!"

"So you took the ship and massacred all aboard to keep silence on the matter," Harlan ground out as he leaned over the desk, his hands planted on its surface. He was so close to the seated captain, he could smell the rum on the man's breath.

Captain Aiken cringed visibly. "They saw our flag afore we could run up the Jolly Roger. But we took a rich haul," he offered, his voice squeaking in fear.

"Aye, and if 'tis ever discovered 'twas my ship, I'll be ruined and all the booty in the world won't signify," Harlan returned sharply. He straightened and paced the cabin for a few moments, pondering the situation.

The captain cleared his throat nervously. " 'Ere's another small matter, sir. As we sunk the sloop, an American ship was spotted in the distance, but I know they couldn't tell who we was."

Harlan cursed softly, mindful of the fact that Amy was on board. He had no wish for his partner's niece to hear any breath of scandal about the Staffords. His plans to snare her fortune would be ruined, and so would he. Placing an iron grip on his temper, he asked, "Is there anything else of major import I should know?"

"No, sir," the captain said, a certain relief in his voice.

"Order the crew to remain aboard and to speak to no outsiders until further notice. I expect you to report to my office in one hour, and we shall go over this disaster in detail and decide what to do. I have a young lady with me and must return her ere I see to this matter," Harlan said in a clipped tone as he departed.

When Thaddeus and the two women returned to Stafford House, Ivy informed them it was time for afternoon tea. Julia was descending the grand staircase, and they waited for her to reach the foyer.

"I take it my brother will not be joining us," Julia said, noting his absence.

"He sent his apologies, but had important business to attend to," Thaddeus explained.

"Of course. Well, we shall try to get on without him," Julia said with a smile that did not reach her eyes. "Ivy, please see to the tea—"

"If you don't mind, Mistress Julia, I won't take tea. There are some papers that need my attention before dinner," Thaddeus interrupted her.

Fiona spoke up as well. "I must beg off also. My ankle is paining me and I would rest it."

Julia glanced at Amy with a raised brow, expecting a refusal from her also.

132

As Amy couldn't think of a polite excuse, she smiled thinly. "I would love some refreshment, Mistress Julia. I shall freshen up and join you in a moment."

Julia nodded. "Since 'tis just the two of us, we shall have it in my private sitting room. Pamela has gone to pay a call." Turning, she addressed the black girl. "Ask Layla to serve in a quarter hour."

Just as Amy smoothed the last stray curl into place, Ivy arrived to show her to Julia's chambers. The hallway was dim, for there were no windows to let in the sunlight, as Amy followed the maid. As far as she could tell, the family as well as the guest rooms were located on this floor, and she asked, "Are the servant quarters within the house, Ivy?"

The slim young woman smiled shyly and shook her turbaned head. "Oh, no, missy. De slaves be out beyond de buttery house. You see dat stone wall out back? De other side be de cabins."

"I thought perhaps the cellars were used as living space," Amy commented.

Ivy's expression grew guarded as she stopped before the door across from Marcus's room. "Oh, no, missy. De massa keeps cargo down dat dark place."

Amy nodded absently, thinking instead about how easily she might have been seen with Marcus that night. Ivy let her in and retreated quietly.

Julia was seated on a worn sofa, a tea service placed on a low table in front of her. There were two carved and gilt chairs in the grouping, and a large fireplace on the near wall. A coffee-colored maid stood beside her mistress and eyed Amy boldly. Julia favored her with the same type of cold look, and Amy wished she had not been so polite in accepting this invitation.

Julia made a slight gesture with her hand toward the chair closest to her. "Don't be shy, my dear. Please sit down. This is my personal maid, Layla."

Amy nodded to the woman and hid her surprise at Julia's unusually cordial tone. She murmured her thanks as Julia passed her a cup of tea and offered some sweet biscuits. Amy searched frantically for something complimentary to say, but it was nearly impossible. Julia was dressed in yet another dull black dress, and even her sitting room had nothing to commend it. The furnishings and trinkets scattered about reminded Amy of a very young girl's tastes, excepting the fact that everything was worn and dated. Her eye chanced to land on an ornate silver music box gracing a nearby table. "What a lovely piece," Amy said. Then she inquired politely, "What tune does it play?"

Julia motioned for Layla to bring the music box to her. For a moment, she caressed the smooth surface and then lifted the lid. The strains of "Greensleeves" filled the room, and Amy murmured, " 'Tis a fine piece with good sound."

"Aye," Julia responded slowly, staring dreamily at the object as if off in another world. Layla touched her shoulder, and, abruptly, Julia closed the lid and returned to herself. " 'Twas a gift from someone special," she said, handing it back to the maid.

Amy sipped her tea and asked, "An admirer?" She could well believe there had been many in Julia's youth, for it was evident that the woman had been a beauty. Julia's mouth tightened for a moment before she spoke in a level tone. "He was more than that . . . we were in love and wanted to wed."

Amy was surprised that the older woman was confiding in her, when she had seemed so reticent since their arrival. "I'm sorry, Mistress Julia, if I reminded you of something painful."

Julia gave her a twisted smile. " 'Tis not your fault, girl. The pain in my life began many years before you were born. My 'dear' brother Harlan — so much like my

134

papa — sent away the man I loved, saying 'twas for my own good. He swore Grayson was a fortune hunter and cared naught for me, but I found later Harlan wanted only to make a slave of me for his own ends."

Amy took a sip of her tea to cover her embarrassment at this outburst. "Perhaps you shouldn't tell me these things, Mistress Julia. I'm but a mere acquaintance and you may regret it later."

"I have a reason for this," Julia said. "Think you I am an empty-headed old woman who babbles?"

Amy's brows rose at the woman's rudeness. "No," she said. "However, it is not my business."

Julia gave her a piercing look. "That's where you are wrong. I am telling you this so you will understand my warning. Harlan intends to use you and Justin just as he did me."

Amy thought she understood Julia's meaning then. Harlan desired a match between herself and his son and Julia saw it as treachery. The poor woman was bitter beyond belief, and, for all Amy knew, Harlan might have had her best interests at heart when he interfered. "My uncle and your brother have, I believe, discussed the possibility of a match between Justin and myself, Mistress Julia," Amy began quietly. "However, Justin and I will make up our own minds on the matter. Besides, they only want the best for us."

Julia gave a sharp bark of laughter. "You foolish girl! Mayhap your uncle cares for you, but rest assured my brother has dark motives for all he does. He cares for himself and no one else — not me, not his children."

Decidedly uncomfortable, Amy rose and said stiffly, "Thank you for the tea, Mistress Julia . . . and for the warning. Though I doubt I will have need of it."

When Amy reached the door, Julia called her name and she turned. "I can see you do not believe me, but know this: I love Justin and Pamela and will not see them used for any purpose."

A chill raced up Amy's spine at Julia's cold words. They sounded much like a threat.

Passing her own room, Amy knocked lightly at Thaddeus's door. When there was no answer, she peeked inside and saw her uncle sleeping soundly on the large bed. Sighing, she closed the door and made her way downstairs and outside. She had wanted to tell him of the strange conversation with Julia. The woman seemed quite unstable, and Amy did not enjoy being a pawn in anyone's game.

She descended the front steps and turned to her right, following the drive to a high stone wall. Curious as to what lay beyond, she found an iron gate and stepped inside. It was a beautiful English garden with bright blooming flowers, shrubs and trees. Everything was well tended, but she saw no one there at the moment. She followed the pathway and discovered a stone bench beside a fountain and sat down. It was a shady spot, and the sound of the water splashing lent an air of coolness to the place.

How her life had changed in just a few short weeks! She had been happy at school and content at her uncle's, playing hostess to his influential guests while she plotted the best method of gaining his permission to open her academy. Then he had become obsessed with the idea a finding her a husband. She shuddered when she thought of Edward Simpson as his choice. The man had been distasteful to her before, but now she realized she could never marry him. Being with Marcus had shown her how intimate the relationship between a man and woman really was, and she knew she couldn't bear Edward's touch in that way. At the thought of Marcus came a yearning

deep inside that suffused her body with a t̶
warmth. She was a woman now, with desires that s̶
not understood before. Those intense needs frightene̶
her, where once she'd been merely curious. It was not
Marcus who frightened her, though, but her own traitorous body that responded to him whenever he was near.

What of other men, though? She was not repulsed by
Justin as she was by Edward, but, on the other hand,
would his kisses make her feel like Marcus's did?

"I would give much to know your thoughts," a deep
voice said.

Amy gave a guilty start and looked up to see Marcus
standing a few paces away. The very idea of telling him
what she'd been thinking made her blush. "Then you
would be wasting your coin, sir, for I was but wool-gathering," she said, angry that he'd caught her off guard.

He ignored her tone and gestured to the place beside
her. "May I share your bench?"

A knot formed in her stomach as she looked into his
expressive gray eyes. Already she could feel the sensual
attraction, and she knew the closer he was, the less she
could trust herself. However, she was loath to have him
guess this. Shrugging, she said, "Why not?"

He sat down and stretched his long, white-stockinged
legs out in front of him and gazed about. After a moment
he said, "My mother had a garden much like this. She
planted it herself and always told me it was very like the
one her family had in Devonshire when she was a girl."

The sound of his deep voice did strange things to her
insides, as did the heat that radiated from his thigh next
to hers. However, his uncaring words of last night rose up
to gall her. She could not bring herself to make idle conversation as if nothing had passed between them.

Another stretch of silence passed before he sighed
heavily. "Amy, please forgive me for what happened. I
would that the deed could be undone, but that is impos-

ell know. I know not how to atone."

though well meant, seemed to cut deeper
ess speech of before. For all her bravado,
d to hear him say he cared about her — that
opened between them meant something to
him.

Amy swallowed a lump in her throat and said lightly,
"As I said before, Marcus, I made my own choice — you
forced nothing on me."

"But I thought you had . . ." he began and then
stopped, realizing how it sounded.

"Had other lovers?" she finished for him. "Is that what
you were going to say?"

Marcus bowed his head. "Aye," he said truthfully, and
then cursed softly. "This complicates my plans more
than you know."

Amy was beginning to get annoyed at his attitude.
"And why is that? I make no demands on you!"

" 'Tis not you but my own conscience that bedevils
me, and I would make it right," he said in agitation, running a hand through his thick hair.

Amy glanced at his handsome profile, and anger
stirred in her. "The only way to do that would be marriage, and I've heard your arrogant views on that. But
know this, Captain Bond: I would not wed you if you
pleaded your case day and night. If you are blue-deviled
about the matter, 'tis no concern of mine."

She rose abruptly and would have stalked away, but he
stood and caught her arm in a firm grip. Turning her to
face him, he said angrily, "I do want you, but you do not
understand! There are circumstances that prevent an involvement with . . . what I mean is, I am not prepared to
take a wife . . ." He stopped short in his explanation,
looking into her angry green eyes. Frustration rose up in
him, for he certainly couldn't tell her about his plans for
revenge. Moreover, his pride was stung over the fact that

he had nothing material to offer a woman, much less a wealthy woman. But he did want her . . . with every fiber of his being.

Amy read the desire in his eyes and felt an answering need in herself. His warm hand on her arm sent excitement racing through her, but she forced herself to remember what they argued about. He pushed her away yet pulled her close each time they met, and she didn't know why. His vague explanation told her nothing, and she could stand no more. She tried to tug her arm free, but he held her fast. "Take your hand from me," she commanded, feeling as if she'd burst into pieces if she stayed.

"I want you to understand—" he ground out between clenched teeth.

She slapped his face, cutting him short, the sound reverberating in the quiet garden. "I think I do understand, Marcus! It seems to me you would like an arrangement but not the guilt."

His face stung where her handprint was already reddening. He pulled her close. "You are a stubborn baggage!" he growled, catching the heady scent of her perfume. "That is not my intention at all."

She was breathless with anger, yet her body ached for his touch. Her mind was in turmoil. Glaring at him, she spat out, "Liar!"

His gray eyes glittered dangerously as he bent his head and took her mouth with a savage intensity, forcing her lips open with his thrusting tongue. His strong hands moved to her back and slid down to pull her hips against his.

Amy pounded ineffectually at his hard chest as her heart fluttered wildly. She felt as if her whole body was on fire, and she suddenly cared not if that blaze consumed her. Her small fists forgot their task as they moved up to encircle his neck and her fingers caressed his thick hair.

Marcus groaned low in his throat as he felt her answering response, and he moved one hand to lightly graze the swell of her breasts above the stiff stomacher she wore. She twisted against him at the exquisite pleasure his touch was giving her.

He pulled back abruptly, panting with desire, aroused almost beyond control. He would have her right there on the grass if he did not stop now. "I . . . cannot," he said, his voice hoarse with passion.

Amy gazed up at him through heavy-lidded eyes, breathing rapidly. Her body was aflame and taut as a bowstring. In a matter of moments he had brought her to a fevered pitch of passion and she had forgotten all else — pride and propriety. Her face flushed at her own wantonness. She stepped back quickly as his hand dropped from her bodice.

"Aye," she agreed harshly, "we cannot do this again." She straightened her stomacher where his hand had pulled it aside, and refused to look at him. " 'Twould be better if we did not see each other outside the drawing room, sir."

He reached out a hand to her, but she stepped back. "I'm sorry — "

Her head snapped up. "Stop saying that! If I hear you apologize one more time, I shall scream! Just leave me be."

She turned and walked stiffly away, letting herself out the gate.

Marcus stared after her, regret marking his expression. He told himself it was for the best, yet there was an emptiness inside him that ached unbearably.

Justin reined in the high-spirited stallion he rode up to a group of low palm trees. He dismounted and turned to lift Amy down from her mare. His hands lingered at her waist a moment longer than necessary, and he smiled. "We'll rest for a space, and then I'll take you to an old pirate's haunt."

Stepping away, Amy stretched her legs and said, "Don't feel you must entertain me the entire morning, Justin. I would not incur your father's wrath by keeping you from your duties at the shipyard."

He admired her trim figure in her green riding coat and skirt, and the natural sway of her hips as she walked. "My position there is suspect, to say the least, Amy. The master builder consults me only on minor details of the daily work, and my dear papa thinks I am fool enough not to realize this," he said, grinning mischievously.

Amy sat down beneath a tree and rested her back against its bole. "And I suppose you have not shared your suspicions with him?" she asked, smiling in return.

He shrugged, arching his eyebrows. "Nay. Why should I? He would but give me a task that consumed more time yet was equally worthless. This way, at least, I may pass part of the day in pursuit of pleasure."

Amy cocked her head to the side and asked archly, "And what pastimes hold your interest?"

He moved to her side and dropped down, pulling a blade of grass to chew at. "Oh, I enjoy an occasional card game with friends, and a horse race now and then. There is also my sloop, the *Margarita,* which I take south marooning at least once a year."

"Marooning—what exactly is that?" she asked.

"We dive on wrecks, fish for turtle and sometimes trade with pirates," he explained, lifting her hand from her lap casually to inspect each slim finger. " 'Tis a wonderful life."

His touch, she had found that morning, was not repulsive, but rather pleasant. However, it did not send shivering warmth through her as when Marcus touched her. Firmly, she put Marcus from her mind and asked, "You actually have dealings with those criminals?"

"Aye. The Spanish pirates we avoid, but aye, the others are glad to trade with us, especially since they cannot chance docking in many ports for supplies." Still, he held her hand, idly stroking the soft flesh of her wrist.

Amy hardly noticed, as she was becoming fascinated with his story. "Why does your vessel carry a Spanish name, pray tell? They are the enemy to all good Englishmen."

He chuckled. "I won her in a card game with a Frenchman who had taken her from a Spaniard. Once I thought to change the name, but seeing how it irritates my father, I left it thus."

"Do you know what I think, Master Justin? I think I would rather have you for a friend than an enemy," she said, her eyes twinkling.

He lifted her hand to place a warm kiss on her wrist, and gazed intently into her eyes. "And I would have you for a friend also," he said, his silky tone holding a challenge.

Amy gently took her hand back and said, "That's settled, then. We shall be friends from here on."

Growing uncomfortable with his attentions, she rose and brushed off her skirt. "Let us be off to your pirate's haunt. I'm growing hungry."

He smiled to himself and rose to walk beside her to the grazing horses. "Your wish is my command, mistress," he said, helping her to mount. He looked up then and grinned. "I had Tante Belle pack a lunch, and we shall dine by the sea."

Amy could not help smiling down at his appealing face, and teased, "That sounds wonderful, Justin. Your thoughtful consideration overwhelms me."

He gave a mock frown. "I believe you are making sport of me, but I shall share my meal with you anyway."

They left the valley behind and topped a hill that overlooked the ocean. They paused for a moment at the crest. "On these islands, Amy, it is impossible to get more than half a league from the sea."

Her gaze swept over the view, taking in a pink beach with a half-moon rim of sand. The beach was backed by a rocky precipice which had been undermined by surf. And then there was the beauty of the blue-green sea. Amy thought she would never tire of looking at it. "How do we get to the beach?" she asked, anxious to explore.

Justin reined his horse to the right, under a tall plantain tree with broad leaves. "There's a trail through here. Follow me."

Amy let her horse pick its way along the lush pathway edged with Spanish bayonets, their spiky leaves brushing her booted foot now and then. As they neared the shore, the grass gave way to rocks and sand, and the trees thinned to a few scrub cedars. Once on the beach proper, Amy noted the precipice she'd seen from the hill was a good distance to her left, and they were actually in a sheltered cove where a small channel led to the open expanse of Castle Harbor.

Justin dismounted and helped Amy down. "There's a story that's been passed down that in 1603 the fleet of Don Luis Fernandez de Cordova was scattered in a storm and one galleon was driven onto the coast near here on the ocean side. The survivors, it's said, were few, but the large cache of gold aboard the ship was retrieved by them and buried hereabouts. They built a small boat and set sail, leaving their booty behind to be picked up later. However, they were rescued by pirates who tortured and then killed them for the information."

Wide-eyed, Amy asked, "So these pirates found the treasure?"

He shook his head and took her arm to stroll down the beach. "No. They came here time and again, looking for it, but apparently the Spanish sailors had misled them, knowing they would die whether they told the truth or not. The cache of gold was never found, but this cove became a nest for those English pirates."

"Do you think there was ever a treasure?"

Justin glanced down at her, a twinkle of amusement in his eyes. "Patrick Cormac and I spent many hours as lads looking for it with no luck, and still I am loath to give up on the possibility."

Amy wrinkled her brow in thought. "I don't recall meeting anyone by that name at the dinner your father gave. Was your friend not in attendance that night?"

Justin chuckled. "Patrick would hardly accept an invitation to one of our social evenings, even if my father extended it, which he would not. The Cormac's are not socially prominent, you see."

She smiled up at him and asked, "Another small rebellion on your part, perhaps?"

His tone was serious for once. "No. Patrick is my closest friend, and it has nothing to do with father. His objection to our friendship is, however, an added bonus."

Amy laughed, "I should like to meet this Patrick, I think."

They had reached the overhanging rock precipice and halted there. Justin took her hand in his and said in a half-serious vein, "I'd not make that mistake, Amy. He's a charmer and would cut me out 'ere he could."

Amy was aware his tone had changed, and she knew he meant to kiss her. For a moment her heart fluttered in anticipation, as she wished to compare his embrace to Marcus's. "We are but friends, Justin," she reminded him gently.

He took both her arms in his hands and drew her closer, his gaze holding hers intently. "I would be more," he said in a husky tone.

Fascinated, Amy watched as his handsome face bent to claim her mouth. She closed her eyes and waited for a stirring of desire, but none came. His kiss was pleasant, his embrace strong, but the warm flood of passion she had half expected did not appear. After a moment, he lifted his head and smiled gently, brushing her cheek with his knuckle. "You're sweet as well as lovely, Amy, and I've wanted to do that since you arrived. I trust you are not angry with me?"

She regarded him with gentle amusement. "You would most certainly know it if I were and not have to inquire."

Smiling, he released her and began talking about his pirates once more as if nothing personal had passed between them. Amy walked about, listening and inspecting the rock formations that reminded her of a chapel with arches and twisted columns. She strove to understand her confused emotions where men were concerned.

For Justin she felt a warm friendship, liking him very much. But his kiss lacked the excitement she'd known with Marcus. And yet, Marcus, while he left her breathless and wanting for more, infuriated her beyond belief, and she, at times, actually loathed him. How was she supposed to know what to do? If only her mother were alive so that Amy might question her on these matters!

Justin suggested they return to the horses and have their meal on the beach. Amy agreed and took his arm, perfectly comfortable with him.

As they sat on a rug, drinking wine, enjoying pork pastries and laughing together over nothing in particular, Marcus Bond sat atop his horse on the cliff, watching them with a jealousy that ate at his very soul.

Chapter Nine

"Do tell me where we might get these funds, Radley? A man cannot draw water from a dry well," Harlan said sarcastically. He sat across the desk from his agent in his town office and, for all his outward calm, felt the clutch of dread in his heart.

John Radley was a small man, thin, with a balding pate. His well-cut suit of clothes was made of fine cloth, and the silver buckles on his shoes were polished. Meticulous with his person as well as his business, he could barely keep from cringing over his employer's alarming state of affairs. 'Twould do no good to remind Stafford that he, John Radley, had advised against the Carolina timber investment, which had been destroyed by fire — and against neglecting the insurance on his costly cargos over the last two years, three of which had gone to marauding Spanish pirates. Nay, Stafford knew these facts but would rather blame his agent than own up to his own mistakes. Radley pushed his spectacles up and, clearing his throat, reshuffled the papers on his lap. "Perhaps we might persuade your creditors to await payment until the profits from the salt arrive," he suggested, knowing the London moneylenders who held the mortgages on Stafford House and the shipyards were tough-minded businessmen and were not disposed to waiting.

Harlan slammed a fist down on the cedar desk and snarled, "You know full well how long it will take to sell that cargo, and I haven't even sent the ships to load it from Turks Island yet."

"In any case, I shall post a letter to them immediately. The notes are not due for two months, and mayhap another solution will show itself, sir," Radley said calmly.

Harlan sat back in his chair and dismissed the man with an irritated wave of his hand. "Keep me informed," he growled as Radley left. He had been counting on the booty brought in by the *Sea Nymph* to tide him over until Justin married Amy. And now the cargo of silks, woolens and jewels that had been confiscated from the British ship was all but worthless, for it had to be hidden. Harlan had instructed Captain Aiken to take on supplies and then hide the smuggled goods on one of the uninhabited islands nearby before he sailed away again. He couldn't risk selling the goods for fear they might be traced back to him. He was responsible for his captain and crew, and all he had worked for all these years would be lost with his reputation.

Why did he suffer such difficulties in his life? He'd had an insipid wife, disappointing offspring, and now he was facing financial ruin. The only bright spot in his existence had been the lovely Sarah Payne, and he deeply regretted the loss of her. A warm feeling stole over his calloused heart as he remembered how sweet she'd been, loving and giving. And she'd had a beauty beyond compare. Of all the women he'd bedded since, none had made him feel more alive — more of a man — than she.

Realizing where his thoughts had wandered, he impatiently pushed them aside to revise his plans for Justin and Amy. Although he had Thaddeus's approval on the matter, they had agreed to let the young people come together in a natural course of events. Now there was not time for that.

Marcus sat alone at a table in the Boar's Head Inn, sipping rum. He'd been observing the patrons, waiting for an opportunity to get into a card game or merely an enlightening conversation. The barmaid, a pretty wench with unusual silver hair, had been watching him curiously ever since she'd brought his bottle. He would have struck up a conversation with her, but the place was busy and she'd been in demand.

A blond young giant of a man entered the long room and made his way to the girl, lifting her off her feet and kissing her cheek soundly. She struggled, but gave a musical laugh at something he whispered to her. Taking a seat with some sailors, he bellowed for her to bring him rum.

Marcus wondered briefly if she was his mistress. At that thought, Amy's bright face intruded on his thoughts and he scowled. He wished his feelings for her were that simple, but she was not a trollop to be dallied with. Nay, their relationship was far more complicated. When she was out of sight, he told himself to forget the little hellcat, even though her memory warmed him like a fire on a winter's eve. Yet, when he caught but a glimpse of her, he trembled with wanting as if in the throes of first love. Seeing her with Justin the day before had fair cut up his peace. So much so that he had absented himself from the family dinner last evening. He couldn't bear to watch his half brother fawn over her all night. It was especially maddening to feel thus when he had a mission to accomplish.

As the afternoon wore on, Marcus continued to drink and wait. The patrons thinned, and the barmaid came to his table and smiled. "Will you have another?" she asked, picking up the empty bottle.

He looked at her lazily, speculatively. "Aye . . . if you will join me."

Normally, she sidestepped amorous attention from the customers, saving herself for Justin, but something about this man fascinated her. And besides, she was piqued over the damning conversation she'd heard in the milliner's shop. Her ire was growing by leaps and bounds, for Justin had not been to see her for days now. She nodded, making up her mind. "Aye, I can use a rest."

She returned with a new bottle and another glass. Sitting down across from him, she filled his and poured a small portion in her own.

"Captain Marcus Bond, mistress, from Boston," he said by way of introduction.

Her blue eyes twinkled as she replied, "By your speech, sir, I could have named your city. There's many who stop here from divers ports, and I've listened to their cant." She smiled, showing white, even teeth, and held out her hand. "I'm Megan Cormac."

He took her hand and, raising it to his lips, murmured, " 'Tis my pleasure."

As he released her hand, she asked, "What brings you to Tucker's Town, Captain Bond?"

"For the moment, I'm waiting for my ship to be repaired. Lately, I delivered my employer and his niece to the Stafford estate," he told her, sipping his rum. He caught a look of surprise in her expressive blue eyes before she could mask it.

"And who might your employer be?" she asked casually.

"Thaddeus Hawthorne of Boston. He and Harlan Stafford are business partners in several ventures, I believe," he supplied, and then added, "I too am a guest of

149

Mr. Stafford, owing to the fact that I am landlocked at the present. You are aware of the family, I'm sure."

She shifted in her seat and smoothed the folds of her simple calico cotton dress in agitation before replying. "Aye. There's not a one hereabouts that don't know them. Truth of the matter is, my brother Patrick and Justin Stafford are as close as two peas in a pod."

Marcus felt a surge of excitement at this news. He could surely glean some valuable information from the girl and, perhaps, her brother. However, he felt that she was hiding something by her nervous manner. "Is that a fact? I understand young Stafford is in charge of the family shipyard."

Her lips thinned with irritation. "That's not the way of it at all. The old man orders Justin about like a lackey — just as he does everyone in his reach."

Her anger was telling, and Marcus pressed his advantage. Innocently, he asked, "Is it possible that Mr. Stafford handles his vast business empire without anyone's aid?"

Megan warmed to her subject, leaning forward. Her ample bosom rose temptingly over the top of the lacings on her bodice, but Marcus was strangely unaffected by the view. "If he trusts anyone, 'tis John Radley, his agent. He's as slick and slimy as an eel, that one. I suppose 'tis why he trusts 'im instead of his own son, for Justin's not deceitful enough to please the old man."

Marcus sipped his rum and tried not to show undue interest in her revelations, yet he wanted to learn as much as he could. "It appears you have no love for Mr. Stafford, Megan. Has he done you some harm?"

She sat back, toying with her glass, and laughed harshly. "None he could be arrested for. Nay, he simply thinks my brother and me are not fit company for Justin. He would have his heir sipping tea in highborn parlors and fawning over government officials to gain favors."

"My host, it seems, is proving an unpleasant subject for us, and your company is too delightful to waste. Let's speak of something else," he coaxed, giving her a rakish smile.

She frowned as she refilled their glasses. His charming manners reminded her of someone else, but she couldn't quite lay a finger on it. The same appeal had led her to accept his company in the first place. Shrugging off the puzzle, she belatedly remembered his earlier comment. "Tell me, is your employer planning a long visit to our islands?"

"A few months, I believe. It's to be a business as well as pleasure trip. His niece, Mistress Amy, has recently come home from school and, never having been here before, decided to accompany her uncle."

Megan gazed thoughtfully into her glass for a moment and then asked, "What is she like?"

"Young, very beautiful . . . fair, with red hair and emerald eyes," he said softly, a faraway look momentarily clouding his eyes.

Megan glanced up at the intensity in his lowered voice. She recognized the longing in his expression and guessed he was enamored of the girl. Her heart sank as she realized that Amy Hawthorne and the beautiful creature she'd seen in the milliner's shop were one and the same and that the girl would be in Justin's company everyday. And Amy Hawthorne was his equal. Was he smitten by her already? The thought made Megan ill. She gulped down the remainder of her rum, letting it warm her cold insides. "Since she was away at school, I take it she's not wedded yet," she said, pretending an indifference she did not feel.

"No, her uncle hinted that she's been painfully selective in choosing a mate. I suppose the right man has not appeared as yet," Marcus said rather stiffly. Although he had accomplished his purpose this day by gathering information, he felt as if a weight sat upon his broad shoulders. Talking to this slip of a girl about Amy had buried his mood deeper than before. Rising abruptly, he placed some money on the table, hardly noticing the dismay on her pretty face. "Thank you for the company, Megan, but I must be leaving. Perhaps we'll meet again soon."

She nodded and murmured an indifferent response, sitting alone for a long while after he'd gone.

As the days drifted lazily by, Amy fell into a loose routine. She took breakfast with the family and, directly after, went riding with Justin. Neither Fiona nor Pamela could be persuaded to join them, but Amy rather enjoyed having Justin's company to herself. He was intelligent and amusing. Most mornings Marcus was absent from the table—to Amy's relief. They barely spoke, but each was painfully aware of the other when they chanced to be in the same room. Amy noticed with unreasonable pique that Marcus and Pamela got on well together and that they spent much time talking in the evenings as they all gathered in the drawing room. She was never close enough to hear their quiet conversations, and her curiosity simmered below the surface.

Some afternoons she went calling with Pamela on friends and neighbors, while other days they made forays into Tucker's Town or took a ferry across Castle Harbor to visit the larger town of St. George. Julia always politely declined their invitations to come along, and Fiona often begged off, saying her small duties and the heat would keep her in the house contentedly.

One afternoon, Pamela, her manner hesitant, invited Amy to accompany her into Tucker's Town. "I'm going to the orphanage to take food and clothing and such. The Reverend Jacobs from Trinity Church tends to the poor waifs, and I do what I can to help."

They had just left the dining room so that the men might smoke after the noon meal, when Pamela revealed her errand. Amy took the other girl's hand and gave it a gentle squeeze. "But I would love to come along. Shall I fetch my hat now? 'Tis all I need to do to be ready."

Pamela looked extremely pleased and nodded. "Aye. I shall meet you out front as soon as I have Moses load the baskets."

Even though Amy had traveled the road to Tucker's Town several times now, the beauty of the tropical scenery still delighted her as they rode along in the open carriage. She was coming to love the islands with the pink and white beaches, beautiful flowers and warm breezes. The bustling life and cold winters of Boston were so very far away now, and she was a different person from the innocent girl who had stepped aboard the *Rebecca* that chilly morning. Marcus refused to be banished from her thoughts for very long no matter how hard she tried, and she supposed that was natural, for he was the reason she was different. Casually, she said, "I've noticed you talking with Captain Bond quite a lot. Do you not find him arrogant and opinionated, Pamela?"

A small smile touched the other girl's lips. "Not at all, Amy. He has been very kind to me and always asks my opinion on any matter we might be discussing."

"The devil you say!" Amy blurted out before she could stop herself.

"Amy Hawthorne! I pray you won't use such language in Reverend Jacobs's company, or I fear he'll swoon," Pamela chided gently, her eyes twinkling.

Amy laughed. "I will try to restrain my tongue. It was

merely my surprise over your misguided opinion of that rogue."

It was Pamela's turn to be amazed. "But he seems to be such a considerate man. I realize I'm not the most perceptive of females, as father has pointed out. However, Captain Bond actually listens to what I say and treats me with respect. Perhaps you received a wrong impression of him."

Amy could not very well tell Pamela how she had reached her opinion, and she did not wish to argue. He had, to be sure, enough charm and virile appeal, when he chose, to talk the birds from the trees. Amy hoped that Pamela's staunch support of Marcus did not mean that she was becoming romantically interested in him. She certainly did not want to see the shy girl hurt. She smiled at Pamela. "I suppose that could be the case."

Their talk turned to the orphanage, and Pamela was enthusiastic in her description. Soon the carriage stopped before a wooden two-story building at the edge of town, directly across the road from Trinity Church. Moses jumped down and helped them from the carriage. He was fairly young, around twenty-five, Amy guessed, and quietly subservient. It was hard for Amy to believe he was Layla's brother. His handsome, fine-boned face broke into a smile when Pamela urged him to visit his lady friend, who was housemaid to a merchant in town, while they were at the orphanage. "Thank you, missy. Soon as I unload de baskets I be on my way. When you want me back?"

"An hour, I think. We don't want to tire Mistress Amy on her first visit," she replied kindly.

Amy followed Pamela inside the house and looked around curiously. They were in a large room that apparently served as a parlor, as it was furnished with several mismatched chairs and a settee. Since there was no one about, Pamela proceeded past a staircase, which led to the second floor, and into a dining room that held a long, rough table flanked by a bench on each side. A door on the far wall led into a spotless kitchen where a rotund, gray-haired woman stood stirring something in a pot on the iron stove.

"Good afternoon, Mistress Alden," Pamela said cheerfully. "I've brought a friend to meet you and the children."

The woman smiled broadly as she put aside the large wooden spoon and came forward. "Mistress Pamela! 'Tis glad I am to see ye — and yer friend."

Pamela made the introductions, explaining that Mistress Alden lived there and cared for the children while Reverend Jacobs tended to their religious instruction and procured funds to keep them in food and clothing.

The older woman immediately set a pot of water on to boil for tea to serve her guests, as Moses carried in the baskets. Amy was drawn to the open doorway by the sound of children's voices outside.

There were roughly twelve children, and by their size, she guessed their ages from two to ten. The children were engrossed in a game of blindman's bluff.

Smiling, Amy remembered her own younger days, playing games with Joseph and Martha Thompson, the cook's children. But that had been before the fire when her parents were alive. She had not engaged in many games afterward, though she counted herself fortunate to have had Uncle Thad to care for her. Turning to the older lady and Pamela, who were busy unpacking the baskets, Amy asked, "Do none of these children have any family left?"

Mistress Alden shook her head regretfully. "Nay, not a one. The two oldest, the twins, Molly and Hope, was orphaned as babies when their folks was poisoned by that no-account slave girl what worked in the kitchen. You remember all that trouble back in '61, Mistress

Pamela, when the slaves was plottin' a rebellion?"

Pamela was removing peaches and plums from a basket as she answered. "I was still too young to dine with the adults, so I really had no notion of what went on outside the nursery. Mama tried to shelter Justin and me from most things, I think."

Mistress Alden clucked her tongue. "Your mama was right to do that. Children shouldn't have to see the ugly side of human nature. I'd wager, though, that young Justin was in the thick of things. That one has ever been a rascal."

Pamela laughed and agreed, " 'Tis true, I'm sure. However, he was far worse than mama about shielding me."

Mistress Alden stopped unpacking her basket to make the tea, and continue her story. " 'Twas luck, I suppose, that I was nurse to the twins when it happened, for the poor little mites had no one to take 'em in. My Peter had died the year before of the fever, and I needed them as much as they needed me. Reverend Jacobs — bless his kind heart — was just come to us from England, and 'twas his notion to let me and the young uns live here. The others came one by one after that, for divers reasons."

Amy took a chair at the scrubbed wooden table and stirred a spoonful of sugar into her steaming tea. "You are a generous person also, Mistress Alden, to care for these children as you do. They are very lucky indeed."

The older woman shrugged off the praise, but her face was pink with pleasure. " 'Tis me who's the lucky one."

Just then, a deep male voice called out from the front of the house, and the three women looked toward the doorway as a tall, thin man appeared. He was dressed casually in a white cotton shirt and black breeches. His thick brown hair was pulled back in a neat queue, and his warm brown eyes smiled at the three of them.

"Reverend Jacobs, good day. Mistress Pamela brought a friend with her," Mistress Alden spoke up, turning then to fetch another cup. Pamela once again performed the introductions. However, Amy noticed Pamela's shyness had returned and that she actually blushed when the cleric spoke to her.

Amy liked the way his eyes crinkled up at the corners when he smiled, as if it were a much-repeated habit. He politely inquired about Amy's voyage and how she liked the islands. Her reply was enthusiastic and sincere. He asked the older woman about the children's welfare, then turned to Pamela. "We do thank you for the food and also the cloth I see here. The children grow so fast it is difficult to keep them clothed properly."

Pamela dropped her gaze and began setting the empty baskets on the floor. " 'Tis not as much as I would like it to be," she said quietly.

The young minister smiled at Amy. "She is far too modest, Mistress Hawthorne. Our angel of mercy visits us, without fail, each week and has been more charitable with her time and goods than any other parishioner I could name."

Amy, seeing Pamela blush once again, diverted the cleric's attention by asking to meet the children. His face brightened at her interest, and he offered his arm to her.

Mistress Alden spoke up. " 'Tis time for the young 'uns naps and the older 'uns chores, Reverend. Would ye remind 'em?"

He chuckled as he led Amy out the door, and replied, "That should make us most popular with them."

At the sight of the beautiful, finely dressed stranger, the children abruptly ended their game. The younger ones hid behind the older children and peeked around shyly.

"Children," Reverend Jacobs said, "Mistress Pamela has brought a visitor with her today. May I present Mistress Amy Hawthorne." He then called each of them by name, and they either bobbed a curtsey or bowed, whichever was appropriate.

Amy was completely charmed by their sweet, albeit dirty, faces. "I am very pleased to meet all of you," she said with a smile.

"Mistress Alden says it's time for naps and chores," he told them, pulling a comical face.

Amy chuckled at their woebegone expressions as they reluctantly trudged away. She let her gaze roam the large yard then, taking in several scattered trees, a vegetable patch to one side, a small flower garden on the other boundary, and a dilapidated stable.

" 'Tis not such a bad place to grow up, I believe," he mused, following the direction her eyes took. "I saw many poor children living on the dirty streets of London, and it would near break your heart."

"I agree," Amy replied, touched by his obvious concern. "Whether one is rich or poor, these islands are a paradise, and the most important things are free—the warmth of the sun, the lovely beaches and the magnificent colors of the sea. Moreover, these children have you and Mistress Alden to care for them."

He looked somewhat surprised. "You are sensitive as well as perceptive, Mistress Hawthorne. Most young women in your position would scarce count these assets. They would see only our shabbiness here."

"Then they would be quite blind, sir," she said lightly. "Mistress Pamela is not in that category you spoke of, Reverend, for she talked in glowing terms of this place."

The cleric's eyes lit with a special warmth. "Ah, Mistress Pamela is another special young lady. I do not know how we should go on without her generous patronage."

As they walked about the yard, he gave voice to Pamela's many kindnesses, unwittingly giving away his feelings in the process.

By the time the two young women left the orphanage that afternoon, Amy was feeling quite satisfied that Pamela and Reverend Jacobs were enamored of each other. She did not realize for a time why that fact made her happy — not until that evening, when she saw Marcus and Pamela laughing together at dinner, did she understand. She was jealous of their friendship.

Marcus must have felt her gaze upon him, for suddenly he glanced up and their eyes locked. The unguarded warmth in his gaze sent her pulses racing madly, and her hand trembled as she picked up her wine glass and looked hastily away.

As they retired to the drawing room, Amy was relieved that there were no other dinner guests outside those who were residing at Stafford House. Every evening since their arrival, Harlan had invited many of his friends and business associates to dine. It had been interesting; however, tonight she was feeling restless and not in the mood to be bright and entertaining.

Thaddeus and Harlan settled down to a game of chess, while the women congregated across the room to gossip and do needlework. Justin and Marcus were left to converse with each other reluctantly.

Amy had chosen a chair that was positioned so she might see the entire room, and she surreptitiously watched the two younger men while pretending an interest in the women's conversation. She mentally compared the two and found them both handsome, muscular and well dressed. At that point, the similarities ended. Where Justin had an easy, amiable charm, Marcus tended to be dark and brooding. So why did she feel such an attraction for Marcus instead of for Justin's more likeable personality? It was a mystery to her.

With half an ear she listened to Pamela and Julia discussing the soirée they were all invited to at Verdmont House on Saturday night. Judge John Green and his wife, Mary, their hosts, had been to one of Harlan's dinners, and Amy vaguely remembered meeting them. As the talk turned to dresses and hairstyles, she let her attention wander back to the two men standing beside the fireplace. Marcus's broad shoulders filled the black broadcloth coat he wore, and the fine, white linen shirt with lace ruffles at the wrists seemed to accentuate his masculinity. She knew beneath the ruffled neck cloth lay an expanse of dark hair on his hard chest. She unconsciously picked up her ivory fan and whisked it back and forth to cool her flushed face. Her eyes dropped lower to note tight, black breeches straining against muscled thighs, and she well remembered the feel of them against her own. He stood now with his legs braced slightly apart, as if he were riding the deck of a rolling ship.

As if he could feel her gaze, he glanced up and met her eyes. Nodding, ever so slightly, he raised an inquiring brow. For a moment the blood raced madly through her veins, and she looked away.

"Are you ill, Amy?" Pamela asked with sincere concern, noting the rosy flush on her guest's cheeks.

Amy gave a guilty start, realizing where her wandering thoughts had been. She smiled thinly. "Not at all . . . nay, I am not accustomed to your warm climate as yet, I fear." She rose and added, "If you'll excuse me, I think I will retire."

Fiona rose also, but Amy bade her stay with the ladies. "There's no need for you to come up. I will have Ivy help me if I need it."

With relief, she left the room and spared not another glance for Marcus—she did not trust herself to do so.

* * *

With mixed feelings, Marcus watched Amy leave. He craved the sight of her, yet when she was near, he could barely keep his desires in check and had a difficult time remembering his mission. He and Justin, thrown together as they had been, were discussing the progress of the repairs on the *Rebecca*. Justin took a drink of his brandy and remarked, "I know 'tis slow going. However, as I believe I mentioned, some of our best men are on Turks Island for the salt raking."

Marcus placed his empty glass on the mantle and replied coolly, "Since Mr. Hawthorne sent our remaining cargo by another ship, I am in no hurry. I've been passing my time pleasantly enough."

Justin glanced around at the quiet, homey scene. "I'm heading for the Boar's Head for a little more excitement than this. You're welcome to join me."

Perversely, Justin's friendly invitation irritated Marcus. He did not want to like the younger man but found himself doing so against his will. "I'm not in the mood tonight," he said shortly.

Justin shrugged and walked away from the taciturn captain.

Harlan chanced to look up and see his son quiting the room. "Justin — I would speak with you later on a matter of some import."

His father's commanding tone halted him and caused a muscle in Justin's jaw to flick angrily. Harlan always made him feel like a young lad being reprimanded for bad manners. His left eyebrow rose a fraction as he stated, "By the time I return, Father, your old bones will no doubt be abed."

An angry stain colored Harlan's cheeks at his son's impudence, but he stifled the harsh rejoinder that came to his lips. He wanted . . . nay, needed Justin's compliance with this plan. "The first thing tomorrow morning

161

in my bookroom, then," he said, keeping his tone level.

Justin nodded and then bade everyone a polite good night as he strode out.

Julia gave her brother a look of intense dislike, quite unnoticed by him, but Fiona caught it. It made her wonder what Harlan wished to discuss with his son and why Julia was so angry about it.

Marcus had also caught the undercurrents between father and son and felt a grudging sympathy for Justin and Pamela. After observing the family for more than a week now, he could see there was no affection between the man and his children. Poor Pamela, he had found by talking with her, was sweet and eager to please, but she realized she was a disappointment to her father.

He refilled his glass and walked over to observe the older men's game of chess. While they concentrated, his thoughts drifted to the information he'd picked up earlier in the day. That morning, he'd ridden over to the town of Hamilton in Pembroke Parish. It was located on Hamilton Harbor, a busy port for trade and gossip. Going from tavern to tavern, he'd finally been rewarded for his efforts. An old man, retired from whaling, seemed to know everything that occurred of any import in the islands. All Marcus had done was mention the Staffords, and old Daniel related everything he knew of them while Marcus kept a supply of rum coming.

According to Daniel, Harlan was heavy into smuggling, privateering, and some said even slave trafficking. Of course, the rumor about slave trading hadn't been proven, for those who dealt in "black gold," as it was called, kept it quiet. Most Bermudians abhorred the wretched business, even though many owned slaves. It was a quirk of the islander's nature, Daniel explained, owing to, he supposed, the fact that their ancestors had been criminals, brought over from England in chains and little more than slaves themselves.

162

Listening to Daniel ramble, Marcus decided to do some checking on the storage of Harlan's cargos. Another conversation he had had with the man who owned the tobacco shop in Hamilton told him that most large houses in the islands possessed deep cellars for just such a purpose. Tonight, when all were abed, he planned to have a look at Harlan's cellars.

Chapter Ten

Justin passed the remainder of the evening at his favorite table at the Boar's Head, playing cards with friends. He lost heavily, for his concentration suffered as his hungry gaze followed Megan around the room while she served the customers. He had been too long without her, he thought, suddenly realizing that she hadn't crossed his mind since Amy had arrived. Amy was quick-witted, amusing and beautiful, but Megan held a fascination for him that no other could lay claim to. There had been many a comely wench who had taken his fancy over the years, but he always returned to the silver-haired vixen, finding what he craved and needed in her arms. Tonight was no different — he wanted her with a desire that was akin to pain.

She stopped by his table as often as she could, leaning over him to refill his glass, brushing her breasts against his shoulder, giving him a tantalizing view of their round fullness pushing up above her bodice. She gave him seductive smiles across the room and promised things with her eyes that made his heart beat faster. By the time the last patron left the common room, Justin was in a fever to have her to himself. He came up behind her as she placed a tray of dirty glasses on the bar, and kissed her bare shoulder. "My little Meggie—I have missed you sorely," he whispered in her ear, his arms encircling her small waist.

She turned deftly in his embrace and gave him a kiss that would have set the island afire. "I've been missing you too, my love," she pouted. Then she asked with feigned innocence, "Has that tyrant of a father kept you so busy you could not get away to see me?"

Justin felt a twinge of guilt over the lie that rose to his lips. "I am afraid so. What with business and some family obligations, this is the first night I could steal away."

Megan gave him a look of warm concern. "Ahh, my poor Justin. And it's guilty I feel now, for I was angry when I heard gossip that you've been squiring a beautiful girl about. A houseguest, I believe, was the rumor."

A small warning sounded in his head at her words, but her expression was sweet and trustful. "Nay, Megan, 'tis not so. 'Tis true we are entertaining my father's business partner and his niece, but she is fat and ugly and has the most awful disposition." When he read the sympathy in her blue eyes, he felt emboldened to expand on the lie. "My father ordered me to take her about, but 'twas merely out of duty I performed the distasteful chore. My only thought has been of you."

Megan pressed her ripe body closer to his and smiled sweetly. "You are truly good, Justin, and 'tis why I love you so much."

He claimed her lips in another passionate kiss and felt himself harden with need.

After a few moments, she gently pushed him away and whispered breathlessly, "I will do this clearing up in the morning. Just let me tell Jonas."

He watched her hurry across the room to the balding, rotund innkeeper. His thoughts turned to the small room upstairs that Megan sometimes used if it was very late when she finished working or there was no one to escort

165

her home. Justin reached across the bar and retrieved a bottle of fine Madeira, calling out to Jonas to mark it on his bill.

He then followed Megan's swaying hips up the stairs. Justin felt a twinge of remorse for the fabrication he'd told her, but the hot excitement that warmed his loins overshadowed his urge to tell her the truth. She would doubtless discover his deception in the future, but he would deal with that when the time came. At present, all he could think of was her warm, soft body pressed against his in passion.

She lit their way with a candle to the end of the hallway and opened a door. The small room contained a bed, a washstand and a small chest. Justin placed the bottle on the chest and took the candle from Megan, setting it down also. He pulled her into his arms and kissed her hungrily. Pulling back, he began unlacing the ribbon that held the front of her dress together, and soon had her pink-tipped breasts filling his hands. He took her mouth again and teased the nipples with his thumbs until they hardened.

Megan gasped at the pleasurable sensation and ran her hands over his muscled shoulders, pushing at his coat. Once more, he pulled back, breathing heavily, and murmured, "Are we in a hurry, little one?"

Her sea-blue eyes had darkened with desire, and her voice was husky. "Aye, my love . . . let me undress you."

He felt a warm rush in his loins at her request and nodded. Taking her hand, he guided it to the hard outline in his breeches and whispered, "Do not be all night about the task, love, for I need you soon."

She smiled with a promise in her eyes and slipped his coat off. Next came his open-fronted shirt, to be dropped on the floor, and then her slender hands worked the buttons on the front flap of his breeches. Justin closed his eyes and gasped audibly as he felt her fingers close around his erection. "God's blood, woman! I'll not be able to wait if you continue thus."

Complying, she stripped the pants from his lean hips and stooped to remove his shoes and stockings and pull the breeches off. He stood naked and proud before her as she gazed at his virile form. For a moment her resolve slipped, for she was becoming as hot as he to make love, but then she forced herself to remember the red-haired beauty as well as Justin's lies.

He reached for her, but she gently pushed his hands away. "Warm the bed, my love, and I'll disrobe for you," she offered in a husky whisper. He smiled and moved to do her bidding, leaning back against the headboard to watch.

Megan retrieved the bottle of wine, popped the cork from the neck and took a long, slow swallow. Holding it forward, she asked coyly, "Do you wish to slake your thirst, m'lord?"

He shook his head, swallowing tightly as he gazed at her naked breasts. "Nay, love, I wish to appease my hunger," he rasped, his blood hot.

Megan drew the bottle back and flung it at him with all her might. "Not with me, you lyin' bastard!"

So stunned was he by her unexpected action, Justin did not move fast enough and the bottle glanced off the side of his head before it shattered against the stout wooden headboard, spraying him with glass and red wine. "Megan!" he gasped, holding his head to keep the room from spinning.

"Stay away from me!" she cried out, her eyes flashing blue fire. She glanced quickly around and spotted the pitcher on the washstand and ran for it.

Justin rolled to the far side of the bed and landed on the floor just as the pitcher whizzed past his head and hit the wall. "Damnation, woman! Cease and desist! What are you doing?" he shouted.

"Fat and ugly, is she, now?" Megan said, panting with fury as she picked up the bowl.

Too late, Justin realized that Megan must have heard a detailed account of his guests and the happenings at Stafford House. He swiped at the red wine that dripped into his eyes, and tried to reason with her. "Megan, love, let me explain—"

The bowl sailed in his direction, and he jumped sideways to avoid it and landed back in the middle of the bed.

"I am not your 'love,' you jackanape! Go home to your fancy house and your fancy red-haired trollop, for I'll not warm your bed this night or any other night!"

The last of her stinging speech had risen to a screech as she threw open the door and ran out, leaving him alone on the bed.

For a moment he was too amazed by what had happened to move. Then his eyes crinkled at the corners, and a wide grin spread across his handsome face. Finally, he threw back his head and gave a great bark of laughter. "What a woman," he gasped.

Rising, he threw on his clothes and left the room. Letting himself out of the inn, he retrieved his horse from the small lean-to adjoining the building. He knew where Megan would be, and intended to settle their differences before the night was out.

At a leisurely gait, he left the town behind and made his way south, along the beach, giving her time to cool off before he arrived. It was a beautiful night, fragrant and warm, with a multitude of stars and a half-moon to light his way. The sound of the surf relaxed him and he smiled again, remembering Megan's surprise attack. She had led him a merry dance, she had! Pretending all evening to woo him—and then nearly knocking his fool head off when his breeches were down.

The beach began to narrow and a limestone cliff rose up to his right before he reached a small, secluded cove.

Dismounting, he tied his horse to a scrubby bush and walked along the base of the cliff until he found the opening he sought. It was a small cave where he and Megan had spent a great deal of time in the past.

"Meggie?" he called softly. The only answer he received was the faint sound of sniffling. By the faint moonlight, he could make out the shadow of her small shape huddled against the wall. "I'm sorry, love, for lying to you. Please don't cry," he pleaded softly. Suddenly he felt remorseful, for she was hurt. He had thought her merely angry; however, her soft weeping was more than he could bear.

"I am not crying — Megan Cormac weeps for no man!" she said in a trembling voice.

He smiled to himself and asked, "You don't by chance, have a large stone to fling at me should I come near?"

"Had I thought to find one, you would already be laid out cold!" she replied, her voice a bit stronger now.

He took that as a good sign and made his way to her side, pulling her to her feet. He held her loosely, for he could still feel her resistance. "I could never bear for you to be angry with me, Meggie," he whispered, his hands gently stroking her back. "I care naught for that other girl, my love. 'Tis you who means everything to me."

"She's lovely to look at — I saw her myself. And your father most surely finds her a fine match for you," she replied stubbornly.

"He has said nothing of the sort. And besides, I will choose my own wife," he assured her softly.

Megan moved closer to him, her full breasts pressing against his chest. "Do you really have a care for me, Justin?" she asked in a small, unsure voice.

"Aye," he replied, his tone husky. "I love you, Meggie girl, and always will." He took her lips and knew deep in his heart that he meant it. All the years he had plied her with sweet words, he had never pledged his love, but tonight he realized that he had loved her all along. Many were the wild oats he had sown, but now he wanted only her.

They kissed and touched slowly, as if drugged by the deep feelings they shared. Their clothes landed in a heap on the sandy floor, and they loved with an abandon they'd never experienced before. A moan of ecstasy slipped through Megan's lips as they soared to a shuddering climax together. For a time, they rested in each other's arms. Then they swam naked in the warm seawater. Again and again they rode the hot tide of passion, whispering sweet promises to each other.

Once the house grew quiet, Marcus slipped out and took a lantern from the summer kitchen. Striking flint to steel, he lit the candle inside and made his way to the north side of the house, where earlier in the day he had discovered the entrance to the cellars. Lifting the heavy door, he played the light over the rough-cut stone steps and descended, careful not to slip on the damp surface. He counted twenty steps before he reached the bottom and found himself in a large room, the walls cut from natural rock. There were crates stacked about, but as he glanced first in one then another, he found nothing more interesting than barrels of molasses, salted cod and flour. And these were in no greater quantity than for the household use. In another room, beyond the first, he found large pieces of furniture stored and several rats scurrying about. If Harlan had been smuggling contraband goods, they were not stored here, he thought. He made his way out and decided to check some of the storage buildings near the stables.

* * *

Roused suddenly from sleep, Amy sat up and glanced around the room, her heart thudding. All was quiet, and her perusal told her there were no unusual shadows. She calmed a bit, deciding that perhaps the cry of a night bird had disturbed her, for she was not yet accustomed to the strange sounds of the island. Getting up, she poured a glass of water from the pitcher and took a sip. The sound of the doorknob turning startled her, and she watched in frozen anticipation as it turned completely and the door swung inward. Swallowing the sudden lump of fear, she told herself it could be Fiona coming to check on her, so she called her companion's name, her voice shaky. There was no answer, nor did anyone enter. Amy glanced about, sidestepped quickly to the fireplace and grasped the iron poker. Slowly, she moved toward the door and, when close enough, yanked it the rest of the way open with her weapon held high. There was no one there, and a quick glance into the hallway showed it empty. Breathing a sigh of relief, she closed the door and leaned on it for a moment. Perhaps she had not closed it properly before retiring and the breeze had pulled it open? As a precaution, she locked it and moved to the French doors to close them as well, but before she could do so, a thin, reedy voice reached her ears. She cautiously stepped out on the terrace to have a look.

Beside the summer kitchen, a woman in a flowing white gown stood, looking up at her. She raised her hands, palms outward and called softly, "Help me . . . please."

Amy could make out no features of the woman and had no idea who she could be or why she was calling for help. Should she raise the household? On the heels of that thought, the woman in white called again, sounding more desperate, and began to move across the wide lawn toward the woods. Quickly, Amy decided to rouse Fiona to go with her to investigate. Running along the terrace a few steps, she was just about to enter Fiona's room through the French doors when she heard a masculine voice from within, along with an answering laugh that belonged to her companion. For a moment, Amy was shocked that her companion was entertaining a man in her bedroom in the middle of the night. Not that Amy was prudish—nay, it was the fact that Fiona seemed so prim and proper. Amy was curious about the man's identity, but at the moment she was far more curious about the mysterious woman in white. Another glance in that direction told her the woman would disappear into the woods soon if Amy did not hurry to catch her. Making a split second decision, Amy hurried back through her room, grabbing her robe. She flew down the stairs and out the back entrance of the house.

The thick grass was damp with dew under her bare feet as she ran toward the woods. The woman in white beckoned once more before entering a thick stand of olive-wood trees and disappearing from sight.

When Amy reached the wooded area, she was breathless, and she stopped to glance around. It was much darker within the thick foliage, and she hesitated to continue, but then she caught sight of a flash of white and decided to pursue it a bit longer. "Please stop," she called out to the woman, knowing they were far enough away now not to wake the household. However, the woman's pitiful sob was the only answer. There was a distinct path to follow or Amy would have been forced to turn back. She picked her way carefully, mindful of her bare feet. By now the woman had disappeared, and an eerie feeling stole over Amy as she realized her vulnerable position. A flock of brown bitterns rose in flight as if startled, emitting peculiar booming sounds, and Amy gasped at the abrupt break in the silence. Strange rustling noises in the underbrush made her wonder what other animals were moving about. An island lizard—a grotesque looking

172

creature, in her opinion — ran across the path, brushing her foot. She jumped back and cried out involuntarily. Shivering, she decided to go back. With no light to guide her or a weapon in case of danger, it was folly to continue.

But just as she turned, she heard a great thrashing in the underbrush deep in the woods behind her. A loud snorting sound alerted her to the fact that a large animal was responsible, and she suspected a boar. Her heart thumped wildly as she began running, heedless of the brambles that tore at her robe and the stones that bruised her feet. The crashing noises left her in no doubt that she was being pursued by the beast, but she was afraid to turn around and look. On she ran, crying out, but knowing she could not be heard from the distant house. Her mind was filled with images of the wild boar she'd seen once when she and her uncle had been on a fishing trip to Dedham. It had come crashing out of the woods, and her uncle's quick thinking had saved them. He'd shot the beast straight through the heart. Amy remembered the size of the animal and the deadly tusks that could gore a person to death. That memory gave her a sudden burst of energy, and she prayed she could make it out of the woods to where her path would at least be clear. That hope died when at the next instant her foot caught on a root and she was flung forward to land face down, the breath leaving her body in a hard *whoosh*. For a few seconds she was stunned, but as her breath came back, her terror doubled, for she could feel the vibration of the ground as the beast thundered toward her.

In a last effort to save herself, she started to rise. "Stay down!" a harsh, commanding voice called out.

Amy looked up to see a dark silhouette aiming a pistol in her direction. It took much courage to drop back to the ground and trust that his bullet would fell the beast. If his marksmanship failed, the beast would be upon her in seconds. The report of the gun was deafening — or perhaps it was her own heartbeat in her ears — as Amy cringed, waiting for what might come. She felt a hoof strike her foot, and then the beast fell upon her, pinning her legs with its weight. For a moment, she thought all was lost, but the boar shuddered convulsively and then lay still.

Her savior dropped to her side. "Are you hurt?" he asked urgently.

Amy lifted her head weakly and eyed Marcus's anxious expression. She gave him a twisted smile. "That was a fool thing to do."

Seeing that she was trapped beneath the boar, he took her arms and pulled her free, saying, "Aye, it certainly was. What in God's name were you doing out here alone at this time of night?"

He helped her to stand, and she immediately swayed, clutching at him for support. "Me? I was speaking of you, sir. If you had missed, we'd both be dead now!"

He shook her, none too gently, and snapped, "Had you a better plan, you addle-witted chit?"

Realizing he did not appreciate her feeble jest, she leaned her head on his broad chest as a sob escaped her lips. "Oh, Marcus . . . forgive me. I owe you my life."

The sound of tears in her trembling voice was his undoing. He shoved his pistol in the back band of his breeches and swept her up into his arms. He whispered soothing words in her ear and stroked her back.

She clung to him and cried tears of relief at their near-miss. The strength of his arms and the sound of his deep voice wrapped her in a protective world she had no wish to escape from. "Don't let me go, Marcus . . . don't ever let me go," she whispered against his neck. His heart lurched at her pitiful plea, and he knew she was in shock, for her fierce pride would otherwise never let her beg for anything. He started for the house, carrying her effortlessly and wishing things were different so he could hold her forever as she'd asked.

He could see lights up ahead in the downstairs windows and knew the household had been roused by the gunshot. Harlan and Thaddeus met him at the back entrance with worried looks and questions. "She's unhurt," he assured them as they moved aside to let him carry his burden inside. "Aside from a few scratches, that is, and shock."

Amy swiped at the tears on her cheeks. "I'm fine, really, Uncle Thad. You may put me down, Captain Bond. I can stand, I'm sure," she said shakily.

Marcus ignored her request as Fiona stepped forward. "I'll help her to her room and get her settled."

Pamela and Julia, clad in their robes, stared in concern and curiosity as Thaddeus agreed, "Of course, but I wish to know what has happened. Why were you outside at this hour — and look at you!"

Amy glanced belatedly at her disheveled appearance. The once elegant satin gown and robe were torn and dirty. Her hands and feet bore bloody scratches and bruises that were beginning to color. With some of her old spirit returning, she said firmly, "It is a long story, but Captain Bond saved my life. If you wish to hear the rest of the tale, you'll have to wait, for I sorely need some brandy and my bed at the moment."

Julia touched Thaddeus's arm and said unexpectedly, "The poor child is right. She has apparently been through an ordeal and needs rest. Captain, please take her upstairs, and I'll send Ivy to assist Mistress Morgan."

Marcus did so and gladly, for he needed time to concoct his own story as to why he was wandering about the estate in the middle of the night, carrying a gun!

Fiona arrived with a bottle of brandy, while Ivy helped Amy to bathe in a warm, scented tub of water. The black girl soaped Amy's hair to remove the dirt and leaves, and after a final rinsing, Ivy stayed to administer salve to the scratches. Fiona brushed the tangles from Amy's thick mass of hair.

While they saw to her needs, Amy related her adventure. Ivy, she noticed, looked frightened when she mentioned the woman in white, but she was too exhausted to question the girl.

When Amy was clothed in a fresh nightrail and tucked into bed, Fiona said, "I will relay the incident to your uncle, Amy, so that you can rest. I know he's anxious about you. Should you need anything, call out, for I will leave both our terrace doors open and will hear you."

Amy murmured her thanks, her eyes feeling heavy already. She was drifting to sleep even as Fiona doused the light.

The dream came almost immediately. There was the sensation of strong hands upon her body sending warm shivers of delight through her. Marcus's handsome face floated above hers and she pulled him close, offering her lips with wanton eagerness. She moaned as his tongue explored the softness of her mouth, while his fingers stroked at the very core of her womanhood. The pleasure became so intense that she awoke with a start.

Her face was beaded with perspiration as she sat up, recalling the vivid dream. Would he forever torment her, even in her dreams, she wondered?

A dark shadow beside the French doors detached itself and moved toward the bed. Amy gasped in sudden fear, but then recognized his familiar outline against the moonlight. "Marcus," she breathed.

He stopped beside the bed and looked down at her, his expression masked by shadows. "I had to see you," he said softly.

Without thought to her action, she lifted her arms to him and he joined her on the bed. He kissed her tenderly as his hands slid her gown up, then pulled back from her swollen lips long enough to lift i̶̶̶̶ Clad only in breeches, he pulled he̶̶ him and reveled in the warm press̶̶ breasts on his hair-roughened chest.

Reliving the dream, Amy parted her le̶̶ hand found her moist opening, gently str̶̶ groaned and moved instinctively against his̶̶ ̶̶until her body began to vibrate with tremors of e̶̶quisite release. Breathing his name, she sighed and pulled his head down for a lingering kiss.

After a time, Marcus rose and divested himself of his breeches. Amy gazed at his well-muscled body outlined in the moonlight, and felt a twinge of feminine satisfaction at the sight of his burgeoning manhood. The soft mattress gave under his weight as he moved above her. Burying his face in her fragrant hair that spilled across the pillow, he murmured, "Amy, Amy . . . my heart nearly stopped when I saw that beast charging you."

Her lips curved as she stroked the corded muscles of his wide shoulders. "It fair worried me as well," she said, more aware of what he was doing than what he was saying.

Rising, he straddled her hips. Gently, his hands cupped her face. "I could not have borne it had my bullet missed its mark." He was trying to tell her he cared for her, but knew he should not. He should not even have come to her room to assure himself she was all right, for it had ended thus, with the two of them in bed.

Amy turned her head and kissed his palm, sliding her hands along his thick forearms in a caress. "But it did not . . . and we are safe. Let us forget the incident and concentrate on the matter at hand," she urged in a husky whisper.

No more encouragement was needed, for Marcus dipped his head and claimed her soft mouth. His knee

...s, and he entered her with a gentle thrust ... took on a frantic rhythm.

...y's hips rose eagerly to meet his, time and time again, until the fire they were building together burst into a hot shower of flame.

Their sweat-dampened bodies lay entwined while their breathing slowed to normal and they shared sweet, tender kisses.

Reluctantly, Marcus rose and donned his breeches. He crossed the room and poured fresh water into the bowl and wet a cloth. Returning to the bed, he wiped Amy's face and gently sponged her body free of perspiration before helping her on with her gown. Oddly enough, this did not embarrass her, but was comforting.

Once he was finished, he sat on the side of the bed and asked, "What were you doing in the woods tonight, Amy?"

She cocked her head to the side and countered, "I might ask the same of you." With all that had happened, she hadn't thought to wonder why Marcus was in the vicinity when she needed him.

He reached out and tucked a stray lock of hair behind her ear and said casually, "I couldn't sleep and was too restless to stay abed. I was taking a walk when I heard you call out."

He looked sincere, but his voice sounded guarded. She wondered briefly what he was hiding, but didn't press the issue. She told him of the strange woman in white. As she finished her story, she said, "If I had not been awakened by my door opening, I should never have heard her."

A frown creased his brow. "If she wanted your help, why did she run away?"

"I do not know, Marcus, but it seemed as if she wanted me to follow her."

Dawn was breaking, and Marcus knew he must return

to his own room before the household began to stir. He took her hand in his and said firmly, "Promise me you will be careful in the future and not wander outside at night alone."

A smile trembled over her lips. "If I am too cautious, sir, I shall miss all sorts of adventures."

He took her slim shoulders and shook her gently. "Your impetuous nature will be the death of you, Mistress Hawthorne. I am not leaving this room until you promise," he growled.

The light of battle flared briefly in her eyes before she dropped her gaze and murmured, "I shall take more care from now on."

Marcus was not fooled by this backhanded promise. He knew her well enough now to realize that no one could force this strong-minded woman into anything. He sighed and tipped her chin up with his finger. Bending forward, he gave her a lingering kiss that made it difficult for him to leave her side.

Amy watched as he slipped quietly out the French doors. Settling back on her pillows, she sighed with regret. Her treacherous body had overpowered her logical mind once more. No matter what sound reasoning she used in regard to Marcus Bond, he had but to touch her and she melted into his arms like hot candlewax. And he committed nothing to her save the fulfillment of her passionate needs. Her face burned as she recalled their lovemaking. It was a potent drug of which she could not get enough.

However, she was mature enough to realize that she could not spend her life at the beck and call of Captain Bond. She had promised her uncle she would find a suitable husband, and that she must do. Surely she could feel about another man as she felt about that rogue, she thought, trying to calm her doubts.

Her eyes drooped heavily as she began to fall asleep

from exhaustion, while a sweet smile of contentment curved her lips.

Fiona rose very early, intending to check on Amy and, if she was awake, have a personal chat with her. She had put Thaddeus's proposal of marriage off by claiming that Amy's future should be settled before they carried out their own plans. She was delighted by his eagerness to wed, but shrewdly guessed that the secrecy of their affair added spice to the relationship and hooked him deeper every day. The other reason she delayed was that if Amy had something to occupy her, she would be less likely to cause trouble over her uncle's choice.

As Fiona finished dressing and began to brush her hair, she felt vaguely dissatisfied. The initial excitement of their assignations was wearing off, and she found Thaddeus to be a somewhat boring lover. Oh, he was sweet and gentle and he tried, but that spark Fiona needed was missing. Pushing such thoughts aside, she told herself firmly it was time she settled on a husband — and a rich one at that. The years she'd spent dallying with exciting men had brought her nothing in the way of security.

After pinning her thick hair in a knot atop her head, she stepped out on the terrace and made her way to Amy's door.

The sound of voices slowed her steps, however, and she peered carefully around the open door. At that moment, Marcus bent forward and kissed Amy. Fiona turned and hurried back to her own door. She stood for a moment in her room, chewing thoughtfully on her thumbnail. In the past she'd encouraged Amy's interest in the captain, but now all that was changed. She wanted her young mistress betrothed to Justin and safely out of the way so her own plans could proceed. Her course was clear now: she would simply have to see that Amy and Justin realized how compatible they were. With some careful planning and manipulation, she should be able to accomplish that.

Fiona made her way downstairs, intending to fortify herself with some morning tea as she planned her strategy.

Ivy placed the tray holding the tea service on the small drop-leaf table in Harlan's bookroom. Her master sat behind his large cedar desk, drumming his fingers on its smooth surface with impatience as he silently watched her.

The black girl's nerves were stretched taut as she poured two cups of the fragrant, steaming liquid and added a touch of sweetening to each.

Massa Stafford had used her for more than a serving wench on several occasions, and she despised his meanness. However, she did not let any of this show as she carefully placed the cups in front of him and his son, who sat on the other side of the desk. The young massa, she thought, was so different from his father—they were like day and night. Or more like good and evil, she amended to herself. She stepped back with her head bowed and waited.

Harlan's dark gaze pinned the slave girl for a few moments before he barked out a sharp command. "Open the window to let in some fresh air, girl, and then leave us."

Ivy flinched and hurried to perform this task, then left, closing the door behind her.

Justin took a slow sip of his tea and asked, "Why do you do that, Father? Does it give you pleasure to have the slaves cower like dogs at your feet?"

"If the darkies don't fear you, Justin, they forget their place. Is your memory so short you've forgotten the re-

181

bellion in '61? More than a few white people were poisoned by their slaves. You would do well to remember that, for someday you will be master here," Harlan directed in a level tone. He kept his temper in check, for he wished to discuss his business this morning without their usual arguments.

The tensing of his jaw betrayed Justin's deep frustrations. "I forget nothing, Father. I merely think you could enlist their loyalty by different methods. They are, after all, human and have feelings."

"You sound like your Aunt Julia now. She was ever their champion — wanting to mollycoddle the lazy creatures," Harlan said, rising to refill his cup. Before his son could argue the point, Harlan turned and said, "That, however, is not why I asked for this meeting. We have something far more serious to discuss."

Justin refrained from reminding his father that he had not "asked" for, but had ordered, his attendance. Having just arrived home from his night with Megan, he was tired and a bit more mellow than usual. He gave his father an expectant look. "You have my attention."

Harlan returned to his seat and asked casually, "What do you think of Mistress Amy?"

Taken aback, Justin stared at him for a moment. He had assumed Harlan wanted to discuss the shipyard, and this question about their guest caught him off guard. "Well, she's certainly lovely. And I find her an amusing companion," he said.

"Good," Harlan said, nodding in satisfaction. He sat back in his chair and took a sip of his tea. "I've been thinking about your future, and I feel Amy would make a fine and fitting wife for you. She's well placed socially and would bring many financial assets to our family."

Justin stared, openmouthed, at his father. He had been expecting a lecture or a dressing down, but not this! All of his life, Justin had borne his father's domination and disapproval, and now the man had even chosen his bride.

Of a sudden, Justin's lethargy evaporated and he sat up straight, his eyes narrowing. "And have you decided how many grandchildren we shall provide you? And mayhap their sexes and proper names?"

Harlan ignored the sarcastic reply and admonished, " 'Tis time you grew up, Justin, and married. And why not the beautiful Amy? God knows, you're not courting any other suitable female."

Justin was furious. He stood up and paced the room in agitation. "You know nothing about me, Father," he spat out. "You never cared enough to ask how I felt about anything, but merely made decisions on my behalf. There is a girl I care about — and what's more, I intend to marry her." Stopping before the desk, he glared at Harlan in defiance.

Harlan bristled at his son's aggressive tone, but reminded himself of what he faced without Amy's fortune. Clearing his throat, he asked, "Are you speaking of that little chit from the Boar's Head?"

"Your spies must be everywhere, Father," Justin sneered, hiding his surprise. He'd no idea that Harlan knew of his affair with Megan.

"I don't believe it's wrong for a father to take an interest in his children's lives," Harlan said, trying to sound reasonable. "And while I can understand your infatuation with the girl's beauty, I can't believe you seriously intend to marry the trollop. She's not socially acceptable. You would be an outcast among your own class."

Justin had not actually gotten as far as thinking of marrying Megan, but had said that to spite his father. Now, however, he realized that the idea appealed to him. What did he care about a group of stuffy society folk anyway? "Hear this, Father: I will not be dictated to by you or anyone else in the future. My life is my own."

Harlan saw the determination in his son's eyes and for the first time felt a stirring of respect for the boy. However, he could ill afford the luxury of giving in. He had decided not to tell Justin about their financial troubles, but now he knew that he must use the knowledge to sway his son to his way of thinking. Shrewdly, he said, "Would you see your aunt and Pamela put out of their home and left destitute to satisfy your own ends?"

Wary, Justin snapped, "What have they to do with my decisions?"

Harlan stood and crossed the room to gaze out the window on the back lawn. The morning breeze ruffled the red figured-banyan coat he wore over his white linen shirt while he absently gripped the informal lapels. Instead of answering the question, he said, "When your grandfather gave this estate to me upon my marriage to your mother, I had high hopes that my son would someday inherit the richness I intended to build here. And I have done quite well — and I do have a son. However, over the last two years, a number of business reversals have left us in dire straits." He turned then and faced Justin, steeling himself to form the words. "If you do not marry Amy and acquire her fortune, we shall lose this estate and the shipyard as well."

Justin sat down and stared at his father incredulously. "I don't understand . . . you never said a word . . ." Justin stuttered in disbelief.

" 'Tis true. We're mortgaged to the hilt, and there is little time to pull the fat from the fire." Briefly, he mentioned each of their losses, starting with the five shiploads of salt that had been confiscated by the captain of a merchant vessel who thought the salt trade should belong to the merchants of the Bahamas. No compensation or redress had been ordered by the lords of Trades and Plantations. Then there was the loss of ships to Spanish pirates, and also the timber fiasco in the Carolinas. "I took out loans in London to cover the early losses, but our luck went from bad to worse," he finished.

Justin digested this information and shook his head. "Why did you not tell me? Perhaps I could have helped. Together we might have . . ." His voice trailed off, for he knew why Harlan had not mentioned any of this. His father had never thought him capable. "I care not for myself in this matter, but Pamela and Aunt Julia should not suffer. About that you are correct," he added, his voice bitter.

By appealing to Justin's sense of honor, Harlan had won his gamble. He felt sure his son would do what must be done. Quietly, he prodded, "You will marry Amy?"

Justin rose and walked slowly to the door. Opening it, he said without turning, "I will think on it."

Once alone, Harlan smiled in triumph and poured himself a measure of brandy. He downed it with a satisfied sigh.

Outside the open window of the bookroom, Fiona sat on the terrace, concealed from view by a large potted plant, enjoying a cup of tea and contemplating the startling information she'd just overheard. A thrill of excitement shot through her as a whole new plan began to take shape in her mind. When Justin married Amy, Harlan would, once again, be a wealthy man. In her opinion, he was far more interesting than Thaddeus. A slow smile curved her lips as she realized that her eavesdropping was going to bring her everything she'd ever wanted . . .

Chapter Eleven

Saturday dawned gray and cloudy. It began to rain during breakfast, and Amy and Justin had to forego their usual morning ride. He suggested a game of whist, and the two of them retired to the drawing room. Julia's maid, Layla, brought coffee.

The handsome black woman smiled warmly at Justin when he thanked her, but her gaze was cool when it rested upon Amy.

While Justin shuffled the cards, Amy glanced across the candlelit room to where Fiona, Pamela and Julia sat doing their endless needlework.

Her companion had brought up Justin's name this morning while dressing her hair and had talked at length of his good looks and admirable qualities. Amy had agreed on each point while wondering if Fiona had become infatuated with the younger Stafford. It had raised the question in her mind that perhaps Justin had been the man in Fiona's bedroom that night.

Amy looked at him over her hand of cards, trying to imagine him and Fiona together; however the idea seemed ludicrous. They seemed quite ill-suited, but then she and Captain Bond would most probably seem mismatched to others as well. It was a mystery not to be solved for the time being, she supposed, turning her attention back to her cards.

"Shall we play for points or coins?" Justin asked, his eyes twinkling.

"I should feel guilty relieving you of all your money, sir," she said.

He chuckled and proceeded to lose the first two hands. Their conversation was desultory, each getting lost in his or her own thoughts from time to time, the silences barely noticed by the other.

Justin could think of nothing but the unsettling conversation he'd had with his father the day before. Stealing quick glances at the woman across from him, he tried to imagine being married to her. While certainly not a distasteful thought, he felt strangely reluctant to commit to the deed. For one thing, he had realized just recently that Megan Cormac held his heart; for another, he was loath to use Amy in such a scheme, for he had come to like her very much indeed.

Glancing across the room, he eyed his sister and his aunt and felt a sinking sensation in the pit of his stomach. Should he decide to follow his own heart, they would suffer, and aside from Megan, they were the two people in the world he loved most. Their love had sustained him throughout his life, and he owed them much.

Amy lost two hands to Justin, and they found themselves in the middle of the next hand at a loss as to whose turn it was. Laying her cards down, Amy suggested, "Let us call it a draw, Justin. I've a headache."

He gave her a sad smile and agreed. "Perhaps you should rest before the soiree tonight at the Greens'. I must speak with my father on an important matter anyway before he leaves for town." He rose and then added as an afterthought, "I would be pleased if you saved most of your dances for me tonight."

187

Amy glanced up at his resigned expression and nodded slowly. "Aye, Justin. I cannot think of a more . . . suitable partner."

The rain continued until midafternoon, and Amy's mood matched the dismal, gray skies. The men had all gone their separate ways to take care of business, leaving the women to ready themselves for the party. Pamela came to Amy's room to chat and see the gown her guest had chosen, taking innocent pleasure in seeing the beautiful jade-green silk laid out upon the bed.

Amy barely attended the other girl's account of who would be at the soiree, until she heard the Reverend Jacobs name mentioned. Pushing aside her own dreary thoughts, she casually asked to see Pamela's gown.

They went at once to Pamela's room, and the girl explained she'd not decided yet. Throwing open her wardrobe, Pamela said hopefully, "I thought perhaps you would help me choose. You always look so lovely, and I would value your opinion."

Thoughtful, Amy sifted through the gowns, finding mostly browns and grays, but spying a pink silk at the back. She pulled it out and held it up to Pamela, noting how the soft color transformed her from plain to pretty.

Pamela began to shake her head uncertainly, "I don't know, Amy. *You* can wear bold colors, but I . . . I feel quite . . . uncomfortable. Justin chose this for me once, but don't you see, I'm very like the little brown sparrow, as father says, and would look ridiculous dressed in bright feathers."

Amy felt a sharp flash of anger at Harlan's careless, unfeeling opinion. She hid it, however, and said briskly, "Nonsense, Pamela! We must all assist nature to look our best. Come here." She pulled the girl toward the dressing table and bade her sit. Taking the dress, she held it beneath Pamela's chin. "See how the color gives your skin a glow? It will look wonderful on you, and you shall have Fiona's help with your hair tonight."

Pamela still looked doubtful, and Amy pointed out, "Reverend Jacobs won't be able to take his eyes from you."

Pamela blushed to the roots of her hair and dropped her eyes. "Is it that obvious? I pray he hasn't noticed!" she said with anguish.

Amy gave her a quick hug and said, "But that is the whole point, dear Pamela!" Laughing, she asked, "I believe you are interested in him, or am I dreadfully wrong about this?"

Pamela took a deep breath and murmured, "I think I'm in love with him. But what would he want with a woman like me?"

Amy gave her shoulder a little shake. "He is a lucky man to have gained your affection. You're very pretty — and warm and caring. You've just been trying to hide it, dear. However, if my guess is correct, I think Reverend Jacobs is interested in you already."

Pamela's head shot up and she pleaded, "Oh, Amy, I pray you — don't say that just to make me feel better!"

Amy assured her truthfully, "When we spoke of you that day at the orphanage, he gave his feelings away in a hundred small ways. And I know what I heard in his voice."

Pamela's face lit with happiness, and Amy was glad she had broached the subject. The poor girl had been browbeaten by her father far too long. It was time she gained some confidence and realized her worth. Looking conspiratorially at her in the mirror, Amy promised, "Tonight Fiona and I will assist you in getting ready, and I think the good Reverend Jacobs will be hard put to resist you."

* * *

After Pamela had donned the pink gown, Amy, true to her promise, arrived to apply some light makeup. A touch of rouge gave Pamela a healthy glow. Fiona came to do the girl's freshly washed and dried hair in a style similar to Amy's upswept curls, and the effect was dramatic. Pamela hardly looked like the quiet, mousey girl who had met them on their arrival. From the pocket of her robe, Amy produced a small bottle of French perfume and dabbed some on Pamela's slim neck and at her wrists. "There!" Amy exclaimed. "You are finished and look just beautiful. Does she not, Fiona?"

Fiona was secretly amazed by the transformation and nodded. " 'Tis true, Mistress Pamela." She turned to Amy and urged, "We must do your hair soon or we'll be late."

"Aye," Amy replied. "I will be right along."

Pamela thanked Fiona as the girl left the room, and then she jumped to her feet and hugged Amy soundly. "I cannot believe it is me! You've been a wonderful friend, Amy, and I wish you could stay here forever."

Amy chuckled and held the girl away, chiding gently, "You'll be wrinkled if you do not stop that. As to my staying here, you will not need me, for Reverend Jacobs will carry you off when he sees you."

Pamela's eyes twinkled at the outrageous jest. "Well, if he doesn't, I shall need a shoulder to cry on."

Verdmont House was located near Flatts Village about a half hour from Stafford House. The rain from earlier in the day had completely dried on the white coral road, as was the way of it in Bermuda. The crushed coral soaked up moisture like a sponge. It was a pleasant change from the muddy conditions of Boston streets after a rain.

The party from Stafford House was traveling in two carriages so as not to crush the ladies' skirts. Harlan and Justin rode with Amy and Fiona, while Thaddeus and Marcus rode with Pamela and Julia.

Amy had been torn when Harlan suggested this arrangement, one moment relieved that she would not share close confines with Marcus, and the next instant longing to do so. He looked so very handsome and debonair dressed in formal evening clothes. The burgundy-colored silk banyan coat, white linen shirt and black velvet breeches fit his muscular frame to perfection, and his warm, admiring look had told her he approved of her appearance. There had been no opportunity the day before for a private conversation between them, but he had sent her intimate messages with his eyes during the course of the evening. That made the ache in her heart all the more unbearable, for she was seriously thinking of Justin as a husband.

Common sense bade her to end the dalliance with Marcus before she became pregnant or before, at the very least, the affair was exposed. If that happened, her uncle would be angry and, more importantly, disappointed in her behavior. Her heart felt like a stone in her chest, however, when she contemplated never seeing Marcus again. She was in love with the rogue and had realized it the night he'd come to her room. But while he could whisper words of love in the heat of passion, she was certain that he cared not enough to make her his wife.

This realization had brought her to her senses and prompted her decision to consider Justin if he offered for her. She had to put a permanent distance between her futile desires and the man who would make a fool of her. There was her pride to consider, she told herself stoutly. But a sick feeling washed over her just the same.

"Are you feeling well, Amy?" Justin asked in concern. She had barely spoken since they'd left, and her face was a trifle pale.

Giving him a weak smile, she said, " 'Tis that same headache I complained of this morning. Don't trouble yourself about it, though, for I shall be fine."

Harlan reached across and took her hand. "Justin could escort you back to Stafford House if you're not up to this soiree, my dear. Say the word and Mistress Fiona and I will transfer to the other carriage and leave this one free for your use."

Amy shook her head and forced a brighter smile. The last thing she wanted was to be alone all evening with her disquieting thoughts. "You are too kind, but nay, I really wish to attend the party. I am sure my first glass of champagne will banish the pain."

Harlan sat back and chuckled. "A refreshing attitude, my dear. Most females take to their beds and plead extreme distress at the slightest pretext. Is she not a treasure, Justin?"

The younger man agreed without hesitation and then teased her with a smile. "She is fearless as well, chasing our ghost through the woods at night without so much as a lucky charm to ward off evil spirits."

"I think you are having fun at my expense," Amy chided with a smile. "There are no such things as ghosts."

Justin's brows rose. "Too many strange things occur for me to disbelieve altogether. However, the slaves are fond of dressing up for their ceremonies. And they have always whispered of the ghost woman in white appearing on occasion. It is quite harmless."

Harlan scoffed. "You know how superstitious the darkies are, Justin. They're like children, seeing things that are not there."

"But Amy's life was endangered," Fiona protested mildly. "That does not sound so harmless to me."

192

Justin shook his head. "I am sure the ghost did not intend for her to follow, but merely wished to elicit a startled reaction." He grinned then at Amy. "How was the ghost to know she is impetuous as well as brave?"

Amy's smile was tinged with relief at Justin's explanations. " 'Twas more foolish than brave of me to go chasing anyone into the night. It was merely a bizarre coincidence that a wild beast nearly attacked me."

Verdmont House was ablaze with lights when they arrived at dusk. Several other carriages were simultaneously rolling up the drive to let their finely dressed and bejeweled passengers out at the wide stone staircase in front of the mansion. Liveried servants stood at attention at the door, and host and hostess greeted their guests just inside the spacious ballroom. Amy and Justin moved through the line, and when she heard Mistress Green compliment Pamela, Amy felt the afternoon's effort had been worthwhile.

The room was already crowded, and musicians played softly to one side. A servant stopped with a tray, and Justin lifted two glasses of champagne and handed one to her. "Your headache remedy, my dear," he said, grinning.

Amy tasted it and chuckled. "And so much more appealing than those awful powders my maid forces on me."

Justin gazed down on her shining copper curls and asked, "Do you often have this malady?"

"Only when I do not get my way," she said, hiding the turmoil of her heart as she noticed Marcus being led to a group of female guests by Pamela.

"If that were my case, my head would have exploded by now, the way my father thwarts my plans," he replied, his attempt at humor sounding quite bitter instead.

Amy stopped a passing servant and exchanged their empty glasses for full ones, handing one to Justin. "I can see we are going to be the life of the party tonight," she said ruefully, taking a large swallow. An attractive brunette had attached herself to Marcus like moss on a tree and was gazing up into his eyes coquettishly, making Amy wish a pox upon the hussy. She finished her second drink in one gulp and seized Justin's arm. "My glass seems to be empty, dear Justin. You may get another for me and then introduce me to your friends."

He glanced down at her flushed face with raised brows and nodded. Her mood was no better than his, but he knew not the reason for her unhappiness.

Justin and Amy mingled, and she kept a surreptitious eye on Marcus. Several beautiful women now claimed his time, vying for his attention like a well-bred pack of dogs trying to procure the only bone in sight. Amy was disgusted with their obvious behavior, especially after noting the fact that he seemed to be enjoying it overmuch.

Belatedly, she looked around for Fiona to make sure her companion was not left alone among strangers. Her worry was unfounded, though, for she spotted her with Thaddeus across the room beside a large potted palm. The two were talking quietly.

Then Amy started as she saw Fiona lay a hand on Thaddeus's chest and his arm go around the young woman in an intimate gesture. Could Uncle Thaddeus have been the man in Fiona's bedroom? Amy suddenly wondered. It seemed odd, and yet he was not really that old — fifty — and was still a handsome man. But Fiona? She was young enough to be his daughter.

Justin brought her attention to the fact that dinner

was being announced, and she decided to speak to her uncle later on the matter.

She found her place card on Judge Green's right at the head of the table and forgot her worries for a time, as she listened to his stories about the booty brought in by privateers under his jurisdiction. Being the judge of the Vice-Admiralty court, he had final say on the prizes seized by these ships. " 'Tis a great boon to our economy here in the islands," he remarked, noting her shocked expression.

"Is there a difference, sir, between piracy and privateering?" she asked candidly.

He chuckled at her blunt question. "Aye — a letter of marque issued by the governor. That makes the whole affair legal and tidy."

"If not morally right?" she suggested with a twinkle in her green eyes.

He smiled at her persistence. "Since all countries engage in the practice, it is universally accepted. Moreover, we do have rules we abide by, and those who break them are considered pirates, my dear." He found her not only beautiful but intelligent as well, and was pleased his wife had placed her beside him. It was refreshing to hear her views on the subjects normally discussed only in male groups. Deftly, though, he changed the subject. "You might be interested to know, Mistress Amy, that today word arrived via a British man-of-war that Parliament repealed the Townshend taxes on March fifth, except for the three-penny tax on tea, that is."

Amy absorbed this piece of information and then frowned slightly. "Well, sir, that news is encouraging, but not as good as a complete repeal. I fear the political climate has been stormy in Boston since the Stamp Act of '65. And even though it was repealed, the Townshend Acts following close behind has been a source of much irritation to Americans."

He nodded. "I have heard of the unrest in America, especially in the seaport towns. I came to Bermuda in '65 from Philadelphia to take up my post here. However, back then in America we were experiencing problems other than the tax laws levied on us by England. The backcountry Scots-Irish rabble and the Indians were causing difficulties."

"I take it you're referring to the Paxton Boys? I heard the story of how they massacred some peaceful members of the Conestoga tribe in revenge for Pontiac's rebellion."

His eyebrows shot up in surprise. "My dear Mistress Hawthorne, you are extremely well informed to be concerned with the political squabbles of another city, and all of five years ago. I must say I am impressed."

Amy smiled. "I was attending Dalton Academy in your fair city at the time, and I confess that I was an avid reader of the newspaper. My studies were a bit tedious, and I found current events far more interesting than needlepoint or French verbs."

They paused in the conversation while a delectable dessert of creamy strawberry pudding was served. Changing the subject, Amy commented on the abundance of fresh fruit on the islands, and Judge Green agreed.

"Although I miss the noble city of Philadelphia, I have come to enjoy life in these islands tremendously. And had I not come here, I would not have met my dear Mary. Verdmount House was built by her great-grandfather, a shipowner, in the early part of the century, you know."

He then told her more of the history of the area, including the fact that nearby Flatts Village was a known smugglers' port. It wasn't until Amy had returned to the ballroom for the dancing that she remembered she had meant to ask Judge Green if he had known Fiona's family in Philadelphia. Since the city was quite large, there was a chance they were not acquainted, for Fiona would surely have recognized her host's name and made mention of it.

She forgot about it, though, as Justin claimed her for the first minuet. When they finished, Justin led her to a seat and commented, "I do believe you have made another conquest, Amy. Judge Green has never been so animated at dinner before. I noticed that he barely conversed with the lady on his left."

A small frown puckered her brow. "I do hope I did not keep him from his duties as host. I tend to talk too much."

Justin laughed, stopping a servant to take two glasses of champagne from the tray. He handed one to her and lowered his voice. "Not to worry, my dear, the lady in question, Madame Livingston, was next to her current lover. I'm sure they found things to talk about."

"How convenient that arrangement was," she said, sipping the drink. "However, I feel pity for Mr. Livingston."

The musicians were playing a jig, and it was sufficiently loud that Justin had to lean down to talk close to her ear. "Do not. He has a mistress tucked away in St. George," he told her.

Amy opened her fan and created a breeze, but the room was crowded and hot and she felt slightly sick. Rising unsteadily, she took Justin's arm. "I need some air. Could we step outside?"

Once on the terrace, she breathed deeply of the cool night air. They leaned on the stone balustrade, and Amy waited for a couple to pass them before she spoke. The amount of champagne she'd consumed, along with several glasses of wine at dinner, was making her quite melancholy. " 'Tis sad, Justin, that men keep mistresses and women take lovers, don't you think?"

He could hear the slur in her voice and realized she was slightly foxed. Her words, though, sent a shaft of pain through his heart. Many marriages among the upper classes were for convenience sake and not love matches. It was a fact of life and, as she had said, quite sad. He had resigned himself to such a marriage, but was not happy about it. Slipping an arm around her shoulders, he gave her a comforting squeeze. "It is sometimes a fact of life, Amy, and you should not fret over it," he counseled wisely. Soon, he would offer marriage to her, but not tonight. The ache inside him was too fresh, and he sensed Amy was dealing with her own devils.

After a while, they returned to the ballroom, where Amy was kept dancing by a multitude of partners. One bright spot during the evening occurred when she saw Reverend Jacobs escorting Pamela onto the floor. He was smiling and she looked radiant. It was nice, Amy thought, that someone could be happy.

During a break in the dancing, Thaddeus claimed her from her current partner and led her to a secluded alcove to sit. His first comment was, "I am very pleased to see you and Justin getting on so well."

"I like him very much," she said truthfully, omitting the fact that she did not love him and probably never would.

Thaddeus nodded in approval. "I was hoping you would feel that way. Harlan and I talked at length about a match between you. Shall I tell him you are receptive to the idea, my dear?"

Amy swallowed tightly as she caught sight just then of Marcus with the brazen brunette on his arm. She nodded and forced her voice to a calmness she did not feel. "Aye, Uncle Thad. It's time I settled on someone."

So pleased was he that everything was turning out to his satisfaction, he missed the pinched look about her mouth. "This makes me extremely happy, my dear. And your parents would have been very proud of this match."

Amy gave him a tight smile. "Yes. Justin is suitable in every way," she murmured. In every way but one, she thought miserably. I don't love him, and he doesn't love me.

"I shall speak to Harlan tomorrow about this," he said, patting her shoulder and scanning the crowd as if looking for someone.

"There is no hurry, Uncle," she said quickly, needing more time to adjust herself to the idea.

He smiled at her absently. "No, I realize that. Now is not the time, but soon I wish to discuss something important with you concerning my future. I hope you will be pleased about it."

Amy was fairly certain she knew what that was, but silently agreed that now was not the time. She sighed. "I'm sure I will try."

He gave her shoulder a reassuring squeeze. "You are a good child. Excuse me now, my dear, but I see someone I must speak with."

Amy watched him move away and couldn't help noticing a new eagerness to his step. She had been so absorbed with her own life that she had completely missed what was beneath her very nose.

A cotillion was announced by Judge Green, and he and his wife stood waiting to lead the dance, giving everyone time to find a partner. Amy was hoping no ardent young man had spotted her hiding place in the alcove, when Marcus stepped up and held out his hand.

For an instant a wistfulness stole into his expression as he gazed at her. Then it was gone as he smiled politely. "May I have the pleasure?"

Conflicting emotions warred within her breast. She felt anger over his careless treatment of her, and yet her heart thumped madly as a delicious warmth suffused her body. Placing her hand in his, she decided to take this opportunity to tell him of her decision.

He tucked her hand in the crook of his arm and bent his head to murmur, "I have been waiting for a chance all evening to have you to myself."

Amy refused to look at him as they moved to take their places with the others. "Aye, Captain Bond, I noticed your lack of companionship."

A smile trembled over his lips at her sarcastic tone. "The way you say 'Captain Bond' when you're angry sends a chill through me. What have I done now, pray tell?"

They chose a square with three other couples, and the music began. It was just as well, for the tart reply that rose to her lips would have given away her jealousy, and his self-esteem needed no boosting.

For a while they changed partners, but finally met to finish the set. Marcus did not release her hand as the music ended, and the gentle pressure of his warm fingers reminded her of what she must do.

"Could we speak privately, Marcus?" she asked in a low tone as they left the dance floor.

He nodded and led her out onto the terrace, but several couples were strolling and some were occupying chairs placed there. Marcus took in the situation and casually led her to the steps, and they descended to the garden below. The fragrance of oleander and roses enveloped them in the tropical night. A night bird squawked, and tiny tree frogs made cricketlike sounds all around them. Amy felt as taut as a bowstring, thinking about the distasteful task ahead of her.

Marcus had been silent as they walked, waiting for her to speak, but when she did not, he stopped under a palm tree and took her in his arms. He bent to claim her lips in a searing kiss that left them both shaken.

Breathless, Amy whispered, "This was not what I intended, Marcus. We must talk."

He stroked her back with slow, sensuous movements and kissed her ear before moving to the slim column of her throat. "I am listening, Amy. Say what you will," he urged in a husky voice.

It was so difficult to think within his embrace. Her arms, of their own volition, circled his neck, and she arched her body as his warm lips left a moist trail down to her bare shoulder. She moaned as he pressed her hips against his suggestively and his tongue danced in slow circles across her delicate collarbone. "Oh, Marcus . . . we cannot continue," she gasped softly.

He lifted his head and pressed small teasing kisses around her mouth. "I know, love. I will come to your room tonight when all is quiet," he promised, misunderstanding her meaning.

For a moment Amy wanted to agree to that, but she knew in her heart that this had to end sometime. Now was the time, she decided, the pain making her voice harsh. "No!" Forcing back the hot tears that threatened, she pushed at his chest and stepped back.

Surprised, Marcus stared at her in the semidarkness for a moment and then reached out. "Amy? What is it?" he questioned.

She turned away, her chin held high. "Our little arrangement, Marcus. That is the problem. In good conscience, I cannot continue this madness. Surely you understand that." Although she'd forced herself to say this evenly, she wrung her hands together in agitation.

Marcus stared at her proud silhouette and found no argument with her logic, save the fact that he wanted her more than life itself. However, he had nothing to offer her, and there was the unsavory fact that he was Harlan Stafford's bastard son. He knew he should have never become involved with her in the first place, but it was done and couldn't be changed. "Madness it surely is," he agreed aloud, almost as if he were talking to himself. "I will keep my distance from now on, Amy. It is the least I can do."

The flat, resigned tone of his voice sent a fresh pain slicing across her heart. She realized that she'd been half wishing he would declare his love for her and insist on marriage no matter what his financial circumstances, but she knew he was a proud man. Then again, perhaps that was not the reason at all. Once, he had told her he did not wish to be trapped by matrimony, and she should have paid heed to his warning. One way or the other, he did not care enough for her, and she had to remember that.

"I must look to my future, Marcus. Soon I will be betrothed, and I do not intend to play false with the man who will be my husband," she said, a thread of steel in her voice.

He felt his insides tighten. He desperately longed to carry her away to a place where they could be together always. But he barely owned the clothes on his back, much less a ship to carry out that grand scheme. He had been defeated by the whims of fate. "I admire you for that sentiment, even though I shall miss you," he said slowly, moving to stand next to her. The heady scent of her perfume rocked his senses for a moment before he forced himself to say, "I wish you happiness, my love."

His nearness was overwhelming, and before her resolve weakened, she nodded and left the shelter of the palm. Without another word, they made their way back to the ballroom. Amy had no memory of the rest of the evening and fell into an exhausted sleep upon reaching Stafford House.

Despite the lateness of the hour, Julia asked her

brother to give her a few minutes in her sitting room after they returned from Verdmont House.

He shed his coat and poured a brandy before knocking at her door. Layla left them alone after admitting him. He sat down in a side chair and stretched his legs out comfortably, in a mood of rare good humor. "What is so important, dear sister, that could not wait 'til morning?"

Julia stood behind the settee, her hands gripping the back in an effort to stay calm. The look she gave him was carefully neutral, due to much effort. "I am worried about Justin. He is quite upset, but I could get no explanation from him. Do you know what ails the boy?"

Harlan's brow drew together in a frown, and he answered evasively, "You worry entirely too much about him and Pamela. They are no longer children to be mollycoddled, Julia."

She fixed him with a cold-eyed stare. "You do know what the matter is, and, as I guessed, it is most likely your doing."

Harlan shrugged indifferently and took a sip of his brandy. "I have merely secured the boy's future. As his father, I want only the best for him."

"And what did you decide that was?" she asked, her voice edged with sarcasm.

"He will wed Amy Hawthorne," he said bluntly, his good mood disappearing.

Julia had been afraid of that since their guests arrived. It was not that the girl was not beautiful or suitable, but Julia did not want her nephew or her niece forced into loveless marriages. They were like her own children, and she loved them with the selfless love of a mother. "By his downcast attitude the last few days, I assume he does not wish this match?" she asked.

Harlan rose, tired of the conversation. "He has agreed, and that's all that matters."

Julia's eyes flashed dangerously. "To you, perhaps, but I won't see him miserable his whole life, as I have been."

His lips twisted into a cynical smile. "Don't tell me you still yearn for that fortune hunter I sent packing?"

"He wasn't wealthy, but neither was he a pauper, Harlan, and you know it. We were in love, and you spoiled that for your own selfish reasons. I have come to realize that you simply wanted me here to deal with Papa's illness and to raise your children in case Martha's unstable side presented itself. You always feared that strain of insanity, didn't you?" Julia was past holding her temper and flung the accusation in his face.

"That's nonsense!" he blustered, but dropped his gaze guiltily. Striding toward the door, he threatened, "Leave this alone, Julia. Justin is my son, and you will be sorry if you interfere."

Julia was shaking with anger as he slammed the door behind him. Hatred flared in her eyes as she said harshly to the empty room, "No, Harlan, you shall be the sorry one."

Marcus stared, unseeing, at his ship while Toby Oakes apprised him of the progress on the repairs. The *Rebecca* had been hauled up and locked into place by several winches on the west side of the wharf, and the men were working diligently to put her to rights.

"Another week, lad. That's me best guess," Toby said.

"Not much time," Marcus muttered to himself. He then turned to his old friend and asked lightly, "Have you been staying out of trouble?"

Toby grinned and slid a hand over his bald pate. "Aye, lad. What kind of mischief could an old goat cause anyway? I have me work here and me rum at the Boar's Head. 'Tis enough."

Marcus frowned in mock disbelief. "Time was, you had a ladybird on each arm for company."

Toby snorted. "Females is too much work and worry. I leave 'em alone. Speakin' of trouble, how're ye gettin' on with that red-haired firebrand? The two of ye was like oil and water on the *Rebecca*."

The mention of Amy caught Marcus off guard, and he struggled to keep his expression bland. "Like you, my friend, I'm learning to steer clear of dangerous waters."

Toby had known Marcus since the latter was on a leading string, and noticed the tense set of his shoulders; but the lad was stubborn and would talk in his own good time. Changing the subject, Toby said, "Saw a friend of yers at the Boar's Head yesterday—Captain Marsden."

"Jeffrey? Is he still sailing the *Hawley* out of New York?"

Toby nodded. "Aye. He had a rare tale too, lad. I'll fill ye in if we find a spot of shade. No use standin' here in this burnin' sun."

The two men stopped by the water tank and filled tin cups to the brim before settling under a palmetto. Toby wiped the sweat from his face with his neck cloth and began, "Seems he was a day south o' the Carolina coast when he saw a pirate sloop sinkin' a British ship, 'er flag still wavin' as she went down. He was too far away to help, and not equipped with the guns needed to take the pirate sloop."

Marcus whistled through his teeth. "Was he able to identify either ship?"

Toby shrugged. "The pirate sloop was flyin' the Jolly Roger, but one thing he noticed, it wasn't Frenchie or Spanish built. He said it was Bermuda cedar as sure as he was born."

"Why the devil would an English privateer or even a pirate attack a British vessel? These waters are crawling with British men-of-war, and retaliation for an act such as that would be swift and terrible," Marcus mused.

Toby shook his head. "Your guess is as good as mine, lad. But when he docked in Charleston and reported it, 'twas decided that the British vessel was most likely the *Edwin* due to return from Barbados. Captain Marsden says they're makin' inquiries now."

"No survivors, I suppose?" Marcus asked.

"Nay, but he fished two bodies out. One was a sailor, the other a woman passenger—both shot through the head."

"That's vicious, even for the worst of those scurvy pirates," Marcus declared, wondering what prompted men to such evil deeds.

"Aye, lad. The sea's not the safest place to be in these times," Toby agreed.

"Did Jeffrey say when he's leaving?"

"Today. Most likely gone by now. He had cargo to deliver in London."

Marcus took his leave shortly after and rode into Tucker's Town. The previous afternoon, he'd seen John Radley, Harlan's agent, procuring the services of a prostitute at the Boar's Head. The little man had followed the girl up the stairs to her room while Marcus was playing cards with some soldiers from Castle Island. By the time he'd been able to break away, she was with another customer, and he had to return to Stafford House.

Today, he intended to speak with her to see what information might have been passed along in the bedchamber. He sought out Jonas, the innkeeper, when he arrived, and learned her name—Rose. She would be available after noon, he was told.

Marcus walked down to the bay and found a flat rock to sit on. Further down the beach, the wharf was alive with incoming and outgoing vessels, but all was quiet in the spot he'd chosen. His last encounter with Amy flashed into his mind, and he felt again the desolation of that night. He'd had no choice but to let her go, but that did not make it any easier. For several days now, they hadn't spoken, and she refused even to glance his way. The nights were worse, when he knew she was but a few steps away along the terrace. He'd had too much time to think about what she'd said that night . . . soon to be betrothed. Justin Stafford was the logical choice, for Marcus remembered her uncle intimating to him that this trip would yield more than business if all went well. Now he understood what the older man meant. A knifelike pain cut through him at the thought. Not only would she be lost to him, but his half brother would be her husband. If only there were some way, he tormented himself, but no solution presented itself. The only thing he had left was his mission of revenge, and it was beginning to taste bitter indeed.

Chapter Twelve

A young stable boy led a roan mare to the front steps, where Amy waited. She smiled at him as she tied the ribbons of her large straw hat under her chin. Already, the sun was growing hot, and she felt a slow trickle of perspiration run down between her breasts. "Good morning, Amos. Where's Moses? And who's this fine filly?"

Amos's black face split into a grin as he patted the mare's neck. "Dis be Lucy, Missy Amy. Moses, he say dat mare, Bess, be steppin' lame dis mornin'." The boy puffed out his chest with importance as Amy mounted from the steps. "Moses, he be busy, an' he says I git yo mount ready dis mornin'."

Amy grasped the reins he held up to her. "I hope it's not serious. Bess and I were getting on so well together."

Amos cocked his head to one side. "Doan rightly know, missy. I never seed her."

"Well, Lucy and I will have a good run anyway. Do you know if she neck reins or has a tender mouth?" Amy asked, patting the horse's neck. "I wouldn't want to upset my new friend."

Amos shrugged. "Doan know dat neither. Massa Stafford, he jes gits her last week."

"Then I'll just take it easy until I know her better," she

said, nudging the roan into a walk down the lane. After passing between the large gates, she turned toward the meadow and urged the horse into a trot. Lucy began throwing her head in a peculiar way, and sidestepped a few times. Amy leaned up and spoke soothingly to the animal and decided to give her her head. The mare stretched into a run and seemed to smooth out.

She was growing accustomed to riding every morning with Justin and missed his amusing banter, but he'd been ill with a stomach complaint and had to stay abed today. Her uncle had objected to her riding alone, but she assured him she would stay to the paths she knew. It was much too lovely to stay inside and do needlepoint.

For a few minutes, Lucy stretched out her long legs, crossing the meadow before Amy guided her to the right where an opening presented itself in the cherry hibiscus hedge that separated the meadow from the road. Pulling gently on the reins, Amy tried to slow the horse, but Lucy put her head down and put on more speed. Sawing on the straps, Amy felt a leap of fear in her stomach, for the mare had veered and no longer was aimed for the opening. Instead, she was heading straight for the hedge. It was not so very high, but Amy was not accustomed to jumping. Instinctively, she leaned over Lucy's neck and gripped her mane in both hands. When the horse left the ground and flew over the hedge, Amy prayed she could stay in the saddle. The jolt of hitting the road on the other side shifted the sidesaddle, and still the beast kept running. Frantically, Amy yanked on the reins and cursed the animal, who seemed hell-bent on a wild chase.

Up ahead was a curve in the road, and as horse and rider made the turn, a carriage met them. The startled mare swerved and stiffened her legs in an effort to stop, sending Amy flying over Lucy's head to land in a heap on the ground.

* * *

When Amy opened her eyes and focused on the cream-colored drapings around her bed, she thought it was morning. A soft gasp to her left side caught her attention. "She's awake," Thaddeus exclaimed to Ivy as he rose from his chair to bend over the bed. "How do you feel, my dear?"

Amy thought it was strange that he looked so worried, but when she shifted her position, she groaned at the pain and soreness in her body. Memory of the accident flashed through her mind then, and she murmured, "I don't know exactly, Uncle . . . did I break any bones?"

He smiled and patted her hand. "No, but it's a wonder. The gentleman you nearly collided with said you were thrown a fair distance. He brought you by luck to Stafford House in his carriage, since it was nearby."

She was cautiously moving her limbs and noticed her right arm felt extremely tender. She must have landed on that side, she thought. "I suppose 'twas lucky he came along, for my horse was out of control." Ivy placed a cool, wet cloth on Amy's brow and offered her a drink of water.

Thaddeus frowned. "What is this about your mount?"

Amy returned the cup to Ivy with a smile and lay back against her pillows. "I could not stop her. She jumped a hedge and was running full tilt down the road without my permission," she said, a touch of humor crossing her pale face.

"But you are an excellent rider," he protested, looking faintly puzzled.

"I was not accustomed to Lucy . . . nor she to me, obviously. Mayhap she took an instant dislike to me."

Amy shrugged and then winced at the pain the movement caused.

"So she was not your usual mount?"

"No. Amos said Bess was lame this morning."

Thaddeus stood up, noticing her drooping eyes. "Well, all that matters is you're all right. We were very worried, you know. The others are waiting impatiently downstairs for news of your condition. Even Justin rose from his sickbed when you were brought home unconscious. I'll let you get some rest."

Amy gave him a sleepy smile and closed her eyes. She napped peacefully through the afternoon and would have been appalled to know that Harlan, after hearing Thaddeus's account of what happened, had had Moses flogged soundly for allowing her to ride out on the unstable mare.

As the sun began to set, Amy roused from sleep and was sitting up when Layla entered, bringing a tray. The smell of the food made her a bit queasy, but she said nothing as the black woman placed it on the bedside table. Layla made her uncomfortable. "Where is Ivy?"

Layla gave her a look that was both aloof and stony. "She be helpin' in de kitchen."

Her tone was sullen, but Amy let it pass, knowing it was no use to question the woman, for she would hide behind a wall of ignorance. Instead, Amy said, "I would like to wash my hands and brush my hair before I try to eat. Could you bring my things?"

Layla nodded stiffly and got what was needed, then waited in silence beside the bed for Amy to finish. After taking the washbowl away, Layla asked almost mockingly, "Missy need me to feed her?"

Amy's left eyebrow rose a fraction. "I will manage on my own, Layla. You may go."

The woman dropped her gaze, as if hiding her expression, and turned to leave. At the door, she stopped.

"Sho be a shame dat boy Amos git you de wrong horse." Letting that statement hang in the air for a moment, she added finally, "Massa Stafford say he be up to see you 'fo' dinner." Without turning, she let herself out.

Amy shivered, even though the air was sultry. There was something in Layla's voice—a warning of some sort. It was almost as if the woman were telling her the accident had not been an accident. But why, Amy wondered, would anyone want to hurt her? She posed no threat to Layla. Getting a grip on her vivid imagination, she shrugged off these fanciful thoughts and turned to her tray of food. She picked at the roasted pork and potatoes, but in the end, she drank her tea and left most of the food.

Carefully, she rose and donned the light wrapper on the end of her bed, favoring her sore arm. Her satin nightrail, she felt, was inappropriate for receiving visitors.

She'd barely gotten back into bed when there was a knock on the door. She called out permission to enter, and Harlan strode in with a vase full of beautiful bougainvillea blossoms. Smiling, he said, "You gave us quite a scare, young lady."

Amy returned his smile. "The flowers are lovely. Please put them here," she said, indicating the bedside table.

He moved the tray and placed the flowers in its place. He sat down and gave her a mock frown. "You didn't eat. How do you expect to get strong?"

"I shall probably have more appetite tomorrow," she hedged. "How is Justin this evening?"

Her interest in his son pleased him. "Fit as a fiddle and wanting to see you, but his aunt thought it improper for him to visit you in your bedchamber."

Amy smiled at his exasperated expression. "You are here," she pointed out.

212

He laughed. "In the first place, she does not know that. In the second, I'm too old to be a threat to your reputation."

A glint of amusement lit her eyes. "I did hear your knees creaking as you crossed the room."

He picked up her hand and squeezed it gently. "Seriously, I had to make sure you were well." His eyes hardened as he added, "Moses knew the animal was unstable. As a matter of fact, I had given orders for the horse to be put down. Your accident was unpardonable."

"I'm sure Moses didn't realize Amos had chosen Lucy for me. And except for a sore arm, I seem to be fine," she assured him, uneasy with his cold anger.

His frown deepened. "Nevertheless, they are very fortunate their heads remain on their shoulders." Letting go of her hand, he rose. "The doctor was here and left some laudanum in case you had pain or could not sleep. Mistress Fiona will give you some if you require it," he said, and added, "I believe she's waiting to see you now."

Amy nodded. "Please send her in . . . and thank you for the flowers."

Fiona entered as he left, and she gave Amy a sympathetic smile. "You are certainly having your share of troubles lately, Amy," she said, and began to straighten the covers on the bed.

"I've begun to wonder if I should have stayed in Boston and married Edward," Amy said.

Fiona laughed and went to refill Amy's water glass. She then sat down beside the bed. "That would have been quite dull, I'm afraid."

Amy pleated the edge of the sheet thoughtfully, her mood growing pensive. "Perhaps a quiet, well-ordered life would be preferable to a love match after all."

Fiona's heart sank. So the girl thought herself in love with the sea captain. That complicated her own plans, but she was in an excellent position to sway Amy's opinions. And sway her she would, Fiona thought determinedly, for if Amy refused to marry Justin, she, Fiona, couldn't have what she wanted — not without the money. Why couldn't the silly chit take her pleasure and keep her emotions intact? Putting on an earnest expression, she said, "We women hope for love, but the fact is, sometimes we must be practical. If a marriage starts out with friendship and respect, love can grow from that."

For all the wisdom in her companion's words, Amy still felt depressed. She had set the course she must take, but a cloud of gloom had hovered over her ever since. At the moment, all she wanted was for Marcus to hold her in his arms. Sighing, she said, "I know you are right, but I cannot seem to be happy about it."

"You're not feeling quite yourself at the moment, Amy. Give it time and I'm sure you'll see what a wonderful husband Justin will make," Fiona encouraged.

Amy's eyes widened. "How did you know?"

Fiona shrugged. "I have watched your uncle and Mr. Stafford push the two of you together since we arrived. I would have to be blind not to see what they intend."

A dull throb had begun in her temples, and Amy pressed her fingers to her head to relieve the ache. "I suppose so. And I think you're right about Justin being wonderful, but I'm not so sure I would make a good wife for him. I cannot imagine being intimate . . . that is, I do not think I can . . ." Her voice trailed off in confused embarrassment.

Fiona clucked her tongue sympathetically. "I would not trouble myself about that, Amy. He will give you time to accustom yourself to that side of marriage."

Amy gazed at her companion curiously. "How can you be so sure, Fiona? In my limited experience with men, I've found them to be very unpredictable creatures — irrational and moody."

Fiona advised, "You must learn to read their character and what drives them, not the superficial signs. Beware of men who fire your blood yet offer no commitment—they're dangerous."

Amy remembered the uncontrollable passion she'd shared with Marcus and knew that Fiona was right. He was the forbidden fruit she longed for, while Justin was what she needed. Amy cocked her head to one side and asked, "How did you grow so wise? Have you been in love with many men?"

"A few, yes. And generally they were the wrong kind. That's how we learn, I suppose—by our mistakes."

"Is Uncle Thad the right one?" Amy asked softly.

Fiona's expression registered surprise before she could mask it. She had no idea Amy had any inkling of what had been going on. However, it would be beneficial to her new plans if Amy thought she and Thaddeus were serious. She took a deep breath and nodded. "Yes. As a matter of fact, we've become very . . . close. Please don't be upset, dear. Thaddeus has asked me to marry him."

Amy had had her suspicions, but it still came as a surprise. But, having grown used to the idea, she could, in fact, picture them together. Fiona was mature and self-assured and would probably make Thaddeus a perfect wife. Amy gave her a wan smile. "I'm not angry. I want Uncle Thad to be happy. He's spent too much of his life alone. But why did the two of you not tell me?"

Fiona had anticipated this question, and her quick mind formulated an answer beneficial to her own plans. "Well, dear, Thaddeus thought it would be selfish of us to announce our plans before your future was settled. He's been waiting for you to make up your mind."

Amy felt a stab of guilt. Her uncle had taken her in when she was ten years old, had been both mother and father to her, had put her needs ahead of his own for years now. He was not old, but neither was he a young man, and he deserved some happiness. "I have been the selfish one, Fiona. I will tell him that your marriage has my blessing," Amy said.

Fiona rose and gave her an awkward hug. "Thank you, dear Amy. I will try to make him very happy." Insisting Amy rest, Fiona left the room.

Amy stared at the door for a long while, as her thoughts swirled round and round. Her uncle and Fiona in love . . . the two of them married . . . herself married to Justin . . . how would she feel . . . 'twas infinitely preferable to being married to Edward Simpson . . . but how would she feel when Justin took her to his bed? She shivered as her mind shied away from that thought. A sharp pain gripped her stomach, and she gasped at the suddenness of it. She bent forward until it eased, and felt perspiration beading on her face. The nausea hit her so fast she barely had time to stumble from the bed to the wash bowl. Once she lost the scant contents of her stomach, she found herself shaking so hard she could barely make it back to bed. She felt hot and cold at the same time, and the room began swirling out of focus. Her last coherent thought was that she should have pulled the bell cord to summon the maid, but now it was too late.

Dark images filled her mind, and then sounds and voices echoed in her ears. Insistent drumbeats and rhythmic chanting came sharply into her barely conscious mind until her body throbbed with the intensity of it. The words were not discernable, only the threatening tone. Her heart pounded wildly as an unnamed fear enveloped her. Instinct bade her run, get away — anything but remain where she was. She struggled up and out of the bed, feeling light-headed once she was on her feet. The French doors offered an immediate escape, and she was drawn to the opening as if in a trance. It was

216

almost as if she were two people. One self watched her moving across the room while the other obeyed some silent command outside her body.

When she reached the stone balustrade surrounding the terrace, an unbidden voice in her mind urged her to climb over it. *Escape . . . escape,* it prodded. One small corner of her mind blanched in horror as she felt herself finding a foothold in the stone.

"Amy!"

The sound of her name harshly spoken jarred her from the strange state she was in, and she sagged against the wall.

Marcus moved forward and picked her up in his arms. "God's blood, woman! What were you doing?" he demanded, striding into her room with her.

Amy wrapped her arms around his neck, trying to clear her mind of the residual shadows. "I think . . . I was going to jump," she said, her voice small and shaky.

"Damnation! Why would you do that?" he gasped, astonished by her answer. He let her legs slide to the floor, but steadied her with his hands on her waist.

She leaned back to gaze helplessly into his eyes. "I don't know, Marcus," she whispered. "I couldn't seem to help myself . . . I felt so strange."

Her answer jolted him, and he felt a chill run down his spine. He studied her eyes and noted that the pupils were enlarged and the pallor of her skin was tinged a faint blue. Her skin also felt clammy and damp. She was disoriented, and he thought perhaps the fall she'd taken had addled her senses. Her body was trembling, and he pulled her close, holding her tightly. "It's all right, love. There's a reasonable explanation for this, and we'll find it," he said, stroking her hair.

Amy closed her eyes and drew on his strength. Her head began to ache again as she tried to clear her mind. "But what reason could I possibly have for jumping from the terrace? It could have killed me."

"People who are ill sometimes get strange ideas. You most likely sustained a concussion from the accident and had a spell of delirium," he suggested.

A lone tear slipped down her cheek. "When I awoke earlier, I felt fine — just sore and achy. I had lucid conversations with Harlan and Fiona. What happened between that time and my . . . strange behavior?" She was feeling apprehensive now as her mind pieced it together.

Marcus continued stroking her hair absently as he pondered the situation. His gaze fell on her food tray. Could someone have given her a drug or poison? Her actions were not those of a lucid person, and he knew the islands abounded with conjure women. However, he didn't understand why Amy would be a target for such sorcery. Perhaps his imagination was getting the better of his good sense. He dropped a soft kiss on top of her head and gently pushed her away. "You should get into bed, Amy, and try to rest."

She complied meekly and let him pull the sheet over her. A wan smile curved her lips. "I must thank you for once again saving my life. You always seem to be there in my time of need."

He caressed her cheek, his smile twisted. "Your white knight, as it were," he said.

Without thinking, she lifted her hand to close over his. She wanted to tell him he was the man of her dreams, but realized their situation was no fairy tale. "At this rate, you will be overworked in no time," she said lightly, even as an unspoken pain glowed in her emerald eyes.

"These accidents are beginning to worry me," he said, trying to ignore the warmth of her fingers on his. "That is why I am not at dinner with the others. I had to see for myself that you were all right. Thank God I did."

Amy was feeling nearly normal again, and the incident on the terrace seemed like a bad dream, best forgotten. She smiled up at Marcus. "So you weren't just out for a stroll and happened by?"

His frown deepened. "This is not in the least amusing, Amy. And I intend to speak to your uncle about it."

Dismayed, Amy blurted out, "Don't do that! Uncle Thad is overprotective as it is, and I'll not be able to take a breath by myself if you alarm him. Besides, I don't want to worry him. He has other things on his mind at the moment."

"I'm sure nothing is more important to him than you are," he insisted with impatience.

Amy reached out and caught his other hand. "Please, Marcus, do not say anything? These accidents, I'm sure, have merely been a run of bad luck. I promise to be more careful in the future."

He started to refuse her plea, but tears pooled in her eyes and her chin quivered. Defeated, he sighed heavily. "For now I will say nothing, but remember your promise," he said firmly, and added, "And if anything else suspicious occurs, you must come to me. Is that understood?"

Amy nodded, relieved. She wiped at the tears and smiled again. "All will be well, you'll see," she assured him.

Two days later, an impatient Amy was allowed out of bed, and Justin suggested an outing at breakfast that morning.

"Devil's Hole? Whatever it is, it sounds deliciously exciting," she said, her eyes sparkling.

Thaddeus frowned. "You are still recuperating, my dear, and shouldn't exert yourself."

Harlan intervened smoothly. "They could take the carriage, Thaddeus, and the cave is quite manageable. Justin would see to her welfare, wouldn't you, boy?"

A shadow of annoyance crossed Justin's face. "Of course, Father. I had intended to go by carriage instead of horseback anyway. I'm not a complete dolt."

Amy smiled brightly on all of them, hoping to avoid an argument. "Justin is most considerate and would not suggest anything that would tax my strength unduly. Furthermore, I feel quite fit now."

Thaddeus capitulated under their barrage. "Very well. I am outvoted," he said, raising his hands in mock surrender.

Hurriedly, Amy finished her meal and went upstairs to ready herself for the outing. As she changed into a blue, flower-printed cotton gown, her thoughts strayed to Marcus. She had not seen him since the day of the accident, and he had not been present at breakfast that morning. It was for the best, she knew, but she missed him sorely.

Thirty minutes later, Justin and Amy were on the south road in the small carriage. Justin had made up his mind to approach her today on the subject of marriage. While he answered her questions about the odd rock formations they passed, the surf, to the left of the road, thundered across the reefs, churning a froth among the boilers. Here and there, high gray cliffs blocked their view of the blue-green ocean, but the sound of the crashing waves was ever present. Normally the music of the sea soothed Justin's spirit, but today it made him feel lonely.

He asked her about her childhood in Boston, and she seemed relieved to talk of days gone by. They passed isolated cottages surrounded by rough vegetable patches and heavy stands of cedar. Presently, they came to a lake where thick trees grew out of the dark, murky water. Justin noticed her interest and supplied, "Mangrove Lake. It's a saltwater marsh."

"It looks so dark and mysterious," Amy commented.

"On a smaller scale, it reminds me of your American coastal swamps in the south. Now there you have dark and mysterious, as well as dangerous," he said, smiling.

Amy was intrigued. "I've heard Uncle Thad speak of the southern colonies, but my trips at home have been limited to Philadelphia and New York. Anything south of that is uncivilized," she said, grinning. "Or so I've been told."

Justin chuckled. "It's vastly different from the northern cities, I'll agree, but also quite exciting. When I go marooning, we put in at various ports in the south as well as the islands in the Caribbean."

"It must feel wonderful to sail off on an adventure," she said wistfully.

They came to a fork in the road, and Justin urged the pair of grays onto the left fork. "We'll soon be there," he said.

The road began to climb, and at the top of the hill Justin drove the carriage off to one side on a grassy verge. Another large body of water was visible in the distance, and he explained it was Harrington Sound, surrounded by land except for one narrow channel to the sea on the opposite side of the island. "We have no freshwater lakes or rivers in the islands," he told her as he jumped to the ground and turned to help her alight.

"Uncle Thad mentioned that and said that is why everyone's roof is whitewashed and clean — so the rain water can be caught in drains and carried into tanks."

"It seems odd to visitors, but we are accustomed to it and have never been without rain for long."

He took a lantern from the carriage and led her up a pathway through the lush vegetation toward an opening in the side of the hill. They entered the natural grotto, where it was instantly cool and dim. Justin lit the lantern and took Amy's hand as they walked.

The cavern's rocky floor echoed their footsteps, and she could hear the sound of water lapping as if it ebbed and flowed. They soon came to a clear pool, and Justin held the lantern high so she could see the fish. Amy was entranced at the odd shapes and beautiful colors. He pointed out parrot fish, small silver-green fry and even an angelfish, which he told her was shy and not seen often. "There are a great many groupers here as well," he said, lowering himself to sit on the rock ledge. Helping her down beside him, he pointed to a wide-mouthed, brown fish whose open red jaws lifted out of the water as if waiting for bait on a hook. "Watch this," he said, pulling a napkin from his pocket. When he unwrapped it, there was a chunk of bread from their morning meal. "I brought this to show you what our groupers are like." He tossed a piece in the pool, and instantly there was a great commotion, and the water was churned into a whirlpool. When the ripples smoothed out, the mottled brown fish had turned black.

Amy shivered. "What gluttonous little beasts," she said, eyeing their red snapping jaws.

"They would do the same to a human," he told her, and then, teasing, said, "They especially like beautiful red-haired ladies."

"I'm afraid they would find this one a bit tart," she returned.

For a time, they rested and watched the fascinating display of fish. Amy, however, was glad when they emerged from the grotto into the warmth of the sun once again.

Justin fell silent as he turned the carriage and headed back the way they'd come. Amy wondered at his strange moods the past few days. Normally, he seemed carefree and went out of his way to amuse her, but lately he'd been taciturn. Finally, she lay a hand on his arm and asked, "What is bothering you, Justin? I'm a good listener."

He smiled briefly and shook his head. "It's nothing. Or I should say, nothing more than usual. My father."

She tucked her hand in the crook of his arm. "Is there anything I can do?"

Justin fought down the urge to tell her what his father had pressured him into, but then he remembered his aunt and Pamela. No, he couldn't sacrifice them to gain his own happiness. How content could he be knowing they would suffer? Instead, he shrugged. "That's most kind of you, but no. I've survived twenty-five years under his influence. I'll manage this."

"Of course you will," she encouraged, and let the subject drop.

Justin swallowed a lump in his throat. She was so sweet, and he truly liked her, but he still found it hard to say what he must. "I wanted to be alone with you today so I could ask you something important."

Amy tensed at his serious tone. Justin plunged on. "I would be honored if you would become my wife, Amy."

His offer was no surprise to her, but this decision was the most important of her life, and she hesitated

Justin did not press her, but drove the carriage off the main road onto a track that wound down to the beach. He halted the horses under a tree at the edge of the sand and waited for her to speak.

Amy had already made up her mind, but now she wrestled with her conscience. Was she being fair to Justin? She did not love him and would not be the virgin he expected. Turning on the seat, she said earnestly, "The honor would be mine, Justin, for you are a fine man. However, before I give you an answer, there are things about me you should know."

He picked her hand and gave it a gentle squeeze. Her green eyes were full of anxiety, and he sought to reassure her. "As long as you have not murdered a previous husband, dear Amy, there's no need for confessions, truly. If you can accept me for what I am, I shall be quite satisfied."

More than his words, his eyes pleaded with her to understand. Amy faltered for a moment, realizing he did not wish to know her secrets or reveal his own. Slowly, she nodded. "Very well, Justin. Then I accept your proposal."

He lifted her hand and kissed it, his resigned gaze holding hers. "I shall try my best to make you happy," he promised solemnly.

The dining room was brightly lit with dozens of candles. The elegantly set table reflected that light, from the polished silverware to the shining crystal glasses. The family and houseguests at Stafford House were gowned and suited accordingly, having been informed by the master of the house that tonight was to be a special occasion.

The assembled company was unusually quiet, each for his own reason, as they waited for Harlan to appear.

Marcus was lost in thoughts of his continuing investigation of Harlan. Rose, the prostitute from the Boar's Head, had been quite talkative after he'd given her some coins. John Radley, it seemed, was a braggart in bed and liked to boast of his most important client. He never let slip anything specific, but intimated that Stafford was in financial trouble that would be his undoing if a miracle did not appear to save him.

Amy felt emotionally drained as she sat staring out the open terrace doors. The pleasant night air drifting in did little to cool the room, where so many candles warmed the air. Mechanically, she'd dressed in a flocked cream-colored dress and applied rouge to her pale cheeks. Fiona had fussed over her like a mother hen, getting her ready for the official announcement to-night. She and Justin had informed Thaddeus and Harlan the night before of their plans, and it had been decided tonight would mark their celebration. Amy's gaze was drawn to Marcus as she wondered what he would think of the news. They had not spoken since the evening he'd slipped in to see her after her spill from the horse. He looked preoccupied, and she wondered what thoughts filled the mind of this enigmatic man.

Harlan strode into the room and took his place at the head of the table. "Forgive me for my tardiness," he said. Placing a velvet pouch on the table, he nodded to a servant. The black man took a bottle of fine Madeira from the sideboard and began to pour. When he had filled everyone's glass, Harlan stood up and said, "We are celebrating tonight a most joyous occasion — the be-trothal of my son to Mistress Amy. I am more than pleased to welcome her as a daughter, and I know I speak for everyone at Stafford House." He paused, and his gaze swept over the group. "May you have a long and happy life together." With a broad smile, he lifted his glass and drank. The others, except for Julia, did the same, and then a surprised outburst from Pamela broke the silence.

"Oh, my dear Amy! I'm so pleased for you and Jus-tin," she said, beaming with sincere happiness. "Now I shall have you for a sister."

For once, Harlan looked on his daughter with ap-proval. Amy returned the girl's smile as best she could and murmured, "Thank you, Pamela . . . and Harlan. I shall try to be an asset to the family."

Justin cringed at her choice of words, then swallowed the contents of his glass in one gulp. He signaled the ser-vant for more. Well into his cups already, from an after-noon spent with a bottle of rum, Justin rose unsteadily to his feet and lifted his replenished glass. "You have no idea how important you are to this family," he said, his words slurring a bit as he gazed pointedly at his father. "To my beautiful bride-to-be." He resumed his seat without saying more, but Amy felt the tension between him and his father.

Thaddeus rose next and made a toast, while Fiona smiled happily. As dinner was served, the conversation flowed, and only Julia and Marcus remained silent. When Amy chanced a glance at him, his expression was tight with strain. A knifelike pain twisted in her heart, but pride forbade her to weaken. She pretended to be happy for Justin's sake.

When the meal was over, they made their way to the drawing room, and Marcus attempted to excuse himself, but Harlan spoke up. "Please stay a moment longer, Captain Bond, if you don't mind."

Marcus nodded stiffly as Harlan took the velvet pouch from his pocket and moved to Amy's side. "A betrothal gift, my dear," he said, smiling. He opened it and extracted an emerald ring, which he placed on her finger. Again he reached inside and pulled out a flawless emerald necklace. Obediently, she turned so he could clasp it around her neck.

"It's beautiful, Harlan. Thank you," she murmured.

"Beautiful jewels should always be worn by a beautiful woman," he said. "These belonged to my wife."

Amy's glance swerved to Pamela. "Oh, dear. Shouldn't these go to your daughter?"

Harlan shrugged negligently. "Martha had other pieces that will go to Pamela. Besides, she could never wear these as well as you."

Amy felt a sudden revulsion for the jewels, in that moment and longed to claw them off and throw them in his face. How could he so callously hurt his own daughter? Pamela appeared at her side and hugged her, exclaiming, "Father is right, Amy. I want you to have them. They were meant for Justin's bride."

Amy took the girl's hand and gave it a squeeze. "Thank you, Pamela. I shall treasure them, since they were your mother's." To Harlan she said nothing, fearing that if she looked at him, she would be tempted to say what she really thought. And that would only hurt Pamela more.

Justin had helped himself to a brandy, and leaning against the fireplace, he gave Amy a twisted smile and tipped his glass.

Marcus had been taking in the scene, his intense emotions masked. He left the room without anyone's notice, except Amy's.

Chapter Thirteen

Amy was sitting up in bed, brushing her thick copper hair in a desultory fashion. The activity soothed her frayed nerves. Fiona had offered to perform this task, but Amy had refused. She couldn't bear her companion's happy chatter over the engagement.

A brief knock sounded on the door, and Amy called out permission to enter. Thaddeus came in, dressed for bed in his nightshirt and robe. He carried a glass in his hand. "I met Layla in the hall. She said Ivy has been bringing warm milk for you at night — that you haven't been sleeping well. I've been concerned about you since the accident."

Amy took the glass from him and moved over a bit so he could sit on the edge of the bed. "I've been restless, but it's nothing to worry about, Uncle."

He smiled. "Now that your future is settled, perhaps you will be more at ease. Justin will make you a fine husband, my dear. The Staffords seem quite happy about the match."

Amy grimaced. "I don't believe Julia approves."

Thaddeus countered, "She has some strange ways, that's all. Why would she not approve of you, pray tell? Especially since you are Justin's choice."

Amy refrained from mentioning that Justin did not seem overly enthusiastic about their betrothal. It was more of a feeling than anything he'd said. She took a sip of the warm milk and sighed. "In any case, she will have to come around. What's done is done."

Thaddeus noted her downcast attitude, but steeled himself against it. He was doing what was best for her, and if he weakened, the willful chit would lead him a merry dance. He was glad that Fiona had helped him put things into perspective regarding Amy's future. "The banns will be posted at Trinity Church this Sunday, and I've spoken to Justin about a date for the wedding. Would three weeks from now be sufficient time to ready yourself?"

Finishing the milk, she frowned at the funny taste it left in her mouth. "That will be fine. I already have a wardrobe full of new gowns. They will suffice as a trousseau."

"You shall have a few more things I think. And then there's the wedding gown to think of. Pamela could call in her seamstress," he suggested.

Amy was beginning to feel a little strange, lightheaded somehow, but she didn't mention it. "Three weeks will be fine, Uncle, but what of your marriage? I half expected an announcement from you tonight."

He patted her hand. "Fiona and I did not want to encroach on your special evening. Once you are married, though, we will proceed with our plans. The two weddings will mean postponing my return home, of course, but I'll send word to my agent in Boston. At any rate, I have plenty to do now, what with settling your dowry and inheritance with Justin."

Amy wanted to point out that she should have some say in the matter of her finances, but an odd buzzing had started in her head, so she pleaded fatigue to put an end to the conversation.

Thaddeus rose and kissed the top of her head. "Sleep well, my dear."

Her sleep, however, was filled with strange dreams. She was on a runaway horse and could hear the thunder of the surf as her mount careened headlong toward the edge of a cliff. The sound of the crashing waves grew until she could feel the vibration in her body. Fear held her fast to the animal's back, and silent screams nearly choked her. She was helpless to stop what was happening, and knew any moment they would reach the precipice. In the next instant, she felt the horse leave solid ground, felt herself falling in slow motion, facedown toward the water below. Suddenly, rising out of the water were hundreds of red-jawed groupers, their teeth flashing, sharp and deadly, hungrily waiting to devour her.

Gasping in panic, Amy woke with a start and sat up in bed. Her heart was pounding heavily in her chest, and a film of sweat covered her body. Raising a hand to her trembling lips, she tried to slow her breathing as she gazed around the room. But something was wrong, as the familiar shapes of furniture grew and moved, almost as if they were living things. Bright bursts of color flashed before her eyes, and in the center of her line of vision, a ghostly white apparition appeared. The woman in white was covered from head to toe in a robe, her face deep in the shadows of a hood. Her white sleeve reached out to Amy and urged her from the bed.

Amy rose without thinking and followed the ethereal figure out of the room, down the stairs and out into the night. She had the strangest feeling that she floated along, her feet barely touching the ground.

The apparition took her hand, leading her rapidly down the driveway toward the open gates, and Amy had no will to resist. They crossed the mangrove swamp and went on to the beach. Along the sand they walked, the ghostly figure pulling her in its wake. Amy had brief flashes of recognition of the landscape, but they ebbed away before she could grasp them firmly. Finally, the woman stopped along a cliff wall and pulled aside a scrubby bush. She motioned Amy inside an opening there and spoke for the first time, in guttural tones. "You'll be safe here. Go in."

A momentary flicker of defiance flashed in Amy's mind as she squinted into the dark opening, but before she could form a protest, she was hit from behind and fell forward into total blackness.

.

"I don't quite know how to say this, but soon I will be marrying Mistress Hawthorne," Justin said quietly.

"You're what?" Megan whispered, feeling as if she couldn't get her breath.

She stood facing him in her little room above the tavern. The last customer had departed, and Justin had shown up wanting to have a talk with her.

Justin pulled her close to him and held her fast. "It's not what I want, Meggie, but what I must do. Try to understand," he said, anguish marking each word.

Megan was too stunned to fight, as she asked, "You will wed another woman, and I'm to understand?" A searing pain ripped through her as his bold statement finally registered in her mind. He was her love, her protector, her best friend, and he was telling her he would soon be another woman's husband.

Justin stroked her back and said harshly, "I know it's unfair — life is unfair. Damn my father!"

Megan pulled back and gasped, "He's making you do this, isn't he? But you don't have to, Justin. We'll run away together . . . we'll have each other, and nothing else will matter." She ended on a pleading note, and Justin groaned aloud.

He caressed her face with a trailing finger and shook his head. "I wish it was so simple, love."

"And why not?" she said desperately. "We could leave on the *Margarita* tonight and be far away before he found out."

The light from the flickering lamp etched the pain on his handsome face. "You don't understand, and I cannot explain it all, but there are others who will suffer if I don't marry her."

"And will they suffer more than me?" She cried, feeling her last hope die as she stepped away from his embrace. She recognized the determination in his voice and knew all was lost. But what of the babe she carried in her womb? Justin's child, the child she wanted desperately, just as she wanted its father. What was she to do? Her mind was in a turmoil, her grief too fresh. She had to have time to think. Slowly, she lifted her bowed head and asked, "When, Justin? When is the . . . wedding?"

His hurt was multiplied seeing the look of betrayal on her face, but he steeled himself to answer. "Three weeks."

She nodded and turned away as he reached out for her. "Leave me now. I cannot take more."

When Amy opened her eyes, she felt a jolt of panic, for the darkness was thick and unfamiliar. She was sitting with her back against a hard wall, and to her horror, there was water lapping up to her waist. Her head ached, but her mind seemed clearer now, and she remembered the ghost woman knocking her unconscious. Getting to her knees, she explored with her hands the place she occupied, and found the ceiling quite low and the walls not more than a few feet apart.

She stifled the urge to scream, knowing it would do

no good. What she needed was to keep her wits about her and find a way out. She sat still and rapidly deduced from the way the water lapped against her body that the tide was moving into her cave from behind. Breathing slowly to discourage the nausea that rose in her throat, she reasoned that all she needed to do was make her way against the tide to the opening and swim out. She turned herself around and crawled against the tide, but after a few minutes, she realized the water was getting deeper. Even as she held her head higher, the water lapped at her chin. The ghost woman must have dragged her far back into the cave, or else she'd have reached the entrance by now.

On she went, desperately hoping to get out before her prison filled completely. She dared not let herself think of that, as the roar of the ocean grew louder in her ears. Her father had taught her to swim when she was very young, and she sent up a fervent prayer of thanks for that. With a dog-paddle stroke, she gained more ground than with crawling, but the strength of the tide pushed against her with greater force now.

Hope dawned when she glimpsed at a distance a pale circle of light in the surrounding blackness. Redoubling her efforts, she surged on, gasping once as she swallowed a mouthful of salt water. Just a bit farther, she told herself, even though her arms and legs felt heavy with fatigue.

Keeping her eyes trained upon the opening, she began to notice it growing smaller and soon realized it would be no more when the tide reached its highest point. Frantic now, she was paddling as close to the rocky wall as she could manage when, suddenly, she felt a cool, slippery body slide along her leg. Forgetting her purpose, she clutched at the wall and screamed as she felt the body once more brush her skin. It felt large, and she was terrified a shark or a barracuda had invaded the cave. Scrambling along the wall, she prayed the creature would move on. All of a sudden, the wall made an abrupt turn into another passageway.

The tug of the current yanked her into the new tunnel before she could get her balance. She flailed her arms, trying to touch the wall, but the water pushed her farther away from the point of light, and she knew this tunnel was larger than the other. Her foot could not find the bottom, and her strength was too meager to fight the tide. Keeping her head above water, she let the current carry her farther back into the cave.

An eerie calmness stole over her as she floated. Death, when it came to her, would not find her a sniveling coward, she thought fiercely. However, she sorely regretted that she would never see Marcus again . . . or be able to tell him she loved him. His handsome face filled her mind, and she could hear again the deep husky tone of his voice. Closing her eyes, she moved with the gentler current now and remembered how his strong arms had held her, how his sensuous mouth had claimed hers with passionate kisses. Would he miss her? Would they even find her body? She felt a moment of sadness for Uncle Thad. He'd lost all his family besides her, and now . . . But he had Fiona; he would not be alone.

A cool breeze blew across her face as she mulled over how few people her death would affect. All at once, her eyes flew open, and she blinked the water from her lashes. She could feel fresh air, and that meant a possible way out! New hope flooded her as she discerned a patch of moonlight on the water ahead of her. Swimming for it, she found a small, slanted, tunnellike opening. Her heart pounded with excitement as she grasped the rocks and hauled herself up. It was wide enough for her to climb using crevices for toeholds. When she reached the top, she lay on the ground, panting from the exertion.

After a few minutes, she rolled over her back and gazed up at the starlit sky, thinking it had never looked so bright or beautiful.

Then reaction set in, and she began to shake. Curling into a ball, she hugged herself as her teeth chattered uncontrollably. What had really happened to her tonight? she wondered. Why had she docilely followed the strange ghost figure out into the night without a protest? It had almost seemed like a dream until she awoke in the cave. That had been more than real. Since she didn't really believe in ghosts, who was this woman in white? And why did the woman want to hurt her?

Shivering, she got to her feet and looked around, trying to get her bearings so that she could get back to Stafford House. Walking to the edge of the nearby cliff, she gazed up and down the beach. Her eye caught sight of the odd rock formations that she had inspected the day she and Justin had picnicked. She could make out the arches and twisted columns clearly in the moonlight. Knowing her exact location now, she found the path to the road and headed for Stafford House.

Pushing open the front door, Amy stumbled into the dim foyer. Seeing her, Fiona hastily stepped back into the shadow of the corridor. She had just left Harlan's bookroom, and Amy's unexpected appearance startled her. What had she been doing out at this time of night? Smoothing her hair, Fiona composed herself and stepped forward, fixing a startled expression on her face. "Amy! Where have you been?" Fiona exclaimed, moving to her side.

Amy stood shivering just inside the doorway, dirty and wet. Her nightrail was torn and limp, while her hair hung in damp tendrils down her back. The tone in Fiona's voice caused her slight grip on composure to

235

snap. "Not to a tea party, I can assure you, Mistress Morgan!" Amy said, her voice rising on a shrill note. "I've been drugged, knocked unconscious and nearly drowned."

Fiona put her arm around her charge. "My God, Amy, come sit down and tell me what happened." She led Amy to a chair against the wall and gently pushed her down into it.

"Oh, Fiona," Amy began to sob, "it was horrible."

Fiona pulled a handkerchief from the pocket of her robe and gently wiped Amy's face. "What, dear?"

By the time Amy finished the tale, she was shivering again, reliving the terror.

"Oh, my dear, I can hardly believe these awful things happened to you! It's like a nightmare," Fiona said, worry lines creasing her brow.

"Its more than that," Amy said, hugging her body with her arms. "Someone is trying to murder me." Breaking into fresh sobs, Amy clutched at Fiona's arm.

"We need to get you upstairs to your bed. Come on, dear," Fiona coaxed.

Obediently, Amy stood and moaned, "I must tell Uncle Thad."

"Of course, Amy. I'll fetch him as soon as I get you settled," Fiona agreed in a soothing tone. She wanted to get this irritating chit to her room before anyone in the household questioned her own reasons for being downstairs at this hour.

"Just hurry," Amy sobbed.

In no time, Thaddeus swept through the door, belting his robe, with Fiona following.

"What's this all about, Amy? Are you all right?" he asked. "Fiona was babbling something about murder, for heavens sake!"

Amy gripped his hand and held back the fresh torrent of tears that threatened to erupt. She began at the begin-

236

ning, telling him about her eerie dreams and about waking up to see the ghost woman in white. "I'm sure I was drugged, Uncle Thad. I felt so strange, and followed that creature without one protest. It was as if I had no will of my own!"

"But who would have reason to drug you?" Thaddeus asked, hardly believing his ears.

Amy shook her head. "I wish I knew." She resumed her story, finishing with, "And if I hadn't found that tunnel out of the cave, I'd be washing out to sea about now."

Thaddeus paced back and forth in front of her, his head bent in thought. Abruptly, he suggested, "Perhaps you were sleepwalking. You did that quite often after your parents died."

Amy jumped to her feet, gasping. "Damnation! Of course I wasn't sleepwalking. Don't you think I would know the difference, Uncle?"

He bristled. "Calm down and remember to whom you are speaking, young lady. Your use of profanity does not lend credence to your story, I'm afraid."

"I can't believe you're taking this so lightly. Don't you care what happens to me anymore?" she asked, her eyes widening.

"Of course I care, Amy, but you must admit, this story is rather bizarre. And besides being wet and dirty, you have no injuries that I can see," he pointed out, one brow raised.

Amy's fear had long since evaporated, as her temper had risen. "This is not a fantasy, Uncle, and I will not be treated like an overimaginative schoolgirl. Whether you believe me or not, what I've said is true. And furthermore, I will not marry Justin and stay in this place if we do not get to the bottom of this."

Thaddeus crossed his arms over his chest and fixed her with a knowing look. "I think we now are at the bottom of this. If you did not wish to marry Justin, why did you not say so? There is always Edward Simpson waiting at home."

Amy stood facing him, her fists clenching and unclenching at her sides. "You may regret someday, Uncle Thad, that you didn't pay heed to what I'm saying," she said coldly.

"I suggest you get out of those wet things and get some sleep. You may reconsider this whole episode by the light of day and realize the events were not as you remembered. Please stay and help her to bed, Fiona." He turned and left the room without waiting for an answer from either of them.

Amy picked up the empty glass on the bedside table and threw it against the wall, causing pieces of glass to fly. "We'll see who reconsiders," Amy stormed.

Fiona took a few tentative steps toward the wardrobe and asked, "Shall I get you a dry nightrail?"

Turning, Amy snapped, "You might as well, Fiona. I'm not going anywhere tonight."

Fiona fetched a garment and a bowl of clean water so that Amy could wash up. "I'm sorry, Amy, that he didn't believe you, but after he thinks it over, he may—"

"He won't," Amy interrupted. "But it doesn't matter, Fiona, for I will take care of this myself."

Amy's companion wisely said no more.

When Amy arose the next day, it was well past the breakfast hour. Ivy, when summoned, helped her to bathe and brought coffee and fresh-baked bread with plum preserves. Amy, remembering her midnight episode with a shiver, abruptly asked the maid, "Have you ever seen the ghost woman in white, Ivy?"

The black girl's hand stilled as she was straightening the things on Amy's dressing table. "No, missy," she whispered, and resumed her task, eyes downcast.

Amy persisted. "I've seen her twice, and both times she led me into danger. If you know anything, please tell me. It could mean my life."

Ivy walked about the room, picking up Amy's discarded clothes, putting them away. "She be evil spirit," Ivy said, her voice so low Amy could barely hear it.

"I don't believe in ghosts, Ivy. I have a lump on the back of my head to prove it. Do you think a spirit hit me from behind?" Amy pressed her.

Naked fear flashed across Ivy's face, and she began backing toward the door. "De spirits be angry wit you, missy. Dey be angry wit me if I speak of dem. Mebe you tink about goin' home."

"I can see you're frightened, so I'll not press you, Ivy. However, I'm in the middle of a situation that prevents a hasty departure, and I need some answers."

Ivy nodded and said, "I be needed in the kitchen, missy."

Amy sighed and gave her permission to leave, which Ivy did with haste. Amy sat tapping her nails thoughtfully on the bedside table. Ivy truly believed the woman in white was a spirit, but Amy had grave doubts about that. However, the frightening thing was that she had no clue as to who this person was or why they intended to harm her.

She had promised to inform Marcus if any more "accidents" happened, but he was no doubt gone out for the day. She needed to collect herself before she saw him else she'd make a complete fool of herself. More than anything last night in that cave, she'd wanted him, but in the light of day, she knew nothing had changed. She might love him to distraction, but he didn't care enough to ask for her hand.

Resolutely, she finished her meal and dressed for her morning ride.

239

* * *

Marcus was halfway between the Stafford shipyard and Tucker's Town when he saw Amy galloping at breakneck speed across the road up ahead. Cursing under his breath, he kicked his mount into a run and left the road to pursue her across the meadow. The stallion he rode was more powerful than her mare, and he soon closed in, shouting for her to halt.

She reined in, and her mare danced sideways. Amy turned to face him.

"Are you intent on killing yourself?" he said angrily.

"No, but someone else is, and no one seems to care," she snapped back, her emerald eyes shooting sparks.

He was instantly alert. "What happened?"

Her anger faded as she saw the genuine concern in his gaze. He was the one person she could talk to without feeling foolish. She sighed heavily. "Someone intended for me to drown last night."

He dismounted and moved to her side. Helping her down, he held her tightly for a moment as her rapid heartbeats slowed against his chest. A bittersweet pain tore at him, at having her in his arms. The warm, fresh scent that was exclusively Amy filled his mind with erotic images.

Urging her to talk, he listened to the entire story before he gently held her away to look into her eyes. "My God, Amy, but you have a dangerous enemy, and we don't even know why."

His concern wrapped around her like a warm blanket as tears pooled in her eyes. She longed for the protectiveness of his arms once again, and her heart ached. "And my uncle doesn't believe me. He thinks I've fabricated the whole tale to keep from marrying Justin."

A bitter jealousy stirred inside him, but he was also angry with Hawthorne for jeopardizing her safety. The situation was growing more complex by the day. Not only was his investigation of Harlan moving irritatingly slow, but he was worried about Amy. His hands were tied in her case, though, for she was his half brother's betrothed now. He struck down the frustration that threatened to choke him. Reaching up, he brushed a tear from her cheek with his thumb and gave her a grim smile. "I believe you, and tonight I'll talk to your uncle. He doesn't know about the incident on the terrace, but I was witness to that and will make him understand. Before I leave, you will have protection, I promise."

She stared wordlessly at him for a moment. All at once, her fears took second place as this new anguish seared her heart. She swallowed past a painful lump in her throat. "You're leaving?"

"Tomorrow. I was on my way to the Boar's Head to alert my crew. The repairs are finished, and your uncle wants a shipment of sugar picked up on St.-Domingue," he said, unspoken pain glowing in his eyes. He didn't want to leave her, especially with the threats on her life, but he saw no way around it. "When I return, you will be married to Justin," he said aloud, as if to convince himself there was no hope for their relationship.

Amy dropped her gaze so that he wouldn't see the torment there. She felt as if a heavy stone sat on her heart, but pride stiffened her spine. She would not throw herself into his arms and beg for his love. Swallowing past the painful lump in her throat, she said, "Yes. Everyone is pleased about it. However, I don't remember receiving your good wishes." She hid her pain with a spark of defiance as she glanced up at him.

Marcus took note of the tilt of her stubborn chin and fought the misery that was so acute it was nearly a physical pain. He wanted desperately to take her in his arms again, but he knew he did not possess enough self-control to do so. If he touched her again, he would not let her go. In a thick, unsteady voice, he said, "Your happiness is more important to me than anything else."

His words wrenched her heart and she turned away. "I'd better get back . . . If you would help me mount."

He cupped his hands and she stepped up, adjusting her skirts over the saddle. She gazed down at him for a moment, memorizing every detail of his handsome face. "Have a safe journey, Marcus. Goodbye."

The finality of her words rang in his ears as he watched her ride away.

Marcus posted a notice at the Boar's Head and also spoke with three of his crew. They promised to pass the word to the others. He ordered rum at the bar and stood there sipping his drink. The unexpected encounter with Amy had left him more unsettled than ever. He had a strong desire to remain in Bermuda to be near her, and just as strong a desire to sail away before she took her vows with Justin.

"Good day to you, Captain Bond."

He turned his head at the soft voice beside him and recognized the blond girl immediately. "Megan," he acknowledged with a nod.

She leaned casually against the bar. "I heard you telling those men earlier that you're sailing tomorrow."

He finished his drink and placed the glass on he wooden surface. "Aye. We're headed for St.-Domingue."

"My uncle, Jamie Cormac, owns a tavern in Cap-François. He wrote to me a while back asking for some of the herbs and rosemary I grow in my garden," she said, cocking her silver head to one side. "Could you spare a bit of room for an extra trunk?"

He nodded. "We've only a small cargo of cotton to

carry there, so I've room. Have it delivered by tonight to the *Rebecca*. She's docked at Stafford's shipyard."

Megan smiled. "Thank you, Captain. It will be a great favor to me."

As dinner progressed that evening, Amy grew more restless. She could barely attend to what Justin was saying to her. He was seated on her right, Pamela on her left. Marcus was directly across from her, and she avoided his glances but could feel his presence as one feels an impending storm in the air.

On the surface, the dinner seemed a perfectly normal family meal. The conversation did not lag, the courses were served unobtrusively, and everyone behaved correctly. Amy glanced at her uncle. He was talking animatedly to Fiona, who was on his left, while she smiled and nodded. Amy was totally bewildered by his behavior. Since Fiona had come into his life, he had changed. No longer was he concerned about her problems or willing even to listen to her. All he seemed to care about was getting her married to Justin.

Pamela touched her on the arm, breaking into her brooding thoughts. "I'll be going to the orphanage tomorrow, Amy. Would you like to go along?"

Amy nodded absently. "Yes. We could also visit the dressmaker while in town. I have a fitting."

Pamela looked pleased. "Good. We shall have a pleasant day together, just like sisters."

Amy smiled then. "I'm looking forward to it."

Harlan addressed Justin from the head of the table. "Will our ships be ready to leave for Turks Island soon?"

"Yes, Father. Three more days at the most, I've been assured."

"Excellent," Harlan replied. He asked, "have you engaged the crews?"

243

A shadow of annoyance crossed Justin's face. "I'm attending to that, Father. We are just a few men short now."

"You didn't hire that worthless rogue of a friend of yours, did you?" Harlan asked, his eyes narrowing.

Justin raised his gaze slowly from his plate and regarded his father with unmasked dislike. "And just which worthless friend are you speaking of?" he asked.

"Cormac, of course. Although you do keep unsavory company other than his. Once you're married, boy, you'll need to develop a more select group of friends," Harlan advised, toying with his wineglass.

Justin's face reddened. "Considering your precarious position, Father, I don't believe you're qualified any longer to choose my friends or dictate my life. Do I make myself clear?"

Conversation around the table had ceased due to the tones father and son were using. Amy looked curiously from one to the other, noting Justin's angry flush and Harlan's tight expression. It was almost as if Justin were threatening his father with something.

With an effort, Harlan recovered himself and smiled apologetically at Amy. "Please excuse our bad manners, my dear. I fear we eat so much pork that our tempers are becoming hoggish."

Amy smiled thinly. "I have been known to display temper on occasion myself, sir, when goaded into it." Although nicely said, her meaning was clear, and the older man knew she took Justin's side.

He nodded and eyed her approvingly. "Touché, my dear. Justin is a lucky man."

The tension in the room dissolved, and the meal resumed. As the group retired to the drawing room later, Amy watched Marcus approach her uncle. They moved to the far end of the room, away from the others, and spoke quietly for a long while. She could see her uncle nodding gravely from time to time. She wondered sourly if he was taking Marcus more seriously than he did her.

Justin appeared at her elbow with a cup of coffee, and she reluctantly turned her attention to him. Sighing, she said, "After we are married, Justin, let's go marooning for the rest of our lives. I can't abide much more of my uncle or your father."

He gave a mirthless bark of laughter. "Aye, my dear. That idea appeals greatly to me."

Fiona joined them, and the conversation turned to general subjects. When Marcus and Thaddeus rejoined the group, Marcus caught Amy's eye and nodded. She took that to mean he'd convinced her uncle that the threat to her was real. She appreciated his efforts, but the thought of his impending departure left her with a feeling of hollow victory.

Chapter Fourteen

Amy retired very early that evening. Taking off her sea-green dress, she left it in a heap on the floor along with her hoops and petticoats. She threw herself across the big bed and stared dejectedly at the canopy top. The group's conversation had turned to the wedding plans, and after a while she'd grown frustrated at having to smile and act happy. She was tired of pretending things she did not feel, so she'd invented a headache and taken her leave.

Amy heard the door open, then close, but she didn't bother to rise.

"Amy?" Fiona's voice was hushed, as if she were unsure of her welcome.

"If my uncle sent you to fetch me," Amy said, "tell him I refuse to come back down."

"He didn't send me, dear, but I know you're upset. I came to see if there was anything I could do." Fiona was sitting on the edge of the bed.

Amy rose to a sitting position and pushed her loosened hair back from her face irritably. "There's nothing anyone can do, Fiona. He doesn't care what happens to me except that I marry Justin. I'm sick of being told what to do, and soon Uncle Thad will turn me over to Justin like a piece of property, and then Justin will have the right to decide my fate! It's not fair what happens to a woman . . . and I might just revolt." There was a glint in her eye.

Fiona bit back a sharp retort, knowing that was definitely not the tack to take with the angry girl. "Your uncle just has your—"

"Best interest at heart," Amy mimicked. "Don't mouth platitudes to me, Fiona. I know you mean well, but I'd like to be alone now."

With a sigh, Fiona rose and walked to the door. "If you should want to talk later . . . ," she offered, and let herself out.

Amy snorted in frustration and lay back down. She almost felt envious of Fiona. The girl might have to earn her living, but at least she was her own person. Making a face, Amy decided Fiona was addle-witted for considering matrimony.

Her thoughts drifted back to her main problem. Since Marcus was leaving, she would be on her own dealing with this lurking danger. Her uncle, she knew, might have listened to Marcus, but he was still skeptical. She had seen it in his eyes. She carefully ignored the sharp stab of loss she felt when she thought of Marcus, and considered telling Justin about the incident in the cave. Would he think her daft? He'd already made it clear he thought the slaves' superstitions were harmless. And Harlan? She could hear him now, chuckling at her childish fancies. A cold knot formed in her stomach when she realized the only person she could really rely on was herself. If I could just find out who is behind this, she thought, pressing her fingers to her temples. The incident with the wild boar could have been a case of being in the wrong place at the wrong time, even though she'd followed the ghost woman to the woods. However, her fall from the horse was a deliberate attempt, she felt sure. Layla had even intimated in a sly way that she knew something about it! But why? What reason did the slave have for hurting her? Then there was the matter of having been drugged and led to that cave. If only she could get a better look at the ghost, but the woman's face was always covered by a hood. That was Amy's problem — she had no positive proof of any kind.

For several hours she lay there trying to sort through the problems that faced her, while keeping the ache in her heart at bay. Try as she might, though, Marcus's face intruded on her thoughts without mercy. Life without him seemed dull and flat, but there was absolutely nothing she could do to stop the unfolding events. It would take a miracle, and she had given up dreaming about that.

A brief knock on her door jarred her back to reality, and she rose to slip on a robe before calling permission to enter.

Layla stepped in carrying a tray with a glass of milk. The woman's usual poise was absent tonight, and she cast her eyes about nervously.

Standing beside the open French doors, Amy gestured toward the bedside table. "Put it there, please." Wary now, Amy decided she would no longer drink the nightly milk. She may not know who was trying to hurt her, or why, but she could protect herself in this small way.

After doing as she was bid, Layla turned toward Amy and dipped her bright-turbaned head.

Amy frowned at the act of obeisance, never having seen this proud woman bow to anyone in the household. When the woman continued to stand thus, Amy asked curiously, "What is it, Layla? Do you want something?"

"Not fo' me — no, missy. It be Massa Justin . . . he sick enough to die," she said without lifting her head.

Amy felt a twinge of alarm at the woman's bald state-

248

ment. She stepped forward, concern in her tone. "Justin? What's wrong . . . where is he?"

Layla looked up then and shook her head. "Not sick in de flesh, missy. He sick in de soul."

Amy's anxiety turned to irritation, and she gripped Layla's arm, giving her a shake. "What are you talking about? Tell me now and stop speaking in riddles."

There was a peculiar flash in the woman's eyes as she answered in a level tone. "He doan want marry wit you. He love another. Dey be soulmates."

Amy stared at her for a moment, registering this information. She didn't trust Layla or even like her, but it made sense. Justin had seemed like a man doomed these past few days, and even his proposal had been stilted and without warmth. Amy had known something was wrong, but her own misery had kept her preoccupied. And perhaps here was an answer to the mystery. Mayhap this other woman was behind the attempts on her life. Amy had to find out. "Where is he, Layla? I'll talk to him."

A thin smile lit the woman's handsome face, and she nodded. "In de garden. He be drinkin' de spirits heavy dis night."

Amy hurried to pick her dress from the floor where she'd discarded it earlier. "Go tell him to stay there. I'll be down as soon as I'm dressed," she ordered.

Layla departed, and Amy fumbled nervously with the laces on the green dress. She was all thumbs, but she finally smoothed her skirts into place. Pulling the pins from her hair, she quickly brushed it out, leaving it to fall over her shoulders. She was in too much of a hurry to put it up into a fashionable style. Besides, she thought, if Justin was in his cups, he wouldn't notice anyway. A faint hope was beginning to sprout in her heart that perhaps she and Justin could mutually decide not to wed. His father and her uncle might crumble before their united front. What would happen to her after that, she didn't know, but it would be a respite. Grabbing a matching silk shawl, she left the room.

The tall clock in the foyer was chiming the hour of two as she let herself out the front door. She hadn't realized it was so late, but that would work to her advantage. There would be no one to interrupt her conversation with Justin, and perhaps by morning they would have everything worked out.

Heavy clouds hid the moon and stars, leaving little light to her path, but she found her way along the drive to the high wall surrounding the garden. Once she was inside the gate, the utter stillness gave her pause, for usually the night creatures and squawking birds rent the air with their raucous sounds.

The garden seemed darker than it was elsewhere, with the swaying shadows of trees and vines that reminded her of grasping arms. As she gazed about, her heart lurched, and for a moment she considered turning back. Her earlier decision to be more cautious leapt into her mind, but at that moment, she heard Justin call her name. The voice sounded slurred, and she let out the breath she'd been holding.

Moving along the path, she decided she would coax Justin to return to the house with her. They could speak privately in the bookroom, since the rest of the house was abed.

As she rounded a bend in the path, the stone bench came into view, and on it was a bent figure draped in a dark cloak. The figure straightened and rose, pushing back its hood. Amy got a brief glimpse of flowing silver hair just as someone grabbed her from behind. Before she could scream, a large hand clamped over her mouth. Sheer black fright swept through her as her captor held her against his big body.

It had been a trap, and she'd fallen for it. This

time, she realized, there would be no lucky escape.

"Quit fightin' now, missy. It'll go easier on your pretty self if you hold still." The man's coaxing voice was low and almost musical, Amy thought, as she delivered a well-aimed kick to his solid shin bone.

He let out a grunt, having buried his face in her hair to muffle the sound. The silver-haired girl had reached their side, and Amy could see her anxious face. It was the girl from the milliner's shop!

"Keep still, you big oaf!" the girl hissed. "Do ya want the household down upon us?"

Amy let her weight drop forward suddenly while he was distracted, and when he bent to hold onto her, she threw her head back and connected with his nose. This time he howled in earnest and let go with one hand to search the damage she'd wrought.

There was a sharp throbbing in the back of Amy's head, but a surge of satisfaction spiraled upward in her chest as she prepared to jerk free of him.

But his accomplice anticipated Amy's action and grabbed her arms, holding her fast while she scolded the whining man. "Take hold of her, man! If she gets loose now, we'll hang for sure."

He pulled Amy tightly against his frame and growled, "Damnation, Megan, she broke me nose. All the brawlin' I've done in me life and never had me nose broke! And her a little slip of a female! How can I ever hold me head up again for the shame of it?"

"Shut up, Patrick!" The girl shed the dark cloak and produced a handkerchief, pushing his hand away from Amy's mouth. Amy drew in a gasping breath and immediately found her mouth stuffed with a wad of material. Before she knew what was happening, the man wound the cloak around her tightly and hefted her over his broad shoulder.

He walked at a brisk pace, making it hard for Amy to

251

breathe as she bounced against his hard frame. She could hear him and the woman conversing in low tones, but couldn't make out what they were saying. What did they want with her? she wondered with fear and nausea clawing at her stomach. Were they simple kidnappers planning to hold her for ransom? Or was their purpose more sinister? God, how she wished she knew what was going on. For some inexplicable reason, she wasn't as frightened of the man as of his accomplice. There had been an odd note of reassurance in his voice when he'd spoken to her. However, she'd felt the dark animosity that poured from the woman. Why? she wondered frantically.

There was no more time to speculate, for he stopped abruptly and lifted her onto a hard surface. Kicking her legs, she tried to get free of the cloak, but once again found herself grasped in his arms.

Her world began moving, and she realized they were in a wagon. She could hear the clop, clop of the horses hooves, and Megan's sharp commands to the animals. After another brief struggle, Amy lay limp, knowing it was little use. On and on they rode into the night, and more than once Amy felt the sharp taste of bile rise in her throat. With difficulty, she swallowed, comforting herself with the fact that there could be a chance for escape later.

Just when she began to wonder how far they intended to take her, the wagon rolled to a halt. The big fellow carefully unrolled the cloak and helped her to sit up. Amy yanked the cloth from her mouth and, glaring at him, took in a deep draft of cool air.

He chuckled and scooted out of arm's range. "You're a spirited filly, you are. 'Tis a grand shame we didn't meet under more, ah, sociable conditions."

"You bastard," Amy croaked, her mouth and throat as dry as autumn leaves.

"Now, now, me darlin', there's no need to be castin' aspersions on me ma," he chided, reaching for a bottle on the bed of the wagon beside him. Uncorking it, he started to tip it up for a swallow and then stopped. He held it out toward her. "Would ya be carin' for a swig o' this, missy?"

Amy eyed him suspiciously and decided she could use a drink. Taking the bottle, she drank enough of the watered-down rum to ease her aching throat. She intended to flay the two of them with her sharp tongue as soon as she regained her voice. They might be planning her demise, but she wouldn't cower like a dog. When she finished, she tossed the bottle rebelliously against a large trunk at the foot of the wagon bed and glared at him. "What do you want with me?"

"We'll not be hurtin' you," the girl answered sharply, "if that's what you're worried about. I just want you gone, that's all."

"But why? I don't understand," Amy said, baffled by these two. "I don't even know you!"

"You ask too many questions. Just be glad I let you live," Megan snapped, turning her back to them.

Patrick spoke up then. "Aw, Meggie, ya know ya wouldn't hurt a fly. She wouldn't, ya know," he said, his gaze swerving to Amy.

Amy's eyes were beginning to feel heavy. She had the wildest urge to giggle at Patrick's sincere tone. She tried to straighten her shoulders and sound firm. "Ranshom . . . that's it, isn't it?" she said, her tongue felling decidedly thick. She swung her arm in a wild arc, trying to point a finger in his face. "Won't pay . . . Uncle's mad at me." The truth penetrated her foggy brain in a final flash of consciousness—she'd been drugged again. That cursed bottle of rum. She groaned at her own stupidity as her body slumped over, and the darkness enveloped her mind.

Strong arms lifted her gently and laid her on a soft bed, as a deep, thick voice murmured, "I'm sorry, me darlin', but I have to be lookin' out for Meggie."

With the help of the sailor on watch, Patrick carried the large trunk aboard the *Rebecca*. Megan, watching from the wagon, smiled in satisfaction. Her troubles would be sailing on the next tide. Justin couldn't marry Mistress Hawthorne if he couldn't find her, now could he?

Patrick offered to help young Jeremy store the trunk in the main hold. "Thank ye, sir. I'd be grateful for the help. The others get quarrelsome if you wake 'em up," the boy said with a cheeky grin.

"No trouble a-tall, lad," Patrick assured him as they headed for the main hatch. "Captain Bond is deliverin' this for me sister to our uncle on St.-Domingue," he said conversationally as Jeremy put his end down and jumped into the open hatch. "Careful, lad, don't let it drop, now. I think there's something delicate in there with the herbs and rosemary."

Jeremy grinned at Patrick as the big man climbed down to help. "I thought I smelled something sweet coming from this trunk."

Patrick helped him settle it in a safe spot against the wall. "That's right. I drilled a couple of air holes so the herbs don't collect moisture and mildew. Come to think of it, you could do us a great favor if you'd open the lid in a day or so to make sure it was stayin' dry in there."

"I'll be glad to, Patrick. You and Mistress Megan were good to me while I stayed at the Boar's Head, and it's the least I can do to repay you," Jeremy replied as they regained the deck.

Relieved, Patrick slapped the boy on the shoulder. "You're a good lad, Jeremy Cooper."

* * *

Marcus brooded silently as he held the wheel of the ship and stared at the horizon. This was his second day at sea, and he'd taken almost round-the-clock duty. Occasionally, he rubbed at his tired eyes, but he felt no urge to sleep. With sleep came tormented dreams of Amy, and he wore a heavy mantle of guilt where she was concerned. No matter how often he reminded himself that it was her decision to marry Justin, he felt he'd abandoned her.

"Cap'n Bond! Cap'n Bond, sir!" Jeremy Cooper's voice held a note of urgency that Marcus couldn't ignore. He saw the young man crossing the main deck below him at a run, and Marcus motioned to a sailor nearby to take the wheel. He reached the bottom of the steps the same time Jeremy did.

"What is it, lad?"

"Oh, sir, you won't be believin' this! Come quick!"

Marcus felt a twinge of alarm at young Cooper's actions. The boy was tugging at his arm, and he knew Jeremy was extremely agitated or else he would never have taken such liberties.

Marcus let himself be pulled along, but barked sternly, "Calm down and tell me anyway, Cooper."

The note of command in the captain's voice penetrated the boy's agitation, and he immediately let go of his superior. "I beg your pardon, sir . . . but I found . . . she's in the trunk!" Apprehension and horror mingled in Jeremy's expression as he stammered, "I helped carry the trunk aboard . . . I didn't know—"

"Who's in the trunk?" Marcus roared, losing patience as he kept up at a trot.

They reached the main hold, and Jeremy jumped down as he answered. "Mistress Hawthorne."

Marcus followed him down and across to a large

255

trunk against the wall. The lid was open, and Jeremy was peering inside with wide, stricken eyes.

Fearful now, Marcus pushed him aside and drew in a quick breath. "Amy!" He would remember the sharp taste of fear in his mouth for as long as he lived, and for a moment he could only gaze down on her crumpled, still form.

The next instant he was searching for a pulse in her throat, and he let out the breath he was holding when he felt a weak response. "Climb up on deck, Jeremy, and I'll hand her up to you," he ordered as he scooped her into his arms.

Jeremy took her slight weight and waited for Marcus to retrieve her. "Go ahead to my cabin and turn back the bed."

Curious stares from the crew followed the three, but no one dared question the situation after seeing the captain's grim expression.

Marcus laid her carefully on the bunk and instructed, "Fetch Dr. Carter at once."

Jeremy, relieved to have something constructive to do, departed, and Marcus pulled up a chair close to the bed to sit. Taking Amy's limp hand in his, he watched her face for any sign of life. How in the world had she come to be inside a trunk aboard his ship? Had she stowed away? She was not merely sleeping, though, for he'd tried to rouse her without success and her pulse was very weak. Perhaps, he thought, her air supply inside the trunk had been inadequate and she'd lost consciousness. Before he could speculate further, the doctor arrived, and Marcus moved out of the way.

"Quite a surprise, eh?" Dr. Carter said grimly, taking her pulse and lifting her eyelid to have a look. "Young Cooper told me how he'd found her."

"I have to admit, I'm baffled," Marcus conceded. "What's wrong with her?"

The brisk, older man continued his exam[ ] finally said, "I believe she's been drugged. P[ ] large dose of laudanum. The question is, who wo[ ] such a thing? Any ideas?"

"No, but you can rest assured I shall find out," Marcus said. "Her uncle is probably beside himself with worry by now, and we've no way at the moment to contact him." The *Rebecca* had left Bermuda two days before, and Hawthorne was sure to be turning the islands upside down looking for her.

"We could turn back," Dr. Carter suggested.

"Aye, we could do that," Marcus said reluctantly, but hesitated to make the final decision just yet.

The doctor asked for a wet cloth and began to bathe her face and slap her hands. He took a bottle of smelling salts from his bag and held it under her nose. After a moment, she began to turn her head away and moan softly.

"That's it, Mistress Hawthorne, open those pretty eyes, now," coaxed the doctor.

Amy obliged, but it was a while before she could hold them open. Recognizing the doctor, she whispered his name. However, her mind was fuzzy, and when he asked how she felt, she said weakly, "I don't know."

Marcus moved into her line of vision. "You're safe with us now, Amy. Just rest and we'll talk later," he said quietly.

Amy gazed into his familiar gray eyes, and a warm sense of security enveloped her. A peaceful sleep claimed her this time as she closed her eyes.

When Amy awoke the next time, the soft glow of a wall lantern lit the captain's cabin. Her gaze found Marcus sitting in his chair fast asleep. Relief washed over her as she realized he wasn't a dream she'd had. The gentle

caused her to wonder how she'd been
[...]d up with him aboard the *Rebecca*.
[...] kidnapping were clear now, but she
[...]s to the reason for it.

[...]at up and pushed back the quilt to dis-
[...]othed in a large white shirt. She assumed [...] [...]d to Marcus, but wondered where her
clothes were and if he had removed them. Not that it
mattered, she thought, for Marcus had seen her naked
before. Wherever this situation eventually led, she was
with Marcus now, and the wedding and her uncle could
go hang.

Quietly, she rose and padded barefoot to the washstand. She washed her face and rinsed the funny taste
from her mouth. Using his brush, she put her hair in order.

When she turned around to get back into bed, Marcus was awake, and the smoldering flame she saw in his
eyes startled her. Quite unsure of what to do, she stood
frozen.

Marcus rose and moved unhurriedly to stand before
her. Amy lifted her gaze and met the warmth in his eyes
with her own. Gently, he slid one hand to the back of her
slender neck and held her fast while his mouth descended to cover hers.

Her calm was shattered by the hunger of his kiss, and
she clung to him, giving herself freely to the passion
they shared. After a time, his mouth left hers to sear a
path down her throat. Impatiently, he pushed her shirt
aside to nibble on a delicate shoulder.

"Oh, Marcus," she gasped, her chest rising and falling with her harsh breathing. Her whole being was alive
with anticipation of remembered intimacies. She
moved her hands along his sides and down over his narrow hips.

Groaning with pleasure at her touch, Marcus reciprocated by slipping a hand inside the shirt to cup her breast. Its weight felt delicious, and he caressed the nipple with his thumb. His lips returned to tease hers. "I thought never to have you in my arms again, little firebrand," he whispered.

"That was my intention, sir . . . but I've heard the road to hell is paved with good intentions . . ." she returned in a husky voice.

A smile tugged at his sensuous lips. "Rather hell with you than heaven without," he said.

Lifting her effortlessly in his arms, he carried her to the bed and watched as she removed her shirt.

She gave a shiver of desire as his seductive gaze slid downward from her flowing copper hair to her bare feet.

A hot rush of passion surged through Marcus, and he quickly stripped off his clothes to join her on the bed. The fire between them was hotter still than the first time they'd made love. Each knew what the other needed, and each one remembered the intense pleasure that resulted from those small intimacies.

Marcus moved his hands possessively over her soft breasts and across her silken belly before going lower to caress her parted thighs.

Amy moaned in pleasure and pulled his head down for a searing kiss. He responded by exploring her sweet mouth with his probing tongue. Their bodies rubbed intimately together until Marcus felt as if he would explode. He pulled away and guided his erection to the soft, moist core of her womanhood. "Tell me Justin will never have you like this—tell me!" he commanded hoarsely, gazing intently into her fiery emerald eyes.

Amy slid her hand between them to close around him boldly. "I'll never give myself to another man, Marcus . . . I'm yours and always will be," she vowed.

"God, how I love you," he said with conviction.

With the promise of that declaration, Amy guided his shaft into the velvet softness of her body and he moved slowly back and forth, barely maintaining control, tantalizing both of them. Amy arched her body upward, needing more of him, and gasped in sweet agony as he obliged with one deep thrust. However, he then resumed the slower pace, murmuring, "Is there some hurry, love?"

Her body trembled with shivers of wanting as she slid her arms around his neck and pulled up to trace his lips sensuously with her tongue. "No, my dark captain . . . but I warn you, if teased overmuch, I could turn into a scratching wildcat," she challenged in a husky voice.

"Ummm . . . sounds dangerous," he said thickly, capturing her bottom lip between his teeth and sucking gently.

Amy felt her blood quicken as he began to move with increased urgency, all playfulness gone now. She clutched his shoulders and matched his rhythm with her own hot need. All thought was blotted out as a force began gathering inside her. She gasped his name as the convulsing tremors shook the foundation of her world.

A short while later, Marcus held her close, the quilt pulled snugly around them. Absently, he stroked her arm and breathed in the sweet womanly scent of her. "When we found you, I had thought to turn back to Bermuda, but I find I have no will to do that," he admitted.

Amy smiled to herself. "It's good we're of like mind, for I have no desire to return. Aside from the fact that continuing with you on this voyage will be an adventure, my presence there was nearly fatal to my health."

"Speaking of which, I have a fair notion of why you ended up in that trunk, but you could supply some details," he urged.

Amy leaned back to look at him with surprise. "But how could you know when I haven't had a chance to tell you what happened?"

"Because the trunk belongs to Megan Cormac, and I know that she's in love with Justin Stafford. It doesn't take a genius to understand her motives," he said.

"She's the one who kidnapped me all right, and a man she called Patrick." Amy's eyes narrowed. "So, she's in love with Justin. That explains something she said about not wanting to hurt me, but wanting me gone. However, Marcus, I could have died in that trunk."

He frowned. "Young Cooper told me that Patrick specifically asked him to open the trunk a day or so after we departed. And I checked the trunk — it had air holes in it. No, Amy, I don't believe they intended you any lasting harm. But they will answer to me for what they've done."

Amy shook her head. "I still don't understand her reasoning. If I'm not dead, I can and will return to Bermuda, and their crime will come to light."

Marcus caressed her cheek. "I don't profess to understand the workings of a woman's mind, Amy. However, I am in one way indebted to the Cormacs for reuniting us."

An impish smile curved her mouth. "I could almost forgive them, come to think of it."

Dropping a light kiss on her lips, he sighed. "Aye, but one thing bothers me. Your uncle will be worried sick about you. We must notify him as soon as possible."

"As angry as I am with him, I feel you're right. How will we do that?"

"If we do not make contact with a passing ship heading for Bermuda, we will send word from Cap-François when we dock," he told her as his mind began to savor the fact that he would have her to himself for a few weeks at least.

"And when we return to Bermuda — what happens to us then?" she asked.

He hesitated a moment and hated himself for it, but it was her well-being he was thinking of. He would not promise anything lightly. "By then I shall have worked something out, my love. Trust me."

Amy leaned forward and kissed him gently. "With my very life," she murmured.

The following morning, a sharp rap on the door brought Amy awake. Marcus was gone, and since she was once again clothed in his shirt and covered with a quilt, she sat up and called permission to enter.

Jeremy came in with a tray and greeted her with a mumbled good morning, his gaze lowered.

Amy wondered briefly if he was embarrassed by the fact that she'd spent the night in the captain's bed, but he soon relieved her of that notion.

Placing the tray on a small table, he said, "Captain Bond said you spent a restless night and to let you sleep late this morning, mistress. He sure was fearful for you and wouldn't let none of us sit by you during the night."

Amy took her cue and said, "That was a generous thing for him to do. I seem to remember waking once and seeing him asleep in his chair."

Jeremy nodded briskly as he poured coffee and took the warming cloth from a plate of eggs and fresh-baked bread. "He's a good man, to be sure."

Amy watched him fidget from one foot to the other for a moment, and then asked, "Is there something else, Jeremy?"

A dull red flush stole over his cheeks, and he stammered, "I'm truly sorry, mistress, that you was in that trunk for two days afore I found you. I shoulda checked it when Patrick brought it aboard — we usually do, you know. But he said it was herbs and rosemary and the like, and since I knew him I didn't bother. It would be my fault if you'd died. I failed in my duties."

Amy understood then. He felt guilty. "That's utter nonsense, Jeremy. The Cormacs are to blame for what happened, and I shall be angry if you continue to feel bad. I'll hear no more about."

He nodded and gave her a shy smile. "Thank you, mistress. Well, I'll be back with a bath and your clothes. I cleaned 'em and stitched a tear. When you're ready, Captain says you're to have the cabin you was in before."

Amy smiled and watched as he scooted out the door. She rose with enthusiasm to eat. All of a sudden, she was ravenous and more content than she'd been in a long, long while.

Amy made her way up to the main deck after bathing and dressing. Without the help of a maid, she'd pulled her hair up in a simple roll atop her head, leaving loose tendrils around her face.

Marcus spied her immediately from the quarterdeck and came down to greet her warmly. "How are you feeling this morning, Mistress Hawthorne?" he asked politely for the benefit of two passing sailors. However, his eyes caressed her bright face in a way that made her heart beat faster.

"Much better, thank you," she responded with a twinkle in her eyes. "Traveling in a trunk has been vastly overrated."

He chuckled. "You're very cheeky about that bit of treachery this morning."

Amy shrugged. "I'm not pleased about the Cormacs' trickery, but it did take me away from a marriage I didn't want. And it explains why Justin has acted so miserable lately. He must return Megan's love. What I don't understand is why he asked me to marry him."

Marcus took her arm, and they began to stroll along the deck, away from the working crew members. "I think I understand. Megan is a barmaid, and the high and mighty Harlan Stafford would not stand for his son and heir to marry that far beneath his station."

Amy remembered when she'd seen Megan in the milliner's shop. Madam Burgess had sneered over the fact that the silver-haired girl was a barmaid. It also explained why Megan had left the shop so abruptly that day. She and Fiona had been discussing Justin, if she remembered correctly. Frowning, she said, "That may be true, but I don't think Justin's so weak-willed that he would let his father choose a wife for him. As a matter of fact, he's quite rebellious where Harlan is concerned.

After a brief pause, Marcus said tersely, "There's a possibility that your money is the reason."

Amy halted in midstride to look at him. "But that's utterly ridiculous. Why, the Staffords are wealthy people in their own right."

Marcus's brow furrowed. "Once, perhaps, but I've been hearing rumors to the effect that Harlan is quite in debt with no way out."

Letting that information sink in, Amy once again started to walk. The thought that Justin would use her hurt more than she cared to admit. "I thought Justin was a friend," she said finally. "Which shakes my faith in my judgment."

Marcus gave her arm a comforting squeeze and offered grudgingly, "I would guess Justin is a pawn in this deception, for I too believe his moral fiber is stronger than that. However, Harlan is a different story."

"I don't know what to think anymore, but when we return, I will have some answers," Amy said with some of her old spirit.

Marcus smiled in approval. "And I will stand behind you, because left alone you tend to land in serious trouble."

"Speaking of trouble, I have been mulling over the 'accidents' I've had and wondering if the Cormacs are responsible for those also."

"Perhaps, but somehow I don't see Megan and Patrick doing anything that treacherous. But again, we won't find out until we return," he pointed out.

They dropped the subject, and Marcus talked of Cap-François for a time, telling her of his other visits there. Soon, though, he was called away to tend to a duty. Amy amused herself by roaming freely about the ship. She stopped to talk to the sailors as they worked, asking questions and getting to know them by name. Later in the day, Mr. Hadley gave her a cup of coffee and a lesson in preparing a delicate sauce for the rockfish that was to be tonight's main course.

After dinner, she played whist with Marcus, Toby Oakes and Andrew Williams, passing a pleasant evening. Finally, she excused herself to retire to her small cabin. Since she had no clothing except what was on her back, she bathed and climbed into bed naked. Tired, but content, she fell into a dreamless sleep.

The mild, sunny days drifted by as Amy occupied herself with many small chores about the ship and learned something of navigation from Marcus. The crew began to accept her as a mate rather than a female passenger. Jeremy Cooper loaned her some breeches and shirts to wear, since he was the only one close to her size. Toby gave her a bandana to wear on her head and tied it sailor-style, which gave her the look of an impish pirate. She no longer seemed like the heiress of a wealthy Bostonian merchant.

One evening, just before dinner, Marcus came upon Amy with Toby, the two of them perched on water barrels. The old sailor was teaching her to tie knots, and their heads were nearly touching as they chattered and worked at the task.

"Not planning a mutiny, I hope," the captain said, a smile in his voice.

Amy looked up, her gaze growing warm as she said with a laugh, "Nay, Captain. I'm not skilled enough . . . yet."

His left eyebrow rose a fraction. "For my own good, I had better leave out a vital lesson in your training," he teased.

" 'Twould be a pity, Marcus," Toby piped up, a twinkle in his eye. "For she's as bright as a new coin and learns faster than any lad I've ever taught."

"I can see I'm outnumbered here, so I'll be about my duties. Carry on," Marcus said in mock exasperation, and strode away.

Amy watched him for a moment, taking note of the broad outline of his shoulders straining against the fabric of his white shirt. His black hair caught the last rays of the setting sun and appeared almost blue. Everyday, her love for him deepened and intensified, and she couldn't imagine life without him. The nights he was not on duty, he came to her cabin and loved her until the wee hours. It was an idyllic existence, and she fervently wished they never had to return to Bermuda.

Chapter Fifteen

The *Rebecca* made a brief stop at the small island of North Caicos to take on fresh water. Amy gazed at the tiny harbor town from the deck of the ship but found nothing to excite her interest. The few inhabitants populating the one visible street consisted of two old men, who were baked the color of worn leather, and a young Indian girl. They were sitting together under the shade of a palmetto, with a basket of fruit for sale.

They barely stirred as Toby and Marcus, heading for the customs house, passed by. Amy had hoped to purchase some clothing, but was discouraged by Marcus. "The most you could hope for would be inferior cloth. Wait until we reach Cap-François," he'd counseled.

It wasn't that she disliked wearing shirts and breeches; quite the opposite was true. They were far more comfortable than hoops and petticoats, and she rather liked the freedom of movement. However, she didn't wish to embarrass him or herself when they reached the more cosmopolitan city on St.-Domingue.

Before noon, they were once again on their way, taking the Caicos Passage due south to their destination. Two days later, the *Rebecca* rode at anchor in the harbor of Cap-François. Marcus spent the better part of the morning settling duty rosters with the crew and speaking with customs officials who came on board. Once the small cargo of cotton was dealt with, he sent word for Amy to meet him topside.

Amy had taken as many pains with her appearance as she could, given her limited resources. Jeremy had cleaned and pressed her one dress, and she had washed her hair and knotted it rather severely atop her head. The style, even if it was not the latest fashion, became her lovely face. Once she reached the main deck, Amy spotted Marcus right away. He was dressed in black breeches and had added a silk banyan coat to the usual white, full shirt. His black top boots had been rubbed to a satiny shine.

When he saw her, he finished his instructions to Toby Oakes and came to meet her. "Ready, my love?" he asked, offering his arm.

Amy gave him a wry smile as she took it. "My toilet doesn't take up much time these days, with only one dress to choose from."

He smiled rakishly. "I much prefer you in snug breeches or nothing at all, if I'm to be truthful."

She laughed. "The civilized world would think me scandalous."

"But definitely ravishing," he teased, leading her to the ladder. "However, for the sake of propriety, we will visit the shops, and you may buy anything you want or need."

Marcus insisted she let him go first so that he could keep an eye on her descent to the launch. Once he found his footing in the small boat, he spanned her waist with his hands and lifted her down beside him. Two of the crewmen rowed them ashore, and Marcus helped her onto the dock.

Amy's excitement mounted as they made their way through the bustling activity surrounding the customs and warehouse buildings. Hucksters and peddlers were doing a brisk business with the merchandise brought ashore from the many ships and sloops anchored in the harbor. Once through this throng, they reached the rue de la Quaie, or high street, where the town proper began. Here, small grogshops rubbed shoulders with drygoods stores and brothels that doubled as rooming houses. Each place of business sported neatly painted signs out front, and boxes of brightly colored flowers adorned doorways and hung from second-floor balconies, mingling their smells with the strong aromas of food cooking and the fish markets.

Marcus suggested they take a walking tour of the town before visiting the shops, and Amy happily agreed. They strolled the cobbled streets past a slave market where an auctioneer was calling for bids on a husky black man who stood at attention on a platform. Never having seen anything like this before, Amy stopped to watch a moment. A small group of white men — obviously wealthy, given their fine dress — stood about calling out bids and sipping drinks.

Several more slaves, men and women, wore chains or fetters of some sort and waited their turn at one side of the platform. There were buyers inspecting this group as if examining prized animals for sale. The goings-on made Amy feel slightly sick. She accepted slavery as a way of life in certain places, but she had never seen anything like this.

Marcus sensed her feelings and patted her hand that rested on his arm. "It's not a pretty sight, love, but a necessary evil on these plantations. Let's go on, shall we?"

Amy nodded as they moved away. "They look so . . . vulnerable."

Marcus sighed. "There is certainly no dignity left for those poor souls, but that is the accepted way here. Did you know their own chiefs sell them to the slave traders? That's as cruel as the men who buy them."

Amy's brow knit in a frown as she looked up at him. "I suppose there are many ways to be enslaved in life, and this is just one of them."

Thoughtfully, Marcus nodded. "Aye, Amy. I have found that to be true." He was reminded of his quest for revenge against Harlan. The need to make the man pay for what he'd done to Sarah and himself had consumed him for the last year.

They passed a horse trading market and then turned down a wide boulevard of elegant town houses. These were whitewashed, with intricate grillwork on the windows, and walled gardens where lush tropical vines of bougainvillea spilled over the tops to please the eye and perfume the air. Black women with colorful scarfs on their heads traversed the street, carrying empty baskets on the way to market or returning with full ones.

Making a circle of sorts, they found themselves once again near the docks. Amy chose a quaint shop with a beautiful red gown gracing the window as her first stop.

The proprietress was arranging an assortment of delicate fans on a low table when they entered. She was a pretty woman with skin the color of café au lait, and her movements were graceful as she came to meet them. "Ah, m'sieur, madame . . . welcome to my humble shop. How may I help you?"

"I am in need of everything. Do you have gowns in my size already made up?" Amy asked, glancing about the shop curiously.

The woman's dark eyes gleamed at the prospect of a large sale. She smiled graciously and gave a small nod. "Oui, Madame. You are a perfect size and I am sure I have several things you will like. Come, *s'il vous plaît,* and make yourself comfortable." She led the way to a velvet settee at the back of the shop and motioned for them to sit. Hurrying away, she soon returned with several gowns and matching petticoats draped over her arm. There was a young girl with her who so favored her that Amy guessed her to be the woman's daughter.

The woman held each garment up for Amy's approval and then draped them over the girl's arms. Amy studied the materials and chose three gowns to try on. The proprietress ushered Amy to a dressing room in the back, behind a curtained doorway. Belle, as she called the young girl, was instructed to fetch refreshments from a bakeshop down the street.

Amy had chosen a deep-green silk gown with a white petticoat embroidered with green roses, a yellow floral taffeta and a cream figured-silk gown. Trying on the green silk first, Amy chatted easily with the woman in French, asking about the town and what it offered. When she was dressed, the madame fetched a pair of shoes to match, and also brought a fan to complement the outfit.

Amy stepped out to show Marcus how she looked and was rewarded with the warm admiration in his eyes. "A beautiful sight, I must say," he complimented.

She opened the fan and coquettishly hid all but her emerald eyes as she took a turn in front of him, hips swaying provocatively.

He smiled at the tempting picture she presented and took a sip of the coffee Belle had brought. "Let me see the others."

He approved all three, and when Amy was removing the last one, the proprietress brought in the red gown that had hung in the window. "Try this one, madame," she urged.

"I don't think so," Amy replied, thinking the color and style would not suit her.

"But m'sieur requested it. I too think you will be irresistible in it," the woman said with a twinkle in her dark eyes.

"Did he say that?" Amy asked, her attention caught.

"Oui. That one is quite a man and knows what he desires."

"Help me with it," Amy said. After she was dressed, she gazed at herself in the mirror and blushed. The bodice was very low, and the brilliant color set her hair aflame. She looked sophisticated and naughty at the same time. She understood now why Marcus wanted to see her in it.

"Come, let m'sieur have a look," the woman urged with a smile.

"Not now. I'll take it, but don't let him know. Just wrap it up," Amy said decisively. There was a wicked gleam in her eyes as she took one last look at the dress.

Before they left the shop, Amy had chosen underthings, a silk nightrail, shoes, stockings, a multicolored silk shawl, a hat and a small velvet drawstring purse. Marcus paid for the purchases and arranged to have them sent to the ship.

"Are you hungry?" he asked, wondering at her solemn expression, since she'd been in a gay mood before.

She blinked in the bright sunshine and then frowned. "I will repay you for the clothes when we return to Bermuda," she said. "I had forgotten I have no coin or accounts as I do in Boston."

"There's no need," he said casually, hoping to prevent one of her fits of temper over the matter.

She glanced up at him with a scowl. "I will not be a kept woman, Marcus Bond. We may be lovers, but I'm not a trollop."

"I didn't intend for you to feel that way. It was merely a gift. However, I will bow to your wishes if it will make you happy," he said in a placating tone. "Now, there's a tavern just down the street. I'm sure we can get something there," he suggested, and she nodded, mollified.

The meal proved to be excellent. There was turtle soup, fresh fish, and bread warm from the oven. Amy smiled at the silly stories Marcus made up about some of his sailing adventures. He had a delightful sense of humor when he wasn't being so somber, she thought.

As he enjoyed her company, Marcus tried to ignore the niggling worry about their future. The day was perfect, she was beautiful and sensuous, and he wanted to be with her forever. Leaving the tavern, he suggested they rent a carriage and see some of the countryside. "It's quite beautiful; I think you'll enjoy it."

"That's a wonderful idea," she said, "I don't want to go back to the ship just yet."

"I sent one of my men with a message to Henri Joubert's estate, announcing our arrival, and, by tomorrow, we should get an answer from him. I'm sure he will invite us to stay for a while. It will take time to negotiate a deal on the shipment of sugar your uncle wishes to buy."

"Does he know who I am? Will he mind my coming with you?" she asked, a frown marring her forehead.

"Henri is an old friend of mine, and he'll welcome you without question. Besides, I would rather explain our circumstances in person," he told her as they reached a livery stable near the docks.

They were soon on their way out of town, and the road rose gradually into the hills beyond. The countryside was lush with trees and heavy undergrowth. Hibiscus shrubs were blooming with clusters of delicate coral flowers, while flowering bougainvillea vines scaled the hillsides and draped the tall trees in vivid hues from red to purple to white. Amy spotted small cottages and an occasional farm as they rode along. They shared the road with other carriages and wagons loaded with produce heading for the marketplace in town. There was color everywhere and especially in the slaves' clothing. The women wore bright bandanas on their heads, and loose cotton dresses.

"They seem so happy," Amy commented after a while, noticing that they were either laughing or singing as they walked along with their baskets and carts.

"It seems to be their nature," Marcus agreed. "Although I don't know what they have to be happy about. Some of the plantation owners treat their slaves little better than they do their animals."

"Does your friend, Henri, have many slaves?" she asked.

"He once told me there were around three hundred on his estate. However, Henri is a fair man and not prone to exercising the cruelties practiced by some of his peers. I think you will like him."

"Is he married?" she asked.

"He's a widower, but he has a mistress who lives in the house with him, although her title is 'housekeeper' for propriety's sake. Solange is a free quadroon, and I think you will like her also."

Amy was quiet for a time as she thought of her own situation. She was little more than a mistress to Marcus, despite her show of independence. He said he loved her, but still there had been no mention of marriage. And although she was far happier being with him, her future was important to her. What if she should become pregnant? The thought gave her a headache.

They soon came to a road that veered off to the left, and Marcus turned onto this byway and drove for a short distance. Finally, he pulled the horses off to the side in a cleared area and helped her down. "There's something I want to show you" was all he'd say when she questioned him.

They walked arm in arm along a path, and Amy inhaled the sweet fragrance of the flowers they passed. The growth was so thick it nearly blocked out the sun, which was rather nice in this humid climate. Brightly colored parrots and other tropical birds squawked and fluttered in the trees as the couple disturbed the quiet of the forest. Soon Amy noticed a heavy droning noise and asked Marcus about it, but he put her off. "You'll see," he teased.

A few minutes more brought them to a clearing where the noise intensified. A large waterfall spilled from high above their heads into the river below. The water was clear and cool looking. "How lovely!" Amy exclaimed.

"I came here once for a picnic with some friends from town, and thought you'd enjoy seeing the falls," he said, watching the interest on her face.

He had carried a blanket from the carriage, and he spread it on the sandy ground. "We can rest a while before we go back."

They lay down together, Amy's head resting on his shoulder. A light breeze from off the water cooled them, and they were silent for a time, just enjoying the closeness.

Finally, Marcus brought up a question he'd been worrying about. "Do you think your uncle will try to force you into marriage with Justin when we return?"

Amy had thought of this already. "I don't know. Uncle Thad has not been too agreeable lately. As I told you, he didn't believe me when I told him about the ghost woman trying to kill me in the cave."

Amy raised up on her elbows and sighed. "Perhaps he's tired of my plots to get my way over the years. However, I am hurt that he can't see the difference here. I may be willful, but I'm not a liar."

"I know he cares for you, and that makes his unreasonable attitude very puzzling. The night I spoke with him about your situation, he agreed to check into the matter, but looking back, I believe he was merely humoring me."

"He's involved with Fiona, you know. They're planning to get married when I'm settled, and mayhap love has blinded him."

"That's no excuse," Marcus said bluntly.

Amy glanced sideways and asked, "What if he does insist on the marriage? What then?"

"I won't let that happen. But I would like to buy some time so that I can pay off my debts and offer you more than a pauper's life," he said quietly.

Amy sat up and laid her hand on his arm. "I *thought* perhaps your pride made you say those awful things to me about not wanting to be trapped into marriage."

"My pride is all I have, Amy. I won't live on your wealth—that's final," he said, gazing at the river.

"I would give up everything rather than lose you," she said softly.

He turned back to her, his expression tight. "I won't see you living in squalor. I'll go away before I ruin your life."

She gripped his arm fiercely. "Don't you ever go and leave me to grieve! Only a heartless bastard would do that."

An inexplicable look of withdrawal came over his face as he stared at her. Harlan Stafford's blood tainted his soul, and he realized for the first time that he was toying with this woman's life just as Harlan had toyed with Sarah's. He was no better than the father he condemned. This sharp knowledge cut through him like a knife. He pulled her into his arms and held her tightly. "I'm sorry, love . . . so sorry . . . ," he said, his voice betraying anguish.

Amy felt his suffering, yet didn't understand it. His plea for forgiveness was more than it seemed on the surface. This strange mood frightened her more than any he had displayed before. "What is it, Marcus? Please talk to me. I know I can help if you'll let me," she pleaded.

He ground his teeth in frustration, wanting to tell her

276

the truth, but he couldn't. He cou~~ld~~ Harlan Stafford's bastard son. It was~~~~ he was penniless and had made her lo~~ve~~ couldn't say the words that must be unacce~~ptable.~~ With her background and social standing, ~~she would~~ surely feel repulsed by the knowledge. Woul~~d she w~~ant her children's father to be a bastard? Even if it was kept a secret from the rest of the world, she would know — it would always be there in her eyes.

"Please, Marcus . . . what is it?" she repeated, struggling to loosen his grip.

"It's nothing — let it be," he said harshly, letting her go.

Amy searched his face, and despite his closed expression, she sensed his vulnerability. Taking his face in her hands, she kissed him softly, then deepened the kiss until he began to respond, almost against his will. He pushed her back on the blanket, kissing her with a hunger that belied the fact that they had made love only the night before.

His hand slipped inside her bodice, and he caressed her breast. She moaned deep in her throat as she squirmed beneath him. Abruptly, he pulled away from her and rose to his knees. With jerky movements, he unbuttoned the flap of his breeches, and in one swift yank with both hands, he settled her skirt around her waist. "I need you now, love," he gasped, torn between wanting her and wanting what was best for her.

Amy welcomed him without hesitation, her breathing ragged with desire. He thrust into her without preamble, finding her more than ready to receive him. Their lovemaking was in no way gentle, as it had been in times past. There was an urgency, a hot fire of emotion that boiled up within Marcus, and he strove to consume her and himself in the terrible heat. Amy's breath came in long, surrendering moans as he lifted her higher and he freed in her a bursting of sensations.

Afterward, Amy held him close, stroking the back of his head with her fingertips. She struggled with the uncertainty he had aroused in her earlier. There was something important he was holding back, she knew. It had shown in his manner, his words, his lovemaking, and the depth of his feelings made her uneasy. Somehow, whatever was bothering him boded ill for their relationship.

Finally, he pushed himself up on his elbows and eyed her warily. "You would have been better off if you'd not met me, love."

It frightened her when he said such things. "Why do you torment me, Marcus?" she asked, a hurt look coming into her eyes. "If I only knew what troubled you, we could solve it together."

He shook his head regretfully. "I wish that were true, but some things are a fact of life and cannot be changed." He tried to smile then as he raised up on his knees. "Come, let's take a swim before we go."

Amy realized he was not going to tell her anything, so she gave up. Her left brow rose inquiringly. "In our clothes?"

He grinned wickedly. "That was not what I had in mind," he said as he began unlacing the front of her dress.

She grabbed at his hands. "But Marcus, someone could come along and see us."

He laughed and stood up to take his own clothing off. "We just made love, Amy, and you're worried about someone seeing us swim?"

She sat up and watched him unashamedly. It was hot, humid, and she felt sticky. He was right, she decided, and threw caution to the wind. The imp in her found this idea deliciously wicked. Following his lead, she undressed and took his outstretched hand as they waded into the cool river.

The noise from the falls kept them from talking, but there was no need for words. They swam, splashed each other and shared sweet, lingering kisses. Their time together had a desperate quality to it that both felt. The sun was turning orange and sliding toward the horizon before they arrived back in town.

Early the next morning, a messenger arrived with an invitation to visit the Joubert estate. Amy packed her new clothes in a small trunk Marcus had loaned her, and they hired a driver and carriage to transport them.

They traveled a different road out of the town than they had traversed the day before. The terrain looked much the same, though, and the land rose into the hills. By noon, they turned off the main road onto Joubert property. Marcus told her Henri owned thousands of acres and all of them were planted in sugarcane.

They passed field after field in different stages of growth. In some cases, the cane stalks were twice the height of a man, with feathery, green tops blowing in the breeze. This mature cane was being chopped down by gangs of field hands with machetes. Amy noticed the presence at each field of an overseer riding a mule and armed with a gun.

After a while, the driver turned away from the fields and into a wide lane lined with royal palms. A good distance down this lane, the plantation great house came into view. Amy was impressed with its size and elegance. The rectangular structure was a combination of yellow brick, cut stone and wood trim, with a dozen arched windows lining each of the three stories.

Several slave women could be seen working on the lawn and in extensive flower gardens surrounding the house. The driver stopped the carriage before a flight of stone steps that reached the second, or main, floor.

Marcus climbed out and assisted Amy, but before they could ascend the steps, a short man came out the mahogany door at the top. He had a plain face until he smiled, and then it bordered on handsome. He was dressed formally in a black banyan coat and linen breeches. His dark hair and swarthy complexion contrasted sharply with the snowy shirt he wore.

He eagerly descended the steps, his smile growing broader. *"Bonjour,* Marcus. Welcome to Maison de Fleur, mademoiselle."

Marcus greeted his friend with a firm handshake and introduced Amy. Henri bowed formally over her hand and then offered his arm. "Come, refreshments are waiting. I am so happy to have you both, and Solange has been beside herself with excitement. Marcus is a favorite of hers, you know," he confided to Amy as they entered the front door.

The entrance foyer was quite large and dominated by a graceful curving staircase of gleaming mahogany. It was dim, but cool after the heat from outside. Several doorways opened off the foyer, and a woman came through one to their left. She was one of the most beautiful women Amy had ever seen. She walked gracefully, wide silk skirts brushing the polished wooden floor. Her regal head was wrapped in a beautiful silk turban that matched the color of her dress. It had to be Solange, Amy thought, for the cast of her skin was an unusual olive color and she carried herself with the dignity of the woman of the house.

"Capitan Bond—how nice to see you again. And welcome to your lovely friend," she said, a genuine smile lighting her dark brown eyes.

Marcus warmly returned her greeting and said, "This is Mistress Amy Hawthorne. Her uncle is Thaddeus Hawthorne."

Solange nodded. "Ah, *oui.* He buys much sugar

from M'sieur Henri, and also much rum. I see his name on the books."

Henri looked at Solange with pride. "Solange is a treasure. Not only does she keep this house running smoothly, she helps me on occasion with the accounts."

Solange's gaze softened briefly at his compliment before she turned back to the guests. "I am having light refreshments brought to the morning room, if you will follow me."

Henri and Marcus launched immediately into a discussion of the sugarcane, while Amy commented to Solange on how lovely the house was. "M'sieur Henri's grandfather bought this estate in 1698 and added to the original house during his lifetime, but it was M'sieur Henri's father who refurbished it with all these beautiful things you see."

They seated themselves on elegant brocade settees in the morning room, which faced the back of the house. Outside the tall windows and French doors, a louvered gallery overlooked a formal garden below.

Henri caught a bit of their conversation and added, "Most of the pieces in this room came from my uncle's chateau outside of Paris. When he died, my father inherited his estate, since he had no children."

Amy smiled. "The French certainly have talented craftsmen, m'sieur. Not only in matters of furniture and art, but in clothing. I must confess to a weakness for French fashions."

Henri laughed and agreed. "My country does have a certain flair, but it takes a beautiful woman like yourself to complement these lovely things."

Amy smiled at his extravagant compliment as a black man in formal livery entered the room with a large silver tray. He placed it on the low table between the settees. Solange spoke softly to him and he departed.

She poured steaming tea from a silver pot into dainty

china cups and offered small pastries to each of them. As they sampled the fare, two black boys entered the room quietly with large straw fans and began to stir the air around the small group.

Henri addressed Amy, who sat beside Marcus, across from him. "Are you representing your uncle in business matters on this trip, Mademoiselle Amy?"

She took a sip of her tea and then said smoothly, "Not exactly, M'sieur Henri. I was kidnapped and put on Captain Bond's ship while unconscious."

The looks on Henri's and Solange's faces were quite worth her decision to be honest. Henri sputtered and lapsed into rapid French until Marcus laughed outright at his friend. Solange's eyes were wide and questioning.

Amy took pity on them. "I must apologize. That was rude behavior on my part to give you such a shocking answer — even if it is true."

Marcus chuckled again, but admonished, "You should be ashamed, Amy."

She proceeded to tell them the story, leaving out her intimate involvement with Marcus. They were shocked and indignant at the treatment she had received.

"Those people should be punished severely for their crimes," Henri declared hotly, missing the secret look that Amy and Marcus exchanged.

Amy cleared her throat and nodded. "To be sure, they will answer for it."

Solange, more perceptive than Henri, sensed the private communication between her guests. "You must admit that Mademoiselle Amy looks wonderful after all that, even radiant. So it has not been too horrible, eh?"

Amy gave her a slow smile. "No, Solange, it has not been too horrible."

Their talk drifted back to the business of sugarcane, and Henri offered to give them a brief tour of the operation in the late afternoon. Amy accepted with enthusiasm. Solange suggested she show Amy to her room while the men continued to talk business, and Amy accepted this suggestion gratefully.

Amy stopped in the foyer to look at several large portraits that hung there. They were of aristocratic men and beautiful women. Solange noticed her interest and explained, "M'sieur Henri's parents and grandparents. That one by the library door is his older brother who died at the age of nineteen. So tragic — it was a riding accident."

"He looked very much like M'sieur Henri," Amy commented as they turned to the staircase. At the top, Solange led her down a long corridor. There were many arched doorways set into alcoves that marked the bedchambers. The walls were paneled in fine wood, and the doors, thick and heavy, were intricately carved with a barley-sugar twist design. Fine paintings hung at intervals, and small, elegant tables held porcelain vases filled with fresh flowers from the gardens.

Solange stopped at the end of the long corridor and opened the door to let her guest enter. Amy found the sitting room and the bedchamber beyond as elegant as the rest of the house. "I hope you will be comfortable here, mademoiselle," Solange said, pointing out the bell cord near the huge four-poster bed.

"Thank you, Solange. I shall be quite comfortable." She walked to the tall louvered window and felt the slight breeze that smelled faintly of impending rain. Her rooms faced the back of the house, and she could see the kitchen compound off to the right, where smoke curled up from a chimney in the smokehouse. There was a tall buttery building, and also a bakehouse. Farther away, across a rolling field, lay a small community of slave huts, set into a neat grid pattern. To her left she could see extensive stables and another large stone building, almost as impressively built as the house itself, with great arched windows trimmed in the same yellow brick and wood. Turning to Solange, she asked, "What is that large building?"

"Our slave hospital. On a plantation of this size, there is much sickness and many accidents. A doctor from Cap-François comes to visit quite often." Solange turned toward the door. "I will send up a bath for you."

As Solange departed, Amy thanked her again, then walked about the two rooms, inspecting the fine furniture and testing the softness of the bed. She wondered idly where Marcus would be placed for the night. Blushing, she realized where her thoughts were heading. Turning to her trunk, she decided not to wait for the maid to unpack. She laid out everything on the bed and chose the yellow floral taffeta to wear for the afternoon and evening.

In no time, a tub was carried in and filled with warm water. The young black girl assigned to her, Rose, brought fragrant bath salts and soap. Amy sent her away and promised to ring when she was ready to dress. She wanted to be alone for a while to relax.

Marcus had been right, she did like Henri and Solange. There was a genuine warmth about them, and they had made her feel very welcome, despite the circumstances. Being with Marcus unchaperoned was next to scandalous, but there was little chance anyone would find out. Her uncle, however, would have a fit of apoplexy if he knew she was going about the countryside alone with Marcus. Of course, there was nothing he could do about it at the moment, and she intended to enjoy herself. Never had she had so much freedom, and it felt wonderful.

Clyde, Henri's black driver, pulled the well-sprung carriage to a halt in front of a long, single-story stone building, which was one of several in the sugar-works compound. It looked like a small town to Amy as she gazed around. Henri stood up and pointed out a grinding mill, a boiling house with a tall chimney, a rum distillery, a cooperage where hogsheads were built and the building in front of them, which was the curing house for the brownish raw sugar crystals and vats of molasses. A stream ran alongside the mill and supplied the power to grind the cane and squeeze the juice.

Marcus helped her down, and they inspected each building while Henri explained the process. Black men and women scurried about, busy at their tasks, while armed overseers watched diligently. When they were walking back to the carriage, Amy asked Henri about this. He clucked his tongue and rolled his eyes. "It is because of the Maroons that we must be alert. *Mon Dieu,* but they are a problem! They stir up insurrections on all the plantations from time to time. We have to be very careful, mademoiselle, for the slaves outnumber us greatly."

"Maroons?" she repeated, not understanding the term.

He helped her into the carriage as he explained. "They are mainly runaway slaves that hide out in remote areas of the mountains, although some free mulattos live with these rebel groups. They were a menace in my grandfather's day as well."

Marcus settled next to her as Henri bade the driver to return to the house. "I've heard they communicate through their drum language and voodoo ceremonies," he said.

Henri nodded. *"Oui,* even though these pagan ceremonies are forbidden, the slaves manage to practice them under our very noses. A few years back, a voodoo priest named Mackandel conceived a plot for the slaves to poison their masters' drinking water, and it would have succeeded had it not been for an informer."

Amy shuddered delicately. "It must be awful to live under a constant threat like that."

Henri shrugged. "It is the only way of life I have ever known. Sugar is king, and without slave labor there would be no kingdom. Though I try my best to treat my slaves fairly."

Their conversation turned to other, less serious subjects for the remainder of the return trip, but Amy felt an uneasiness she hadn't had before. She could almost sense the presence of watchful eyes in the wooded areas they passed.

Dinner that night consisted of eight courses served by liveried servants in the enormous dining hall. For the sake of conversation, the four of them were seated at one end of the twenty-foot mahogany table. Hundreds of candles were lit on the crystal chandelier that hung from the center of the high ceiling. Fine china, delicate crystal and heavy polished silver graced the white linen tablecloth.

Solange looked elegant in a silk gown of royal blue with a matching turban on her regal head. She told them a little of her life as they sipped Madeira and sampled the delicious dishes that followed one after the other. "My papa owned a small indigo plantation in the south, near Port-au-Prince, and I was educated in Paris. Mama was mulatto and Papa white. In those days it was not against the law to marry someone of color." She glanced briefly at Henri, and he gave her an encouraging smile.

Henri explained. "About ten years ago, the colonial government passed some very restrictive laws concerning the free *gens de couleur*. They are forbidden to carry weapons, enter certain professions, or marry whites.

The insult was carried even further by making them sit in separate sections of the churches and theaters."

Amy grew indignant on Solange's behalf. "If these freedoms were enjoyed before, why were they taken away?"

Henri sighed. "There are many narrow-minded whites in this colony who began to fear the increasing wealth and prestige of another social class. I voted against these measures at the assembly, but alas, I am one voice."

"Several members of the assembly are married to women of color or at least have 'outside' families of color, but there are more who do not want the power of the aristos diluted," Solange said. "My father and M'sieur Henri became friends while serving on a committee, and Papa invited him to stay at our plantation several times. We fell in love, and here I am."

Henri laid his hand over hers on the table and smiled at her. "Unfortunately, I cannot marry Solange legally, but she is the wife of my heart."

Before Amy could comment that they seemed very happy despite their problem, the majordomo entered the room and announced the arrival of some visitors. Henri was starting to rise when two men walked unceremoniously into the room. A frown settled on Henri's face.

"Forgive us, Henri, for interrupting your dinner," the older of the two men said, "but we have a problem at Vaudravil. Ten of my best field hands escaped today. I wanted to find out if perhaps you were having problems as well."

Henri's brows rose. "*Non,* all is quiet. But we will speak of this in my study, gentlemen. First, let me present my guests to you. Capitan Marcus Bond and Mademoiselle Amy Hawthorne, my neighbors, Jean Claude Bonat and his son, Chandler."

The two men made the correct responses, as did Amy and Marcus, but before they turned to follow Henri from the room, Jean Claude gave Solange a disapproving look. Amy saw it and half rose from her chair in anger. Marcus placed his hand on her arm and shook his head.

Solange gave Amy a grim smile once the three were gone. "I am accustomed to the slights, Mademoiselle Amy, but thank you for caring." Giving a shrug, she dismissed the matter. "There is always a price to pay for flaunting the rules of society, but for M'sieur Henri, I will pay it."

Marcus gazed at Amy thoughtfully for a time while she commiserated with Solange. She was so beautiful, and he wanted her badly, but their situation, though different from Henri and Solange's, would be similarly unacceptable in the elite circles in which Amy traveled. By taking her as his wife, he would be placing her in the position of having to defend her choice at every turn. The gossips would sneer over the fact that he was an adventurer in pursuit of her fortune. He nearly cringed when he thought of the problems they faced.

"I wish you were going with us, Solange," Amy said to her hostess, picking up her fan and drawstring purse from the bed. She was referring to the governor's ball at which Henri had asked them to be his guests. It was to be the last social function at the governor's palace in Cap-François, for the capital was being moved to Port-au-Prince in the next few weeks. Her clothes were packed once more in the trunk and already loaded atop the carriage that would take them back to the city.

"So do I, *chérie,* but you know why I cannot. I expect you to have a wonderful time at the ball and write to me about it. In that way, I can be there," Solange said with a smile.

Amy hugged her and promised she would. "Henri doesn't want to go without you, you know. When you weren't watching today, he looked quite miserable."

Solange laughed, her dark eyes twinkling. "I know, *chérie*. He thinks to fool me with a brave front, but we women are very perceptive, eh?"

"Very," Amy agreed, returning the smile in spite of her sadness at leaving Maison de Fleur. "I always know when something is bothering Marcus."

Solange picked up Amy's shawl and draped it around her shoulders. "There now, the only thing that will bother M'sieur Capitan tonight is the attention you will receive from all the men at the ball. That red dress is ravishing on you."

Amy pulled a face. "A little competition might do him some good. He's much too sure of himself."

Solange laughed and walked with her guest out of the bedroom and down the corridor. The men were waiting below in the drawing room, dressed in evening clothes and looking very handsome. Marcus's eyes swept over her approvingly as he came forward to claim her hand. "You are full of surprises, my love," he whispered, lifting her hand to kiss the tender skin of her wrist.

It sent delicious shivers through her, and she smiled into his warm gray eyes. "That was my intention," she said.

"I'm wondering how I will be able to keep you to myself this evening." He arched an eyebrow in mock seriousness.

Henri walked up with a glass of Madeira for Amy. "I am afraid that won't be possible, my friend," he teased.

They finished their drinks, and Marcus and Amy took their final farewells of Solange and then left the couple alone for a few moments.

They were leaving for town early so as to travel while the light lasted. It was not as safe to move about the countryside after dark without an armed escort. Amy felt relieved to see the sun was still high, for the stories of attacks by Maroon rebels left her nervous.

When they were on their way, Henri's mood became somber. "If I were not required to attend a meeting of my committee, I would not go to the ball where my Solange is not welcome. However, when one participates in government, there are obligations, eh?"

Amy gave him a sympathetic look. "I'm sorry, Henri. I like Solange very much and wish things could be different for the two of you."

He gave her a grateful smile. "You are very kind, chérie, but I knew what I was getting into when I brought her home with me under the guise of a housekeeper. But *mon Dieu,* sometimes it rankles!"

"It was thoughtful of you to invite us to the ball," Marcus put in, deftly steering the subject away from Henri's problem.

Mercurial of mood, Henri smiled broadly. "I must confess, it was Solange's idea. She said Mademoiselle Amy would find it quite amusing."

"I am looking forward to it, if for no other reason than as an excuse to wear my new dress," she said.

It wasn't long before they left the countryside behind and reached the more populated area surrounding the city. Their driver maneuvered the large carriage with ease along the wide boulevards where stately mansions, cathedrals and ornate theaters vied for attention with their elegant charm. The governor's palace was set back from the street with a high stone wall surrounding the property. An armed group of soldiers in formal uniform stopped each carriage at the large gates to check the occupants against their list of guests. Henri was recognized at once, and he informed them of his unexpected guests. They passed through without a problem. At a question from Amy, Henri replied as they drove down the wide driveway. "There are always many guards at these functions, Mademoiselle Amy. The governor is an important man."

The sun had dropped below the horizon, but it was not quite dark yet, so Amy was able to enjoy the extensive flower gardens that graced both sides of the drive. When the stately mansion appeared, she was impressed by its size and grandeur. There were several carriages in front of them, and still more behind. As each one pulled to a stop in front of the wide stone steps, liveried footmen came forward to help the guests to alight.

Large torches lit the front of the limestone mansion and the grounds. Amy could see the parade of elegantly dressed ladies and gentlemen as Henri's carriage stopped. They stepped down, and Henri gave instructions to his driver. "Deliver their trunks to the wharf and see that they're transported out to the *Rebecca,* Clyde. And then return here to wait for us." Reaching into his waistcoat pocket, he took out a slip of paper. "Here is a written pass for you so there will be no problems." He handed the paper to the black man and turned to his guests. "It is not safe for a slave to travel about, especially at night, without permission."

The three of them ascended the steps to the open double doors at the top.

Many people had stopped inside the well-lit foyer to chat while others moved on into the grand ballroom to the right. Prince De Rohan, the governor, his wife and several members of the Assembly were receiving each guest cordially.

The musicians were playing softly as small groups of people talked and moved about. A royal ball in Paris could not have been more elaborate, Amy thought, as she took in the sight. Lavish jewels — diamonds, emeralds and rubies — adorned the throats and ears of most of the ladies present, and the men sported rings and pins with huge stones. Even the glitter of gold and silver threads was shot through some of the dresses and embroidered on men's stockings. It was a dazzling and somewhat excessive display of wealth.

Henri introduced them to several people and escorted them to another room where food tables were set up. "I apologize for leaving you, but I must meet with my committee. *S'il vous plaît,* enjoy yourselves."

They assured him they would be fine, and when he departed, they helped themselves to some of the rich foods provided. Finding a small table for two in an alcove, they sat down, and Marcus fed her bites from his plate, insisting she try some of the more exotic fare.

Amy found his attentions erotic and licked his fingers after each bite while staring deeply into his gray eyes. Her pulse raced disturbingly as she felt his hard thigh pressing against her own. "I'm suddenly very . . . hungry," she breathed in a husky voice.

His gaze fell to the creamy skin of her breasts, which rose above the red dress, and his heart began to pound a little harder. "So am I, my love. And if we weren't in the midst of a crowd, I would do something about it." He caught her hand and pulled her closer, his mouth descending to capture hers. It was a deep, drugging kiss.

The raucous sounds of laughter nearby broke them apart abruptly. They were secluded, but not invisible. Marcus gave her a devilish smile. "That was rather fortunate, for I had just about forgotten where we are."

"Perhaps we should return to the ballroom," she suggested with a twinkle in her eyes.

He sighed and rose to his feet. "It won't be as interesting, but it will be safer. And I must speak to Henri after his meeting about our sugar shipment."

Despite the many attractive ladies present at the ball,

Amy received more than her share of admiring looks. She little noticed this, though, for her attention was centered on Marcus. They danced a cotillion and a jig before stopping to have another glass of champagne. Marcus found her a seat and went in search of a servant with a full tray.

There was a becoming flush to Amy's cheeks as she fanned herself and watched a cotillion in progress. A large portion of the male guests were French officers, but she spotted a few English ones as well. One particular gentleman caught her attention as he moved into her range of vision. He wore the uniform of King George's navy, and although his back was to her, there was something familiar about his stance and mannerisms. When he turned, Amy gave a gasp and tried to hide behind her fan, but it was too late — he had seen and recognized her. It was Edward Simpson.

Chapter Sixteen

Edward's startled expression would have been amusing if Amy hadn't been so dismayed. He stumbled against his partner before he gathered himself to continue the dance. Frantically, Amy looked around for Marcus, and when she could not find him, she rose and hastily made her way to an exit. Finding herself on a covered terrace, she clung to the balustrade and let a welcome breeze cool her flushed cheeks.

What was she to do now? Edward moved in the same social circles she did, and her reputation would be in ruins if he found out she was in St.-Domingue alone with Marcus. Even if the situation was explained to him, she knew he would not believe her. What had seemed unimportant to her before suddenly took on new proportions. She realized it mattered to her what her friends at home in Boston thought. Chewing nervously at her thumbnail, she tried to think of a plausible story to tell him — that is, if she could not avoid him altogether.

Before that thought had left her mind, a voice at her elbow startled a cry from her. "My dear Amy! I simply couldn't believe my eyes. What are you doing in St.-Domingue?" Edward said, grasping her hand. He carried it to his lips and left a wet kiss there before she could yank it away.

"Why, Edward, I'm surprised to see you as well," she gasped. Smiling brightly, she asked, "Is your ship still on patrol?" Ask him about himself or his affairs and the foppish baboon would talk all night, she reminded herself.

"Oh, yes. Just yesterday, we routed a Spanish privateer that had been preying on decent shipowners like your esteemed uncle. Gave us a devil of a fight, but we boarded her with only two lives lost. However, she did some damage to our port bow and one of our best cannon. We stopped here to make repairs."

As he talked, his chest puffed out perceptively, and Amy had to hide a smile. Taking his arm, her eyes widened as she said, "How very dangerous it sounds! Would you be a dear, Edward, and get a glass of champagne for me? It was growing so warm in that crowded room, and I'm very thirsty."

He looked down on her with an adoring expression and nodded. "Of course, my dear. Why don't we step inside and—"

"Please, Edward, do bring it out here. I'll just sit on this bench in the fresh air and fan myself," she pleaded with a slight pout.

He seemed torn for a moment. "Well, if you wish, but I hate to leave you alone out here. Is your uncle—"

Amy cut him off with a frown. "Don't be a ninny. I'm perfectly capable of taking care of myself, for heaven's sake. After all, this is the governor's palace, and there are soldiers everywhere."

He hurried to keep up with her as she made for the bench. "If you're sure, I'll be right back," he agreed, not wanting to incur her displeasure.

Amy watched him disappear through the open French doors and expelled a deep breath. She absolutely had to find Marcus and get away from here, for if Edward returned and found her, he would eventually want to know why she was on St.-Domingue and whom she was with.

Rising, she gathered her skirts and raced along the terrace, looking for another door through which she could enter the mansion. She finally saw a light coming from a room that had another set of French doors, and she tried the handle. It was not locked, and, without thinking, she swept inside. Seated around a rectangular table were several gentlemen in the midst of a discussion. Henri was one of them, and he rose to his feet with a questioning look as the group stopped speaking. "Mademoiselle Amy . . . is something the matter?"

Amy came to an abrupt halt, looking faintly flustered. "Oh, Henri, please forgive this intrusion. I became separated from Captain Bond and was looking for him." She advanced to the door on the other side of the room and turned to smile sweetly. "Gentlemen, I'll leave you to your meeting and find my way back to the ballroom." With that, she let herself out into a corridor. There were two soldiers standing guard at the doorway, and she requested directions. They eyed her with admiration and interest, interrupting each other to give her the information she needed.

She thanked them and, with a coquettish flutter of her dark eyelashes, made her way down the well-lit corridor to a door that led into the spacious foyer. As she was moving through the crowd, looking for Marcus, she received several invitations to dance. Declining each politely, she finally reached the ballroom. Keeping close to the wall, she found a small alcove and stepped back into it so that she might scan the room without being noticed. She saw Edward once, his gaze darting about as he circulated. Amy flattened herself against the wall in the shadows and cursed her ill luck. Of all the islands scattered about the Caribbean, why did the *Beaver* have to stop here? And where was Marcus? The object of her thoughts came into view that moment, when she chanced a peek around the wall. He was coming toward her alcove with a beautiful brunette on his arm. Something the woman was saying to him made him throw back his head and laugh.

Amy's eyes narrowed as she watched them together, and a sharp jab of jealousy caused her to grip her delicate fan until it snapped. Glancing down in surprise at the broken object in her hands, she dropped it onto a chair and stepped out of her hiding place.

"Oh, Marcus *chérie,* it's been much too long since you've visited us," the brunette said, clinging to Marcus possessively. "Papa would say the same thing if he was here tonight. You should think about staying another week, *s'il vous plaît.*"

"Not this trip, Tempest. I must return to Bermuda shortly —" He stopped abruptly as he came face to face with an irate Amy. "Amy! I've been looking for you."

"Yes. I can see how frantic you are," Amy said, one thin brow lifting.

Marcus belatedly realized how this must look to her, and he gently disengaged his arm. "Tempest Galliard, meet Mistress Amy Hawthorne."

Amy nodded politely to the woman, but her eyes were frosty. "If you are finished with your conversation, I wish to leave."

Mademoiselle Galliard glanced from Marcus to Amy with gentle amusement. "Forgive me for delaying Marcus, Mistress Hawthorne, but we ran into each other while he was searching for you. We simply had to catch up, no?"

Amy gave her a thin-lipped smile. "Of course, but if you will excuse us now?"

Marcus bid his friend farewell and asked to be remembered to her father. Taking Amy's arm, he turned toward the foyer and missed the sympathetic look Mademoiselle Galliard bestowed on him.

"Hurry up, Marcus. We must leave immediately," she hissed as she tried to pull him a bit faster.

"You were very rude to Tempest . . . and just where were you?" Marcus said, digging in his heels and refusing to go any farther. "I was beginning to get worried. And why are we in such a hurry? You know I must speak to Henri before I leave," he chided.

Amy's temper flared in the face of his chastisement, especially after finding him with another woman. "I'll explain later. For now, let's go. Henri is still in his meeting, so just leave him a note," she said testily.

Finally, the urgency in her tone communicated itself to him. He began moving through the crowd, pulling her after him. "All right, Amy, but I want an explanation, and soon."

At a reception desk beside the front doors, Marcus stopped and found paper and an inkwell. He quickly composed a note, folded it and sealed it with some hot wax from a candle that burned on the desk. Handing it to a liveried servant, he instructed him to give it to M'sieur Joubert. Amy had been chewing at her thumbnail and glancing furtively around while he was at his task. "Ready?" he asked finally.

She nodded and they departed. Henri's driver had returned, and he drove them to the wharf. Marcus hired a mulatto with a small boat to transport them to the *Rebecca*. From the palace to the ship, Amy refused Marcus's pleas to explain her abrupt behavior. She sat thinking over the whole situation and realized how Marcus would react if she told him about Edward. It would be one more argument for him to make against their relationship. Even her anger at seeing Marcus with the beautiful Tempest could not override her fear of losing him. That was it! Let him think she was angry over that woman, she thought. It would serve him right if she sulked for days, and maybe she could figure a way out of their dilemma.

Very early the following morning, Marcus and Toby Oakes ordered a launch to go ashore. The first mate had informed Marcus that he'd seen Stafford's Captain Aiken at a tavern on the docks the day before. The man was well into his cups and crying to anyone who would listen that he was sorry for the terrible deed he'd done and he deserved to die. And, Toby said, the man was ranting on about how Harlan Stafford's greed was the reason he'd been driven to such a horrible act.

"What do ye make of it, lad?" Toby asked as they reached the wharf.

"I'm not sure, but it could be the information I've been looking for," Marcus said grimly. Toby knew that Marcus was set on avenging some wrong done to his family by Harlan Stafford, but he did not know the nature of that wrong. Marcus had not trusted that information to anyone.

They made their way to Cormac's Tavern while dockworkers silently went about their early morning chores. The small establishment was located two streets above the harbor, and when they entered, the dim interior was quiet save for a black boy sweeping the floor. He looked up at the two men and said, "De place be closed."

"Where's the owner—Mr. Cormac? Does he live upstairs?" Marcus asked, digging a coin from his vest pocket.

The boy's eyes livened up at the sight of the money, and he nodded his head. *"Oui,* m'sieur. He be sleepin'."

When Marcus tossed the coin, the boy caught it neatly and put it in his pocket. He looked pointedly at the stairs and mumbled, "First door at de top." Quietly, he went back to his chore.

Marcus and Toby climbed the steps and knocked at the door. Marcus took the grunting sound on the other side as permission to enter.

The man on the bed had a shock of red hair and an equally red face. He was supporting his weight on one elbow as he looked at the strangers with bleary eyes. "And what would ya be wantin' in the middle of the night, gents?"

"We're sorry to wake you, Mr. Cormac, but it's important that we speak with you. I have some questions about a Captain Aiken," Marcus said, watching the man's reaction to the name.

Jaime Cormac yawned then and sat up rubbing his chin. He pulled a gun from under the cover and laid it on the bedside table. "I know the man, but why should I tell you anything now?"

"Because it's important . . . and I'll pay for the information if need be," Marcus said in a level tone.

Jaime nodded. "We'll talk downstairs. Go on down and tell the boy to get some coffee. I'll be down in a bit."

Marcus had no idea whether he could trust the Irishman or not. The man's expression had given nothing away. But after a while, the tavern owner came downstairs, face washed and hair combed, and sat at the table with Marcus and Toby. The black boy brought him a cup of coffee and asked if he should fetch breakfast from the boardinghouse down the street.

"No, me stomach's still full of last night's rum. Go on about yer business," he said with a sour smile. Looking Marcus directly in the eye, he asked, "Now, who are ya and what do ya want to know about Aiken?"

Marcus introduced himself and Toby and also mentioned he knew Megan and Patrick.

Jaime's eyes brightened. "Me own brother's children! How are they faring? I've not seen 'em for five years now."

Marcus decided that a bit of leverage wouldn't hurt. "They were fine when I left a few weeks ago, but they're going to be in a little trouble when I return. You see, they kidnapped a wealthy young lady and stowed her on my ship unconscious."

Jaime's eyes grew big. "You don't say! And just why would they be doin' somethin' like that?"

Marcus shrugged. "I have a good idea, but it's just a theory. However, the young lady in question is very angry and doesn't care why they did it."

Jaime chewed at his lower lip for a moment and toyed with his coffee cup. "The girl's not hurt, is she?"

Marcus shook his head. "Just her pride."

"Would ya be havin' some influence with this colleen, Captain Bond?"

It was what he'd hoped for. "I might, if there was some incentive."

Jaime sighed. "Captain Aiken has been in here for the past three days drinkin' himself into a stupor. I did talk to him one night about his problems, and he told me a hair-raisin' tale I thought never to repeat. At first I thought it too freakish to be true, but I've never known the man to be a liar. And after I thought about it, I decided no man would tell somethin' that damning if it wasn't the truth."

Marcus and Toby quietly listened as Jaime repeated the story told to him by Captain Aiken. The Irishman finished with, "And Aiken swears he would not have done the deed except for the fact that Stafford has been drivin' him of late to bring in more booty."

Toby whistled between his teeth and glanced at Marcus's grim expression. "The man is a spineless murderer," Toby declared.

"Where can we find Captain Aiken?" Marcus asked.

Jaime rubbed his chin a moment. "Well, gents, if I tell ya, I want yer word ya won't be tellin' him where ya heard this tale."

"We'll keep your name out of it," Marcus promised as he rose.

"He's stayin' at Madam Facone's boardin'house, down the street."

Toby followed Marcus to the door, but they stopped when Jaime spoke. "You will be rememberin' to speak to yer lady friend about me niece and nephew, won't ya?"

"Aye, I'll see what I can do," Marcus said as they let themselves out.

That afternoon, Marcus stood on the quarterdeck and watched as the last of the sugar was loaded and stored in the main hold. He had not been able to find Captain Aiken that morning. A trip to the boarding-house proved fruitless, for the man was not in his room. His bed had not been slept in, and the woman who ran the establishment could shed no light on his where-abouts. Marcus was frustrated, but he consoled himself with the valuable secondhand news he'd received from Cormac.

His eye fell on Amy as she stood at the rail, staring across the harbor. She had been pointedly ignoring him since their argument the night before. After they'd re-turned to the ship, he'd confronted her about her actions at the ball, and she'd finally told him that seeing him with Tempest had made her angry. Somehow, her excuse hadn't rung true, but he could think of nothing else to explain her strange behavior.

When Marcus gave the order to set sail, he watched as Amy went below. She hadn't given him so much as a glance. He sighed and decided to give her some time to cool off. Later in the day, he went in search of her and found her in the galley with Mr. Hadley. There was a huge apron tied around her middle, and she was pounding a lump of dough with her small fists. A dusting of flour covered her face.

"I thought you might like another lesson in navigation, but I can see you're busy," he said, standing in the doorway.

Amy looked up and smiled, her anger forgotten. "Mr. Hadley is teaching me to make bread. If I'd known what fun it is to cook, I'd have been in the kitchen with Mistress Pierce long ago."

The burly cook merely grunted and continued stirring his pot on the stove. Marcus leaned a shoulder against the door frame and grinned. "This domestic side of yours is a real surprise, Mistress Hawthorne. I thought you wanted to command ships and quote law in the Assembly."

"And why can't I do it all?" she retorted briskly. "Besides, you never know when the art of cooking might be useful."

Marcus felt a cold lump form in his stomach. He knew what she meant, and it was distasteful to him. If she gave up her fortune and married him, there would be no servants to do the daily chores. He loved her and wanted her more than life itself, but how could he wrench her away from the life she'd always known?

His expression darkened. "I'll be on the quarterdeck if you finish before dinner," he said, abruptly leaving the room.

Amy felt more than his physical withdrawal and sighed. She couldn't understand why her wealth had to be such a problem. His damnable pride was going to ruin everything between them, she realized, even if she gave up her fortune. She had three weeks at best to make him see what was important. After that, they would be back in the Bermudas.

The days sped by as if pushed by the same brisk wind

that filled their sails. Marcus and Amy loved each other with fierce abandon every night and tried vainly every day to hide their dread at what was to come. They did not speak of it, but it loomed like a malignant growth between them.

Finally, the night before they were to reach Castle Harbor, they lay in bed, sated from lovemaking, and gazed at the full moon out the windows of his cabin. He kissed her tenderly and raised himself on one elbow to look at her. "I've thought about our situation until my head is near to bursting."

A small knot of fear formed in her stomach, but she gazed lovingly up at him and stroked his cheek with her hand. "What is there to think about, my love? We shall spend the rest of our lives together."

"Shall we do it on my pauper's wages or with the Hawthorne wealth? Truly, Amy, I cannot ask the one of you, nor can I as a proud man stomach the other. Henri and Solange are good examples of what happens when one flaunts the dictates of society. There must be a payment of some kind, and I don't want you to have to pay that price."

Amy rose to a sitting position and pushed her mass of loose hair back in agitation. "So what is the answer, my proud Captain Bond?" she asked with sarcasm borne of a deep hurt. "You go your way, holding onto your useless pride, and I marry Justin Stafford, who is most probably interested in my money? That will solve the problem, won't it? Then there will be three lives ruined — no, four, if we count Megan Cormac, who loves Justin enough to risk prison. Yes, I think that is the perfect solution!"

Marcus sat up and grasped her arms. "You don't understand — you don't know the whole story," he said, his voice pleading yet harsh. "If you knew, you would not want me — take my word for it. There is something I have to do for my mother and myself, and until it is done, I am not fit for anyone."

Amy's hopes and dreams of the last few weeks died quietly with his words. She almost hated him at this moment, for he'd given her reason to believe that everything would work out, and now there was nothing. She shouldn't have trusted him, would not ever trust him again.

Pulling away from his grasp, she got out of bed and slipped on her satin robe. Belting it, she looked at him and said calmly, "I really am sorry we met, Marcus. I thought I knew you, but obviously I didn't. However, I want to thank you, for I was a romantic dreamer before, but now I realize how silly I was. It could have been worse, I could have fallen in love with a blackguard adventurer instead of a coldhearted bastard with principles." She turned and left his cabin, head held high. It wasn't until she reached her own cabin and bolted the door that she cried as though her heart would break.

On the heels of the rising sun, the *Rebecca* entered Castle Harbor through the narrow channel without a problem. Amy had been awake and ready to disembark for hours. In fact, she had slept very little and had finally arisen to dress. The beautiful clothes Marcus had bought for her were hanging in the wardrobe as she dressed in her own green dress. She would see that he received payment, but did not want any reminders of him. Carefully, she folded Jeremy's shirt and breeches to return to him. Her brief adventure was over, and she did not intend to look back once she stepped ashore.

They dropped anchor inside Stafford's private cove, and a launch was lowered almost immediately. Amy made her way topside and spoke briefly with Toby Oakes before she let Jeremy help her down into the launch. Halfway across the small expanse of water, Amy glanced back at the ship and saw Marcus standing at the rail. She turned her head and missed the small salute he gave her.

At the wharf, she thanked Jeremy for all the kindnesses he'd shown her, and accepted his help getting out of the boat. He ordered a workman there to fetch a carriage for Amy and then, with a final farewell, climbed back into the boat and returned to the ship.

When Amy arrived at Stafford House, she expected a tearful welcome from her uncle. Marcus had sent news of her safety back to Bermuda by a ship captain he'd sought out when they'd arrived at Cap-François. That captain had sailed the day they arrived, so Amy was sure the news had reached them by now. However, when she entered the foyer unannounced, Julia was coming down the stairs and gave her a look of disdain. "So you're back. I'm surprised you'd show your face here, young woman, after what you've done."

Amy stared aghast at her for a moment. "What I've done? I beg your pardon, Julia, but what is it I'm supposed to have done?"

"Running off with that sea captain, you shameless harlot. And your betrothal to Justin not a week old! Why, your poor uncle went into a decline, and he's near death," the older woman said coldly.

Amy's angry retort froze on her lips as she realized the implications of Julia's last statement. "Uncle Thad? What is it — he's not! You're a hateful old woman to make up such a horrible thing." Still, Amy felt the cold hand of fear clutch at her heart. She started up the stairs and pushed past Julia. "I'll see for myself," she said angrily, but the fear had crept into her voice.

She hurried to her uncle's room and opened the door. It was dim inside because the heavy curtains were pulled on the windows. Fiona sat quietly beside the bed, and

Amy could make out a shape under the covers. When she closed the door, Fiona looked up and, seeing Amy, jumped to her feet. She met Amy halfway across the room, her brow knit with worry.

"Uncle Thad—what is it, Fiona?" Amy asked, gripping the other girl's hands in her own.

"Thank God, you're back! He has a fever—some sort of tropical malaise, the doctor says," Fiona whispered as tears pooled in her eyes. "He's been unconscious for two weeks . . . I just don't know what to do." The desperation in Fiona's voice caused Amy's heartbeat to quicken. If levelheaded Fiona was that worried, it had to be serious.

"There has to be something!" Amy said with more assurance than she felt. She let go of Fiona's hands and made her way to the bed. Leaning over the quiet form of her uncle, she was shocked at how gaunt he was. There were two bright spots of unnatural color staining his cheeks, and his thick hair was damp and plastered to his head. Amy lifted his limp hand, noticing how warm it felt. "What is the doctor doing for him?" she asked anxiously.

Fiona moved to her side and shook her head. "We feed him spoonfuls of water and broth, and the doctor has left some noxious medicine we give to him twice a day. For now, he's resting comfortably, but sometimes he thrashes about in delirium. That's how Layla found him that first morning."

Amy smoothed the hair back from his brow tenderly, as tears pooled in her eyes. "Oh, Uncle Thad, it's Amy. I'm back now, and you're going to get well . . . please try," she pleaded, her voice starting to break.

Ivy entered the room quietly and stopped beside Amy. "Massa Stafford says he wants speak with you. Missy Julia, she tells him you home." The black girl touched Amy on the arm. "I's happy you back, missy."

Amy turned to the girl and patted her hand. "Thank you, Ivy. Is it Master Harlan or Justin?"

"Massa Harlan, and he be in de bookroom," the girl said.

"I do want to speak with him, Fiona, but I'll be back as soon as I can," Amy told her companion as she followed Ivy to the door.

When Amy entered the bookroom, Harlan was standing beside the French doors. He crossed the room and took her in his arms. "My dear Amy! I'm so glad to have you back and so sorry your return is marred by Thaddeus's illness." He led her to the settee and seated himself beside her.

His reception was so different from his sister's that Amy was surprised. "Julia seems to think I went off of my own free will, but that is far from the truth," she said.

He shook his head. "Don't pay any attention to her. She's overly protective of my children and has imagined a terrible slight to Justin. I, on the other hand, felt there was more to your disappearance than that, and when you're up to it, I would like to hear what did happen. All we knew was that you were safe, because Captain Bond sent word of that, but nothing else." He took her hand comfortingly. "By then, though, your uncle had fallen ill, and we could not even tell him you were all right."

"I appreciate the fact that you did not condemn me without knowing the facts. But my main concern now is Uncle Thad. What is the nature of this fever? Is it common?"

His dark eyebrows slanted in a frown. "I don't wish to alarm you, but the doctor has done all he can for the fever. He has also said the effects of it are taking a great toll on Thaddeus's heart. I thought you should know."

Her earlier fear returned to envelop her at his damning words. Her mind, however, refused to believe that something could happen to her uncle. He was all she had in the world, and she loved him dearly. "What would I do without him?" she breathed, not realizing she spoke aloud.

Harlan took one of her hands in both of his. "I truly hope it doesn't come to that, but, my dear Amy, I pray you would lean upon me as an uncle of sorts. Thaddeus would want you to, you know. He has even made provisions in his will, naming me as your guardian in the unhappy event of his death."

For a moment Amy stared at him, trying to assimilate this information, while in the back of her mind, a small voice was reminding her of what Marcus had said about Harlan. If Uncle Thad died, Harlan would have control of her fortune as well as her life. If he were indeed the devious person Marcus believed him to be, she would be in a very precarious position. But she couldn't worry about that now, she thought with agitation. Uncle Thad's recovery was her main concern, and she would see to it that he had the best of care. Pulling her hand back, she gave him a strained smile. "Thank you, Harlan, but I know Uncle Thad will get better." She rose to her feet. "I must get back to him, if you'll excuse me."

He stood up beside her and laid a hand on her arm to detain her a moment. "One more thing, Amy. Thaddeus wanted very much for you to marry Justin, so I believe the wedding should take place as soon as possible."

Her mood veered sharply to anger as she replied through stiff lips. "There will be plenty of time for that when Uncle Thad is up and about. I would like him to be at the ceremony."

Harlan smiled and released her. "Of course, my dear. We'll discuss it later."

Amy fumed all the way back to her uncle's room. She didn't like being pushed by Harlan, and thought it very insensitive of him to suggest such a thing while Uncle

Thad lay so ill. Amy sent Fiona to her room to rest and took her place beside the bed. Periodically, she bathed his face and hands and spooned some water into his mouth. His breathing was so shallow that at times she placed her ear on his chest to listen for a heartbeat.

Just before noon, Pamela came into the room. "Oh, Amy! I'm happy you're back and safe. I was so worried about you," she said with tears in her eyes.

Amy rose and gave the girl a hug. "Don't cry, Pamela. I'm fine, as you can see. It's my uncle I'm worried about."

Pamela stepped back and dabbed at her eyes with her handkerchief. "I know — we've all been worried. The poor dear man. One day he was fine, and the next . . ." Her words trailed away as she shook her head. "When I was in town this morning, Reverend Jacobs told me there were a few cases of this fever among some people who arrived on a ship from South Carolina a few weeks ago. Some have recovered," she offered hopefully.

Amy turned back to the bed and straightened the covers with trembling hands. Her small chin rose a fraction as she said, "And Uncle Thad will also, Pamela. He'll be fine now that I'm back to nurse him."

Pamela felt a painful lump in her throat at Amy's show of bravado. She slipped her arm around Amy's shoulders. "Of course he will, dear, and I'll help in any way I can."

Pamela went off to fetch a cup of tea for her, and Amy sat down and began to talk to her uncle. She talked of her childhood and the happy times they'd had together. She urged him more than once to wake up, promising a bright future for them both if only he would open his eyes.

Instead of going to her bedchamber, Fiona made her

way to the bookroom and slipped in quietly, shutting the door behind her. Harlan stood looking out the French doors and turned when he heard the lock click. He gave her a slow smile as she glided across the room and into his arms. He took her mouth with savage intensity, and Fiona responded fiercely. She clawed at his back with her fingernails and ground her breasts against his hard chest until she felt her sensitive nipples swell.

Feverishly, he slid one hand between them and unlaced the front of her dress. Filling his hand with one soft breast, he teased the hard nipple and kneaded her flesh. Breaking the kiss, his voice held a rasp of excitement. "You're a hot-blooded wench, Fiona, and I'm going to give you what you want."

She gave him a challenging look. "The midday meal will be ready at any moment."

He pulled her over to the red velvet settee and pushed her down on it with a gleam in his eye. "This won't take long, my dear." With a swift movement, he yanked her skirts up around her waist and unbuttoned the flap on his breeches. Taking his swollen member in one hand, he moved between her legs and guided it in.

Fiona gasped and closed her eyes as he lifted her hips and drove into her again and again. Gusts of desire shook her as a low moan slipped through her lips and they were hurtled beyond the point of return. When their tremors ceased, he rose without a word to straighten his clothes. Fiona lay there watching him with more longing in her eyes than she realized.

He grinned rakishly. "Don't tempt me to do more, wench."

She smiled languidly. "When we get married, we won't have to steal moments like this. We can stay in bed all day doing delicious things to each other."

His eyes narrowed briefly before he turned to shuffle

311

some papers on his desk. "You don't have to remind me of my promise."

Fiona rose and smoothed her skirts back into place. "I know that, darling. We're two of a kind, you and I. I knew it from the moment I laid eyes on you. And when I found out how important Amy's money was to you, well, I realized that with my influence with Thaddeus, you and I could both get what we want." She came up behind him and put her arms around his waist, laying her head on his back.

He absently stroked the soft skin on her hand. "Getting Thaddeus to name me as Amy's guardian after she disappeared really was a stroke of brilliance, my dear. Especially now that he's near death." His lips curved over his good fortune. "How convenient for us that he contracted that fever. It saved me the trouble of planning his demise."

She rubbed against him suggestively. "I had a feeling that Amy was not going to cooperate with the marriage plans, and although I didn't know where she'd gone, I knew she'd turn up again. And Thaddeus was so easy to manipulate, it was hardly any work at all. I merely told him that Amy had hinted that she would run away rather than marry Justin. So my suggestion about the changes in his will landed on fertile ground. I can hardly wait to see the look on her face when you tell her she must marry Justin whether she wants to or not."

Harlan chuckled. "That fiery temper of hers will surface, no doubt."

The tall clock in the room began to strike the noon hour, and Fiona sighed, letting go of him. "Tell me you want to marry me, and not just because it was part of the deal we struck," she said, a note of doubt creeping into the question.

He turned to look into her large brown eyes. "Fiona my love, it's tiresome to keep reassuring you on the mat-

312

ter. However, I will tell you that I cannot be forced into anything I do not truly want, so . . ." The implication of his words had the desired effect on her, and she nodded happily.

"Just so I know you really want me. I wasn't sure before," she said, the uncertainty clearing in her expression. Walking toward the door, she said lightly, "I'd better go before one of the servants finds us together behind a locked door. We wouldn't want them to start gossiping before we announce our wedding plans."

Harlan's eyes were cold and distant as they bored into her back. If she had turned and read his thoughts, she would have been surprised and a little frightened.

Amy sat patiently beside the sickbed through the afternoon, occasionally talking to her uncle as if he could hear. She spoon-fed broth and water to him and wiped his fevered brow. The doctor came and went, shaking his head when Amy asked his opinion on the patient's status. It was depressing, and Amy could not hold back a few tears after he left. Justin found her thus and took her in his arms.

"Go ahead and weep, dear Amy," he urged. "It will make you feel better."

For a time she did just that, but she finally pulled out of his embrace and accepted his handkerchief. "I can't believe this is happening, Justin," she said with a catch in her voice. "He always seemed young and strong . . ."

Justin took her hand and led her out onto the terrace. The sun was setting, and the breeze had grown cooler. They stood at the balustrade and looked out over the wide lawns at the back of the house. "It is not over yet. The fever could break anytime, and—"

"Or he could die anytime," she cut in, her voice thick with more tears.

"You must not think that way," he admonished, tipping her chin up with his finger to look into her eyes. "If it's any consolation, the doctor told me yesterday that he could wake up at any moment." He neglected to tell her that the man had said it could go the other way as well.

Amy looked hopeful. "But your father said Uncle Thad's heart was weakening."

Justin frowned. "Perhaps father has not spoken to the doctor in the last day or so," he suggested. Her look of relief made him glad. "Anyway, come back inside and we'll talk while we sit with him. You can tell me where you've been these last weeks. I was worried, you know. And I have some things to tell you also." He took her arm and led her back into the room. Pulling up another chair beside the bed, he sat down beside her.

She told him exactly what had happened, and for a few minutes he looked stunned. "Megan did that? And Patrick?" He groaned and dropped his head in his hands. "Oh, Amy . . . I'm sorry."

She touched his bent shoulder. "Why don't you tell me everything now, Justin. You should have before, and perhaps this whole thing could have been avoided. You didn't really want to marry me, did you?"

He straightened and looked at her miserably. "Forgive me, Amy, but no, I didn't." He told her how Harlan had coerced him into proposing. He also told her how he felt about Megan. "And after you disappeared, Megan told me she's pregnant. We got married secretly a few days later. I couldn't let her face that alone, and I do love her. I'm sorry."

Amy gave him a wan smile. "Don't apologize for doing the right thing, Justin. I respect you for that. However, you could have trusted me with the truth from the beginning. But I understand your concern for Pamela and Julia."

"I felt I was betraying our friendship the whole time," he confessed miserably. "And now I have no right to that friendship."

"Nonsense. I will decide when you may stop being my friend," she said with some of her old spirit. "And I will keep your secret. A solution to your problem will present itself soon, I'm sure."

He leaned over and kissed her cheek. "If I did not love Megan so much, you would be my choice above any I could name."

They talked in quiet tones for a time, and then he rose to leave. "I fear I shall have to take Megan and Patrick to task for what they've done," he said solemnly.

She gave him a brief smile. "Don't be too hard on them. I came to no real harm, and I better understand her plight now."

He nodded and left the room. Shortly after, Pamela entered with a tray of food. She sat with Amy for a long while, but Amy could not eat. Fiona came later and took Pamela's place, but Thaddeus's condition did not change.

Harlan stopped in after dinner, urging Amy to seek her own bed for some much needed rest, but she refused. Hour after hour, she sat there willing her uncle to get better. Sometime after the clock struck midnight, she fell asleep in the chair, dozing fitfully.

A strange choking sound brought her awake with a start, and she realized it was coming from the bed. She jumped to her feet and bent over her uncle. His face was mottled, and a low constricted rattle came from his throat.

"My God . . . Uncle Thad . . . please don't—" she gasped, gripping his hand.

Amy was hardly aware that Ivy had materialized from the deep shadows of the room. "Missy! Missy . . . is he—?" the black girl asked frantically,

315

grabbing Amy's arm.

Amy shook her off and cried, "Go get Master Justin—now!"

By the time Justin arrived, however, it was too late. Thaddeus had died before her eyes, and Amy still held tightly to his hand, staring at his face in shock.

Someone put her to bed and gave her a dose of laudanum. She slept until noon, when she awoke with a throbbing headache. A picture of her uncle's face flashed before her eyes as she relived the terrible ordeal. A painful knot in her throat held back the tears for just a moment before they squeezed past, and she sobbed into her pillow. Uncle Thad was gone and she was alone. Though they had had their problems of late, she loved him and would miss him terribly.

Her eyes were red and swollen when a little while later, Fiona knocked and entered. Her companion came to the bed and took Amy's hand in her own. "I'm so sorry. Is there anything I can do for you, my dear?"

Amy shook her head miserably. "I simply can't believe he's gone, Fiona."

The older girl nodded sympathetically. "I know, dear. I'm having trouble believing it myself."

In her misery, Amy had quite forgotten that Fiona was to have been her uncle's future wife. Now she looked at the older girl critically. There were no traces of grief marring Fiona's attractive face, no red, swollen eyes, no deep pain etched in her countenance. Her companion's eyes were clear and only faintly troubled. It struck her as odd, but Fiona was a reserved person and did not show her feelings openly. Sending Fiona on her way, Amy rose and dressed herself. Since she had no black dresses, she chose a navy-blue gown instead and wound her hair into a severe bun at the nape of her neck.

When she got downstairs, Ivy told her the family was in the dining room for the noon meal. At her entrance,

316

the men rose respectfully, and Justin held a chair for her beside his. Once she was seated, Harlan addressed her. "We can't begin to tell you how sorry we are, my dear. You've lost a dear uncle, but we've lost a dear friend." He bowed his head as if he needed a moment to collect himself before continuing. "You must think of us as your family from now on, Amy, and as for the days ahead, we will be your strength. After the meal, I would like to confer with you in my bookroom about the arrangements, if you feel up to it."

Numbly, Amy agreed. She forced herself to eat a few bites of the roasted pheasant, but mainly sipped her wine. It seemed to soothe the dull ache behind her eyes. Justin gave her hand a comforting squeeze from time to time, and Pamela offered to loan her a black dress until some could be made by the seamstress. Amy accepted her offer.

Once the meal was finished, Harlan took Amy's arm as they made their way toward the bookroom. Marcus was admitted when they were halfway across the foyer, and he came immediately to her side. "Amy, I'm sorrier than I can say," he said softly, genuine concern in his voice. "Mr. Stafford sent word to me, and I came as soon as I could."

Along with the fresh grief that was squeezing her heart, the sight of him added the pain of another kind of loss. Raw hurt glittered in her eyes, but she nodded briefly. "Thank you," she said stiffly.

Harlan gave him a nod of greeting and suggested, "Amy and I have some important matters to settle just now, but I would like to speak with you when we're finished, Captain Bond."

"Aye, I've a need to say a few things myself," Marcus agreed, his gray eyes narrowing as he watched them walk away.

* * *

A short time later, Amy, seated across the desk from Harlan, stared aghast at him. "But I cannot allow that," she sputtered in anger. "Uncle Thad would wish to be buried in the family vault at First Trinity in Boston. My parents are buried there, and I insist."

Harlan rose and came around to sit on the edge of the desk next to her chair. He patted her hand soothingly. "My dear Amy, I understand your feelings, but under the circumstances, it would be better if we conduct the services here. And you shall remain with us."

Amy jerked her hand away in agitation. "Why would it be better?"

"Well, I cannot accompany you to Boston at this time, and I certainly cannot allow you to go unattended. As you know, our own Trinity Church is Episcopalian, and I'm sure Reverend Jacobs will conduct a fitting service that does justice to our dear Thaddeus. And wouldn't you rather have your uncle buried here in our family cemetery, since this will now be your home?"

He was insufferably sure of himself, and Amy felt her temper rise in response. "Why are you asking me, if you've already made up your mind?" She rose and stalked to the door, throwing it open.

Harlan came after her. "Amy — my dear, please come back and let's talk about this in a reasonable manner."

She turned and glared at him. "I don't find it unreasonable of me to try to see to my uncle's wishes."

He halted a few feet from her, his brows drawing together in an angry frown. "I've tried to make this easier for you, Amy, but you're being difficult. The truth is that Thaddeus named me as your guardian. He also wanted you to marry Justin, and you will do exactly that, young woman. And furthermore, I will attend to the funeral arrangements with or without your cooperation. Those were his wishes."

318

Her green eyes blazed with emerald fire as she promised, "We shall see about that." Turning, she strode rapidly through the foyer toward the stairs. She was so angry she could feel a flood of tears trying to burst free, and she was determined not to cry in Harlan's presence.

"Amy — wait! What is it?" Marcus called out. He had stepped into the foyer from the drawing room just as she took flight on the stairs.

"Leave me alone," she flung over her shoulder.

Marcus watched helplessly as she disappeared from sight. He wanted to go after her, but decided to give her some time alone. Her strange behavior spoke of more than simple grief over her uncle's death, and he had a suspicion that Harlan had somehow upset her. Turning toward the bookroom, Marcus's expression hardened as he thought of the man who had caused so much unhappiness to so many people. It was going to be a pleasure at last to bring Harlan Stafford to his knees.

Chapter Seventeen

Julia Stafford entered the foyer from the dining room after conferring with the cook's assistant about menus for the next few days. There would be a lot of callers and numerous mourners after the funeral, and food and drinks must be served. The Staffords were influential and had a reputation to uphold in the community, and even those who had not known Thaddeus would come out of respect for—or fear of—Harlan. Not that Julia cared whether everything went well for Harlan, but public opinion reflected upon Justin and Pamela as well.

She noticed Captain Bond entering the bookroom as she started toward the stairs, and would not have paid any further attention except that she overheard him say flatly, "I'm going to talk, Stafford, and you're going to listen."

Julia glanced around and, finding herself alone, hurried out onto the terrace to listen at the bookroom window.

Harlan glanced up in surprise at the tone of Captain Bond's voice. He had resumed his seat behind the desk and opened a ledger book after Amy had departed. Curiosity more than anything else prompted him to gesture toward one of the chairs across from him. "Everyone seems to be displeased today," he said. "What's on your mind, Captain?"

Marcus ignored the jibe and the offer of a seat, instead resting his hands on the back of the chair. The two men stared at each other for a moment. Finally, Marcus spoke. "When I came to Bermuda to find you, I didn't dream I'd be able to put you in jail for the rest of your days. I merely wanted to avenge my mother in some small way."

Harlan's eyes narrowed at the threat. "Why does that prospect delight you so, Captain Bond? And what in hell does your mother have to do with me?"

"I doubt you will even remember her, but her name was Sarah Payne. Does that sound familiar?" His voice was quiet, yet it held an undertone of cold contempt.

This time, Harlan couldn't hide the astonishment that flashed across his face. He half rose and sputtered, "Sarah . . . Sarah Payne is your mother? I . . . she told you about our . . . attachment?"

"On her deathbed," Marcus said. "She told me everything — including the fact that you took her innocence and then left her behind to marry an heiress."

Harlan stared at Marcus without really seeing him. His mind was years away with a young, lovely Sarah. He shook himself after a moment and said in a husky voice, "You say she's dead? I thought of her not long ago, and now I find she's gone. How strange life is." He mused and then pulled himself together, straightening to his full height. "Why would she tell you about me? That was so long ago."

Marcus's eyes darkened like angry thunderclouds. "I personally wish she hadn't, but mother felt it was her duty to inform me that I am your son." His bald statement startled Harlan, and the older man's eyes bulged for a moment.

"My son?" Harlan croaked, his mind reeling with the

unexpected news. He took careful stock of the man in front of him and saw for the first time the resemblance to himself in the younger man's countenance. The same square jaw, the same gray eyes, the same jet-black hair. He sat down heavily in his chair.

"Aye, your *bastard* son. Jonathan Bond claimed me as his own and raised me, but you sired me."

Harlan passed a hand over his eyes. "I don't know what to say . . . I never knew . . ."

"I don't believe you gave her a chance to tell you, did you? She told me she received a note from you of your impending marriage and never saw you again. And the thing that makes me want to kill you with my bare hands is that she didn't blame you, nor was she bitter," Marcus said, biting each word off in cold fury.

Harlan looked up at Marcus with a bleak expression. "I wouldn't have . . . I mean . . . had I known—"

"Don't try to tell me you would have married her, Stafford. I know you for the kind of man you are — ruthless and self-serving. Which brings me to my second revelation. I know Captain Aiken pirated an English vessel and killed everyone aboard, which makes you responsible, even if indirectly."

Harlan's face turned ashen at this news. His hands started to shake, and he clasped them together in an effort to calm himself. God's blood! Was his whole world going to crash in on his head in one day? he wondered in panic. The one tender spot in his heart had been reserved for Sarah Payne, and he had long regretted his desertion of her. And now his and Sarah's son was standing before him with hatred in his eyes. How ironic, he thought bitterly, to have a son like Marcus — a man a father could be proud of — and never hope to have his love or respect. He sighed and decided there was no use denying any of it. "What do you intend to do with this information?" he asked.

"I haven't decided yet," Marcus said.

"You realize that technically I will not be blamed for what Aiken did?"

Marcus's lips thinned in a grim smile. "Perhaps not, but if I make this public, your reputation as a business-man will be ruined. That will be enough revenge for me."

"You hate me that much?"

"More," Marcus said, turning to leave the room. At the doorway, he stopped. "I will let you know what I decide before I take action. After all, I was raised by an honorable man, a man quite unlike you." With that last salvo, he quit the room.

Harlan stared after him, deep in thought. Fear at what this sordid news would do to his life was tempered by a faint hope that he could win some forgiveness from his son. Marcus Bond would never disappoint him, he felt sure, as Justin and Pamela had done.

While Harlan sat pondering his desperate situation, Julia left her hiding place and went directly to her room. She rang for Layla and paced in agitation as she waited. Something had to be done about this problem. Her brother had been involved in some unsavory things in the past, but he was always discreet, saving the family embarrassment. Now, however, there was nothing he could do to stop Captain Bond from making formal charges, not to mention perhaps leaking the facts about his own bastardy. She had heard in Captain Bond's voice the need for revenge, no matter the cost.

Had it been anyone else threatening her brother, Julia knew Harlan would not have hesitated to permanently silence him. But this bastard son and his mother meant something to him — she had heard the emotion in his voice — and that frightened her. Justin and Pamela's future was at stake, and she was going to see that nothing or no one destroyed their happiness.

Amy sat in the small parlor for two days, hour after dreary hour, receiving mourners who were more or less strangers to her. Thaddeus was resting in a beautifully polished cedar coffin that sat upon two side chairs. The room was filled with flowers from the garden, and the overpowering scent reminded her of death. Reverend Jacobs had been in constant attendance, and she appreciated his caring concern, but she would have preferred to be left alone. Pamela and Justin tried to comfort her; however, it was her anger at Harlan that most dulled her grief. Marcus hovered nearby, but after her initial sharp rebuff, he had kept his distance.

Bitterly, she watched Harlan play the grieving friend and cordial host to his neighbors and associates who came to pay respects. Her stony silence in his presence was barely noticed, most thinking her grief-stricken.

On the afternoon of the second day, Reverend Jacobs touched her on the shoulder and said softly, "Mistress Hawthorne, it's time to begin. Are you ready?"

Amy looked up at him blankly, having been lost in private thoughts. He repeated himself and she nodded. He stepped up beside the casket and called for everyone's attention. Justin came quietly to her side and laid a comforting hand on her shoulder, while the minister offered up a prayer and bade the mourners to ready themselves for the service. While Justin helped Amy to her feet, four of the younger men in the group took up positions beside the casket to bear it out to the family cemetery. Amy could not bring herself to watch as the clergyman closed the lid forever on her uncle.

The group made slow progress out the French doors and down the steps to the back lawn. Amy felt she could not have made it had it not been for Justin's strength as they crossed the wide lawn to the stone wall that enclosed the graveyard.

When all had taken their places beside the open grave, Reverend Jacobs stepped up and opened his Bible to read. While some part of Amy's mind registered his words as the Twenty-third psalm, her thoughts shied away from the finality of the occasion. She was remembering happier days with her uncle: the fishing trips to Dedham, the sleigh rides round Jamaica Pond, dancing assemblies at Concert Hall. In her heart, she had already forgiven him for pressing her marriage plans. She knew he had only wanted the best for her, and it was not his fault he had misjudged Harlan. Hadn't she made an error in judgment concerning Marcus?

She was jolted back to her dreary present circumstances when Justin touched her arm and spoke softly to her. They stepped back and watched as, with ropes, the pallbearers lowered the coffin into the raw, yawning hole. Amy stepped up first and dropped a single rose atop the coffin. She let Justin lead her away while the other mourners followed suit. At the gate of the cemetery, Reverend Jacobs caught up with them and again offered his condolences.

"Thank you . . . and I do appreciate your concern and support, Reverend," she said quietly.

"If you have need to talk to someone, I will be at your disposal anytime," he said, taking her black-gloved hand in his for a moment.

Amy nodded and moved on with Justin. They entered the house once more, and Amy went through the motions of eating from the plate of food Pamela brought her, but the whole day seemed like something out of a dream. A horrible dream from which she wished she could awaken. Marcus, she noticed, was never far from her, but did not intrude to say even a few words. His presence was at the same time comforting and painful. By evening, sheer exhaustion claimed her, and she fell into a heavy sleep.

The following day, Amy finally roused herself to appear at the noon meal. Her countenance was pale and drawn, but she could feel some of her strength returning. The whole family was in attendance in the dining room, including Marcus. A sudden silence fell on the group as she walked into the room and took a seat next to Justin. "I am not so fragile that everyone must cosset me. Please continue with your conversation . . . life does go on," she said, glancing about the table.

Harlan spoke up. "I'm glad you feel that way, my dear, because I was just saying that your marriage to Justin should take place soon. I know there are the proprieties to observe, but the banns had already been posted before Thaddeus's unfortunate death. I don't believe polite society will think ill of you if you do not wait a year."

"I'm not going to marry Justin, so it is a moot point," she said firmly, unfolding her napkin and placing it on her lap. She glanced up at him with a challenging look in her eyes.

Harlan stared at her for a moment as a flush rose in his cheeks. "It's already been decided, and lest you forget, I am now your legal guardian. You will do as I say."

Justin broke in before Amy could reply. "I am in agreement with Amy, Father. We've discussed it and have mutually decided to dissolve the betrothal."

Harlan's gaze jerked to his son. "I think you've forgotten how important it is to us to unite our two families — how important it was to Thaddeus." His words, though calmly spoken, held a double-edged meaning.

"I haven't forgotten, but there are other considerations now, and one of them is Amy's feelings. I certainly wouldn't want to force a marriage on her she doesn't want," Justin said, keeping his tone reasonable.

"You're both too young to know what's best for you, and I will not accept this rebellion on your part."

Marcus had been sitting silent through this exchange, but decided to intervene. "Your attitude leads one to believe there may be other reasons you're demanding this marriage take place, Stafford," he suggested in a cool tone.

Harlan seemed to back down visibly at this goading. "I merely have their best interest at heart, Captain Bond."

Justin and Pamela stared at Marcus with astonished expressions, while Julia's eyes narrowed at her brother's meek reply. She had never seen him so passive with anyone. It reinforced her fear that he might, if given the chance, favor this bastard son over his own lawful children.

"It is a simple fact that I do not love Justin and he does not love me. And I don't wish to discuss it any further, Harlan. If you persist, I will be forced to take some action you will not like," Amy said, a veiled threat in her voice.

"And I shall see that Amy's wishes are carried out," Marcus put in.

Harlan looked from one of them to the other, and frustration got the better of his good judgment. "I beg you both to remember that this is my table and my house, and I will not tolerate your insolence. Moreover, I have no patience with threats, so if you have anything to say, spit it out now."

Marcus stood up at the challenge, his face a stony mask. "When I am ready, Stafford, and not before. However, I'd like to inform all of you that Amy will be marrying me."

There was a general chorus of gasps around the table,

Amy's being the loudest. She jumped to her feet, color staining her cheeks for the first time in days. "How dare you make such an absurd announcement, Marcus Bond! Marry you? I would not marry you if my very life depended on it!" She began to shake with anger and delayed reaction to the stressful interchange she'd just been a part of. Justin placed a hand on her arm, but she shook it free. "Leave me alone—all of you!" With that, she stormed from the room and up the stairs. She ripped off her dress and jerked her riding habit out of the clothes cupboard. Fuming to herself, she dressed rapidly and pulled on her boots. Marcus's bald statement had brought her out of her lethargy, and it had also hurt her. He had not come to her gently with words of love to ask for her hand—no! He had declared his intention in an effort to best Harlan. She didn't know why he harbored such ill feelings toward the man, but she was determined not to become a pawn in their game.

As she slammed out of the house, she heard Marcus calling to her from the foyer. As luck would have it, Moses had just saddled the mare, Bess, to exercise her leg after her forced inactivity. Amy took the reins from his hands and ordered him to help her mount. The black man was surprised at her abruptness and worried over the fact that Bess bore a man's saddle, but he obeyed without a word. She galloped past Marcus as he rounded the house in pursuit of her.

How dare Harlan and Marcus fight over her like two dogs with one bone, she thought angrily. She was halfway across the meadow when she heard a shout from behind. Turning, she saw Marcus galloping after her, but she was sure she could outrun him riding astride. Her lead was considerable, but she leaned over Bess's neck and encouraged the mare to fly faster.

Leaving the meadow behind, she took to the road and flew like the wind for a couple of miles before slowing her horse to turn off onto a track she recognized. Hidden from view by the dense foliage, Amy slowed to a trot and headed for the beach. How she wished there were a fleet sailing vessel waiting for her in the pirates' cove. She would sail away from this place and these horrid people and never return! But, alas, when she reached the sandy beach, all that marred the surface of the blue-green water was a black-and-white longtail diving to catch a fish.

Amy dismounted and walked Bess along the sand to cool her, while she herself welcomed the breeze off the water. Her cheeks were flushed, and her hair had escaped the simple bun atop her head, leaving long tendrils of copper tresses to brush her shoulders. She was trying desperately to think of a way out of the situation she found herself in. Her twenty-first birthday was not until August — more than two months away — and even then, she had her doubts whether Harlan would turn over her inheritance. Marcus had said Harlan was having financial difficulties, and that would certainly explain his eagerness to marry her to Justin. Perhaps she could employ a lawyer to check into Harlan's handling of her money and thus prevent him from using it for his own debts.

As she neared the spot where the secret cave was, a slight tremor shook her as she remembered her near-drowning. The rock face jutted back in an inverted vee, while tough scrubby bushes hid the opening. With the more picturesque rock formations down the beach, it was no wonder this stark rock face was generally ignored. Being here reminded her of that horrible night. Somehow, she couldn't quite see Megan and Patrick as murderers. The woman in white had to be someone else, she decided . . . but who?

The sound of a horse snorting nearby caused her to turn and look. Marcus came into view before she could pull Bess out of sight.

He walked his stallion leisurely up to her and dismounted. The sight of her stirred his senses as it always did. "We need to talk, Amy," he said, a frown marring his face. His stomach knotted at the important task ahead of him.

Refusing to look at him, she snapped, "Is it to be a discussion, or do you merely wish to pass on to me any other decisions you've made concerning my future?" The sound of his voice evoked a flood of despair and yearning in her breast. She was angry with herself for the weakness.

Stay calm. Be reasonable, he told himself, taking a deep breath. "I'm sorry about that, but this is no time for misplaced pride. I don't think you realize what Harlan Stafford is capable of."

"Why don't you tell me? And while we're on the subject, why don't you tell me why you hate him so much?"

Marcus turned away to tie his horse to a bush, then took her reins to secure Bess. Finally, he spoke. "I've found out many things about him, and they're all bad. For one thing, he's going to lose everything if he cannot secure your fortune, and I could almost swear he's using your money right now. But that's not the worst." He paused for a moment and urged her to sit down on a boulder with him. Grudgingly, she did, and he continued. "In St.-Domingue, I spoke with a man about one of Stafford's ship captains and learned about an atrocity that is ultimately Stafford's doing."

"You didn't say anything to me about that. Why?" she asked, trying not to notice the warmth of his thigh next to hers.

He shrugged. "I intended to warn your uncle of Stafford's black deeds and thereby provide protection for you, but with your uncle dying before I could talk to him, I was desperate to keep you out of his clutches."

She still looked doubtful. "Well, what is it Harlan is responsible for that I should know about?"

Marcus repeated the story Cormac had told him and watched the horror settle on her features. "How terrible!" she breathed. "But Harlan did not order this massacre, did he?"

"No. However, Captain Aiken told Cormac that Stafford had been pressuring him to bring in more and more booty, whether it be by legal means or otherwise. And then there's the fact that Stafford knows what was done and has hidden the loot from that ship as well as keeping quiet about it."

Amy shook her head regretfully and gazed out over the cove. "I'm sure Uncle Thad did not know what kind of man Harlan is, or he would have never had any connection to him. Nor would he have wanted me to marry into the Stafford family."

"Stafford was very careful to present a respectable face to the world. We, however, have a problem now, and that is the fact that he says he's your legal guardian."

"We will know for sure this evening when Uncle's will is read. I know for a fact that my uncle carried a copy of his will on this trip, because he mentioned it to me aboard ship. I think he had hopes that Justin and I would get on well together, and he intended to legalize all the details even down to his will should we become betrothed. And Harlan has intimated that Uncle made some changes to it while you and I were away in St.-Domingue."

Marcus wished he could erase the worry lines from her beautiful face, but he knew there was no way to shield her from the ugly side of the situation. He was merely relieved that she had not pressed him further about his personal feelings toward Stafford. "I doubt Stafford would say it if it were not so. A lie would be found out soon enough."

He had put into words what she had already feared. She stirred uneasily and sighed. "I realize that, but I don't know what to do about it. I can't marry Justin . . . I just can't." She was thinking more about Justin's secret marriage to Megan than anything else, but didn't intend to give away his secret to Harlan or Marcus.

"And you won't," Marcus said, standing and pulling her to her feet. He took her in his arms, claiming her mouth before she could protest. His tongue traced the soft fullness of her lips and pushed inside to explore there. Even though she struggled, he felt an answering need in her. He deepened the kiss until her resistance turned into heady response. Reluctantly then, he broke the kiss and whispered hoarsely, "Marry me . . . it's the only solution."

Amy turned her face away. Her heart fluttered wildly under her breast as she fought to control her roiling emotions. She loved him with every fiber of her being, but she knew he wasn't making this gesture out of love . . . and that hurt. There had to be another way to break free of Harlan, and she would look for it. "No, Marcus. I wouldn't want you to sacrifice your precious pride for me," she said quietly. Her traitorous body had betrayed her, but she didn't want him to know how much he mattered to her, so she quickly sought a change of subject. "The cave where I nearly drowned that night is here. I want you to see it."

Marcus let her pull away, deciding to give her some time to think about his proposal. He knew from experience that she could not be bullied. "Lead on," he said.

As Amy climbed through the opening, she felt a chill of apprehension, but it seemed harmless enough in the daylight. She pointed out the tunnel to the right, where she'd found herself when she awakened, and also the tunnel to the left, where she'd found the opening an

332

eventually climbed out to safety. He suggested they explore it, but she declined. "I'm going back to the house," she said, turning toward the opening. "Are you coming?"

"Yes, but then I'm coming back to have a look around. There may be some dry tunnels where Stafford could hide illegal booty, and since I haven't found it anyplace else, I'd like to check," he said, following her outside.

An hour later, Marcus was deep inside the cave with a lantern he'd gotten from the kitchen at Stafford House. He knew that many of the caves on the islands had several entrances and contained very large rooms—large enough to hide entire cargos. He knew also that the loot could have been hidden on one of the many uninhabited islands in the vicinity, but he couldn't overlook this cave, so close to Stafford's property.

The cave was riddled with tunnels, and he explored each one, leaving a trail of white powder so as not to become lost. In most he could tell by the walls that water filled them at high tide, but after a while he discovered one tunnel that climbed higher than the rest and was completely dry. Several yards along, it widened into a room that was quite large, but empty. It would be the perfect place to store booty; however, there was none there. He was disappointed, even though he'd known it was a long shot.

Feeling tired, he sat down to rest a moment before he made his way back out. Amy's beautiful face intruded on his thoughts, as was often the case, and he prayed she would see reason and marry him. It was the only way he could think of to keep her safe. Harlan was a desperate man, and Amy's willful personality might soon drive him to a desperate act. Again he felt a helpless shame at being this man's son and at not being able to bring himself to tell Amy the truth.

While he pondered the situation, he dug idly at the dirt with the heel of his right boot. After a few moments, he realized his heel was striking something metal, as the sound penetrated his thoughts. Curious, he moved the lantern closer and took out his knife to scrape away more dirt. He was intrigued to find that it was a square chest he'd unearthed, black and very old looking. Setting to work now with more energy, he dug away at the sides until he could lift it out of the dirt. His heart beat a little faster at the heaviness of it, as he pondered the possible contents.

Taking his handkerchief, he cleaned away as much of the dirt as was possible and inspected his find. It was solidly built, each corner reinforced with a metal he suspected was tarnished silver, and the whole was trimmed with an intricate filigree design. The lock and hasp were carved, but he could not make out a distinct design, due to the embedded dirt. However, it had the look of Spanish work.

Taking his knife, he wedged it in the lock and pried until it gave way. Holding his breath, he lifted the lid and then gasped at the sight. A sea of gold doubloons filled the chest to the brim. They had lost much of their shine, but as the chest had been sealed fairly tight, they retained much of their color. He picked one up to study the markings, but in the dim light of his lantern, it was too difficult.

Burying his hands in the coins, he gave a shout of laughter. His sheer pleasure at the unexpected find was only beginning to surface past his initial surprise. For a short time, he savored the knowledge of what this was going to mean in his life: the payment of his debts, ships of his own and marriage to Amy on equal terms. He decided to leave the chest behind and retrieve it the next

334

day, for it was too cumbersome to carry on his horse. Putting several doubloons in his pocket, he closed the lid and carefully made a trail back out of the tunnel with the white wig powder he'd brought from the house. It was a trick his father had taught him while on their travels. Exploring caves had been one of Jonathan Bond's passions. Marcus's lighthearted feeling vanished for a moment as he remembered his father. How he wished Jonathan and Sarah were alive to share in his good fortune. And he knew they would love Amy as he did and be happy he'd found the perfect mate to share his life.

As he emerged into the sunlight, he looked around to make sure no one was about. Satisfying himself on that score, he retrieved his stallion and rode for Tucker's Town to have an expert look at his find.

Amy paced back and forth in her bedchamber, waiting to go downstairs for the reading of the will. Ivy had come up an hour ago to let her know Harlan's lawyer had arrived and was closeted with him in the bookroom. What was keeping them so long? she wondered irritably. She wanted to hear the will with her own ears and see any changes her uncle had made, along with his signature, before she would believe Harlan. And if what he said was true, she would implore the lawyer to keep a strict eye on her inheritance until Uncle Thad's lawyer could be notified.

She wiped her sweaty palms on her black skirt for the tenth time and rechecked her appearance in the tall mirror standing in the corner. After returning from her ride, she had bathed, changed and had Fiona do her hair in the cluster of sausage curls atop her head. Her companion had been quiet, yet somehow serene. Not at all like a woman who had just lost her betrothed.

Amy didn't know why, but Fiona must have lied to her — the woman had never loved Thaddeus. Her attitude spoke volumes, but at the moment Amy didn't have the time to delve into the mystery. Her own problems were mountainous and required all her attention.

Unconsciously, she touched her lips as she remembered the kiss she'd shared with Marcus on the beach. It had reopened the wound in her broken heart, and she trembled when she thought of how much she'd wanted him to make love to her. Tears of frustration glistened in her green eyes at her inability to control these feelings. One minute she wanted to claw his arrogant face, and the next she wanted to be in his arms.

His proposal of marriage had come too late, she thought angrily. And it was not love that had prompted it. She could not forgive him for that.

A knock on the door ended her reverie as she called permission to enter. Ivy stepped inside and informed her that Master Stafford required her presence in the bookroom.

When she arrived there, Harlan was sitting behind his desk, Julia and Pamela were seated on the brocade settee, Justin and Fiona flanked the desk in chairs, Marcus was standing beside the fireplace, and a stranger stood by the open French doors and looked out over the lawns. He turned as she entered, and Harlan introduced him as Daniel Bainbridge, his personal lawyer. "So sorry to make your acquaintance under these sad circumstances, Mistress Hawthorne," he said, bowing correctly.

Amy murmured a response, but did not like his oily voice or the calculating look he gave her. Justin rose and seated her in the chair he had occupied, then stood behind her.

Mr. Bainbridge moved to stand beside the desk, taking up the will to read. There were the usual bequests to old and faithful servants in Thaddeus's household, as well as gifts to some of his favorite charities. He left a goodly sum to Trinity Church in Boston, but the bulk of his estate he willed to Amy. Here, though, the lawyer took a new sheet of paper from the desk and informed the group, "Mr. Hawthorne called for me to visit him here at Stafford House just a few short weeks ago so that he might add a codicil to his will. It reads thus: 'In the event of an untimely death, that is to say, should I die before my niece, Amy, is married, I hereby name my friend and business associate, Harlan Stafford of Bermuda, to act as her legal guardian and also executor of my estate in her behalf. The aforementioned appointee knows my wishes regarding my niece and will, I'm sure, carry out his duties admirably.' "

Amy heard this with a sinking heart. It was vague, to say the least, and gave Harlan complete control. "May I see the document, please?" she asked, holding out her hand.

The lawyer glanced at Harlan and received a nod before he handed it to her. Amy studied the signature at the bottom of the page and had no doubts that it was her uncle's. As she handed it back, she asked, "What happens if I am not married by age twenty-one?"

Mr. Bainbridge shrugged. "The original will does not make provisions for that specifically. Your uncle intended for you to marry by that time. Legally, Mr. Stafford will be your guardian until such time as you marry, and then your guardianship will be turned over to your husband."

Harlan spoke for the first time. "Thaddeus wanted you to marry Justin, Amy, and I was in complete agreement. But if the two of you refuse, then I shall manage your estate as I see fit."

"Which means that you will be using Amy's money to pay your own debts, I'm sure. I don't think Thaddeus

337

intended that when he made you her guardian," Marcus said.

Harlan turned to him, his sharp eyes narrowed. "I gave permission for you to attend the reading, Captain Bond. Please keep your opinions to yourself."

"I'm here to see to her interests, Stafford. If you are an honest man, you will let the courts keep an accounting of all transactions within her estate. Are you willing to do that?" Marcus asked.

Harlan's face grew red with the effort of holding onto his temper. "I think you are more interested in her fortune than her welfare, if the truth be known." He turned to Amy and asked point-blank, "Are you considering marrying this man, as he so boldly stated at the table today? If you are, I must tell you I will not permit it."

Amy bristled and stood up. "I'm sick to death of being treated like a bank account! I am a person with feelings and would be treated as such." She burst into tears and rushed from the room.

Marcus's gray eyes blazed. "I don't care what slurs you cast upon me, you coldhearted blackguard, but if you hurt her one more time, I'll kill you." And with that he strode angrily from the room.

Chapter Eighteen

For two days after the confrontation with Harlan, Amy kept to her rooms, alternately sunk in despair or storming about in anger. Try as she might, she couldn't come up with a solution to her problem. Now that he had control of her fortune, Harlan was not as interested in seeing her marry Justin, which she could not do anyway. She could not bear, however, to remain under his autocratic thumb while he squandered her family's hard-earned money. Reluctantly, she admitted to herself that the only solution was to marry. It would remove all power and money from Harlan's hands. In her most frustrated moments, she vowed to do just that, but when reason returned, she feared she would be trading one tyrant for another.

On the third morning of her self-imposed exile, Ivy brought a message from Justin. Amy read it and instructed the black girl to get her riding habit. She dressed and hurriedly ate the bread and tea Ivy had brought. Though impatient, she sat still while Ivy did her hair, since Fiona had been suspiciously absent. Some activity was just what she needed, and she was glad Justin had suggested a ride.

As she stepped out into the hallway, she glanced at Fiona's door with narrowed eyes. Her companion had not once come to her room in the last two days, and she had to wonder why. Amy decided to pay her a visit after the ride.

Justin suggested they ride into Tucker's Town on an errand he needed to see to. For a while they galloped along the road, giving the horses some exercise. When they slowed to a more sedate pace, Justin turned to her with an apprehensive look. "I had an ulterior motive for suggesting this ride today," he said.

Tipping her face up to the sun, she sighed. "I don't care, I was going mad in that house."

"I'm taking you to see Megan and Patrick," he blurted out.

Her gaze swung abruptly to him. "What do they have planned for me today, pray tell?"

He grinned at her skeptical tone. "An apology."

"A fitting punishment for rendering me unconscious and stuffing me in a trunk," she said.

His eyebrows rose a fraction. "Somehow, I got the impression you did not mind spending a few weeks with Captain Bond. Am I right?"

Amy flushed and turned away. "I think that man is odious."

He chuckled. "He seems to like you—even wants to marry you. As a matter of fact, he threatened to kill my father if he hurt you again. I would say those are fairly strong feelings."

Amy's head jerked up at that. "What do you mean, he threatened to kill Harlan?"

Justin's brows rose. "After the reading of the will—when you left the room. Captain Bond exploded."

Amy looked away. "He had no right. I once thought myself in love with him, but no longer."

"Nonsense. My advice is marry him. If you don't, my father will make your life a living hell—I should know."

"And what would my life be with Marcus? He's arrogant, opinionated, and has far too much pride. The man would have me tearing at my hair inside of a week!"

"What a stubborn little baggage you are, Amy. Can't you see you're still in love with him? I recognize the signs, having come to the knowledge lately that I have loved Megan for a long time and didn't realize it. You won't be happy without him," he predicted smugly.

She frowned at him and changed the subject. "When do you plan to tell your father about your marriage?"

He grimaced. "I'm thinking never would be a good time."

"Her condition will be showing before then," she said with a half smile.

They were nearing the outskirts of town, and Justin pointed to a track that led off to the right. "The Cormacs live this way," he said, adding "I want Megan to come to live at Stafford House and have our child there, but Father would never agree."

"You don't think a grandchild will make any difference to his thinking?" she asked as they neared a small cottage in a clearing.

Justin shook his head. "Absolutely none. His heart is made of stone, I'm afraid."

He was helping her dismount when Megan came out the front door and ran to throw her arms around Justin. He laughed and kissed her soundly. A sheepish look settled on Megan's face as she turned to Amy. "Welcome to our house, Mistress Hawthorne. Please come inside for tea," she said formally, holding onto Justin's hand.

Amy inclined her head in a brief nod. "I am parched from the ride." Her bland expression gave nothing away, and she saw Megan glance quickly at Justin. He smiled at her reassuringly and offered his other arm to Amy.

"Is Patrick here yet?" he asked as they entered the front door.

"Aye, he's out back talking to Mum. She's hanging clothes on the line, as always," Megan replied. She glanced at Amy and explained in a slightly belligerent tone, "She takes in washin' for folks and does such a fine job, she has to turn down offers."

Amy did not rise to the bait as expected. "It's very hard work, but takes skill, I know."

Megan looked slightly mollified. "I'll be tellin' Patrick you're here. Make yourselves comfortable."

When she left the room, Amy looked around at the worn, but clean, furnishings. There were beautifully crocheted lace scarves on the tables and on the backs of the two chairs and the settee. Two elegant silver candlesticks graced the mantel above the fireplace, and a cross hung on the wall above.

Justin led her to a chair and then seated himself on the settee. "Megan is a proud woman, Amy, and it wasn't easy for her to agree to meet you face to face with an apology. Even though what she did was criminal. Please don't be too hard on her," he pleaded.

Amy smiled. "Don't worry, Justin. I shan't gobble up your little Irish rose, but I do think an apology is in order. After all, I could have had the two of them arrested."

He held up his hands in a gesture of surrender. "I know, and I can't thank you enough for not doing so."

A moment later, Megan returned with Patrick in tow. The tall blond man came straight away and took Amy's hand and, bowing low, kissed it. "You're more beautiful than I remember, sweet lady, and that's goin' a far piece," he said with a flourish and a wide grin.

Amy found herself smiling at his outlandish behavior in the face of what had gone before. "How is your nose, Mr. Cormac?" she asked, an amused twinkle in her green eyes.

His grin widened as he rubbed his nose with his

thumb. "I'm thinkin' the new hump in it gives me a bit more character."

The other three burst out laughing, and Patrick joined in. When they gained some sense of sobriety, Megan, wiping her eyes, said, "He also limped for days after that kick in the shins, Mistress Hawthorne. The customers at the Boar's Head thought he'd been attacked by ruffians."

"And he let them believe it rather than having it known he'd been bested by a slight, red-haired female," Justin put in.

"And that, me darlin' brings us to the reason we asked Justin to bring you here today. We do truly and humbly beg your forgiveness for what we did," Patrick said sincerely.

"Aye, Mistress. We meant you no harm, but I was desperate," Megan added, holding onto Justin's hand for courage. "I know you haven't told the authorities yet, and I was hopin' you wouldn't, especially since I'm in the family way and all."

She eyed them both sternly. "I should be very angry with the both of you, but somehow I'm not. I accept your apologies and will not report what happened. However," she added, a slow smile curving her lips as her gaze rested on Justin and Megan, "I want your promise you'll be happy for many, many years."

Patrick jumped up from his chair. "This calls for a toast. I'll get that bottle of Madeira we've been savin'."

The morning sped by as the four of them toasted, laughed and talked of the future. Amy found herself truly liking the brother and sister. And the love she saw between Justin and Megan eased the pain of her bruised heart. She was subdued during the ride back to Stafford House, thinking of how things could have been between her and Marcus.

At midmorning, Fiona knocked on the door of the bookroom and entered. Harlan was sitting behind the cedar desk, his head in his hands. Finally, he looked up and grimaced. "Sit down, Fiona. We have problems, and I need your help."

She sat down and smoothed her black skirt. No longer did she wear the severe hairstyle or the spectacles. And her cheeks were tinted becomingly. In short, she did not look like a woman in mourning. "Anything, my darling," she answered.

He leaned forward and frowned. "Marcus Bond is getting in the way. If we don't do something, Amy will probably marry him, and we'll lose her fortune."

Fiona rested her elbows on the chair arms, her fingers making a pointed steeple in front of her. "But Amy has already said she will not marry Justin."

"They have both been extremely stubborn," he said in disgust. "However, it's not necessary that they marry. I simply do not want her to marry anyone else. Especially Bond, who has his reasons for disliking me."

Her eyebrows lifted delicately. "Perhaps he could meet with an accident. Don't you have a trusted lackey who could arrange something?"

"No!" Harlan flared, half rising from his seat. "I don't want him touched—do you understand?"

Fiona was taken aback by his vehemence. "Whatever you say, Harlan. But I'm surprised you care. Moreover, I'm shocked you have allowed him to remain in your household, given the way he treats you."

He sat back down and composed himself. "He's my son . . . illegitimate, of course, but my son all the same."

Fiona was speechless for a moment at his totally unexpected revelation. "Your son?"

"Aye," Harlan said, running his fingers through his

dark hair. "It's a long story that I won't go into. And even though he hates me, I would keep him safe. What I propose we do is this. You could tell Amy about his relationship to me and intimate that he is only interested in her as a means to get revenge. That should put sufficient doubt in her mind."

"That will be easy, but what if it doesn't work?"

"Then I shall ship her off to England to await my pleasure in the matter of her future," he said bluntly.

"Do you have the poison ready for tonight, Layla? I heard Captain Bond say he would be back for dinner," Julia asked in a low tone. She and the black woman were in Julia's sitting room, awaiting the bell for the midday meal.

Layla nodded, her eyes distant. After a moment, she blinked and asked her mistress, "After dis be over, you send Moses an' me to be with our babies?"

Julia smiled. "You know I will—I promised. I would have freed you and your brother years ago if I could have. And yes, I'll make sure you get your children back to live with you."

Layla gave her a rare smile. "I never forget you."

Julia studied the attractive black woman as she moved about the room performing small tasks. She and Layla had been friends since their youth, and she had felt her friend's pain at the loss of her two children when Harlan sold them off to a planter in Jamaica. Moses had fathered a child by one of the young slave girls, and Harlan had sold the woman and child to the same planter. He was a coldhearted bastard and had hurt a lot of people. Julia was glad she was alive to see him receive payment for those deeds.

* * *

When Justin and Amy arrived home, Marcus was waiting for them outside the stable. "I need to talk to you, Amy," he said, frowning at her and Justin.

Justin dismounted and turned to help Amy, saying over his shoulder, "My father is a dangerous enemy, and you have been irritating him lately for some reason. I would watch my back if I were you."

Marcus nodded grimly. "I know what I'm doing, Stafford," he said, watching the younger man lift Amy down to the ground with a twist of jealousy.

Justin faced Marcus and shrugged. "Just friendly advice, Bond, because for some obscure reason I like you. But I am puzzled as to why you and my father are at odds . . . and why he has allowed you to remain in his house when you have clearly shown your feelings toward him."

Amy watched this exchange with interest. She too was curious about the situation.

"It's not something I wish to discuss at the moment, but rest assured everyone will learn the facts in time," Marcus said, turning his gaze on Amy. "Could we have a private conversation . . . please?"

On this last plea, Amy relented. "If it's that important. Why don't we talk in the garden? I need to walk a bit to work out the stiffness. Thank you, Justin, for the outing," she added, smiling at the younger man.

Justin nodded and left them. Marcus took her arm as they walked across the back lawn toward the stone wall that surrounded the garden. At first, Amy held herself aloof, but the touch of his hand did strange things to her senses, and she admitted to herself that Justin was right. She did love Marcus, and try as she might, she couldn't ignore that fact.

Once inside the walls, she relaxed as they followed the pathway to the stone bench and fountain. She remembered the other time they had met there and what had ensued. It brought an ache to her heart. So much had happened since then, and she had become thoroughly disillusioned. She wanted to weep for those lost romantic dreams she'd harbored, but she had to be practical. Her situation was fast becoming desperate, and only cold reason would see her through these times.

Seating herself, she glanced at Marcus with a significant lifting of her brow. "What is it you wish to speak of?"

He placed one booted foot on the bench beside her and leaned an arm on his knee. "I'm asking you again to marry me," he said without preamble.

"Stubborn man," she murmured. He certainly had dogged persistence. "How many times are you going to ask me that question?"

"Until I get the answer I want," he said.

She sighed. "Then I accept." The surprised look on his face almost made her smile, but she refrained. "I think we should do so immediately, before Harlan can stop us."

"Why are you doing this?" he asked, suspicious, as he raised up and glared at her.

"You're never happy, are you? First you don't want to marry me, and then you do, and now you're asking for reasons?" She threw up her hands in exasperation. "Yes or no?"

"Yes, of course, but you're up to something, I know it," he said, his attitude testy.

"Just what is *your* reason for marrying me, pray tell? There is something you're not telling, and I would like to know what it is."

He stared at her for a long moment, trying to decide if he should reveal his secret, but in the end, he couldn't bring himself to do so. His fear of losing her when she was ready to capitulate was too great. "All right, I'll ask no questions if you won't — agreed?"

She nodded and held out her hand to him. "Agreed." Instead of shaking her hand, he took it and pulled her into his arms. Bending his head to hers, he kissed her possessively, his heart singing for the first time in weeks. She was his, and that was all that mattered.

Amy felt weak by the time he released her, and truth be told, she wished the kiss could have gone on forever.

"Reverend Jacobs would probably perform the ceremony without too many questions," she suggested breathlessly.

Marcus still held tightly to her hand as he replied, "Aye. Let's go now, before you change your mind."

For the first time, Amy smiled, stirring his blood. "I shan't change my mind, but, yes, we might as well do it now."

They began walking back through the garden, and she said wistfully, "I wish I could ask Pamela to come with us."

He nodded. "Why don't you. I think I know her well enough to say she'll not give us away."

In lieu of the kind of wedding she'd always dreamed of, having dear Pamela there would be a consolation. Marcus waited at the stable for her while she went in search of her friend. After Amy revealed their mission, Pamela swore to keep the secret and quickly changed into riding clothes. They encountered Ivy as they left the house, and Pamela asked her to tell Harlan that the two of them would be going to town to shop and would take the noon meal there.

Amy's spirits rose with every mile they traveled. She was glad she'd had that talk with Justin. The only cloud on her horizon was the fact that Marcus still did not trust her enough to share his secrets. But perhaps that would come in time. She knew she loved him and felt sure he loved her. Wasn't that all that mattered?

They found Reverend Jacobs in the church working

348

on a sermon, and when they explained their mission, he readily agreed to officiate, without asking any awkward questions.

He and Pamela lit several candles on the altar, and Reverend Jacobs stood in front of them instead of in the high pulpit. Pamela took her place beside Amy and smiled with sincere happiness as the minister spoke the words of the sacred ceremony.

The promises Amy made, however, gave her pause, as she realized how lightly they had entered into this union. Even though she loved Marcus with all her heart, they were taking their vows for the wrong reasons. It sobered her to think about it, but all too soon the minister was asking Marcus to place a ring on her finger. She glanced quickly at him, knowing there hadn't been time to get one, but he was fishing in his waistcoat pocket. He produced a wide gold band and slipped it on her finger with a smile. "It was my mother's," he whispered. After that, Reverend Jacobs pronounced them man and wife, and Marcus was kissing her tenderly. In that moment, she truly felt like a beloved bride, and it brought tears to her eyes.

The minister shook Marcus's hand, and Pamela hugged her soundly, whispering, "I wanted you to be my sister, but I still have you as a friend."

Reverend Jacobs went to his office and came back with a bottle of fine Madeira and four glasses. "It was a Christmas gift from one of my parishioners, and I was saving it for a special occasion. I believe this could be called that," he said with a laugh. He toasted the bride and groom, and Pamela added her good wishes. Before they left, the cleric fetched paper and pen and filled out a marriage certificate, having them both sign next to his signature. "I will post the banns today and announce it in the worship service tomorrow. Again, congratulations to you both."

When they emerged into the afternoon sunshine, they decided to go to the Boar's Head for a celebration meal. Amy was far too excited to eat, but she picked at the food Megan brought to them. When Marcus asked the silver-haired girl to bring their best champagne, Amy impulsively told Megan what they had done. Megan's eyes lit up, and she gave the couple a broad smile. "I'm thinking this is a good thing. Justin has been tellin' me that the two of you were meant for each other."

She went to fetch the champagne, and when she returned, they asked her to share a glass with them. Raising her glass, she said solemnly, "May the sun always shine upon your face and the wind be at your back."

As they drank several more toasts, Amy stole secret glances at Marcus. He seemed truly happy. It gave her hope for their future.

The drawing room was well lit with candles by the time everyone arrived for drinks before dinner. Marcus stood beside the fireplace, and Harlan had come to stand beside him. "I know how you must feel, Marcus, but could we not talk in a reasonable manner and settle our differences," the older man said in an undertone while everyone else was engaged in conversation.

Marcus, with a look of disgust, turned to the man who had fathered him. "Do you think a few words between us will make up for what you did?"

Layla was unobtrusively handing out glasses of Madeira to everyone, and she kept her expression bland as she served the two men.

Harlan tried again. "No, but perhaps you could learn to accept me in time if you gave yourself a chance."

Marcus drained his glass and placed it on the mantel. "I don't think so," he said bluntly, and he moved away to stand behind Amy, who was seated in a chair next to Pamela. He touched her shoulder in a caress, and she smiled up at him.

Fiona was watching this exchange. She alone had seen the ring on Amy's finger. It gave her a start, but she quickly gathered her wits and reasoned that even if they had gotten married, Harlan could use some influence to have it annulled.

The butler announced dinner, and they made their way to the dining room. As Harlan seated himself at the head of the table, he suddenly started to gasp and clutch at his throat. His face turned red, and he made a choking noise.

Pamela cried out and rushed to his side while the others looked on in stunned silence. Marcus rose and hastily loosened Harlan's stock, but it didn't seem to help, for the man's eyes bulged out and he clawed at the empty air.

"Help me get him to the drawing room," Marcus ordered Justin, who had rushed to stand by his sister.

Justin, glad of something to do, pushed Pamela out of the way and helped Marcus lift Harlan. The older man's limbs were jerking, and his face was more engorged with blood. The rest of them followed the two men as they carried Harlan. Marcus shouted over his shoulder, "Send someone for the doctor."

By the time they deposited Harlan on the settee, his jerky movements had ceased and his eyes had drifted closed. Marcus finished removing the snowy stock at his throat and felt for a pulse. His grim expression told the story, and Pamela began to sob.

Amy was stunned as she realized the man was dead. Just moments ago, he had been standing in this very room talking, and now he was gone—just like Uncle Thad. Fresh grief washed over her at the thought, and she looked around at the faces of those who stood by. A slight chill gripped her when she saw a look of pure triumph on Julia's face. The woman was staring at her brother, but glanced up and caught Amy's eye for a moment before she masked her expression. But what surprised Amy more was the awful grief on Fiona's face. Tears were rolling down her cheeks unheeded as she stared at Harlan, oblivious to those around her.

Marcus covered Harlan's face with his handkerchief and bade everyone return to the dining room to await the doctor. Julia ordered a servant to bring coffee, and she moved between Justin and Pamela, speaking softly. Marcus took the chair next to Amy and held her icy hand in his. "It was so sudden, I wonder if his heart gave out." he speculated quietly.

"I can't believe he died right before our eyes . . . it was just like Uncle Thad," Amy whispered, and then dissolved in tears at the memory of her uncle. She had not particularly liked Harlan, but never had she wished his death. This visit to Bermuda had proved to be tragic in many ways, and she felt as if her hold on sanity was starting to crack.

Marcus drew her close, and she wept into his shoulder, clinging to him for strength. When the doctor arrived, Justin suggested the women retire to their beds, and he and Marcus would talk with the man.

Julia took charge of Pamela, and Amy found herself holding Fiona up as they climbed the stairs. Her companion's quiet sobs were barely controlled, and Amy had the feeling that the girl was near collapse. Fiona hadn't been nearly this upset when Thaddeus died, Amy thought, her earlier suspicions returning. There had been no time to talk to her companion, what with all that had been going on. Amy gave her a gentle shake. "Please get hold of yourself, Fiona. This has been a terrible shock for all of us, especially after losing Uncle Thad."

"You don't understand!" Fiona responded brokenly,

her eyes lifting accusingly to Amy's.

As they made their way down the deserted corridor, Amy challenged in a silky voice, "I'm afraid I don't. Why don't you explain?"

They had reached Fiona's bedchamber, and Amy led the girl to a chair and began unloosing the laces on the front of Fiona's dress. Fiona wiped ineffectively at her wet cheeks and glanced up to see the probing query in Amy's eyes. Cold reason reasserted itself and she looked away. "Could we talk about this tomorrow?" she mumbled, subdued for the moment.

Amy walked over to the bell cord and answered. "To be sure, Fiona. Tomorrow I want some answers." As she left the room, she said, without turning, "Ivy will help you to bed."

Amy made her way wearily to her own room. There, she undressed and sought the comfort of her bed. She was propped up on several pillows, wondering if Marcus would come to her. After all, their marriage was based on reasons other than love. Before the thought was finished, he let himself into the room. She sat up straight and asked anxiously, "What did the doctor say? Was it his heart?"

He sat down on the side of the bed and took her cold hand, his face pale in the muted candlelight. "Poison. The doctor said he'd been poisoned."

Amy's grip tightened in his as she stared at him. "No, it can't be . . . who would . . . how — ?"

"I don't know," he said, shaking his head. "He seemed fine before dinner in the drawing room. I . . . we talked for a moment, and I didn't notice anything out of the ordinary about his appearance or manner. He seemed fine," he repeated, as if he still couldn't believe it had happened. "The doctor will be notifying Sheriff Campbell, and I expect he'll be out here first thing in the morning."

Amy's thoughts tumbled over each other as her mind tried to accept this news and find an answer. Finally, she said, "Harlan had a lot of enemies. It may be difficult to find the murderer."

Marcus stood up and ran one hand distractedly through his hair. "I will most likely be a prime suspect. We have had several clashes in the past week," he pointed out.

"No!" Amy blurted out, her green eyes widening at this frightening thought. She scrambled from the bed and threw herself into his arms. "A few disagreements cannot be construed as a motive for murder. You were hardly more than an acquaintance of his."

Marcus held her close and rested his chin on her head, closing his eyes. He should tell her, he knew, but still the words would not come. Harlan had been the only one who knew, and now he was dead. Did he really have to tell her . . . ever? She was his wife, and he loved her desperately. Should he risk the chance they had to be happy by telling her a truth that no longer mattered? She was so soft and warm in his arms. He wanted to make love to her, wanted to banish the bad memories, the need for revenge.

Amy swallowed a lump in her throat. Harlan was dead, and she no longer needed Marcus's protection. Her pride urged her to offer him his freedom. "I've been thinking, Marcus. When this is over, we can seek an annulment."

He stiffened as her words cut through him like a knife. She cared for him. He'd been sure of that . . . until this moment. His heart thumped painfully against his ribs as he asked, "Is that what you want?"

Amy hesitated and then spoke the truth, setting her pride aside. "No," she whispered.

Marcus let out the breath he'd been holding and gently pushed her back to look into her sea-green eyes.

Tears glittered behind the dark fring[...]

"Then why, pray tell, did you suggest su[...]
lone tear slipped down her cheek, and he s[...]
with his thumb as he waited for her answer.

"I had no wish to hold you against your wil[...] aid
in a shaky voice. "With Harlan gone, there is no longer
any need to protect me."

A warm smile curved his mouth as he caressed her
cheek. "And you thought that was my only reason for
marrying you?"

She dropped her gaze and murmured, "You once said
you did not wish to be trapped by matrimony."

"Ahhh, I do remember saying something ridiculous
like that once, but it was a lie," he said, his smile growing
broader. "I have wanted you for mine since the moment
I saw you. I love you, Amy, and that is the only reason I
married you."

Her pulse quickened at his declaration. She wanted to
believe him, but a shred of doubt remained. She raised
her eyes to his imploringly. "Why, then, did you turn
away from me when we returned from St.-Domingue?
It near broke my heart."

He sighed heavily, knowing he didn't deserve Amy.
He'd taken her innocence and hurt her many times, all
because of his insane need for revenge against Harlan.
"If I could undo the damage I've done, my love, I would
do so gladly. The truth is, I believed you would be better
off without me." He leaned forward to brush her lips
with his. "I'm sorry, Amy. My damnable pride nearly
cost me the one thing I want most in this world." That
same pride kept him from revealing his secret. It was
over, he reasoned; there was no need.

"Oh, Marcus," she said, her voice catching on a sob.
"We have wasted so much time . . . and I love you so
much. Let's start over and forget the past."

"Aye," he agreed, his voice husky. Tipping her chin

355

claimed her lips. Her arms slid up to encircle his neck as she pressed even closer to his rock-hard body. The kiss became an urgent hunger they shared. His thrusting tongue sent shivers of desire racing through her, while his hands moved to cup her rounded hips and pull her hard against him,

It seemed like forever since he'd made love to her, and he found he couldn't wait to have her beneath him. Breaking the kiss, he pulled her satin nightrail over her head and dropped it to the floor. He picked her up and laid her on the bed and began undressing.

Amy watched him in the dim glow of the candlelight and felt a stirring of pride as her gaze traveled up his well-muscled body. There was an inherent strength in his face that spoke of well-molded character, and she knew in her heart that he was not capable of murder.

When he joined her on the bed, he wrapped her gently in his arms and whispered his love in her ear. She moaned with pleasure as he caressed the soft curves of her body. All of the hurt he had caused her ebbed away as they touched, kissed and spoke softly of their deepest feelings. His love was the balm she needed to soothe her bruised soul, and she gave it back to him tenfold.

His warm lips explored her breasts, lingering a moment at each pink nipple. She shivered with desire as he moved down her silken belly to the sweet valley between her legs. She cried his name out softly as he loved her intimately with his mouth, and a molten wave of passion enveloped them when she exploded in a downpour of fiery sensations. He quickly moved up to join his body to hers. He felt the last of her tremors as he entered into the warm, moist core of her, touching off an uncontrollable passion in him like the hottest fire. She was his woman now and forever, and nothing would ever change that. She rose up to meet his every thrust until they soared together to a shuddering ecstasy.

For a time they lay without moving, their breathing gradually slowing to normal. Then Marcus dropped gentle kisses on her face as she whispered, "Oh, Marcus, please tell me everything will be all right. I'm so afraid, and I can't help it."

He turned on his side and pulled her into the shelter of his arms. "I will never let anything hurt you again, my love. If you trust me, you'll believe that."

She nestled in the curve of his shoulder and with a new maturity said, "But we cannot control everything that touches our lives."

She was the reason for his very existence, and he felt fiercely protective of her. "I won't allow anyone or anything to come between us again," he said sharply. Then he added more gently, "Sleep now, my love. We have much to face tomorrow."

Chapter Nineteen

Before the sun rose, while the morning was still dim, Sheriff Campbell and two soldiers from King's Castle arrived at Stafford House. The servants were instructed to rouse everyone and bid them to appear downstairs as soon as possible.

Ivy, when she came to wake Amy, was startled to find Captain Bond in the bed as well. The black girl gently shook Amy awake and gave her the message, careful to avoid looking at the man next to her.

Marcus raised up on one elbow and yawned. "Bring your mistress some hot water, Ivy, and tell the sheriff we will be down shortly." After the girl left, Marcus turned to Amy and brushed her tangled hair away from her neck, where he placed a warm kiss. "I love the way you look in the morning, all sleepy and desirable. It was what I missed most from our time on the *Rebecca*."

"We were free then . . . and happy. I wish we could stay in bed all day and forget all that has happened," she said, sliding her arms around his neck.

He kissed her gently and then pushed her away to rise from the bed. "That would be my choice also, love, but unfortunately we cannot." He dressed quickly and smiled at her as he opened the door. "I need to freshen up, but I will knock on your door before going downstairs."

Twenty minutes later, he was back, and they walked arm in arm down to the drawing room. Justin came forward, his face haggard, and gripped Amy's outstretched hands. "Oh, Justin, this is all so terrible. How is Pamela?"

"I checked on her a few moments ago and she's still sleeping. The doctor gave her something last night before he left." He turned as the sheriff came up to them. "Amy, Marcus—you remember Sheriff Campbell."

The older man nodded politely and shook hands with Marcus. " 'Tis a shame we meet again under these sad circumstances." He called the two soldiers over and introduced them as well. Marcus nodded and Amy murmured polite responses. As they moved away to find a seat, she heard the sheriff ask about anyone in the household who was not present.

Ivy brought them coffee and offered warm bread and butter, but they declined the bread. Amy felt as if the food would stick in her throat if she tried to eat. As she sipped the steaming coffee, she felt a bit better, more able to face what lay ahead. Before she finished the cup, Fiona walked in, looking haggard. Julia appeared on her heels and spoke privately with the sheriff.

When all were seated, Sheriff Campbell spoke. "This is an official investigation, and each of you should answer the questions you're asked as if you were in a court of law. Mistress Pamela is the only one excused from the questioning this morning, due to her prostrate condition, but even she will be expected later to come forward." He paused then as all the house servants filed into the room behind Ivy to stand uncomfortably against one wall. "I want to talk to each of you individually in the dining room. Captain Jones will escort you back and forth." He then nodded and left the room with the other soldier.

When it was Amy's turn, she sat on the edge of her

chair in the dining room and faced the sheriff quietly, even though her insides were churning.

His voice and expression were both bland, and Amy could not tell what he was thinking. The soldier sat on one side of her with a paper, pen and ink pot.

"For our records, please tell me what your relationship was to Mr. Stafford and how you got on with him," he said.

Amy cleared her throat. "He and my uncle were business partners for many years, and we came for a visit — my uncle and I — as well as for business reasons. When my uncle died, Harlan became my guardian."

He said nothing for a moment, then prompted, "You forgot to mention how you got on with him."

Amy glanced down at her hands and realized she was twisting her lawn handkerchief in agitation. Smoothing it out, she returned her gaze to him and said quietly, "At first, we were on friendly terms, but after a while, I found I didn't like him very much, for several reasons."

He nodded. "I see. What were those reasons?"

"He didn't treat his family very well, for one thing. He also tried to force me into marriage with his son, and I believe it was to gain control of my fortune. I had heard rumors that he was in deep financial trouble," she said truthfully.

The sheriff nodded again, his expression never changing. "So, had he lived, your fortune would have been in jeopardy, since he was your guardian?"

Amy blinked at his bald question, and then relief washed over her. She understood what he was implying. "Not after what I did yesterday morning. Captain Bond and I were married at Trinity Church. Upon my marriage, control of my inheritance went to my husband, according to my uncle's will."

"As your legal guardian, did Mr. Stafford approve this marriage?" he asked with interest.

"No, he knew nothing about it. We were going to tell him today so that he couldn't obtain an annulment," she answered.

He stood up then, signaling an end to the interview. "Thank you, Mistress Hawthorne, uh, I should say, Mistress Bond. After I've talked with everyone, I may have further questions."

She nodded and rose, relieved to have the interrogation over with.

By noon, every person who lived or worked in the house had been interviewed. The servants laid out a hasty buffet meal in the dining room once the sheriff had removed himself to the drawing room to contemplate their depositions.

Julia had ordered two of the servants to wash and dress Harlan's body and place it in the bookroom until further notice.

When the family gathered for the meal, Marcus tapped his glass with a fork. When he had everyone's attention, he said, "We're all shocked and saddened by the tragic deaths that have occurred in one short week. And I know this is not the time or the place for a happy announcement. However, I think you should know that Amy and I were married yesterday at Trinity Church." One hand rested comfortingly on Amy's shoulder, and he gave her a gentle squeeze.

Amy had been watching the reaction of the others as he spoke. Fiona stared blankly at them and then turned away to pour a cup of coffee. Justin strode forward after a moment, and held out his hand to Marcus. "Congratulations, you are indeed a lucky man," he said, his manner subdued but sincere.

Marcus's attitude toward him thawed completely at this last gesture. All along, he had fought the urge to like his half brother, but now he realized that Justin was a good man, quite unlike their father.

Justin kissed Amy's cheek. "Be happy, love. You deserve it."

Amy nodded and assured him, "I know that I will be."

Pamela, who had come down later in the morning to answer questions, was, of course, not surprised by the news. She drew her aunt forward. "We consider you family, and want you to stay with us for as long as you want. Don't we, Aunt Julia?"

The older woman regarded them with impassive coldness. "You are far too naive and trusting, Pamela. I, for one, don't wish to harbor a murderer in our home."

Amy blanched. "What do you mean by—"

Marcus interrupted, his eyes locked with Julia's, "Aye, Mistress Stafford, I can see that you think I killed your brother."

Pamela gripped her aunt's arm in agitation and protested, "No, Aunt Julia! Captain Bond could not have done such a thing."

Julia pulled free and moved to Justin's side. "All of you heard him threaten Harlan. I say he did it."

Justin placed his arm around her shoulders. "I know you are upset, Aunt Julia, but please, don't do this." Julia turned her face into his shoulder and began to cry. He looked apologetically at Marcus.

Amy trembled with a mixture of anger and fear, clinging tightly to her husband. She bit her lower lip in an effort to keep from lashing out at the distraught woman.

At that moment, Sheriff Campbell and his two companions came into the room. Justin helped his aunt to a chair and then spoke as if nothing untoward had happened. "Would you gentlemen take the noon meal with us? It's a hasty affair, but there's more than enough."

The sheriff looked pained as he declined. "Thank

362

you, but we've official business to attend to. After discussing the information we've gathered this morning, we've decided Captain Bond should come to King's Castle with us."

Amy gave a start. "But why, Sheriff? You could not possibly think—"

The sheriff held up his hand for silence. "I didn't say we were charging him, Mistress Bond. However, at the moment, all we know is that he is the only one who actually threatened to kill Mr. Stafford."

"That's ridiculous! Captain Bond did not even know Harlan before this trip! Where did you get an idea like that?" Amy said, her voice rising with each word. She turned her gaze on Julia and knew, from the smug expression on the older woman's face.

Marcus pulled her close for a moment. "It will be all right, Amy, don't worry. I didn't do it, and the sheriff will discover that." Letting her go, he walked over to stand with the two soldiers.

Tears were streaming down Amy's face unheeded as she pointed to Julia. "She had far more reason to kill Harlan than anyone, Sheriff. Ask her about how she hated her brother!"

Justin came to Amy's side and placed an arm about her trembling shoulders. "Everything will be all right, and Marcus will be cleared. Let's not accuse anyone unjustly."

Amy barely heard his comforting words as Marcus turned to leave with his escort. "I'll find the person responsible, Marcus," she promised in a broken whisper as he disappeared through the door.

That afternoon, Amy and Pamela paid a visit to a lawyer in the town of St. George. Harlan's lawyer was out of the question, and Amy wanted Marcus to have counsel as soon as possible. She drew a draft on her uncle's account at the bank and employed the man immediately. They then boarded a ferry at the harbor and reached Castle Island in a short time. The boat docked on the eastern side of the island, where King's Castle overlooked the water. One of the soldier's on duty escorted them through the ground floor of the huge stone building to the office of the commander. As they waited in the anteroom, Amy turned to Pamela. "I don't know what I should do without your support, Pamela. And at a time when I should be thinking about you instead of the other way around."

Pamela gave her a wan smile. "I'm fine now, Amy. It was just such a shock to see Father . . . go in that terrible manner. In my own way, I loved him and always wanted him to love me, but he didn't — I know that. And I want to help Captain Bond in any way I can, for I know he didn't do this awful thing. We must help each other, you and I. After all, you had a grave loss just days ago, and now your husband is in trouble. We shall be strong together."

Amy hugged her and thanked the good Lord for such a loyal friend. Shortly thereafter, they received permission to visit Marcus from the commander.

The room he was in was not exactly a cell, but was simple and cold. It contained a cot, a table and two chairs. A single lamp burned on the table, and a recess in the wall contained a window overlooking a sheer rock cliff that slanted down to the water.

Marcus turned as they entered, and Amy ran across the room and into his arms. He stroked her back in a comforting gesture and smiled grimly at Pamela. "This is no place for the two of you. However, I'm glad to see you just the same," he said.

"Amy was so distraught, and I couldn't let her come alone," Pamela explained.

Amy pulled back and began telling him of the lawyer she'd engaged. He urged her to sit down and offered the other chair to Pamela. "I haven't been formally charged yet, but I am being detained. Perhaps the lawyer can have me released until they decide."

Pamela shook her head in confusion. "I don't understand why they think it would be you, Captain Bond. You barely knew my father."

Marcus walked over to stare out the window. "They were told that twice I made threats," he said, once again shunning the opportunity to reveal his relationship to Harlan. Since Amy was now his wife, there was a chance she could be implicated if the truth were known. He couldn't take that chance, and so maintained his silence.

"But no one could possibly have taken that seriously. People say things they don't mean in anger every day," Amy exploded.

He turned to look at her with a tender expression. "Don't get upset again, my love. It will do no good."

Pamela was staring at her hands, which were clasped in her lap. "I personally think it was one of the slaves. This sort of thing has happened several times in the past where the master was . . . shall we say, unkind." She glanced up then at Marcus, her chin lifting a bit. "I told Sheriff Campbell this."

Marcus moved to stand beside Pamela and laid a hand on her shoulder. "Thank you for your help . . . and for believing in me."

The three of them discussed other possibilities until the guard returned to inform the women that the last ferry would leave the island in a few minutes. Pamela turned discreetly away while Marcus embraced Amy and gave her a lingering kiss before they parted.

* * *

365

Fiona sat quietly in her bedroom, staring out the open French doors. She was not aware of the setting sun, the squawking birds or the cool, evening breeze that drifted into the room. If asked, she would not have remembered that Ivy had helped her dress early that morning after the black girl had come in to wake her. For the first time in her life, she'd lost something she really wanted — Harlan Stafford. He had been exciting, a wonderful lover, and by far the most interesting man she'd ever known. In short, she'd actually been in love with him. She knew she would have made him happy, given the chance.

What was she to do now? she wondered. Her lips curled scornfully at the thought of being a lady's companion for the rest of her days. Thaddeus was gone, and now Harlan — where did that leave her? And now Amy had made this ridiculous marriage and would soon realize she did not need a companion. One had to be practical, she thought, as Justin crossed her mind as a substitute, but she discarded him almost immediately. His financial situation was worse than hers, and she didn't intend to be poor.

A discreet knock on her door brought her back to reality, and she called permission to enter. When Amy stepped into the room, an unreasonable anger enveloped Fiona. This whole thing was Amy's fault. She might have married Thaddeus sooner and been wealthy beyond her dreams had not Amy been so stubborn about marrying Justin. She and Harlan could have remedied his problems and married if she'd been left a rich widow. She turned away so that Amy wouldn't see the hatred in her eyes.

"How are you feeling, Fiona? Ivy told me you haven't stirred from your room," Amy asked.

Fiona bit back a sharp retort and said evenly, "I'm fine."

Amy moved to stand beside the French doors and feigned sympathy. "I know how hard all of this is—two deaths inside of a week, and one of them murder. It seems like a nightmare. And now Marcus locked up at King's Castle . . . It's truly dreadful."

Unable to help herself, Fiona pressed her fist to her lips as a sob escaped. "I miss him so much . . . you cannot imagine how alone I feel," she cried.

Amy watched Fiona's genuine display of grief and asked suspiciously, "Who, Fiona? Who do you miss?"

Fiona called in all her reserves as she raised her startled face. "Why, Thaddeus, Amy! What sort of question is that?"

There was a mixture of shock and hurt on Fiona's face that seemed sincere. Amy didn't know what to believe all of a sudden. Perhaps she'd misread the whole situation? She had, after all, been under a great strain herself. "Never mind, Fiona. I'm terribly worried about Marcus, that's all."

Fiona had to think of her future, and right now she needed Amy. Wiping her eyes with her handkerchief, she said, "I will heal in time, I know, but I wish I could have stopped you from marrying him. I feel just awful that I didn't tell you in time."

A cold knot of dread clutched Amy's stomach as she asked, "Tell me what?"

Fiona lifted her tearstained eyes. "I . . . perhaps I shouldn't have said anything. You're his wife now, and it would do no good . . ."

Amy's fear doubled as she moved to grasp Fiona's arm. "You cannot leave me to wonder—what are you saying?"

Fiona sniffed again and dabbed at her eyes. "Well, after you left with Justin yesterday morning, I overheard an argument between Harlan and Marcus. I was on the terrace outside the bookroom, and they did not realize I was there."

"Get to the point, Fiona!" Amy prompted in agitation.

Fiona dissolved in tears again and sobbed, "I wish I hadn't heard or at least hadn't kept it from you. Oh, dear, I just don't know what to do!"

Amy wanted to shake the girl. Her heart was pounding with anxiety, but she managed to urge calmly, "It will be fine — just tell me what you heard."

"Marcus is Harlan's son," she blurted out, and then amended, "his illegitimate son. And that was the reason for the argument. Marcus hates him and told him so."

Amy's whole world rocked for a moment before she could speak. "His son?" she whispered in disbelief. How could Marcus have kept that from her? She thought they had finally come to love and trust each other.

Fiona felt a surge of elation at having pricked Amy's happiness. Careful to keep her expression grave, she said, "He also told Harlan he was going to marry you to get his revenge. Marcus said he knew Harlan was in deep financial trouble and wanted Justin to marry you to save his empire. By marrying you, Marcus could destroy the one thing Harlan cared about."

Fiona broke down and began to sob again while Amy absorbed this information. The cold knot inside her dissolved into a searing pain as her face turned ashen. He had used her for his own ends. She shivered with conflicting emotions and rose to her feet. "I need to be alone to think," she said in a distant voice.

Fiona grasped her hand and pleaded, "Please don't be angry with me, Amy. I was going to tell you last night, but then Harlan . . . I was so stunned by what happened . . . I forgot. And then, well, Marcus announced that the two of you had gotten married. It was too late then."

Amy pulled her hand free and said, "Perhaps it's better that I know the truth now." Slowly she made her way to her own room and curled up on the bed in a tight little knot. Marcus had not used her as Fiona had said . . . he couldn't be so cold, she reasoned miserably. But she felt as if the foundation of her life was on shifting sands, and she wondered if she would ever be truly happy and secure again.

The following day, an endless parade of people came and went at Stafford House to pay their respects. Julia and Pamela handled the social interchanges, while Amy took over supervision of the servants and the food. Amy felt guilty at Pamela's gratitude and praise for her help, for she was staying busy more for herself than anyone else. She knew she would go out of her mind if she contemplated her own situation too long or too hard.

Amy glanced at Justin and Megan across the large drawing room, where they were talking quietly with Judge Green. She couldn't help but be glad that Justin's problems with his father were over. He had installed his new wife in the house that morning, to the surprise of everyone but Amy.

While breakfast was being served, Justin had arrived with Megan in tow and made his announcement. Julia had recovered herself quickly and kissed Megan on the cheek, welcoming her to the family. Amy had watched and realized that the older woman did truly want Justin's happiness.

A soft voice at her side put an end to her thoughts. Looking up, she saw Reverend Jacobs. "I'm sorry, what did you say?" she apologized.

He nodded in Pamela's direction. "I'm concerned about Mistress Pamela. Do you think she's all right?"

Amy followed the direction of his gaze and nodded. "This has been awful for her, but she's a strong person. She loved him, despite the fact that he cared little for her."

Reverend Jacobs sighed. "I know. The man must have been blind not to have valued a wonderful daughter like her."

Amy glanced up at him, her expression gentle and understanding. "Have you told her you love her?"

He blushed to the roots of his thinning hair. "Is it that obvious?"

Amy smiled. "No, I'm just perceptive. She's in love with you, you know."

His face brightened as he asked softly, "Do you really think so? I was just working up the nerve to talk to her father about courting her when this . . . happened."

"Tell her how you feel. I think she could use your support," she coaxed. "And I'm sure Justin and Julia will approve."

"Thank you, Mistress Amy. Pamela is lucky to have you for a friend, and so am I," he said quietly. Changing the subject, he asked, with concern knitting his brow, "How are you faring? I heard they have Captain Bond at King's Castle. They haven't charged him, have they?"

Amy let her gaze slide away, and her hands momentarily fisted at her sides. "No. I engaged a lawyer on his behalf, but I'm worried."

"I pride myself on being a good judge of character and your husband, Mistress Amy, does not strike me as a man who could commit murder. I would be happy to speak for him."

Calmer now, Amy smiled wanly. "I'm sure he would appreciate that."

Judge Green stopped at her side as Reverend Jacobs

moved away. "Gruesome business, Mistress Amy," he said, shaking his head. "Can't tell you how sorry Mary and I are for the Stafford family. And you too, my dear. Your loss being so recent."

Amy felt tears sting her eyes, but she blinked them back and murmured her thanks. She had been pushing her own grief away the last few days and concentrating on the matters at hand. However, Judge Green's sympathetic words brought it to the surface again. Fiona's revelation had torn her apart as well. Was it true . . . or not? She wanted desperately to believe it was not, but until she could talk to Marcus, she couldn't be absolutely sure. When she realized the judge was saying something to her, she pushed her tormenting thoughts aside. "Pardon me, Judge Green?"

"I was just saying young Justin mentioned your companion to me last week — Mistress Morgan — that she is from Philadelphia. I knew her father quite well through business. Although we did not meet in the same social circles, we belonged to the same political club. It surprised me to find she'd sought employment," he said with a raised eyebrow.

"I understand her father got into some financial difficulties and had to move back to Ireland," she said. "Rather than go with the family, Fiona decided to seek a post."

He peered askance at her. "How very strange. I received a letter from my brother the other day, and he mentioned Leland Morgan had bested him on a wager over a horse race. Ethan, my brother, has kept me abreast of anything newsworthy from home these past years. He's never said a word about the Morgans having any financial difficulties."

Amy glanced swiftly across the room to where Fiona was sitting alone, staring out a window. All of her suspicions about the girl came flooding back. If she had lied about one thing, chances were that she would lie about another. Relief washed over her as welcome as rain on a summer day. Abruptly, she turned back to the judge and gave him a smile. "I must have misunderstood. Sometimes, I'm afraid, I don't attend properly to what's being said."

The judge took his leave shortly thereafter, and girding herself with resolve, Amy muttered, "We shall have the truth from you, Fiona, and soon."

The rest of the day was interminable for Amy, as people came and went and she waited for word from King's Castle. She desperately wanted to see for herself that Marcus was all right and to speak with him about Fiona's shocking news. Sheriff Campbell dropped by and spoke with several people while there, including Justin and Amy. He gave only noncommittal replies to her questions, though.

By the following day, the tension in the household was like a coiled spring. Amy was sure everyone felt it, as the mourners once again made their way to the walled-in graveyard. Pamela wept silent tears, while Fiona sobbed openly. Amy watched her companion through narrowed eyes and clamped down on her own frustration. In deference to Justin and Pamela, she had decided to wait to confront Fiona.

The reading of the will was set for late afternoon, and when the last of the mourners departed, everyone gathered in the bookroom. Layla was the only servant present, excluding Ivy, who was serving coffee.

Harlan's lawyer, Daniel Bainbridge, was sitting behind the desk, spreading his papers out. He looked up once and said, "We will begin shortly. I'm expecting someone else." Bending his head to his task, he didn't enlighten them.

Before Amy could guess who it might be, Marcus and Sheriff Campbell entered the room. Marcus came straight to Amy's chair and bent to kiss her cheek. "I have much explaining to do, my love. Just don't pass judgment yet," he pleaded in her ear before he straightened.

All Amy could do was nod, for Mr. Bainbridge had begun to speak. "I know you are wondering why Captain Bond was sent for, but I assure you, he is just as important to these proceedings as the rest of you. Since Mr. Stafford died so precipitously, I will explain the codicil he added several days ago because I'm sure he thought all of you would know who Captain Bond was long before he died."

Amy glanced around the room and noted that Justin and Pamela wore puzzled expressions, while the others looked quite interested. She had been observing everyone in the household since Harlan's murder, trying to detect the guilty party. There was still the unresolved matter of who had been threatening her own life. Could they be one and the same person?

Marcus laid his hand on her shoulder and gave a gentle squeeze as the lawyer went on. "Captain Bond is Harlan's firstborn son. He was never married to the captain's mother and, in fact, did not know until a week ago this son existed."

Although Fiona had told her as much, Amy couldn't help flinching. He had begged her not to judge him, but she was hurt just the same. Her gaze lifted to his in question, and she saw an unspoken pain glowing in his gray eyes. Pamela gasped, and Justin's eyebrows shot up in surprise. They all turned to stare at Marcus.

Justin recovered himself and gave a mirthless bark of laughter. "Well, I'll be damned! Welcome to our happy family, brother," he said. Megan placed her hand on Justin's arm, looking vaguely disturbed, but he smiled

373

at her reassuringly. "Not to worry, Megan. I'm not upset—quite the contrary. Pamela and I have discussed the fact that we quite like the captain. Although we didn't know he was our brother."

Pamela rushed in with, "That's quite true, Captain Bond. It's just such a shock . . . I can barely take it in."

Marcus was in no mood to be welcomed into the family, however sincere they were. He straightened his shoulders and scowled. "I did not come here to intrude on your family circle."

Mr. Bainbridge coughed and said firmly, "I will begin reading, if you don't mind."

Burning with curiosity, everyone settled back once more to listen. Unlike with Thaddeus's will, there were no minor bequests. The bulk of the estate—the house, the shipyard, the ships, the salt contracts—was left to Justin. Julia was to have a home for life, and Pamela was to have her mother's jewels. "However," Mr. Bainbridge said, glancing up at the group. "The codicil Harlan added changes one bequest. That is that Marcus Bond shall share in half of Justin's inheritance."

Julia jumped to her feet at this and glared at Marcus. "Half for a bastard son! It's not fair to Justin!" She turned her wild gaze on the lawyer and demanded, "You must do something about this travesty—it cannot be legal. Especially as he is a murderer."

Sheriff Campbell cleared his throat, covering the tense moment. "We haven't even charged Captain Bond, Mistress Julia. Holding him for questioning has been more of a formality."

Mr. Bainbridge's left eyebrow rose a fraction. "And I'm afraid, Mistress Stafford, the point is moot, since Harlan was on the brink of financial ruin anyway."

His words took a moment to soak in, and then Julia sank back into her chair. "What do you mean?" she asked in a voice that trembled.

He stood up and let his gaze touch each occupant in the room. "I hate to be the bearer of bad news, but Harlan's creditors in England are beginning to call in their loans, and there is no money to pay them. The estate and the shipyard are forfeit in another month or so."

Justin slipped an arm around Megan and gave his aunt and sister a confident smile. "Don't worry, I will take care of all of you. We'll find a place to live and be far happier than we were living under Father's iron fist."

Pamela nodded. "I'm not worried, Justin."

Amy spoke up for the first time. "How much would it take to pay the creditors? I would be happy to loan Justin the money."

Justin smiled at her, but shook his head. "Thank you, Amy, but no. My father never gave me credit for any sense, and I would like to prove him wrong by taking care of my family. I still have my ship and my wits."

Julia rose from her chair again, her wild eyes trained on Marcus. "It's not enough, Justin. You should have had it all — and you would have, if it wasn't for this upstart, Captain Bond!"

Justin started to rise. "Please, Aunt Julia, it's not his fault — "

Her gaze never wavered from Marcus. "Oh, yes it is. Him and his blackhearted bastard of a father — my dear brother!" She spat out the words like venom. "Without Captain Bond's interference, Harlan would have had control of this chit's fortune. You would have been saved, we all would have!" Her voice rose on a note of hysteria, and her eyes burned with a strange light. "Why do you think we killed Harlan? He had to be silenced! And now it's all for naught. You — " she growled at Marcus, "you should have hanged for the murder as we planned, but since that's not likely now, I will see you dead myself!"

Her confession and hysterical threat stunned th
group. Layla was trying frantically to still her mistres
grabbing at her arm. Sheriff Campbell started to mov
forward just as Julia broke free of Layla and lunged a
Marcus. The flash of something silver in her hand mo
bilized Marcus. He grabbed her arm just before sh
sank the sharp scissors into his chest. Amy screamed a
Marcus struggled to subdue the crazed woman.

Chapter Twenty

"A week ago, I thought my whole world was coming apart," Amy mused, lying in Marcus's arms in the big bed. The moon was on the wane, and its soft light glowed in their bedchamber. "When I saw Julia with those scissors, I realized your secret didn't matter to me nearly as much as your life."

Marcus sighed and held her tighter, as if he were afraid she'd yet get away from him. "I'm sorry, my love. I'll say it every day for the rest of our lives and gladly. I should never have kept that from you, especially once we were married, but I was afraid of losing you."

She smiled contentedly. "I know that now, but when Fiona told me you were Harlan's son, I was devastated that you didn't trust me." She raised up then to look into his eyes. "Still I think deep down I knew even then she was lying about the reason you married me. I just couldn't make myself believe it was true. What I don't understand is her hatred."

He pulled her head down and kissed her deeply and then smoothed the hair back from her face. "I don't think she hated you, Amy. It was more jealousy than anything. She had everybody fooled for a while, first Thaddeus, then Harlan. The woman was an adventuress and very devious. Your mind doesn't work that way, so you accepted the facade she presented."

"I'm just glad you put her on that ship for Boston and she's gone," Amy said with a sigh. "I shudder to think of the trouble she could have caused if we hadn't found her out."

"Forget her, my love. The important thing is we have each other now. Do you know I fell in love with you the moment I saw you?" he said, his voice husky with emotion. "I fought it for a long time, though, because I wanted the best for you, and I had nothing to offer."

"I won't stand for any disparaging remarks about the man I love," she said in mock sternness.

He chuckled and caressed her bare satiny hip. "I was penniless, in debt, and bent on revenge. Those are not admirable qualities in a man," he pointed out.

She traced the square line of his firm jaw with her fingertip. "I saw the real man inside. And I've never been prouder of you than this last week."

His expression grew pained. "I'm merely looking out for my own interests," he said stubbornly.

She smiled at his discomfort. "You're far too modest, my darling. You didn't lay blame on Harlan when you reported what you knew of Captain Aiken and the massacre, which spared Justin and Pamela the shame. And using the treasure you found to pay Harlan's debts was a very generous gesture."

"I inherited half of this estate, and I couldn't let it go to ruin," he defended modestly.

"You could have bought another estate and half a dozen ships. You were thinking of Justin and Pamela and what would happen to them, weren't you? Why won't you admit you're softhearted?" she teased.

His expression grew serious. "They are my brother and sister, and I've found I care for them . . . I didn't intend to, but . . ."

"They're not like Harlan—they're worthy of your love. It's amazing really, that a man like Harlan could be the father of three such wonderful children," she said gently.

He sighed. "My mother and father—stepfather, that is—were good people. They raised me with solid values, and I suppose that's what counts. And Julia taught Justin and Pamela to be upright and moral even though her soul was twisted with bitterness. She did love them."

"Julia's trial will be very hard on them, and I wish they could be spared that," Amy said, her voice sad.

"They know that Julia and Layla will get the death penalty—it couldn't go any other way. However, my brother and sister are strong and will survive. They have happiness ahead," he pointed out.

Amy smiled faintly. "Megan's baby will come in the autumn. I'm looking forward to it almost as much as they."

Marcus kissed the tip of her nose. "You will be a most beautiful aunt," he predicted. He then asked, "Did I tell you Reverend Jacobs approached me yesterday asking my permission to court Pamela?"

Amy raised up to frown at him. "Marcus Bond! How could you forget to tell me something that important? What did you say?"

His eyebrows rose at her pique. "I said I would have to speak with Pamela first. She may not be interested in him, you know."

Amy groaned and shook her head in despair. "Men! You are such dull-witted creatures. Of course she's interested, Marcus—she's in love with him!"

His eyes widened. "Oh. Well, I shall tell him yes, then."

Amy smiled. "I'm happy for Pamela. They are the perfect couple."

Marcus pulled her down onto the soft mattress and rose above her. "No, my darling, we are the perfect couple . . . and I will show you." His lips claimed hers in a demanding kiss before she could comment further.

On a sultry Sunday toward the end of August, Amy and Pamela decided to pick some flowers to place on the graves in the small cemetery behind Stafford House. Services at Trinity Church and the noon meal were past, and the men had retired to the covered terrace to smoke. Megan, who had grown large, had decided to retire to her bedchamber to rest.

The two women gathered their colorful bounty from the enclosed garden and crossed the wide lawn to the graveyard. Passing through the iron gate, they paused by each grave and placed a few flowers next to the headstones.

"Moses takes great care of this place, don't you think?" Amy said, moving on to her uncle's grave. The mounded plot was thick with growing herbs — parsley, thyme, sage, sweet marjoram — as were the other graves. She placed a bouquet of tiny, blue Bermudianas near his name on the stone.

Pamela smiled. "Aye. He takes great pride in the work he does with the plants." She moved to distribute flowers among the three newest graves along the back stone wall. They belonged to her father, her aunt and Layla. "I think it was very fitting that he planted medicinal herbs on these," she said, nodding toward the new plots. "Perhaps in death their spirits will draw from the healing plants and they'll rest."

Amy nodded and said hesitantly, "I want you to know I don't hold a grudge over the things your aunt did to me. We haven't spoken of it before and won't again, but when she posed as the woman in white, she was misguided and thought I was a threat to you and Justin. It's forgotten as far as I'm concerned. And I'm glad you're at peace about everything. I know it was difficult for you, though having Reverend Jacobs by your side must have helped."

Pamela blushed and dipped her head. "Samuel is truly wonderful, and I'm anxious for the wedding." Her color deepened as she glanced up. "Is that very brazen of me?"

Amy chuckled as she looked fondly at her sister-in-law. The changes in the shy girl were nothing short of a miracle. Gone was the drab, mousey look, and in its place was a young woman with sparkling eyes, rosy cheeks and more confidence. "I don't believe we can relegate you to the class of harlot just yet, dear Pamela. You are merely in love with the man you're going to marry — nothing wrong with that."

Pamela stood up and brushed her hands off. "Sometimes I feel guilty because I'm so happy," she mused.

"Don't," Amy advised wisely. "Life is for the living, and besides, your aunt would have wanted you to be happy. She loved you and Justin very much."

Pamela smiled then and linked her arm with Amy's as they walked away. "She certainly has her wish then. Marcus has seen to that. We owe him so much — saving our home and business as he did. And he's been a wonderful brother to both of us."

Amy nodded. "I agree, but the gain is not all on your side, sister dear. You and Justin have given him love and acceptance . . . and a reason to leave behind his bitterness. I think it was a fair trade."

They fell into discussing a layette for Megan's baby and soon reached the house. Climbing the steps to the back terrace, they heard deep voices in conversation and followed them. Marcus, Justin, Reverend Jacobs and Patrick Cormac were reclining in the shade, sipping cool Madeira. When they saw the two women, they rose hastily. Amy smiled to herself as she watched Samuel pull a chair next to his for Pamela. Marcus kissed Amy's cheek and seated her. Megan stepped out onto the terrace through the French doors just then and complained, "Young Justin wouldn't hear of me sleepin' in the middle of the day. He's kickin' up a fine fuss." She patted her bulging tummy with a smile.

Justin moved to her side, placing his hand beside hers. He grinned as he felt the child kick. "Feels like a determined little girl to me," he teased, helping his wife into a chair.

Marcus rang a bell and ordered more drinks for the ladies. "We were just discussing building three more ships to add to our fleet. The trade between the colonies and the islands is growing daily, and we should be ready for expanding markets."

Amy smiled at them. "Since we've become a family and thrown our lot in together, we should expand. After all, as the years go on, our children will need some diversity in the business."

Marcus, standing behind her chair, stroked her cheek. "Male and female," he added seriously. "I have a feeling our daughters will not be satisfied to sit at home and sew."

Amy turned her head up to look at him, a twinkle in her green eyes. "And I used to think you arrogant and narrow-minded."

He struck an innocent pose and answered in an injured tone, "I have no idea where you got that ridiculous notion."

Everyone laughed, and the discussion resumed with sketchy plans for the future. Marcus had made a point early on of telling Pamela and Samuel that they would share equally in the business, even though the major part of their lives would be devoted to the church. Amy spoke up with her own plans for a free school for the children of Tucker's Town, and Marcus teased her about the curriculum that would be offered to the girls.

"They shall learn everything the boys do and more,"

she assured him smugly.

"Will you be teachin' the art of self-defense, Amy?" Patrick asked as he rubbed his crooked nose and grinned.

When the laughter died down, the conversation turned to the news of a Spanish galleon that had been wrecked during a storm the night before. Under cover of the excited chatter about more chests of gold doubloons, Marcus bent to whisper in Amy's ear, "Come, walk with me." She nodded and rose. The others paid no attention to their departure as the couple descended the steps to the lawn.

A fresh breeze from the east lifted the loose tendrils of hair around Amy's face, and she sighed with contentment. Her hand rested in the crook of her husband's arm. She glanced up at him. "Are we going anyplace special?" she asked.

His gaze, which had been moving over the green lawn and the woods beyond, swung to his wife's face. He smiled. "No. I just wanted you to myself. Besides, when you're by my side, anyplace I happen to be is special."

She returned his smile with a wicked gleam in her sea-green eyes. "How gallant! When we first met, I had no idea how charming you could be."

He chuckled. "Are you implying my wit was lacking?"

They had reached the edge of the woods, where a bird squawked raucously to its mate and the air was perfumed by oleander and hibiscus. No longer were these sounds and smells foreign to Amy—this was home. They paused and Marcus pulled her into his arms, hungry as always for her. She turned her face up and said softly, "I've never found you lacking, Captain Bond . . . not in any way."

He saw the same hunger in her eyes just before his mouth descended to take hers possessively. When the

383

kiss ended, Marcus vowed in a husky voice, "And I've never been happier in my life."

Amy leaned into his broad chest and rested her head on his shoulder. How could she have known on that cold day when she'd first seen Marcus on Long Wharf that her life would take this turning? Her heart swelled with love for him. The only thing she was missing was a child who looked like its father. If Fate continued to look kindly upon her, she was sure that would come in time